Millie's Treasure

Center Point
Large Print

Also by Kathleen Y'Barbo and available from Center Point Large Print:

The Secret Lives of Will Tucker series
  Flora's Wish

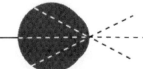

**This Large Print Book carries the
Seal of Approval of N.A.V.H.**

Millie's Treasure

KATHLEEN Y'BARBO

CENTER POINT LARGE PRINT
THORNDIKE, MAINE

The text of this Large Print edition is unabridged.
In other aspects, this book may vary
from the original edition.
Printed in the United States of America
on permanent paper.
Set in 16-point Times New Roman type.

ISBN: 978-1-62899-413-1

Library of Congress Cataloging-in-Publication Data

Y'Barbo, Kathleen.
Millie's treasure / Kathleen Y'Barbo. —
    Center Point Large Print edition.
    pages ; cm
    Summary: "The notorious Will Tucker is passing himself off as a
British gentleman while he is really seeking a hidden treasure map
connected to heiress Millie Cope's family. It's up to Pinkerton agent
Kyle Russell to determine if Millie is an accomplice or a victim"
    —Provided by publisher.
    ISBN 978-1-62899-413-1 (library binding : alk. paper)
    1. Mistaken identity—Fiction. 2. Large type books. I. Title.
PS3625.B37M55 2015
813′.6—dc23
                                                        2014037687

To my Lord and Savior,
Jesus Christ,
My all and all.
You alone are my treasure.

And thank you to the "real" Kyle Russell
for letting me borrow your name.

The youth gets together his materials to
build a bridge to the moon, or, perchance,
a palace or temple on the earth, and, at length,
the middle-aged man concludes to build
a woodshed with them.

HENRY DAVID THOREAU

Where your treasure is,
there will your heart be also.

MATTHEW 6:21

One

December 24, 1888
Chicago, Illinois

"I'm a Pinkerton agent, not a treasure hunter."

Agent Kyle Russell knew he had raised his voice far louder than was proper when speaking to a superior officer, but he didn't care. In previous cases, pleading his passion for the topic might have been a sufficient excuse, but this time he offered no apology. He was a man accustomed to working cases that mattered, not a flunky being used to further another man's political career.

Henry Smith ignored the breach of conduct to point in Kyle's direction. "The president has requested I put my best man on this case, and, unfortunately, you are he."

If this was Henry's way of praising him, the compliment fell short. Nor did it matter that it was Christmas Eve, and he had agreed to a meeting in Chicago when his mother wished him home in New Orleans to celebrate the holidays with his family.

"March fourth." Henry shrugged. "Your time on this case lasts only until inauguration day. When the president leaves office, you can leave this case behind." He removed his spectacles and pinched the spot where they rested on his nose. "What if I allow you to return to the Will Tucker case after this is all over? Would that sweeten the pot for working this one until the first week of March?"

Will Tucker.

The name held memories of a case that had become personal. Of a man whose exploits had wounded hearts and caused losses beyond the jewels he stole from his victims. That he had escaped from Angola Prison in Louisiana had been a thorn in Kyle's side for more than a year.

"Before I answer you, can I ask why a president who was voted out of office is suddenly interested in Confederate treasure that may or may not have existed?"

With a lift of one shoulder, Henry put on his spectacles once more. "I would only be guessing, but I think he is looking to add some money to the government's coffers. To leave on a high note, as it were."

"Meaning?"

"Meaning he is promising to be back in four years. To be responsible for adding a substantial deposit of gold to the Treasury without taxing the people might help him get there."

"Confederate gold for reelection?" Kyle shook his head. "Not seeing the point in it."

"We do not have to see the point. And who knows? Maybe it is not Cleveland himself who's asking. It could be anyone who runs in his circles. A cabinet member, one of his political backers, anyone."

Henry walked to the door and closed it. "The assignment comes from William Pinkerton himself, son, so I suggest you take it seriously and respond accordingly."

Kyle accepted the folder his boss offered and then opened it to give the pages a cursory glance. Though William Pinkerton ran the Chicago office with an iron hand, he rarely intervened in individual cases to make specific requests. Despite his misgivings, Kyle nodded. "All right."

"That's it? Just 'all right'? Nothing else?"

Kyle tucked the folder under his arm. "What else is there to say, sir?" He paused to offer the beginnings of a smile to the man he had worked under for the better part of ten years. "Unless Mr. Pinkerton would be willing to write a note to my mother explaining my absence during her holiday celebrations. Not that it would do much good."

Henry chuckled. "No, if she is anything like my wife, I would imagine not." His expression sobered. "The agency appreciates you, Kyle. You are the best we've got. Mr. Pinkerton said so, and I will echo the sentiment."

A compliment neither man bestowed lightly. "Thank you, sir."

"Look on the bright side," he said. "Maybe you will come up with some sort of invention that will uncover buried treasure." At Kyle's grin, he continued. "You already have one?"

"Borrowing on the theory of induction balance put forth by Bell, I . . ." Kyle shook his head. "The short answer is yes, though it's not yet ready to patent until we have done more research in the field. At least, that is the opinion of Mr. Toulmin."

"Toulmin?"

"Our patent attorney."

"I see. Well, perhaps you will get your field research out of this assignment. See, a positive aspect to hunting treasure and calling it Pinkerton business."

Henry returned to his chair. "Any chance you will ever leave us to work on those inventions of yours full time? I admit I am intrigued with the idea of the personal flying machine."

"Ah, the flying machine," Kyle echoed. Until recently, no one at the agency knew of his inventions beyond the rare mention of one in the reports he turned in after completion of his duties on any particular case.

Then came this particular project, and his cover as an inventor had been blown. One of the investors, an Ohio lawyer by the name of Taft, was a close acquaintance of Henry's and had shared his excitement in the invention without realizing he had breached propriety in the process. Henry had since been brought into the fold and was following each step with enthusiasm.

Kyle gave the question of his retirement only the briefest amount of thought. "As to when I will leave the agency? Not until the time is right."

"And when will that be?"

"When the Lord says so, I suppose."

"Fair enough." Henry reached out to shake Kyle's hand. "Just know I am going to be praying He remains silent on the job change for many years."

They shared a laugh and then parted ways. A few hours later, Kyle was on a train heading south.

Unfortunately for Henry Smith and the Pinkerton agency, the Lord had already been making it quite plain to Kyle that his exit from the agency would come sooner rather than later. At least he hoped it was the Lord and not his own wishes that gave him hope he would soon spend all of his days and most of his nights working on the inventions that he and his best friend, Lucas McMinn, wished to patent.

Kyle wondered if he might pay a quick visit to Brimmfield Plantation, where Lucas, a retired Pinkerton agent, had settled with his wife, the former Flora Brimm. Perhaps Kyle could dig up a reason for the detour in the documents Henry had given him. After all, Natchez, Mississippi, was as likely a prime spot for hidden contraband gold as any other place in the Southern states.

Two months would not allow him time to delve into all the possibilities, nor could he visit all the locations where treasure had been claimed to exist. Somehow he must decide which were the stronger leads and follow them.

He dove into the file. Clipped to the second page was an envelope with his name written in Henry's scrawling handwriting. Inside Kyle found a letter, a match, and a key.

While I cannot be absolved from keeping you away from family on Christmas Eve, I can at least make up for the fact by providing a brief respite before work on this case begins in earnest on January 2. Arrangements have been made for rooms at the Peabody Hotel in Memphis from tomorrow night through the aforementioned second day of the New Year. Should you find that your work on the missing gold case requires it, of course the agency will pay for as many nights past that as you deem necessary.

Our friend Taft suggested that the rooftop of the as-yet-unopened Cotton Exchange building on Second Street might prove just the venue for your test flight. To that end, he has secured access for you and assures me the three of us are the only ones who have knowledge of this. Thus, I hasten to warn that you must not be caught lest you alone will be forced to explain. And, per Mr. Taft, please remember to leave the key in the Weather Service office on the third floor before the service employee arrives at work after the holiday and realizes it is missing.

Consider this a small measure of thanks for your dedication to the agency. And no, I have not cleared this with Mr. Pinkerton, thus the need for the match. I am sure you will make good use of it, as always.

Best regards,
Henry

Kyle scanned the letter once more before folding the document in quarters and setting it alight. A quick toss out the open window and the flaming remainder of Henry's correspondence was gone on the afternoon breeze.

Kyle leaned back against the seat in the sleeper car and grinned. So he would have time to make a stop at Brimmfield after all. And he would bring the flying machine to Memphis for its first official test of the steering mechanism they had been working on. In all, a good trade for taking on the ridiculous assignment of digging up Confederate gold more than two decades after the war had ended.

He arrived at Brimmfield Plantation in the dead of night to find the McMinn and Brimm families away for the week. That was a disappointment because he had hoped to convince Lucas to accompany him for the test flight.

Letting himself into the cottage Lucas had claimed as his workshop, Kyle packed a bag with the items he would need for the tests and then left a note before departing.

Come January 2 he might be chasing treasure, but he would be chasing the wind on New Year's Eve.

December 24, 1888
Memphis, Tennessee

Cook was right. The best thing about marrying Sir William Trueck and beginning a new life in London was that Millie Cope would leave Memphis and everything she knew and once loved behind. And this was no small thing.

In fact, taking this step to marry and leave Memphis entirely was a thing so large in scope that Millie could scarcely take it in on those occasions when she made the attempt. And thus she had settled into a habit of not making the attempt.

For she knew she could not stay, not when her life in this house was merely the wisp of a shadow slipping into darkness. As Sir William Trueck's American bride, she could step out of that shadow. She tried to recall that when fear rose to make its attempt at choking out good sense. And Millie Cope was nothing if not sensible.

After the death of her mother and two elder sisters, Julia and Sarah, to a yellow fever epidemic a decade ago, the distance that yawned between her and her father had become unbearable.

In England, Millie could be odd. She could be thought a bluestocking or some other antiquated term used to define a woman bent on pursuit of intelligence and scientific thought rather than the gentler things in life. Even better, she could finally put the rumors of family treasure to rest by actually finding it. For a married woman with a secure trust fund and a husband who was busying himself elsewhere could travel at will and without explanation.

If only she could bring Cook with her. But as much as Cook loved the Cope girls, as she called Millie, her sisters, and Mama, Cook was dug deep in Memphis soil and would never be uprooted.

At least that is what she told Millie every time she broached the subject. In fact, the only time the woman was absent from the Cope home was the week she took off each year in mid-February.

To go home, was the cryptic response to anyone who asked where Cook went. Beyond that, she refused to say.

Cook was wise beyond her substantial years, a woman whose words were sprinkled with refer-ences to people long dead and places shielded by

Spanish moss and reached only by pirogue through the narrow expanses of the bayou.

Father liked to claim she dallied with voodoo, but Millie knew the truth. The woman whose kitchen brought forth unmatched delicacies three times each day had taken up the task of teaching her about the Lord Almighty through the ancient Bible she kept behind the breadbox just as soon as Millie could read.

So when Father brought his new business partner, Sir William Trueck, home for dinner, it was Cook's idea for Millie to smile sweetly in his direction. To allow him to court her when he asked. And, finally, to accept his proposal of marriage, but only if it came with the assurance that she would be allowed to live in England and have complete freedom to do as she pleased.

Millie slid Sir William a sideways glance. Of course, he was deep in conversation with Father. The topic, as always, was business.

And though she ought to pay at least some modicum of attention to the things that interested her future husband, Millie just could not manage the feat. Perhaps it was Father's fervor for the topic that put her off.

Instead, she allowed her covert gaze to wash over the Englishman's handsome features. He was tall and fair, with eyes of stormy gray that sometimes turned green when the light was right. While he spoke of business deals and building empires, his voice bore an authoritative quality that women who liked that sort of fellow might adore.

In truth, Millie could easily imagine falling in love with Sir William. He was kind, and when occupied with a topic other than business, interesting and quite well spoken.

He caught her looking and smiled. She returned the gesture easily. Though she had to admit hers would be an arranged marriage and not a love match, the thought of life with Sir William was not altogether unpleasant.

"Mildred," Silas Cope said, cutting into her thoughts. "I trust you have chosen your gown for the announcement. You have just a week, you know." He looked away as if no response was required.

Which, of course, it was not. Millie could count on one hand the number of times since the funerals that he had actually wished for her opinion on any matter.

His companion, a horse-faced widowed heiress with a reluctance to marry that merely challenged Father to try even harder to wed her, lifted her glass and offered a toast to the newlyweds.

Not-yet-weds, Millie was wont to remind Mrs. Freda Ward-Wiggins. And yet she remained silent, mute to words that wished to bubble forth like the effervescence dancing to the top of a glass of champagne.

"Indeed, to my bride." Sir William slid her a look that promised a warmth they had not yet achieved in their brief moments alone. "Or, rather, to the woman who shall be my bride very soon."

Her father added his sentiment, brief and emotionless as usual, before downing his entire glass in one lengthy gulp and then motioning for the nearest servant to fill it again. As he lifted the champagne flute once more, he was speaking now of London, of something he recalled from a visit he made some years ago.

Mrs. Ward-Wiggins joined in, offering glimpses of some anecdote that caused her to smile. With the smile, the woman lost a little of her harsh features, and for a moment looked almost as if she might be pleasant. Which she was most decidedly not.

It was the one thing Millie and her father did agree on regarding her. The difference being that he quite enjoyed being seen with someone whose bank balance would long outlast any remnants of beauty or personality.

She is exactly who she says she is, and you could learn much from her, Mildred. The statement ended every conversation on the woman. Millie tuned out the conversation swirling around her and thought about her father's statement. Was she the woman she said she was?

Most decidedly not. Not as long as she lived in Memphis.

But in England she could be the woman God made her to be with no expectation of simpering silences or sipping sweet tea on a stifling afternoon without any hope of allowing so much as a bead of perspiration to dot her forehead.

Perhaps she would be branded as unusual there as well, but weren't most Americans thought of as just a bit off center?

She glanced past Mama's Waterford candelabra, the embroidered linen tablecloth, and Limoges platter that held the as-yet-untouched Christmas ham. The topic had moved past England to tackle some sort of travel debacle involving Father missing a train on the way to a safari.

Mrs. Ward-Wiggins listened with what appeared to be single-minded attention, and yet Millie had the distinct impression she was being watched from across the table as she set her napkin beside her plate.

"Mildred, do pay attention. It is Christmas and we've not yet begun to celebrate." Her father offered a glare than held no trace of holiday cheer. "Freda was just telling us of her trip down the Nile. Interesting stuff. Perhaps you and Sir William might want to accompany us someday. If you're thinking of pleading an early exit, do think again."

And so Millie picked up her napkin along with the remembered thread of her internal discourse on the benefits of leaving Memphis for greener and decidedly more northerly pastures.

Unfortunately, much as England was her solution, England was also her punishment. It was her penalty for surviving to look at Father across the breakfast table each morning and know he had done nothing to save Mama, Julia, and Sarah. For knowing he had gone off with yet another of his women the night Mama pleaded for him to stay. Pleaded for him to call for a doctor for her girls.

Being shipped abroad like a parcel mailed off to a distant relative was Millie's penalty for being the one to greet him at the garden gate as the sun was only just beginning to glisten upon the Mississippi to tell him his wife and two of his three daughters had succumbed to the fever during the long dark night.

Indeed, England was her punishment for surviving. A punishment she readily accepted, for she should not have escaped the fever that took the others.

Instead, she sat beside Father in the family pew and knew she was more like him than them. She would forever be reminded that God had chosen to usher Mama and the girls to their heavenly home while leaving Millie with Father.

So to England she would gladly go, for she knew something her father did not. Knowledge Mama had been entrusted with by her mother-in-law early in her marriage. For Grandmother Cope knew the son she had raised, and she knew Mama might need something more than what he could offer.

So she told Mama, and with her dying breath, Mama told Millie.

About the treasure.

Cook knew too, though she refused to confirm this. But Millie had heard snatches of conversation through the fireplace grates, a trick of the flues in their home that allowed a person in one room to hear someone speaking a floor or even two beneath.

When the time was right, when Father thought her well and truly gone, Millie would return from exile to claim her treasure. To live the life she promised Mama she would live.

"Just think, Mildred," Mrs. Ward-Wiggins was saying. "Next Christmas you will be having dinner in Sir William's ancestral home in the English countryside." She batted eyelashes that were almost nonexistent at Sir William and then turned what was likely intended as a charming look toward Father.

"A brilliant idea," Millie's future husband said. "Do you not think so, Mildred?"

"Brilliant," she echoed.

Mrs. Ward-Wiggins returned her attention to the Englishman. "You have a London home, do you not? Country life is wonderful, but I so adore the city."

"Of course he does," Father said. "A grand place

near Kensington Gardens, if I recall correctly. Three levels and a garden where he once hosted the Prince of Wales and his entourage. Isn't that right, my boy?"

Sir William nodded and opened his mouth to speak, but Father's companion beat him to the punch.

"Oh, my. I hear such naughty things about that group. I do hope our Mildred's delicate sensibilities will not be shocked by their behavior, should she be introduced." She gave Father a playful jab he pointedly ignored.

"A rumor, I promise you," Sir William insisted. "Nothing but top-notch, those fellows. Quite the educated bunch of chaps."

"Top-notch, indeed? Perhaps our girl here could discuss cryptology with the prince," Father offered. "Mildred is a student of the topic and she longs for further education."

Millie looked up sharply. That her father knew even this much about her interests came as quite a surprise.

"Cryptology?" Mrs. Ward-Wiggins looked to Millie as her thin lips formed the word. "What is that exactly, dear?"

"It is the study of—"

"Puzzles," Father interrupted. "The girl has an affinity for solving puzzles. I blame my mother for it. I should not have allowed her to give Mildred that infernal cypher charm. It was the start of what has become an obsession."

Cryptology was nothing of the sort, though Millie could not deny that her interest came from the lessons she learned at Grandmother Cope's knee. She reached to touch the chain that held her most precious possessions, though she was careful not to allow the pair across from her to notice.

Sir William reached under the table to grasp Millie's hand and give it a quick squeeze. "Personally, I find the science of puzzle solving fascinating."

"Is that so? Well, I must warn you. She has a few other affinities, all nonsense."

Mrs. Ward-Wiggins turned her attention to Millie. "Such as what, dear?"

"Things no woman should concern herself with," Father responded, his expression giving no doubt as to his feelings on the matter. "If I let her, she would sit on that blasted balcony out front all night and stare at the stars."

Many nights, especially when the absence of Mama and her sisters fell hard around her in the awful silence, she had counted the stars and wondered which ones they could see from heaven.

Perhaps that is why the maids had offered up a tiny corner of their domain for her use. Why Father's valet and his underlings kept their silence on the matter, even when they ought to be tattling to Father about the furnishings she had borrowed to cozy up the room.

"Oh, but the prince." Her father's voice interrupted Millie's thoughts and thankfully stole Mrs. Ward-Wiggins' attention. "Mildred had best keep clear of him. Not that she is one to lay claim to coquetry or any of the feminine arts. That, my dear," he said to Freda, "is your specialty, and skills you have definitely mastered."

Father laughed first, a loud guffaw that shook the champagne flutes and caused the turtle soup to ripple in the tureen. His companion joined in, leaning across the distance between them to grasp his forearm with her bejeweled fingers.

Millie bit back on a retort that she only allowed voice as a sigh. England was a small price to pay. A choice and not a banishment.

She is exactly the woman she says she is, and you could learn much from her, Mildred.

Indeed, she intended to do just that.

Two

December 31, 1888
Memphis, Tennessee

The Cotton Exchange would not open until two days hence, but owing to his position as a cotton trader of some importance, Father already had a key to the building downtown. And thus so did Millie.

She made her way around the corner of the roof and then back again, certain now she was alone. Two days ago she had braved a visit up to this rooftop in search of a better vantage point in which to sketch the stars. She had expected that construction debris might impede her, but what she had found instead was a space clear of all but a few clusters of materials stored in stacks, barrels, and boxes.

Along with these she had also found a most interesting crate. Opening it had been a chore, and she had been careful to replace the lid exactly as she found it.

Inside was a most interesting collection of items, along with a drawing that seemed to show that these things were part of some sort of grand experiment. Possibly some sort of machine. What sort she had yet to ascertain. She returned tonight to see if perhaps she might have another look. Or better yet, might find the owner of this crate and ask a few questions.

Millie inhaled deeply the crisp night air and thought for just a moment of what it might be like had she the ability to explore the world of science without fear of being called an embarrassment to the Cope family. Without fear of being sent away penniless or, worse, to some far-flung relation who would pay far closer attention to her and her scholarly interests than Father ever did.

The thought of her father made Millie frown,

but he would not find her here tonight. Not until she was ready to be found.

Far below, the intersection of Second and Madison Streets looked dizzyingly small. The stars above, however, seemed quite close thanks to the lack of a moon to dim them. Tonight the sky was clear, the weather just cold enough to need more wrap than she had thought to bring. It wasn't as warm as Christmas Day, but a great improvement, nonetheless, from last year's tornado and torrential downpour.

Millie had always hated the rain, but never so much as that awful night when the wind turned deadly and lives were lost, though those under the Cope roof were miraculously spared.

Millie squared her shoulders, allowing the reminder of memories of last year's New Year's Eve to slide off like raindrops down the gutter. About now Father would be wondering where she had gone.

Making an appearance at the Peabody Hotel was all she had promised, and she had kept her word. Even now, though the hotel was several blocks away, she could hear lively music drifting up toward her rooftop perch as partygoers awaited the countdown to the new year.

All that remained was to arrive at the gala tonight and make the announcement of their impending nuptials. Well, she *had* arrived. She had smiled and made polite conversation while offering an occasional attentive glance at her husband-to-be.

Millie frowned again. She had left before Father could take the stage and beg the attention of those assembled. Before he could claim his spot as the future grandfather to nobility.

Her escape from the ballroom did not mean she would refuse to keep her end of the deal. She would, though she preferred a more private announcement. She had come to the roof to think, not to hide. To remind herself of why she must go through with the marriage. To sit under the stars and pray and remember Mama, Julia, and Sarah.

And possibly to meet the owner of the secret crate.

Millie shifted positions to lean against the rough stone wall. A chill wind sent her tunneling deeper into her velvet-and-silk opera coat. Like her, the coat was meant to be more decorative than useful.

Going home would be best, but the solitude she found here warred with knowledge of the warmth she would find beside the fireplace in her bed-chamber back on Adams Street. Millie toyed with the chain that rarely left her neck, the legacy passed down from grandmother to mother and then to her.

Two charms lay hidden at the end of a length of chain resting beneath the fabric of her gown. A gold locket held a miniature portrait of a dark-haired man whose identity was shrouded in mystery. A distant relation, Mama had been told, though her mother-in-law refused to say any more.

The other charm, no broader than a dime, was no less mysterious. A gold cylinder with notches and an odd metallic rattle when shaken, this device had been an early source of Millie's interest in cryptography.

She ran her thumbnail over the edges of the cylinder's metal rings, seven in all. Some combination of alignment was needed to reveal whatever had been hidden inside. Though she had become quite adept at solving all manner of puzzles, the charm with its hidden treasure had proved as yet unsolvable.

Thanks to Mama, however, she knew that its contents were important. Life changing, perhaps. That she owned the piece and Father did not vexed him something awful. Another bonus.

The rooftop door opened and then closed again. Tucking the charms back into her bodice, Millie darted to hide behind a stack of wood left by the construction crew. Heavy footsteps echoed above the muted sound of the Peabody's orchestra, each one bringing the intruder closer to her.

Her heart pounded. Could this be the crate's owner?

A pair of black boots stopped just the other side of her refuge. Carefully peering out, she spied long legs and the tails of what appeared to be a formal coat. Inching slightly to the left, she could see one broad shoulder, a hint of ebony-colored hair, and a hat suited to an evening at the opera house.

How did he get in and, of all the places in the building, find his way up here? She had been careful to lock the door behind her lest Father or Sir William had seen her exit from the hotel and attempted to follow.

Either this man had a key as well or was a trespasser up to no good. Another peek revealed him holding some sort of metal and glass object in the air and then making notes in a small note-book.

Perhaps he was the person she sought. Millie watched intently as he leaned forward and disappeared from sight only to straighten again and heave some sort of carpetbag atop one of the barrels. The bag must have been heavy, for the barrel swayed as the burden landed on it.

Though the stranger's face was hidden in shadow, Millie could just make out the outline of a dimpled chin and a pleasing smile. Opening the bag, he pulled out an array of items and set them at his feet.

"Benchmark of practicality, indeed," he muttered, his voice deep and low. "Let's just see what Mr. Toulmin says once I provide him with the proof."

Something clattered to the ground with a metallic sound, and he reached down to pick it up.

His fingers grazed the round object, sending it rolling to a stop at Millie's feet.

With that simple incident, the moment of truth came. She could have easily grasped the object and stood.

And yet Millie found she was frozen in place. So much for being a brave scientist looking to find another kindred soul with whom to swap experiments.

She gathered her knees to her chest and held her breath as his hand reached for the ball and grasped it, missing her shoes by mere inches. Heart pounding, her eyes darted around the small space for a means of escape but found none.

All right, Lord. Please just make him leave.

Almost immediately he walked away, his footsteps sounding as if he were heading for the edge of the roof. Millie leaned over and looked at the empty bag lying on the ground. Inching forward, she saw the man step into the far edge of the pale light from the street below.

Indeed, he was quite tall, his broad shoulders balanced nicely with arms that appeared muscled even beneath the formal cut of his suit. Slung over one shoulder was something that looked like a length of cloth or perhaps an oversized cloak, and in one hand was what appeared to be several pipes or perhaps a cluster of sticks.

He moved with purpose, stepping around the puddle of light from the streets below to disappear into the shadows on the other side of the building. Was he going to fetch the crate?

Millie waited a moment before darting to hide behind a stack of construction materials on the far end of the structure. From her vantage point she could just make out the fellow's movements as he easily slung the crate onto one shoulder and carried it over near the edge.

She inched closer. What was he doing with those ropes? Her foot caught on something, and she stumbled hard against the brick wall.

Despite the pain, Millie managed to stand absolutely still as she watched the fellow stop to look around before returning to his work. Tomorrow she would probably pay for the collision with a nasty bruise, but tonight she bit her lip and maintained her silence.

He paused at the roof's edge to slip the cloak over his shoulders and then fitted the sticks into a cage of sorts. Once he had slipped the object beneath the cloak, he turned his back to her and began working in earnest on something Millie could not see.

A flash caught her attention, and she realized he was holding a small torch that he also slid beneath his cloak. What in the world was he doing? The stranger stepped up onto the rail and stood very still. After a few moments he straightened and stretched both arms out at his sides and then up over his head as if preparing to dive.

And then he jumped.

Millie screamed and raced to the edge of the roof. Her fingers gripped the bricks but she could not make herself look down. Instead, she closed her eyes and waited for the sound of the man's body landing on the pavement below. To her surprise, only the music of the orchestra over at the Peabody combined with an odd hissing noise was audible.

The noise grew louder until it sounded as if someone were boiling water for tea just out of reach. She remained quite still, fear at what she might find keeping her eyes shut tight.

"What are you doing here?" a deep voice asked.

Millie's eyes flew open. There, just a few feet away was the dark-haired man in the formal suit and beaver hat. Floating. In midair.

A rope tied to his waist stretched to the building and across the roof to disappear behind the wall. This explained how he managed to hover so near the edge of the roof. It did not, however, explain how he could remain suspended with his feet four stories up from the sidewalk. Or was it five?

He continued to watch her, one hand on the rope and the other resting at his side. Her gaze traveled up to the black device hovering above him. Of course. The contents of the crate could easily have been assembled to form this device.

"Is that a balloon?" She shook her head. "But it is so small. How do you manage to keep it in the air?"

Something akin to annoyance crossed his features. "This is no balloon."

"And yet you are floating." She looked up. "Attached to something that looks very much like an extremely small balloon. I would hesitate to call it a dirigible, what with the size being such as it is. Of course, the real question is what is powering the lift and how are you managing to steer it?"

Her courage emboldened, she asked more questions, most having to do with the gas involved, the materials he used, and the like. During the barrage of queries, the aviator merely stared at her.

He leaned forward, his posture threatening despite the odd location of his person. "I repeat: What are you doing here?"

"*I* have a key," she snapped. "What are *you* doing here?"

"I also have a key." Kyle would tell her nothing more than that, especially given the fact she appeared to know how to ask intelligent questions.

The idea occurred that she might be some sort of spy sent to find out what he had learned about steering mechanisms and flight. He would not rule that out. Not yet, anyway.

She scoured him with a haughty gaze. "You have no good reason to be here, sir. Nor do you have a decent explanation for . . ." She made a sweeping gesture in his general direction. "For this."

Wasn't she the spunky one? Had their meeting occurred elsewhere and under other circumstances, Kyle might have found her imperious attitude amusing.

Tonight, however, she was either a threat or an interruption. He aimed to decide which, and quickly.

"Go back to your party, miss," he said as evenly as he could manage. "I am sure there are a dozen Memphis boys waiting for their turn on your dance card." He gave her a slow looking over— what he could see of her, which was not much thanks to the absence of moonlight. "And my guess is your father does not know you have gone off alone."

Silence.

A thought occurred, and he laughed. "Oh, I think I see what is happening here. You have slipped away to meet someone, have you not?" He paused to watch her closely. "Or are you hiding from someone?"

"Don't be ridiculous."

Though her face was hidden in shadows, her tone told Kyle he had struck a nerve. Then she leaned forward.

There. Her expression showed the truth. The girl was on the run.

A chill wind whipped past them and rocked the equipment overhead, causing him to grasp for a better hold on the rope.

"Having a problem with your plaything?"

"This is no plaything," he said as he checked the altitude reading. No problem there. A glance at the gas levels, and he frowned. He had used more than his calculations indicated he might expect to, an issue in need of further exploration.

Kyle released his grasp on the rope to pull out his notebook and jot down the numbers. When he finished, he tucked the book away, only to realize he had drifted up and now hung suspended at the far length of the rope and well above the roof.

"I will need a promise of confidentiality from you before I can allow you to leave." He paused only a heartbeat. "It is a matter of national security."

It was. Of a sort. According to Mr. Taft, the War Department was interested, as were several other government agencies. All would be for naught should someone catch wind of the fact he had managed to get this close to perfecting the device.

To his surprise, the woman rested her hands on her hips and gave him a withering look. "Who said I was going anywhere?"

"You have no business here," he said as he pulled on the rope and began to descend.

"But here I am, and I am very interested in

what you are doing. That is an experimental flying machine, which explains the crate I found two days ago."

So she had found his equipment. Kyle bit back the words he wished to say in favor of not responding at all.

"I understand the need for secrecy." She moved to the left and appeared to be studying the device. Or possibly him. "What with national security and all," she added with an obvious note of sarcasm. "But, I truly am curious. How does this work?"

When she stretched to touch the rope, he yanked it out of her reach. "I will thank you not to play with the equipment."

"Play?" Her laughter was haughty and yet her expression was not. "I assure you I am not interested in amusing myself with your rope. I only wanted to see what sort of device this is. You cannot possibly be using hot air to keep it afloat as there is no flame, so what is providing the lift? Or is that a matter of national security too?"

Her questions continued as her gaze swept the length of the flying device and then landed on him again. When he didn't respond, she grew silent.

"Are you finished?" he asked.

"For now. Oh, wait. Just one more thing." At his chuckle, she continued in a more conciliatory tone. "Take me with you on a flight."

"Absolutely not. *Now* are you finished?"

Her expression answered for her. Kyle returned to his notes in the hope she might lose interest. When she remained in place, he looked at her again to find her watching him closely.

"As you can see, I am busy here," he said as firmly as he could manage. "I suggest you leave now."

The hurt in her eyes was unmistakable. "You are not going to answer my questions?"

Again, he remained silent.

"Oh, I see. You are one of *them*. And I had hoped we might talk as one scientist to another."

The woman shook her head and turned to walk away. She reached the door without sparing him so much as a backward look.

He studied her. He had never seen a scientist who could wear a ball gown so successfully.

She gave the door a jerk and then another. Apparently it was locked. Or jammed.

Turning around to face him, her stance told him how she felt about the matter. "You have locked me up here. I demand you come down here this instant and release me."

"I have done nothing of the sort," he said as he pulled against the wind now whipping up around him.

"You have, and you will remedy the situation immediately, especially as the reason for my departure is your lack of cooperation in answering the simplest of questions."

The tremor in her voice might have been anger, but Kyle decided it was more likely attributable to the completely unsuitable wardrobe she had chosen for her visit to the roof.

Fighting the wind was proving a bigger problem than the woman glaring at him from below. Slack in the rope allowed the flotation device to bob upward, not the direction he intended.

"You will not fly away and leave me here." She took a step forward, and then another, all the while looking up at him with one hand on her hip and the other pointing in his direction. "Understand that there will be repercussions from this . . . this . . . oh!"

Her foot tangled in the rope, sending her plummeting. When she did not immediately rise, he called down to her. No response.

Kyle bit back on the words he longed to say as he maneuvered himself toward the building. When his feet touched the roof, he slipped off the device and set it aside to hurry to her side. "Miss?" he said as he knelt beside her.

A cursory examination told him that while she might awaken with a headache, there was no blood to indicate a serious injury. Just beyond the edge of the roof, the flotation device bobbed slowly up and down at the end of its rope.

Thanks to the building's height and Kyle's insistence that black silk be used in its construction, the apparatus would be virtually invisible to passersby down below. Also, given the lateness of the hour and the fact it was New Year's Eve, few would be about and even fewer would likely think of looking up.

He lit his pocket lantern, and instantly the lamp cast a wash of golden light over thick dark lashes that brushed high cheekbones. Lips of soft pink pursed as if she might be trying to speak, but otherwise she remained still and quiet. His gaze swept the length of her.

Unless he missed his guess, her gown was made by the society ladies' favorite, the House of Worth, and the pearls at her ears and circling her wrist were the real thing. It did not take a Pinkerton agent to determine she was a woman of quality and wealth.

A woman who did not belong on the roof of the empty Cotton Exchange building on New Year's Eve. And yet she claimed to be a fellow scientist with a key.

What was her story? He would find that out. But first he must figure out how to get her back on her feet. He knew from experience that these society girls could be overly delicate, though this one apparently had no trouble ordering strangers around.

"Miss?" he said softly. "Can you hear me?"

There was no response, though her breathing remained deep and regular. He touched her cheek with the back of his hand and found it chilled.

Slowly her eyes fluttered open and her lower lip quivered.

"All right, then. You did not dress for the roof, but I did. So, being a gentleman . . ."

Kyle slipped out of his coat and instantly he felt the evening's cold.

"Time to get you downstairs."

A soft murmur was the only response when he wrapped her in his coat and lifted her into his arms. Carrying her down four flights of stairs in this condition held little appeal, nor did leaving the flying apparatus, but he could hardly abandon her here. He shifted her in his arms, and a golden chain slid into view beneath the coat. At the end of the chain was a gold locket and what appeared to be a brass Jefferson wheel cypher.

He turned to allow the light from the street below to illuminate the device and decided that what he'd initially thought to be brass was actually gold, possibly doubloons, unless he missed his guess. With seven rings instead of the usual twenty-four, the cypher was smaller than others he had seen. And then there was the lack of letters on the wheels, which were no bigger than dimes.

While President Jefferson created the wheel cypher to encode messages, the purpose of the device, which substituted bumps and plateaus rather than letters, was unclear. Unless there was something inside being protected, the only answer was that the piece was purely decorative.

The society scientist stirred, and eyes the color of Café Du Monde's café au lait flecked with gold stared up at him. However, the scream that issued from those pretty pink lips a moment later was anything but delicate.

Though he stumbled, Kyle managed to hold on to her until he could release her on steady footing. His coat fell to the ground, and her foot tangled in it. Lurching forward, she aimed her fist in his direction.

"Leave . . . me . . . alone." The words were uttered in a voice that held nothing but contempt. Or was it fear? Whatever the reason, the woman thought it just fine to continue a barrage of mostly poorly aimed punches in his direction.

"Calm down, lady," he said as he ducked his head. "I am only trying to help."

"You, sir, will stay back. I insist," she said as she yanked her arm away and landed a single glancing blow on his shoulder. Though she stumbled again, she ignored his reach to help her and quickly righted herself. "Why does my head ache? And, oh, it is chilly up here."

"Sit down and gain your bearings in case something more has been damaged." Kyle snatched up his coat as he watched her glance around looking dazed. "Here," he said as he held out his coat to her. "You are going to catch your death up here."

She jumped away as if he had tried to hand her a live snake. "Stay back. Oh, my head hurts."

"You tripped on that rope and hit your head. That is why you have a headache. You may want to be careful about moving around too much."

She reached into her skirt to remove a tiny double-barrel pistol, which she aimed in his direction. "No," she said slowly. "*You* might want to be careful."

"Hey, now," he said as he attempted a smile. "I am not here to hurt you. If this coat bothers you, I will put it on."

"It is not the coat," she snapped. "It's you. Now get back and do not try to come any closer or you will regret it. That is a promise."

The pistol never wavered as she began to walk backward.

"You may want to look out. That is how you fell," he said gently. "There are uneven spots and—"

She upended herself again. The gun went sliding. Kyle pitched the coat at her, causing the woman to have to stop and toss it aside. They both made a grab for the gun, but Kyle came up victorious. He quickly removed two bullets from the small but dangerous pearl-handled Remington before handing it back to its owner.

"There is no need for shooting," he said as he dropped the bullets into his vest pocket. "How about you take my coat too? You must be cold."

"You are the scientist," she said as she shook her head. "I am sorry. I did not think . . . that is, everything went black and I thought you might have been trying to hurt me."

"Hurt you?" He held out his arms and put on his most innocent expression. "Do I look like a man who might hurt a woman?"

"I don't suppose so . . ."

"Exactly."

"But my head throbs right here." She rested her palm on the side of her head. "And the last thing I remember is I was quite insistent on finding my way out the door."

"Because you were unhappy with me. I was not keen on answering your questions, and you were not keen on ceasing to ask them."

She thought a moment and then nodded. A small groan followed. "Yes, you are right. I do remember being perturbed at your infuriating attitude. Arrogant is perhaps a better word."

"I prefer otherwise occupied."

"That would be two words," she said with a smile.

"You have me there." He once again held out his coat. "Here, please take this. Call it a peace offering, if you must."

Shivering must have trumped pride, for she took it and slipped it on. "Thank you."

"I am a gentleman," he replied with a shrug. "Even when I am otherwise occupied."

"Arrogant," she countered, though her expression told him she might be teasing.

"Losing his patience," Kyle said, though he was careful to lift a brow in mock irritation lest she think he was serious. "And yes, I know that is three words."

He walked back to where he had tethered the rope before she spoke.

"I remember it clearly now. You were over there." She gestured to the roof's edge. "Floating. Or hanging from that device. Or . . . oh, I do not know. You were certainly up here doing something secretive or else you would have answered my questions, and you certainly would not have hidden a crate up here in anticipation of this event. Am I wrong?"

"Not exactly," he said, though he preferred not to tell her any more than he had to about the experiment she had interrupted.

"Well, whatever the situation, I just want to leave now."

He tried to ignore an unexpectedly chill breeze. "As do I."

"Well, as you are the expert in machinery and such, could you open the door? Apparently it is locked."

"I did not lock it."

"Nor did I." She glanced over at the door and then back at him. "You were the last one to use it."

"The building is new. Perhaps it's stuck."

She seemed to think about that as she replaced her pistol in the pocket of her gown.

"Correct me if I am wrong, miss, but Monsieur Worth does not design pockets into his dresses, does he?"

The pretty lady almost smiled. "It is a custom feature, one I am happy I requested."

"I can see how you would need the weapon, especially if you frequent dark roofs regularly."

"I will ignore that comment and plead a headache." The woman went to the door and once again yanked on the knob. "Stay right where you are," she said when he moved to assist. "You may be a fellow scientist, but you are also a stranger to me. You have my bullets, but you have no idea whether that was my only gun."

He took her bluff. "It is."

Kyle had to give her credit. She maintained a haughty expression even as indecision crept across her eyes.

"I might have a knife," she blustered as she tugged again.

"You might, but I assure you I'm harmless." He was not, but he held out his hands in the hopes she would believe that. "How about I promise not to give you any reason to use it?"

"You already have. What harmless man manages to jump off of a building and then float back onto the roof while refusing to answer questions about the experiment?"

"You have me there," he said as he fought to keep a straight face.

"And locks the door."

"No, I did not do that."

She jerked on the knob once more and it came off in her hand. Her expression gave away her shock. "Now what?"

"Would you like me to see if I can repair your damage?"

"My damage?"

He gestured to the knob. "You were the one who broke it."

She opened her mouth to say something and then apparently thought better of it. Rather than respond, she merely nodded toward the door before moving out of the way.

He took the knob from her outstretched hand. After several attempts, he turned to find her watching intently. "Sorry. You have done an excellent job of breaking it," he said as he tossed it aside.

Brown eyes widened. "But that is impossible! It cannot be broken." She hurried to the door and began to hit it. "Someone surely can come and rescue us."

"On New Year's Eve?" He pulled out his pocket watch. "With less than fifteen minutes until midnight? Not likely."

She huffed and leaned against the door. "I suppose someone will come eventually."

"Eventually, yes." Kyle met her eyes. "But the building does not officially open until January second. My guess is you have a forty-eight hour wait, and that is not taking into account how long it would be before anyone decided to visit the roof."

She groaned. "What awful timing. I would choose the one night of the year when the building is completely empty." She gave him a look. "Well, almost empty."

"Oh? I suspect you came up here for exactly that purpose. I know I did."

She glanced over at the flotation device. "So you could play with your balloon without interruption?"

"That was the idea, though it is not—"

"A balloon," she interrupted. "Yes, so you said, and yet it bobs about like a child's toy. An oversized toy, but a balloon all the same. Unless you would prefer I refer to it as a dirigible, though that would not be an accurate description, would it?"

"If you insist," he muttered. "Although, no. Technically it would not."

"No matter how it may appear, I did not expect to find myself in this predicament. Eventually I will be missed. And then what will happen?"

A rhetorical question, he assumed. Yet he could not imagine that a woman as pretty as she was not already being missed by someone, and not just an overprotective father.

The society scientist laughed as she found the answer to her own question. "Well, there is another way down."

"Oh?" He gave her a hopeful look. And then he guessed her intention. "Oh, no. Never."

Three

Millie watched the man gather up his things and return them to his carpetbag. "What are you doing?"

He spared her a glance, offering a glimpse of eyes that held more than the appropriate amount of mirth given their dire situation. "I am preparing for my exit."

"*Your* exit?"

He shrugged before returning to his work.

"Fine," she said as the last of her patience threatened to evaporate. "Go ahead and leave without me, but make me one promise."

"What is that?"

She winced as her head throbbed. "Do not tell anyone I am up here. Just come back and open the door."

"I can't do that," he said as he closed the bag and set it aside. "The only way is to inform someone. To whom should I—"

"Of course you can," she insisted. "If you are worried I will say something about your little plaything there, rest assured I will not." When he did not immediately respond, she hurried to continue. "Believe me, sir. The last thing I want is for anyone to know I've been up here."

His grin was swift and quite disarming. "Because you may want to hide up here again?"

"Not if I will be encountering you," she snapped.

"You will not. Unfortunately, I do not make it my habit to test my devices atop the Cotton Exchange building." He shrugged. "I prefer to do that closer to home."

"And yet you are here. And not home, wherever that is. On New Year's Eve, no less."

"Yes, I am." Obviously he would say no more about that. "How is your headache?"

The question came as an expected diversion.

"Improving." Millie gave him a sideways look. "Where exactly is home?"

He sighed. "You will not let the topic go easily? Fair enough. I have been questioned by better inquisitors and survived."

"Is that so?" She laughed but sobered quickly. "Where exactly did that happen?"

He slung the carpetbag over his shoulder and moved toward the roof's edge. "I did not say, did I?"

"*Please* open the door once you are down on the ground," she called as she huddled against the wall out of the worst of the wind.

"As I just said, I cannot do that." He turned to look at her. "I'm not being deliberately uncooperative. The fact is, I left the key in . . . well, suffice it to say that per a prior agreement I returned it to its owner by way of leaving it on his desk." He gestured toward the door. "Which is several floors beneath us."

Her heart sunk. "I see."

"Wait . . . you said you had a key. I do not mind using that to get you out."

"Not possible," she said. "I left it downstairs so I would not lose it."

"Then I will just go down and get it," he said, as if that were the simplest thing in the world.

"I left it under the rug on the inside of the building," she amended. "And to be sure I was not followed, I locked the door behind me."

"As did I," he said as he slipped the device's leather straps over his shoulders. "Do you wish me to tell your family, or should I go straight to the police? Perhaps I should find a doctor as well, unless you are certain you are not gravely injured."

She groaned. "None are options I would choose. And no, my injuries are minor at best, and mostly to my pride."

The truth on all counts. She would never allow her father to find out where she had gone, and except for an occasional twinge, her head already no longer ached.

"No?" He pulled an object from his pocket and

held it up a moment before returning it there. This time the eyes that stared back at her held no amusement. "Well, if you are certain then."

Was she? Temperatures were plummeting, and she would likely catch her death up here before morning even with the man's coat. Then there was the issue of what Father would say when she finally was found.

Mildred Cope found shivering on the roof of the Cotton Exchange building? Surely the headlines would not be favorable?

MEMPHIS HEIRESS FREEZES TO DEATH WHILE ENGAGEMENT PARTY GOES ON WITHOUT HER.

She might not actually freeze to death, but she would be most uncomfortable. Hypothermia was a potential threat, though she might find something in the construction rubble to form a makeshift covering until . . .

Until when?

Until Father arrived to officially join the other members of the Exchange and tenants of the building for the grand opening ceremony? Indeed, she might be able to alert them and the assembled guests and newsmen through her screams.

Then the headline would read:

DISTRAUGHT FIANCÉE OF BRITISH NOBILITY PLUCKED FROM COTTON EXCHANGE ROOFTOP.

How would that look? Of course, that assumed

Father and Sir William had made the announcement just prior to midnight as scheduled.

"Wait!" she called to the aviator, who was now standing on the edge of the roof.

He turned, the balloon bobbing a few feet from his head. "What is it? A message you would like me to pass on to the police?"

"No." She walked toward him. Though her insides quaked at the thought of what she was about to do, Millie kept moving, propelled by thoughts of what might happen should she choose to allow him to leave without her.

"Are you certain we both cannot fit on that thing?" She gestured to the board that held his feet. "I could place my feet inside yours with my back to you. And that strap," she said as she lifted her gaze to meet his. "Could not it just as easily hold two as one?"

He seemed to consider the idea a moment. "The prototype is only made to accommodate one person." He retrieved his notebook and turned a few pages. "All right, from what I see here, I think it might be possible for both of us to fly together."

"Think?" She shook her head. "I am not so keen on that."

He chuckled. "How quickly you change your mind. Typical woman."

"I take offense, sir. I am a scientist, and a scientist bases decisions on facts, not suppositions. What you have offered is the supposition the machine will fly with both of us attached to it."

"All right, I will tell you this much. One of the fellows bankrolling the project—"

"So this *is* a project," she interrupted as she gave one of the ropes a yank. "What sort of project?"

"Something I am not at liberty to discuss due to issues of national security. However, I can say that one of the backers is a certain Mr. Taft, currently of Ohio but soon to be serving our country in a federal position."

"And?"

"And Mr. Taft is . . . well, he is not a small man, and he had no trouble on a prior flight."

"Your flying machine, does it work like the balloons I have ridden aboard in France?" She held up her hand to wave away any protest. "And yes, I realize you prefer I do not refer to this flying machine as a balloon."

"A similar premise. If you close your eyes, you would likely not know the difference."

"And yet you appear to be able to steer it with a precision my French aviator friend could not." When he said nothing, she continued. "All right, I can see you have secrets of your own and are not keen on sharing them yet. But one promise," she said as she stopped just out of reach of the stranger.

"And what is that?" he asked, amusement crossing his devastatingly handsome features.

"Should I die and you survive, I would like you to tell anyone who asks that I was kidnapped."

His laughter swirled around her like the icy wind. "I will do nothing of the sort."

"Well, then," she said as she moved a step backward. "May I at least request that you not tell anyone where you found me or how I came to be attached to that contraption with you?"

The stranger seemed to ponder the question a moment. "I am a God-fearing man, miss, so I will not lie. However, should you die and I survive, I can promise I will offer nothing of the circumstances as to how we came to be companions in this adventure. How is that?"

"What assurance do you offer?"

"The assurance that I have both the experience and the training to prove my claim."

The way he spoke convinced her he was telling the truth. "I suppose that is fair enough. How do we proceed?"

"First, I need your promise that you have no more weapons hidden on your person. I do not want any nasty surprises should we hit the ground a little harder than expected."

"Just how hard do you expect we will be hitting the ground?"

"I hope it will not be hard at all, but I will not leave this roof unprepared. Answer the question."

"I have no other weapons." She looked up at him. "At least none with bullets."

He quirked a dark brow. "Or blades?"

"Or blades."

"All right, then. Let's begin." The stranger gestured for her to come close, and reluctantly she complied. "It might be a little windy." He glanced around and then yanked on the leather straps one more time before releasing what appeared to be a length of wood attached with wires. "You will place your feet here between mine," he said, and she did. "Oh, and it could be a little bumpy, but I am fairly certain we will make it."

"Fairly certain?" She froze where she stood.

"A figure of speech. Now, come on. Would not you like to be off this rooftop before next year?"

"Next year? Oh, I get it. It's almost midnight."

He pulled a gold watch from his vest pocket. "By my calculations we have just about seven minutes to spare." Snapping the timepiece closed, he returned it to his pocket and then held out his arms to Millie.

"Just so we are clear, there is nothing holding me up here except you, a footrest, and that strap?"

"Sorry, but no." He reached for her hand and she allowed him to take it. "I have a strong interest in arriving on the sidewalk without damaging this device and without either of us acquiring any further injuries."

"As do I." Taking a deep breath, she allowed the stranger to position her in front of him and draw her close.

The feeling was not altogether unpleasant, nor was the masculine scent of soap and woody spice that clung to him as she rested her back against his chest.

"All right," he said as he wrapped what appeared to be a leather belt around her waist and then cinched it tight. "This may be slightly awkward, but you need to be securely fastened in."

Millie knew a woman like herself with such gentle breeding should not have felt so comfortable in such a possibly compromising situation. She rested her hands atop the belt and gave it a tug. "It appears to be secure."

Warm hands topped hers to repeat the test she had just performed. Indeed the gesture was most pleasant, though enjoying it lasted only until she remembered their plan to plummet off the building together.

"Expect the sensation of falling quickly followed by a tugging motion that will temporarily lift us up. That will be the rope holding us to the building. Once I am certain we are safe to fly, I will release the rope and we should float down safely to the sidewalk."

"Should?" she somehow asked through teeth that insisted on chattering from the cold. And yet it was she who wore the coat.

"Will," he corrected. "Unless you would like me to fly you around some first. My calculations show we have at least another twenty minutes of flying time left."

"Thank you, but no."

Even as she said it, however, Millie could not help but feel the least bit intrigued with the possibility.

"No?" he paused. "You have changed your mind so quickly, have you? And you call yourself a scientist."

She had seen him effortlessly flying the machine. And she had watched him land without any trouble. It was a lovely night. But what if someone saw her as she floated past with a man who was not her fiancé in a contraption that was, per the stranger's own admission, merely being tested and not yet safe for the masses? And then there was her companion's lack of proper outerwear, thanks to her.

"I will take your lack of response for a no. You are certain of your health?"

"My health is fine," she assured him as she rested her head on his shoulder. "Let's get this over with, please."

He shifted positions, alerting Millie to their imminent departure. "On the count of four we will be off. For your part, just hold on tight and try not to make any sounds that might alert anyone to our flight. Can you do that?"

Millie glanced down from the dizzying height to consider the distance to the ground. *Other than scream,* she wanted to ask.

"I will try," was what she said instead as she closed her eyes again.

The stranger turned them around so that they were facing away from the rooftop. The next maneuver would likely be to jump.

Or float.

Or fly.

Or whatever one called releasing all good sense and suspending oneself five floors off the ground tied to an experimental plaything.

Lord, please carry us down. I do not want to die yet, and I simply cannot do anything to prevent my move to England.

"Praying would not hurt," the man added. "If you are of a mind."

Millie opened her eyes and swiveled her head to look up into his face. "I am. And I already have."

His expression faltered a moment, and then his smile returned. "Good. So have I. Now, on four. One—"

"Wait!"

"What?"

"I do not even know your name."

He gave her a thoughtful look. "No, you do not. Nor do I know yours." He was silent for a moment. "Propriety would demand that we exchange names, but for reasons I prefer not to discuss, I am not keen to share mine. What about you?"

She thought of the ramifications of the stranger knowing where to find Father to tattle on her. Of what her father might think. Or say. Or do.

At the best he would be horrified. At worst, her

engagement to Sir William would be ended and her deportation to England derailed.

"Good point," she said. "Do forget I mentioned it."

"Mentioned what?"

"Exactly. So how do you guide this contraption?"

His hand pointed toward a collection of pulleys hanging beneath the bottom opening of the balloon. "I can lift or lower the device by using these two and create a forward or backward speed by—"

"You are telling me you can fly this thing backward?" Millie shook her head. "Stop teasing me. That goes against the theories of air resistance as put forth by Cayley . . ."

At the man's apparently stunned silence, Millie paused. "Do you not know the theory?"

"Of course I do."

She had the distinct impression the man thought she was joking. "I told you I was a fellow scientist. Are you surprised a woman would be interested in a man's field?"

"I find it most interesting, actually."

"Me or the field?" she dared ask.

"Yes." Affecting a serious expression, he shrugged. "Suffice it to say I have added features that will allow me to maneuver in and out of tight spots if need be. It is part of the design of the . . ." She felt him shake his head. "Never mind. All you need to know is that it works, forward or backward."

Millie shook her head. "If that is true, then what were you testing?"

He let out a long breath. "Fair enough. In order to secure a patent, certain criteria must be in place, including test flights in different locations and at different altitudes and atmospheric conditions."

"And Memphis on New Year's Eve fit the criteria?"

"An empty roof of an empty building on a night with a slight wind, no moon, and no precipitation fit my criteria. I just happened to find all that in Memphis. Now, if there are no more questions?"

She shook her head. There was no point in delaying the adventure any further. She took a firm grip on the belt and rested her head against his chest once again, squeezing her eyes closed.

"All right," he began. "One . . . two . . ."

And then he jumped.

"You said four!" she uttered before speaking became impossible and the sensation of falling caused an odd lurch in her stomach. Then came the yank upward as the rope caught. At least she hoped it was the rope.

"Look around."

Millie did as the stranger said. Turning her head to glance behind her, she could see that the edge of the roof was almost close enough to touch. She dare not look down.

"Looks like we are doing fine. Hold on tight while I release the rope."

She felt the rumble of the aviator's voice against her ear. *Lord, please do not let us die,* she prayed as she renewed her grip on the leather strap.

A peek down and fear instantly held her immobile. Even the breath in her throat froze. So much for being a brave adventurer.

The device jerked into motion, and she gasped as she slammed her eyes shut once more. This time there was no sensation of flying upward or jolting downward. Instead, she felt little beyond a slight rocking motion.

Opening one eye just a bit, she determined their speed of descent was indeed quite slow. Emboldened, Millie opened her eyes and swiveled her head to look up. The balloon, or whatever the stranger preferred to call it, blocked her vision completely.

How could such a thing, bereft of hot air or any other type of gas that she was aware of, keep them afloat? The science of it defied all she knew of lift and drag, though her study of the subject was most incomplete.

"It works with the same gas that powers street lamps," he said as if he heard her thoughts.

"And it is safe?"

"Extremely." He shifted positions, his arm

reaching to pull down some sort of gauge. "I have not crashed it yet."

Her toes tingled inside her dancing shoes as she kicked one foot against the chill air. The sensation of floating felt oddly exhilarating.

She spied the Haverty Building and could also see the spires of the Customs House. There was the Masonic Temple, and, if she looked closely, she could see Queensware Building. And was that Mr. Robinson's apothecary?

"Ready for landing?"

"Actually," she said as she angled a look up at the handsome stranger, "were you serious when you asked if I might like to fly around with you a bit first? If that is part of your testing, that is."

"Now you want to fly with me." A statement, not a question. "Are you known for changing your mind?"

"Yes," she said, emboldened by the prospect of the once-in-a-lifetime moment. "I believe I am." She shook her head. "What I mean is, I am ready to continue flying if you are not too cold. I feel awful that you've given me your coat."

His grin became laughter. "I'm fine, my brave society scientist," he said as he made an adjustment to his machine that caused them to cease their downward drift. "Let's see Memphis together."

They rose on a gentle breeze, drifting past the

open windows of the Peabody Hotel just as the crowd inside began their countdown.

"Is it that time already?" Millie tried not to think of who might look out and see her.

"As my watch is in a pocket I cannot reach without disturbing your person, I will have to bow to the timekeepers at the Peabody."

The way he spoke made her laugh. "No, we certainly could not disturb my person, could we?"

They drifted past the far end of the Peabody just as the crowd called out, "Three . . . two . . . one . . ."

A symphony of sounds rose as a collective "Happy New Year!" came rolling toward them on the breeze. Somewhere inside the ballroom, Father likely stood with a champagne glass lifted. Was he toasting the first few moments of 1889 with her husband-to-be? Perhaps they were toasting the wedding to come.

"Happy New Year," her companion said as he nudged her arm. "This is not how you expected to spend the midnight hour, I suspect."

"Happy New Year to you," she said as she craned her neck to try to see him. Failing that, Millie leaned back against his shoulder and looked at the stars, which appeared much nearer tonight than they ever had before. Snuggling into the stranger's coat, she grinned.

"I wager the coming year will prove most

interesting," he said as he reached to make an adjustment to one of his gadgets.

Indeed, 1889 would be a most interesting year. It already was.

Four

January 1, 1889
Memphis

With only the occasional bump of wind to propel the flying machine, it floated at a lazy speed toward the western horizon, bobbing over the wide Mississippi River and the collection of steamboats, barges, and other assorted river craft moored some distance below. Here the stars glinted silver on brown as the muddy river flowed toward the Gulf of Mexico hundreds of miles to the south.

"What a nice night for flying," he said. "The breeze has died down enough to make traveling pleasant."

"Pleasant," Millie echoed. "Do you do this often? Test flying devices, I mean."

His response was a chuckle and then a swift, "No."

"No, I do not suppose you would." She snuggled deeper into the stranger's coat. "So, what is this

64

machine's purpose? Other than flying around Memphis in the middle of the night."

"That is classified."

"I see. Sounds very official."

"No comment," he responded with what sounded like a healthy measure of humor.

It occurred to Millie that she should feel some measure of fear despite her knowledge of aerodynamics. After all, her feet rested on a narrow board a great distance above the water, and there was no good or discernable reason in established theory why she or her companion should remain aloft in this creation.

And yet there was something compelling about this adventure. Something memorable, yes, but also something extremely peaceful about gliding about beneath a carpet of stars God hung in their places.

Millie let out a long breath. Perhaps she was meant to fly. She had certainly enjoyed her Parisian adventure and had even gone back several times before the ship sailed for home. So why not take this leap to a smaller craft? A giggle escaped her.

"You are enjoying this."

"I am, actually," she said. "I am no stranger to flying, though the balloon I insisted my father buy was much larger and certainly not this much fun."

"Is that so?" She felt his hands moving as if

adjusting gadgets or possibly changing directions. Still, they remained on course.

"He never bought it, of course," she felt compelled to add. "He claimed I might get into trouble with it."

That he had also insisted she would bring further embarrassment to the family by drawing attention to herself with the contraption went without mention.

"That necklace of yours," the stranger said, changing the subject. "It has a Jefferson wheel cypher on it, does it not?"

"Of sorts. Are you familiar with cyphers?"

"Somewhat." He paused to fiddle with one of the strings hanging from the balloon. "They are a hobby of mine."

Interesting. "Remind me to ask you how to open this one when we are back on the ground."

"I can tell you that now. The rings are coded. The only way to solve the cypher is to figure out the numeric code."

"And that is the puzzle I have been trying to solve. Something is inside and I would love to know what it is."

"Where did you get it?"

"My mother gave it to me. It was hers." Her fingers reached to toy with the chain, now hidden beneath the stranger's warm coat. "It belonged to my grandmother before that."

Making a wide arc, the stranger turned the

balloon back toward the city itself, gliding soundlessly over the spire of the Central Baptist church. Millie giggled again in spite of herself as she stretched her toes to see if somehow she might snag her shoe on its topmost point.

She could not, of course, but the effort was a memory she would likely never forget. And then she spied a familiar poplar tree, a road sign she knew and, beyond that, the chimneys that soared above her home on Adams Street.

It was a grand pile of bricks built to erase the shame of her father's less than stellar personal conduct. The home, though breathtaking on the outside, was museum-like on the inside.

And yet the imposing edifice had done its job. Amazing that the image of wealth could do just as much as actual money in the bank.

Father certainly would not have secured his place at the Cotton Exchange if it became known that, depending upon the moment, he was all cotton and no cash. That much Millie had learned courtesy of the quiet demeanor that caused her father to forget she was about while speaking of business matters.

But Sir William would save the day . . . unless he changed his mind.

With that thought, her good mood plummeted. An obligation for another day, she decided, and not one worth ruining a perfectly spectacular evening over.

She mentally shrugged off the remnants of the thought to give the house a closer look. A fire had been laid in all but one of the chimneys, and the smoke that curled up wove around them in wispy gray plumes.

The lone chimney without a flame was the attic room she had claimed as her own private sanctuary for the practice of reading, science, and the arts. There was never a fire there unless she was in residence and requested it.

Lamps had already been lit in her bedchamber, but Father's end of the house remained dark. Likely he had taken rooms at the Peabody tonight, the better to keep his evening entertainment discreet. For he was nothing now if not conscious of his image as an upright citizen. All that work for nothing? Millie sighed. Were she to be spotted floating across Memphis in this contraption, all her father's work to regain his status would be for naught.

At least the stranger had used black for the fabric encasing the balloon, and his clothing was of a similar hue. If only Millie were wearing the same. Unfortunately, even with the covering of the aviator's black coat, her gown would be easily spotted even by the most myopic of Memphis citizens if they happened to look up.

"Perhaps we have ventured far enough," she said.

"Yes, of course." He once again reached up to

fiddle with the gadgets. "I assume you do not wish to be returned to the roof of the Cotton Exchange, so where might I leave you?"

Where indeed?

She glanced around but could find no place where they might land the craft without being spotted.

"I know," he said. "I have just the place."

"I hope somewhere private so as to keep this evening's trip just between the two of us."

"I prefer that as well," he said as Millie felt his arms moving behind her. "In fact, I will have to ask you to promise not to repeat any details of this trip to anyone. I probably should have mentioned that before we left the Cotton Exchange."

"You will have no trouble from me on that account," she said as she watched the moonlight filter through the lacy fretwork of a building under construction at the far end of downtown. "Actually, I would require the same promise from you."

"Considering I have no idea of your name, telling anyone of our adventure would prove difficult, would it not?"

"Agreed."

They drifted back toward the center of the city and then the stranger began to send the balloon into a slow descent. Any of the buildings nearby might have made a decent landing place. However, the nearest was the dreaded Peabody.

"Sir," she said as she noticed several downtown buildings that might be his chosen landing target. "May I ask where we are stopping?"

His chuckle was low and soft. "The Peabody Hotel, of course," he said as he set his course and maneuvered toward the expanse of roof now so very near. "I happen to know they never lock the roof access door. Do not ask how I know this."

She hauled in a deep breath and held it. Of all the places to make a landing, he was heading for the last place she wanted to be. Possibly the most populated building in all of Memphis on this holiday night.

It was too late to say anything, however, for they were practically there. Instead, she closed her eyes and tried to pray, but no words would come beyond a swift plea for safety and secrecy.

"And we are here," he said as they hit the rooftop with a soft thud. "Go ahead and release the belt. I will tell you how."

Millie did as he asked and then stepped forward. Turning around to face him, she watched him check his dials and gauges, ignoring her completely.

The man's preoccupation with his gadgets gave her the opportunity to study him openly. The wind had ruffled his dark hair beneath his stylish hat, leaving him with a slightly unkempt scientist-gone-mad look not altogether unpleasant.

He caught her staring and grinned. "This is where we part."

"Yes, right." Millie waited for him to cinch up his restraining belt and fly away. "Well," she said a moment later, "thank you for an interesting evening."

"Indeed. However, I really could not leave without my coat."

"Oh!" She quickly slipped out of the garment and handed it back. The chill that followed had her rubbing her arms for warmth.

A floor below, the orchestra had long since completed its rendition of "Auld Lang Syne" and moved on to a more sedate tune. Meanwhile, her companion shrugged into his coat and then resumed what she assumed was his postflight inspection of his floating machine.

"You are cold," he said when he completed his work. "And I have already made you miss your kiss at midnight."

"I have missed nothing of the sort."

"Perhaps you have not, but I guarantee that whichever of the fellows on your dance card who had been planning on taking that honor likely thinks he has."

Sir William would wonder where she had gone, but he was not the one she was concerned about. She thought of her father and what she would say when he demanded an answer to her lengthy absence this evening.

The dark balloon bobbed above the stranger's head as he looked down at her. Slowly a grin lifted the corners of his lips.

"What is so funny?" she demanded.

"Oh, nothing." He shook his head. "I am just wondering why a woman as pretty and intelligent as you seems reluctant to go down and rejoin the ball she ran away from."

Her eyes widened. "How did you know—"

"That this was the party you had come from?" He paused to give her a sweeping glance. "I didn't until you just admitted it, though I had my suspicions."

"Oh!" Millie turned on her heel and headed toward the center of the roof. Surely there would be a door somewhere. Then she stopped short. What was she doing?

"Change your mind?" he called.

She fixed him with a glare but said nothing.

"Now you have got me curious. What did you do? Break a man's heart? Or maybe you were in the middle of a lovers' quarrel and ran off before he could fetch you back?"

Millie ignored him.

"Never mind. It doesn't matter. Go get that New Year's kiss, my society scientist," he told her when he settled back into his harness and belt.

"And if he does not want to kiss me? Then what?"

"Then he is a fool."

She smiled. "Actually, *I* am the fool."

"Because you chose to go flying with me?" he asked as he reached into his coat and pulled out his notebook and a pen.

"No," she responded, emboldened. "Because I am glad I did not get that midnight kiss."

"Is that so?" He continued to scribble in his notebook. "Not fond of kissing, are you?"

"I like kissing just fine—" She bit back the remainder of her statement. "I have said too much. I will just let you fly away to wherever you are headed next."

The stranger shrugged out of the shoulder straps that connected him to the pack on his back. "My flying is done for tonight," he said as he reached to yank the balloon down within reach. "I don't have enough fuel to power the system after our adventure."

"Oh, I am sorry."

"Don't be." As he toyed with instruments in the pack, the balloon began to deflate. "This is where I was planning to sleep tonight."

"At the Peabody?"

Another grin. Oh, how handsome he was when he smiled like that. "Well, yes. You do not think I chose to land here by chance, do you?"

"I guess I . . ." A chill wind blew across her neck and made her shiver. "I guess this is where we part ways then. I will just leave you to your . . ." Her gaze swept the device and then returned to his eyes. "To whatever it is you do after you fly that thing."

He had the audacity to wink. "All right. Enjoy your evening."

It was her turn to smile. "I did, thank you," she said as she left him to walk toward the exit.

"Hey there," her companion called just as she opened the door.

Slowly Millie turned to see he had paused in the process of dismantling the flying device. "Yes?"

"About that New Year's Eve kiss?"

An odd thrill of something unfamiliar and yet quite nice jolted her. "What about it?"

"I owe you one."

Oh, my. His return to work told Millie no answer was expected, and that was just as well, for she had no idea what she might have said.

Instead, she fumbled her way down the dark stairwell to pause at the bottom landing. She must look a fright, but there was little remedy for it.

The wind had wreaked havoc on her hair, so she made an attempt at returning the pins to their proper places. Then, despairing of the project, she shrugged out of her coat, intending to fetch it back later, and turned the doorknob to emerge into the hall. A moment later, she steeled her spine and walked into the ballroom as if she had never left.

"There you are."

Oh, no. Millie pasted on a smile and then slowly

turned toward the sound of his voice. "Hello, Father."

Though no longer a young man, Silas Cope, when dressed in his best formal attire, was still a handsome man. At least society ladies thought so, as witnessed by the attentive Mrs. Ward-Wiggins, who smiled up at him and kept a tight grip on his arm. Her Parisian gown and the sapphires at her ears and neck had definitely caught Father's eye.

"Did you and Trueck enjoy your stroll?" he asked as his fingers absently stroked the young widow's gloved hand.

"Actually—"

"We had a wonderful stroll, did we not, darling?" Sir William edged up beside her looking far too handsome for his own good. As their gazes met, he had the audacity to wink.

From the cut of his coat to the shine on his shoes and the crest on his gold ring, there was no doubt the Englishman was of the nobility, a fact that never failed to remind Millie she was not.

But she would not lie, even if her fiancé allowed for it. Nor would she continue the conversation unless forced to. Silence, her faithful friend, served her well. She met her father's gaze and simply smiled.

Father muttered something likely meant to serve as parting words before ushering his companion away. Millie watched her father disappear into the crowd with a mixture of relief and disappointment.

Being invisible to her father had its advantages, especially on a night when she had escaped the ball to fly away—literally. She suppressed a sigh. She must learn to be more careful.

Sir William pressed his palm to her back and gently urged her forward. "We should dance, Mildred," he said, his breath warm against her ear, "lest anyone suspect we have not been together this past hour."

"Wouldn't it be best if we were not suspected of such a thing, Sir William?"

He whirled her around to assume the correct position for dancing the waltz and then fitted them into the already crowded swirl of dancers.

"I think a couple on the verge of marriage might find it difficult to cause more than an uplifted eyebrow or two should they seek a bit of privacy." He paused to sweep the length of her with his warm gaze. "Or are things different here in Memphis?"

"Maybe they are. Would you be gossiped about back in England for that kind of behavior?"

Her fiancé smiled. "Back in England I would be envied." He paused to twirl her around and then his smile faded. "Where were you, Mildred?"

The swift change of response stunned her. Thankfully, the press of dancers around them prevented intimate conversation.

When William maneuvered them past the crowd and onto a less populated section of the dance floor, Millie knew she must say something.

"I went out for some air." The truth, and much nicer than admitting that the thought of their engagement announcement had nearly stifled her.

"I see." Again he deftly whirled her about. "Who is he?"

His question stunned her as much for his accuracy in guessing that she had not been alone as for the icy tone he had so swiftly and easily adapted.

"There is no 'he,' " she said evenly. "I went out for air."

Millie met his stare and tried to decide if he had seen her on the roof. No, she deduced. The Englishman had no idea she had been flying around Memphis just moments ago.

"As you can imagine," she continued. "I am about to embark on an undertaking that will require many changes. I confess to feeling a bit overwhelmed with it all."

"So I am an undertaking, am I?" Sir William's tone was light again, almost teasing. "Yes, I suppose my mother would agree. If she were alive she would have adored you, though she might wonder why you would agree to take me on." He glanced around the room and returned his attention to the woman in his arms. "Likely many of your friends here would feel the same."

"So the announcement was made?"

"Your father hinted at an upcoming announcement during his remarks prior to the midnight hour, though he did not specify what that might be."

"I see." When the music ended, Millie allowed him to escort her away from the dance floor. "Why don't I fetch you something to drink?"

"Yes, please," she said as she spied Father chatting with his lady friend near the windows.

Perhaps now was the time for a discussion. She made her way in that direction and then stopped short when she saw her aviator friend watching her from the door.

Kyle could not help himself. He had to peek in on the beautiful society scientist and her ball before returning to his room for the night. But now he was good and caught.

Acting as if he had intended for her to see him, he shed his coat and hat and made his way across the room to offer a curt bow. "May I have this dance?"

With an almost desperate glance at an older couple too deep in conversation to notice anyone else in the room, she nodded. Her expression evened out and the beginning of a smile dawned, likely meant for anyone watching and not actually for him.

"What *are* you doing here?" she muttered as she allowed him to lead her onto the dance floor.

The band was doing a passable job of playing one of Chopin's lesser-known waltzes, so a quick spin around the floor seemed completely harmless. But with one look into those beautiful brown eyes, Kyle knew there was nothing harmless about this woman. What had not been revealed in the starlight was absolutely plain under the chandeliers in the ballroom. The society scientist with the adventurous streak was stunning.

And quite a dancer.

"Just passing by, actually," he said. True enough. "I thought I would see what was so awful about this party that caused you to flee."

"I did not *flee*." Her desperate glance around the room told him she had something to fear. Or someone. His Pinkerton training had him looking around the ballroom for the source of her angst.

A fair-haired fellow carrying two glasses of punch stopped short to stare openly. Something about him looked familiar, but before Kyle could figure where he had seen the man before, he disappeared into the crowd.

No one else paid her any attention. Though she seemed uncomfortable, Kyle could see no discernable threat.

The song ended before he realized his flying companion had danced him almost to the exit. While the others applauded the orchestra, the lovely lady yanked him out the door and into the passageway.

"You really should go," she insisted.

He opened his mouth to argue but thought better of it. "Yes, I should. But I have one question. Did you hide atop the Cotton Exchange because you were afraid of someone here?"

"No," she said without missing a beat. "I ran from the spotlight."

"I see." Kyle stared down at her, memorizing eyes the color of café au lait, a nose that tipped slightly at the end, skin of flawless porcelain, and mahogany curls. "But you came back."

"Thanks to you."

He registered her gratitude, though his focus was on watching lips the color of rose petals move.

"You *must* go," those lips said.

He forced his thoughts away from recalling how she felt in his arms as they flew over the Memphis rooftops. "Yes," he said slowly. "I suppose I must. One more question?"

Her perturbed expression gave way to a nod. "Just one."

"Would you have returned had I not deposited you on the roof of this hotel?"

Their gazes met. "I don't think I know the answer to that." She gave him a discreet push. "Now go."

Kyle reached out to draw her further down the

hall with him. Another step to the left and they were in a dark corner completely hidden from view.

Brushing back a curl from her forehead, Kyle once again studied her. "Not until I have your assurance that your insistence on my departure has nothing to do with anything illegal or with anyone who might intend to harm to you."

"I assure you."

Barely a blink and she had continued to look into his eyes. Kyle knew a liar when he saw one. She had spoken the truth.

His gaze fell to her neck and the gold chain glittering even in the shadows. His fingers itched to lift the chain and make his own attempt at solving the unusual cypher. "I have been toying with an invention that might solve your puzzle," he said. "Perhaps someday . . ."

She inhaled sharply. "Yes, someday . . ."

"All right." He released her. "Then I suppose there is nothing left to say except Happy New Year, Miss . . ." He paused. "We never did exchange names, did we?"

Her lips turned up in a smile. "We did not. And Happy New Year to you as well."

Kyle made good on his escape only doubling back long enough to retrieve his coat and hat. Another moment in her presence and he would be sorely tempted to make good on that promise of a celebratory kiss.

The notion was ridiculous, of course. Even considering it defied logic. And yet why was it when he turned to catch her still watching him did he feel an overwhelming urge to ignore logic in favor of the ridiculous?

Because the society scientist was dangerous. And though a Pinkerton agent never ran from danger, he held a healthy respect for it. He also knew better than to follow when danger left town. Or, in this case, left the hall in favor of rejoining her party.

Kyle headed to his room, shaking his head as he stepped inside and closed the door behind him. Later, when there was less chance of being observed, he would go back up to the roof and retrieve the carpetbag and the components of his flying device. For now they were stowed away and safely hidden from view.

"Took you long enough," said a voice he did not recognize.

Reaching for his revolver, Kyle took a step back to connect with the door. Slowly, he inched his free hand along the wood until it collided with the doorknob.

A flash of light temporarily blinded him. Then he heard familiar laughter.

Five

January 1, 1889
Memphis

"Mildred, it's time."

Millie glanced back at the empty hallway and sighed softly to herself. He was referring to the purpose of the evening, the reason everyone who was anyone in Memphis had dined and danced until well past midnight.

Turning to face him, she offered a curt nod. "Yes, Father."

"Now, to find that fiancé of yours," he muttered. "The man was right here, but it appears he has gone somewhere and . . ."

The orchestra resumed their playing, preventing further conversation this close to the musicians. Millie offered a weak smile to Father's companion that was not returned.

Ah, so it was to be like that. Once the heir was safely married off and bundled away to England, the funds Millie's marriage would bring in would be spent on a woman who found it impossible to manage a smile?

"Not while I have a say in the matter," Millie muttered.

"What is that?" the object of her thoughts demanded.

"I was just thinking about England," she responded sweetly.

"I understand it is cold there. And the castles are drafty." Mrs. Ward-Wiggins shook her head. "I am sure it will be a fine place for you to live, but it is not a place I am keen to visit."

You're not a person I intend to invite for a visit, Millie longed to say. Instead she kept her thoughts unspoken and schooled her expression to stay as neutral as she could manage.

"Perhaps the chap will buy you that balloon you pestered me to purchase." Father began to describe to his companion the ballooning trips Millie had convinced him to take her on while in France.

Millie momentarily ignored her father as thoughts rose of a certain dark-haired balloonist, or aviator, or whatever the handsome fellow could be termed. Then she said, "I thought you felt a balloon was an unsuitable means of transportation for a Cope. Do not you find it unseemly?"

Eyes the color of her own narrowed. "But you will not be a Cope then, will you? Nor will you be running about the Memphis skies for all to see and comment upon." He opened his pocket watch, and then snapped it shut, muttering something about the lateness of the hour.

Millie waited for the familiar feeling of disappointment—that heavy blanket she carried about her shoulders even when the summer sun shone. Odd, but it failed to arrive. Not even a thin scarf of guilt to toss over her shoulder.

Interesting.

He was still muttering. Still looking around the room with a perturbed expression.

"Has my intended gone missing?" she asked lightly, for of course Sir William was in the room somewhere. Only then did she realize he had not returned with the beverage he had promised to fetch. Or had he?

Millie considered exactly when he might have returned and decided the time fit square in the middle of the most wonderful dance of the evening.

Her dance with the dark-haired aviator. She sighed. Had the Englishman taken offense to her attentions being stolen by another?

"If you will excuse me, Father, I think I will go see where Sir William has gone."

But gone he was, for Millie scoured the ballroom and could not find him. Just as well, she decided as she returned to find her father still looking quite perturbed.

"Odd business, this disappearance. I suppose our announcement will have to wait for another day unless he returns soon." He glanced down at her wrist. "Are those your grandmother's pearls, Mildred?"

"They are," she said as she slid the strands

around to reveal the intricate gold clasp. Imbedded in the center of what could arguably be a stylized family crest were three yellow diamonds set in triangular fashion. In the center of the triangle was a single sapphire.

Land and sea. That is what Mama had termed the piece. A nod to the family's seafaring past had been her mother's best guess.

The way Father's gaze lingered on the piece gave Millie an uncomfortable feeling that she would not continue to own it should she fail to keep it under lock and key. Stranger things had happened than to find a bauble or two missing at the end of a month that had failed to produce enough revenue to keep her father's business funds flowing.

Another thing she would no longer worry about once her marriage to Sir William was finalized.

The idea should have been a relief to Millie. She had so few reminders of her mother, and with each loss of a pin or bracelet, necklace or earring, she felt another link to Mama slip away.

Her fingers went to her neck and the thin gold chain her father would never have. The cypher and heart shifted, reminding Millie there were still secrets left to uncover.

Her flying friend had boasted of his ability to solve Jefferson wheel cyphers. She also had a bit of talent there, though her grandmother's puzzle had no solution as yet.

"You have gone and done it," Father said as he removed his pocket watch again and pointed it in her direction. "Sir William was ready to proclaim his intentions publicly, but something has obviously delayed his statement. I have nothing left to do but send you home and pray your disgrace goes unnoticed."

Disgrace? So Father was blaming the man's disappearance on her. Of course.

"Not actually pray, of course," Millie said under her breath as she turned to look away. "For that might be worthy of your time, speaking to the Lord on my behalf, that is."

For all the Cope family members who had graced the tufted and pillowed pew in church each Sunday, the only one who had kept Millie in prayers was Mama. And that had been far too long ago.

"Home with you, then," Father said, oblivious to her mutterings. "I will do what I can to remedy the embarrassment you have once again brought to this family."

Embarrassment, indeed. She bit back a retort. What was far more likely was that the town matrons' tongues would be wagging tomorrow because Silas Cope was seen staggering into yet another hotel room with a woman to whom he was not married. And likely a woman of an age that Millie could call sister.

This time when she left the ballroom, Millie

remembered her wrap in addition to her evening coat. And though the carriage ride home was brief, the peace she had hoped to find in the solitude of her bedchamber proved elusive.

She was tempted to escape to her third-floor hideaway to take up a book where she had left off this morning or perhaps sketch the stranger's flying machine before she forgot some of its detail. Neither idea held any appeal.

When one of the maids came to remove her hairpins and assist her in changing into her nightgown, Millie waved her away and moved to the window. Had it been only a little while ago that she had drifted over the rooftop beneath the dark silk balloon of a flying machine?

It all seemed like a dream dreamed while awake and experienced from a faraway place. Oh, but the aviator had been real. His arms were sturdy and his smile quite lovely.

And he had claimed he could solve cyphers.

Millie paused just long enough to exchange her evening coat for a warmer and sturdier garment. Unless she missed her guess, it was quite possible the stranger had returned to the rooftop of the Peabody Hotel for his flying equipment.

And if he had, she intended to join him. Not because she wanted to know more about the elusive inventor, but because the need to solve her grandmother's puzzle was becoming stronger each time Father checked his pocket watch.

Kyle returned his revolver to its hiding place and then walked over to shake hands with his surprise guest. "Do you have any idea how close you were to getting shot?"

Lucas McMinn had the audacity to grin as he set his personal torch device on the table next to him and then leaned back to make himself comfortable. "None at all," he said. "You would never take a shot in the dark. My guess is you were about to open the door and then aim."

His best friend knew him well. And yet the fact Lucas had got the jump on him irked Kyle.

"Happy New Year, my friend," Lucas said.

"I return the sentiment."

A thought occurred. Though his friend sat there, it had not been Lucas's voice he heard. "How did you change the sound of your voice?"

Lucas retrieved what appeared to be a brass tube with a cap at one end and handed it to Kyle. Upon closer inspection, he noted a small speaking tube with some sort of reed inside.

"All right." He returned the device to the former Pinkerton agent and then sprawled on the chair across from him. "Show me how it works."

After an impressive demonstration, Lucas set it aside. "Like it?"

Kyle grinned. "Much better than the last harebrained idea you showed me. I cannot imagine there is need for an automated postage machine. Who is in that much hurry, Lucas? Honestly, if a man cannot be bothered to stop and put a stamp on a letter, then he is just lazy."

"Hey, now," Lucas protested with a laugh. "We agreed to disagree on that one. You will thank me when the patent is approved." He paused. "Any news on the big case that brought you to Memphis?"

Kyle shrugged. "I personally think it is a ridiculous waste of time to go hunting after lost treasure. The war ended twenty years ago. Anything claimed to be hidden has either been quietly found or never existed in the first place."

"And yet someone cared enough to hire the Pinks to settle the question for certain. Any idea who that might be?"

Kyle thought carefully before he spoke. "Henry says the assignment goes all the way to the top."

"President Cleveland?" Lucas made a face. "You're joking. Why? He has been voted out and will vacate the White House in a couple of months."

"On the fourth of March, which happens to be the same day my assignment ends."

Lucas let the silence lengthen. "So," he finally said, "have you asked?"

"Asked if I am working for the president? Of course. The boss says he cannot confirm, but he does not deny it either. Apparently Will Pinkerton himself agreed to take on the case."

His friend let out a low whistle. "It must be a big deal to someone then."

"Agreed. And as to Cleveland being a one-term president, he's claiming he'll be back in four years."

Lucas chuckled. "Don't they all? But, seriously, what purpose would it serve a president to have Pinkertons out hunting for missing Confederate gold?"

"Henry's guess is the president believes the gold belonged to the Treasury. What better way to leave than by being the man who deposited rebel gold in federal coffers?"

"I suppose so, but why Memphis?"

"I got a tip that some of the gold passed through a bank here in town under the guise of a woman whose name did not end up appearing in any of their records."

"Not that someone trying to hide gold would use a real name."

"I thought of that. And I have another lead that will eventually take me home to check out the main branch of the Bank of Louisiana." He paused as he allowed his interest in the topic to shift. "What are you doing here?"

"I got your message," Lucas said as he shifted positions. "And as I was heading back to Natchez, I thought I would bring the flying device back with me unless you have further use for it."

"Actually, I would prefer to give it another test run before I depart."

He had not planned on another test run. He hadn't even given it a thought. However, if he could find the society scientist, then maybe another flight was not such a bad idea.

"All right." Lucas grinned. "I bring greetings from New Orleans. Cousin Winthrop was married this afternoon."

"Is that so?" Kyle thought of Flora's cousin and the woman to whom he had been engaged. "I'm guessing that might have been a little uncomfortable for some of you, given that the bride's father died in a shoot-out trying to kill your wife."

Lucas shook his head. "That was almost two years ago, and no one is going to hold the man's wife and daughters responsible for bad decisions they did not make. But let's change the subject. How did the test flight go?"

"It went well. I think it's time to go back to the lawyers and complete the patent application for the steering device."

"That good?"

"Better."

"About our patent attorney . . . I bring good news."

"Oh?" Kyle's hopes rose. They had at least a dozen inventions awaiting approval and twice that under consideration by the patent attorney. "Which one?"

"The weapons noise reduction system," Lucas said with a look of satisfaction.

"That *is* good news. I have not yet had reason to use mine in the field, but having the noise of gunfire reduced or eliminated completely is going to prove useful."

Lucas nodded. "Apparently we should also get good news on the crystal oscillator, the electrostatic precipitator, and the radio direction finder soon. But enough of that. Tell me more about the flight tests. Were we correct in our fuel calculations?"

"I was able to sustain flight for a quarter of an hour with fuel left for at least another ten minutes."

He continued to field questions from Lucas, carefully avoiding any indication he did not take the test flight alone. Finally his old friend stopped to regard him with an amused expression.

"All right, Kyle, what are you not telling me?"

Shrugging, he shifted positions to pick up the brass voice tube. As he pretended to study the piece, his mind conjured up and discarded several possible answers.

"Come on, buddy." Lucas leaned forward to rest his elbows on his knees. "What are you keeping back?"

Scientifically, the information was significant. Personally, he would catch all sorts of grief once his best friend knew he had taken a woman on his test flight. A beautiful woman who carried a revolver, quoted aerodynamic theory, and danced across a ballroom like—

"Who is she?"

Kyle snapped to attention and banished his errant thoughts. "She?" He cleared his throat. "All right, she was an unexpected copilot on tonight's flight. And before you start making jokes, we were not given much of a choice. We were locked out on the roof of the Cotton Exchange and the only exit was by air."

"Go on."

"That is all there was to it. I just helped a lady out of a situation that was not of our making."

"You expect me to believe you and a young lady on the roof of the Cotton Exchange is a situation not of your own making?"

Kyle's eyes narrowed. "I expect you to take me at my word, yes."

"One more question." Lucas's expression turned serious. "Is she pretty?"

Kyle picked up the nearest pillow off of the sofa and threw it at him.

Lucas dodged and then laughed. "I will take that as a yes. And now to the other reason I decided to crash your little New Year's Eve party." He paused only a second. "Tucker."

Among the Pinkerton Agency's list of missing fugitives, Will Tucker's name stood out because of his personal connection to Lucas McMinn. Not only had Tucker scammed Lucas's sister Mary in a false bid to wed, but he had also done the same to Flora Brimm, now Flora McMinn.

Unlike Mary, all Flora lost was a pair of earrings. Mary McMinn had a watch and her life stolen from her, though technically she died in an accident. If Will Tucker had not failed to arrive at the church, Mary would never have run directly into the path of that New Orleans streetcar.

When the criminal was finally caught and sent away for an extended stay at Angola Prison, both Kyle and Lucas had celebrated. In a cruel twist of irony, Tucker escaped his prison transport vehicle on the same day Lucas married Flora.

Now, more than a year later, Tucker still had not been caught. But he would be.

Lucas reached into his pocket and retrieved a small black box, which he opened to reveal a pair of jeweled earrings.

"Are those—"

"The earrings Tucker stole from my wife? Yes, they are."

Kyle recalled the last time he had seen a pair that matched these. Flora had worn her grandmother's identical set to try and catch her thief. And she had almost succeeded. It had taken Lucas to snatch Flora from certain death after falling off a New Orleans balcony and then to snatch Tucker from what had been a certain escape.

A wave of relief passed over Kyle. "So he has been caught."

"No, but a Miss Abigail Danders of Mobile, Alabama, took exception to his absence and came forward to file a missing persons report on her fiancé. She had a photograph to go along with her report. Definitely Tucker or someone who could be his twin."

"Another victim of the man who somehow manages to collect fiancés but not wedding rings? And this time from Mobile?"

"It appears so."

"Did Miss Danders also report jewelry missing?"

Lucas snapped the box shut and returned it to his pocket, his expression grim. "Pearls. A triple-strand bracelet and matching earrings."

Pearls. Had his flying companion not worn exactly that sort of set tonight? But as soon as the suspicion rose, Kyle cast it away. How many other Memphis belles had worn pearls to their New Year's Eve celebrations? Around this town, young ladies were practically handed their pearls before they left the cradle.

"What are you thinking?" Lucas asked.

"That we need to catch this guy. Other than the missing persons report, have there been any other sightings?"

"None." Lucas let out a long breath. "Tucker's something, I will give him that. Somehow he manages to convince these women he is the answer to all their troubles. He's good. Really good."

"He is, but we are better. It's just a matter of time before he is caught again. Henry told me that as of March fifth I'll be back on the Tucker case full time."

"I'm glad to hear it." Lucas rose and ran his hand through his hair. "If anyone can catch him, Kyle, you can." Exhaustion curled around his eyes and tugged at the corners of his mouth. "I should have realized he would not go to prison easily. But I was thinking of Flora, and Tucker had already been tried and convicted. Still, I should have . . ."

"Where is Flora tonight?" Kyle asked, mindful that his friend sorely needed another change of topic.

"She's traveling to Brimmfield," he said as his grin lifted. "It appears our daughter will have a brother or sister in late summer."

Kyle closed the distance between them to offer a hearty handshake and a congratulatory slap on the back. "All is as it should be," he commended. "Please offer Flora my best wishes for continued good health."

"Why not tell her yourself? You have not seen the half of what I have been working on, and she will be home in a few days. Cannot the Confederate gold treasure hunt wait a week or two?"

"I admit I am curious. Of course, it would help if you were actually harboring Confederate gold. Then I would be able to explain why I headed to Natchez when the next lead is in New Orleans."

Lucas laughed. "Given the fact my wife's

grandmother told General Grant himself to keep on marching down the road, I would not doubt it."

Kyle smiled. Indeed he had met the formidable Millicent Brimm and had no doubt the oft-told story about the Union general was true. However, a second visit to Brimmfield would have to wait.

Lucas's departure from the agency had been as much a result of the gunshot wound that had nearly killed him as a desire not to spend time away from his bride. However, he had used his retirement well, and now the two men had an impressive array of inventions patented between them.

Kyle envied his friend's life. He had days to spend perfecting inventions and creating plans for others. Nights to spend with a wife who loved him and a tiny daughter who was Flora's image in temperament as well as in beauty. But until Tucker was caught, there was nothing for it. Kyle would stay on with the Pinkertons. What had begun as a matter of honor had become a matter of justice.

"Duty calls then," Lucas said as his expression sobered. "Flora and I appreciate what you are doing for us." He paused and swallowed before continuing, "And for my sister."

"It's nothing you would not do for me under the same circumstances."

Lucas suppressed a yawn and then gestured toward the door. "I'm exhausted and I leave at dawn."

"Until we meet again then, my friend."

They said their goodbyes and parted ways. Shutting the door, Kyle walked over to retrieve his copy of the newly signed patent. Though his eyes read through the familiar words, his mind returned to the dark-haired stranger who had been brave enough to float through the night sky with him.

Finally he set the papers aside and reached for his coat. Though he had intended to wait until morning to retrieve his gear, now was as good a time as any. At least it would take his mind off the woman he could not seem to forget.

Six

Rather than risk detection by remaining party-goers or, worse, by Father, Millie bypassed the main staircase to seek out the Peabody's staff corridor. Slipping past two chambermaids and a valet, she found the back stairs and hurried up to the topmost floor.

Though the orchestra was packing up as she slipped past the entrance to the ballroom, a few couples were still milling about. After a cursory glance to be certain her fiancé had not returned to search for her, Millie headed to the rooftop staircase.

Opening the door allowed a draft of chill air to rush past. She gathered her coat around her and pressed forward, being careful not to allow the door to close completely behind her.

The sky was an inky black with pinpoints of stars thrown across it. Indeed, the first hours of 1889 had produced a sky lovely to behold.

In the distance, a clock chimed twice. She should be sleepy. And yet all she could think about was the possibility of finding the mysterious man who had claimed he could solve cyphers.

That she did not even know his name did not bother her. Given the secrecy surrounding Grandmother's cypher, anonymity was preferable. She only hoped that, should she find him, the stranger would be amenable to continue being just that. A stranger.

Moving toward the spot where their flight had ended, Millie found the carpetbag and pieces of the flying machine still stowed in the shadows. While she nursed disappointment at not finding the aviator there, at least she knew she had not missed him altogether. Eventually he would return for his things, and then she could ask his help.

The wind whipped at the edges of her coat and teased at her bare neck, sending Millie huddling close to the brick wall nearest the door. An assortment of wooden boxes and barrels provided an almost-comfortable place to wait, so she settled there and drew her coat in close.

Wishing she had remembered her gloves, Millie dug her fists into the folds of warm fabric and then leaned her head against the bricks and closed her eyes.

"You seem quite happy to be sitting alone beneath the stars."

The unexpected voice of Sir William jolted Millie from her reverie and sent her scrambling to her feet. In the process one of the barrels overturned and a stack of crates fell.

"Oh! I have made a mess," was the only response she could muster, such was the furious beating of her heart.

"No matter," he said as he reached for her hand. "May I join you?"

"You may." Millie indicated the crate next to hers and then returned to her seat. "What brings you up to the rooftop at this late hour?"

The Englishman leaned forward on his elbows and then slowly pivoted to face her. "I could ask the same question of you, Mildred Cope."

What to say? For a moment she allowed herself to study him rather than respond.

He was certainly handsome, even more so in the golden glow of the lamplight. And yet his question seemed at once innocent as well as calculated. It was an odd combination that left her without an answer while she sorted her thoughts. He had come seeking her. Of this she quickly became certain.

"Actually, I am stargazing," she finally said. "It is a lovely night, is it not?"

Both were the truth, though Millie left out the part where she admitted she preferred the view of the stars from a little higher up.

Sir William studied her a moment longer before turning his attention to the horizon. He shifted his position slightly, though he still spared her no glance.

"It is indeed a lovely night, though I fail to see what has captivated you well beyond the hour when decent ladies are abed."

"Decent ladies?" Her chuckle died when she realized he was serious. "Surely you are not making the assumption that I am breaching propriety by enjoying the evening sky."

"Technically this is the early morning sky, and yes, I am concerned that propriety has been breached." He paused once again as he swung his attention to her. "Possibly for the second time tonight."

"I will have an explanation for that, Sir William," she said as her ire rose.

"Funny. I was about to demand the same of you."

"My absence earlier?" she said as she guessed at his meaning. When he nodded, she continued. "I might ask the same of your absence, but I have already admitted to a bout of nerves over the planned announcement of our engagement. The ballroom felt quite closed in, which I fully recognize sounds ridiculous as I now say it, and yet it is very much the truth."

"Go on."

"Well, the truth is, as I told you earlier, I fled." She paused to choose her words carefully, determined to speak the truth while offering as few details as possible. "I found a quiet place to think about it. And to pray."

"Pray?" he echoed as if the idea was a strange one.

"Yes. Do not you—"

"Yes," he hastened to say and then punctuated the statement with a lift of his shoulder. "Of course I pray." He pressed back a lock of straw-colored hair and looked away. "So you have changed your mind?"

"No," she said as she caught up to the switch of topic. "But I suppose it would be accurate to say I am still getting used to the idea."

Her fingers itched to touch his sleeve, to offer something that might indicate to him that he should take no personal offense. Instead, she kept her hands inside her coat and her sentiments unspoken.

"As am I."

She had not expected that. Apparently her expression gave that away, for he shrugged.

"It's the truth. I am to wed, and I have always known this. After all, that is what is expected of the eldest. Marry a pretty girl, sire an heir, and keep home and hearth safe for the next generation."

"You make it sound awful." Her tone was light, teasing. "I had not imagined it that way."

"No?" He reached to close the distance between them by resting his palm atop her sleeve. "I had imagined it would be that way. Until I met you."

Warmth spread through her despite the chilly temperature. "Thank you," she said, and meant it.

"You ruined my gift tonight," he said abruptly.

"Your gift?"

He reached into his coat and then opened his palm to produce a tangle of pearls similar in size to the ones she was wearing on her wrist and in her ears.

"Yes," he said as he returned the pearls to his pocket. "Now I suppose I will have to find something else to give you to celebrate our engagement."

Millie waved away the statement as she thought of Father and what he would likely do with anything Sir William might offer. "Truly, it's not necessary."

"Oh, but it is," he said slowly, almost as if he were speaking to himself. "I am sure I will find something."

"Really, there is no need to trouble yourself," she insisted. "I have all the stars in the sky and no need for anything else that sparkles."

The comment was meant for humor, but Sir

William seemed to take it with a strong measure of seriousness. "Yes, I see. Well, that would be different, would it not?" was his odd and mumbled answer.

He settled back into place and seemed to be contemplating something. Whether it was her statement or the beauty of the night sky or something altogether different, Millie could not say.

"The man you were dancing with earlier." His eyes met hers, his expression unreadable. "Who was he?"

Millie felt her fingers begin to tremble and hid them in the folds of her coat. "Which man?" she asked in a bid for more time to consider her response.

"I believe you know to whom I refer, but allowing that you might not, I will help you to recall him. This would be the fellow who danced you out of the ballroom while I was left standing with the beverage you requested."

"I do not know."

"You do not know?" Now his expression was easily read. Disbelief. "Am I to understand I returned from my errand to find you in the arms of a total stranger?"

"We were dancing," she countered. "In a ballroom full of people, most of whom have known me since I was a child."

"With a man who was not your fiancé."

She let out a long breath. Years of Father's

accusations of bringing embarrassment to the family had taken their toll. Millie knew she could not marry a man who did the same.

"Officially you are not my fiancé, nor will you be if you continue to treat me in this manner." She held up her hand to prevent his retort. "And perhaps you did not notice, but I danced with others as well. Shall we go down the list of names?"

He barely blinked. "No. I would only ask the name of the last fellow."

"Which I have told you I do not know." She paused but only to gather a breath. "Perhaps you need to find another fiancé, sir. I do not wish to impede you from wedding someone suitable."

Millie made to rise, but Sir William tugged her back down beside him. "You do not know him?"

"I have said more than once I do not," she snapped. "And I am not in the habit of lying, though you appear to be in the habit of dis-believing me."

"All right, then. Unless you wish to add anything, the subject is considered closed."

"I do not."

Blood still pounded at Millie's temples. His look of contrition, if that was what he now offered, held the promise of soothing her racing pulse. Still, the damage had been done.

She thought of the pearls in his pocket, of the

title and ancestral home. And yet all of it paled in comparison to her desire to feel as if she were loved just as she was.

No embarrassment. No changes needed. Just as perfectly imperfect as she was right now . . .

"I have offended you."

Millie's chin lifted and her backbone straightened. "Yes, actually. You have."

Sir William's hand grasped hers. His grip was warm, strong, and yet gentle. "Truly," he said softly, his voice husky with emotion, "I did not intend such an offense. Will you forgive me?"

She would, of course. A properly bred Memphis belle never held a grudge, not when the source of those ill feelings was the man who soon would be her husband. Still, Millie decided she would make him wait. Just a bit, anyway.

"I shall consider it."

He rose abruptly and reached to lift her to her feet. "Excellent. It is time to go downstairs now. I assume you have taken rooms for the night."

"Father has." The truth, and yet her mind and heart were still back on their previous exchange of words.

Sir William nodded. "Then I will escort you down. You will catch your death if you remain up here much longer."

"No," she hastened to say. "I am fine, really. My coat is warm, and I was rather enjoying the solitude."

He offered a quizzical expression and then shrugged. "I suppose it is good our home in England will offer much in the way of solitude. It is rather large. Sprawling, actually."

Something about the way he bragged did not set well with her.

"If your father is fine with your stargazing, then I surely will not dispute his authority." He leaned toward her and winked. "Yet, anyway."

The audacity. A wink? When she was still upset over his treatment of her?

"Yes, well, all right," she said stiffly.

"About your father," he said in a rather offhand manner, "is it too late to pay him a visit? I have no idea what time he left the party."

"And that would be because you were not there." She paused. "I am sorry, that was awfully snappish."

But as soon as the apology was out, Millie wished to retrieve it. What was it about her that sought to soothe even when her own feelings still felt trampled?

"No, I deserved that." He fixed her with what she assumed was supposed to be a pitiful look. "I did not explain my own absence, did I?" When she shook her head, he continued. "I was summoned away to answer a telephone call."

"After midnight?"

One pale brow rose. "I admit the hour was late here but early in Britain. I have business contacts that tend to ignore the time difference when making the attempt to reach me."

A plausible excuse, so Millie decided to accept it. Still, she could not resist adding, "Then perhaps it would not be too late to pay Father a visit."

"I would like very much to offer an apology and a proper thank-you for hosting the evening."

"I think that would be just perfect."

"What room did you say he is in?"

Millie froze. "Do forgive me, but I have completely forgotten. I am afraid you will have to check with the desk clerk."

He moved toward the door and rested his hand on the knob. "And you are certain you are fine up here?"

"Perfectly fine," she said, though she knew the fact she was sending Sir William to Father's room meant she could not wait around very long for the flying stranger to reappear. At some point Father would learn of her location and come to fetch her. Or, failing that, send someone in his place.

"All right," he said. "As the hour is indeed late, I will not bother you any further. Once your father and I have come to an agreement, we will reschedule the announcement."

She didn't know what to say about that. Instead of responding with enthusiasm she didn't feel, she bid him a good night and then watched him disappear inside, leaving only the slightest glow of gaslight as the door slid shut.

A moment of panic sent Millie racing for the door. As soon as the knob turned and the door opened, she exhaled in relief. To be locked out twice in one night would be most inconvenient, even though she did have the use of a flying machine.

She turned to look up at the stars and then slowly lifted her fingers toward the sky as if to touch them. The thought made her giggle. Imagine making that sort of attempt. To fly. Alone.

Millie's giggle died in her throat as the rumble of footsteps echoed against the other side of the door. She stepped back to greet, she hoped, her flying companion.

Or perhaps it was Father. No, there had not been sufficient time for the Englishman to find a clerk, ascertain Father's room number, and then pay Mr. Cope a visit.

Millie edged her way out of sight of whoever was heading toward the door and then waited to see if she would have to hide until he or she left. When the dark-haired stranger stepped out onto the roof, she let out a breath she had not realized she had been holding.

She watched him take long strides across the roof. Only when he had almost moved out of her sight did Millie decide to follow.

Keeping to the shadows, she made her way carefully toward him and then watched while he knelt down. He set to work, his moves swift but methodical. After what seemed like only a few minutes, the flying machine had been packed up. Now all that remained of the wondrous device was a carpetbag and some sort of sack that likely held the black silk balloon. Eventually he would go back and fetch the crate from the Cotton Exchange, or so she assumed. However, without a key that feat could not be accomplished until after the second day of January.

Millie hoisted up her courage and then said a quick prayer for favor. If she could get the stranger to agree to help her open the cypher, perhaps her troubles with Father would be over . . . and without having to marry an Englishman she barely knew.

Keep it safe, Millie. Your treasure lies inside.

Begging Mama for details had not done any good. Instead, she quoted the Bible's warning that where your treasure is, so was your heart, or something to that effect.

Millie knew better, though. She had guarded her heart even more carefully than the ancestral necklace. Someday she might solve the puzzle of how to open the cypher, but no one would come near to solving the puzzle of how to reach her heart.

The stranger straightened and lifted the sack over his shoulder. When he reached for the carpetbag, Millie knew it was time to act.

She stepped boldly from the shadows and softly

drew in a deep breath of chilly air and then let it out slowly. Finally her dark-haired flying companion turned to face her.

Their gazes collided. He froze, seemingly at a loss for words.

"I had begun to wonder if you would keep me waiting all night," she said in her most casual tone.

Though cast in shadows, it appeared he was studying her before formulating a response. "How long have you been up here?" he finally asked, his voice soft, almost gentle. His expression, however, was not as he conducted what appeared to be a survey of their surroundings.

"Not so long that I had grown weary of waiting," she said when his attention returned to her.

He shifted the bag off his shoulder and allowed it to drop to the ground before setting the carpetbag beside it. One hand reached into his coat while the other rested at his side.

"What do you want?" he demanded, his tone much firmer.

"Well," she said as she squared her shoulders and feigned a casualness she did not feel, "I thought perhaps I might ask a favor."

One dark brow rose, but he said nothing.

"The cypher." She lifted the chain to show her grandmother's prized possession. "You mentioned you had some skill in solving this sort of puzzle."

"Yes." He glanced around again and then returned his attention to Millie. "Do you mean now?"

She thought of Sir William, possibly in conversation with Father. Or Father, alerted to the fact his only living daughter was on the roof and heading this way. No. He would send one of his minions, but the result would be the same.

"I know the hour is quite late, so I fear I cannot stay long . . ."

"Nor can I." Even in the moonlight, she could see his eyes narrow. "Are you a guest of this hotel?"

Millie shook her head. Though she felt no threat from him, she thought a reminder that there was indeed someone awaiting her descent from the rooftop seemed in order. "I am sure Father will want to know where I have gone."

The truth, as Sir William had probably told him the truth of her destination already.

A grin began. "So you are asking me to solve your puzzle, only I must be quick about it?"

She met his smile. "Yes, that is it exactly."

Having his daydream inexplicably appear was disconcerting at best. Now that she had charmed him with her smile and her suddenly shy demeanor, Kyle knew he would have agreed to almost anything she asked of him.

He watched as she slid the chain containing

the cypher and a smaller heart-shaped locket from her neck.

"The light here is poor. Perhaps if we went inside, then I—"

"No!" She clutched at the lapels of her coat and appeared to be formulating a further response. "That is, I have a good reason for not being seen."

His Pinkerton instincts went on alert. They were alone on the roof, of this he had no doubt. Still, many a pretty woman had been used to accomplish ugly purposes.

"Want to tell me what that reason is?"

She met his steady gaze and barely blinked. "Among my set, Memphis can prove to be a very small town. I cannot risk any sort of . . . misunderstanding . . . should you and I be seen together at this late hour."

"You are afraid of what the gossips will say if you are seen with me?" He handed the necklace back to her and she slipped it on again. "And yet you did not give flying with me a second thought once you determined my craft was worthy of flight."

"That is completely untrue," she quickly responded. "I was simply presented with dire circumstances and had no choice."

"No choice?" His laughter echoed in the quiet of the early morning. "As I recall, you are the one who asked me not to land as planned."

She waved away his protest. "Much as I would love to debate the details of our evening together, as I said, our time is short."

A rumble of footsteps on the other side of the door he had remembered to wedge shut caused his companion to scramble for the shadows. When he stood firm, she returned to grasp his wrist.

"Please do not let them find me up here!"

"Them?" he said as he pulled away to snatch up the pieces of the flying device and then allowed her to lure him into the shadows. Only when he had stowed his gear did Kyle give thought to the fact he could have walked right into a trap.

Seven

January 1, 1889
Memphis

After the aviator had stowed his gear behind a stack of wooden crates, he snagged Millie's wrist. With long strides that had her hurrying to keep up, he moved into the depths of the shadows.

"Who are they?" he said, his breath warm against her ear.

His demeanor required a response. The truth. Millie thought only a moment before answering.

"Most likely my father. And possibly my fiancé."

His grip relaxed as he released her to step away.

The man's sweeping glance left her no question as to what he thought of being asked to protect a daughter from a parent or a woman from her intended.

"Give me a good reason why I should not remove the lock from that door, and make it fast."

She shook her head. "But how can you lock the door from the outside?"

A pounding on the door attested to the fact that his claim was quite possible. The speed with which he left her to stride toward the exit showed her he would brook no delay in a response from her.

"An answer," he said simply, ignoring her question entirely. "And I will allow no diversionary tactics."

"Who is that?" came a male voice from the other side of the door. Definitely not Father, nor did it sound like Sir William.

Millie hurried to the stranger's side and then motioned him away from the door. "Think of how it would look to my father and fiancé if you and I are caught up here with the door locked," she whispered. She nodded toward the odd metal object her companion had used to secure their privacy. Or at least his.

His expression softened. Still, he made no move to open the door. At least for the moment the pounding had ceased.

Millie groaned softly and reached to touch his

sleeve. She would have to tell him everything quickly and quietly. "Had I not been flying over the rooftops with you, my father would have announced my engagement tonight."

"My recollection is that you found me atop the Cotton Exchange building and then you asked that we continue our flight when I was happy to take you straight down to the ground. Do *not* hold me responsible."

"Yes, all right, I agree to all you have said. But I . . . I panicked and ran away, but only just down the street, and I had intended to return after . . ."

"Just one good reason and I will help you." He held up his hand. "One."

"There are many. But the one I will offer is this." She gave him a pleading look. "I must not ruin this engagement."

The pounding resumed, and Millie jumped back. "There are good reasons," she said softly. "*Very* good reasons to marry. May we just leave it at that?"

The stranger leaned against the brick wall, his arms crossed, and his gaze unwavering. Something in his stance told her he had faced down greater challenges than her. And won.

"If what you say is true, why risk coming back up here to find me?"

She pulled the chain from her bodice again. "I thought I might find help with the cypher. You said—"

Demands that the door be opened came louder now, interrupting Millie's response. Any moment whoever was knocking could call out her name and ruin the only chance at anonymity she had. Once he knew her to be Mildred Cope, she certainly could not ask the stranger to help her with the cypher.

He studied her a moment and then nodded. "Find an empty barrel and climb in. Hurry."

She did as he asked, knowing that in the process she would be hopelessly soiling a House of Worth gown of extravagant cost. And yet a stain on her reputation would cost much, much more than the value of a ball gown.

So she crouched down inside the dirty barrel and did her best not to sneeze as she heard the door slam open. Deep voices rose, one speaking in calm, almost hushed tones and the other much louder and insistent.

The dust settled around her as she tried not to inhale the earthy scent. Tried not to think of what the barrel might have held before she climbed inside. What might still be crawling around.

Something skittered across her shoulder, and she bit back a cry as she swiped at it. An ant, it appeared, though an overlarge one. But where there was one . . .

She closed her eyes against the image of horrible little insects marching across her shoes and climbing up her legs. They weren't, of course, but the longer she remained inside the barrel, the longer she listened to the raised voices of the men some distance away, the easier it was to imagine the worst.

And then silence.

Millie waited, her view of the world limited to the bent wooden slats of a barrel and the oval of star-dusted sky above. Then came footsteps. Heavy, even, a measured stride that indicated neither hurry nor a leisurely pace.

Finally the barrel tilted and the aviator's face appeared. He looked less than pleased. In fact, he looked downright angry.

"I will have an honest answer out of you. What do you know of a theft in the hotel?" he demanded.

"What are you talking about?" she asked as she tugged at the gold chain now caught on a nail inside the barrel. As she struggled with the necklace, Millie looked up to find her inquisitor's handsome face masked with an expression of irritation.

He reached in to yank her out of the barrel, and she easily slipped out. "I repeat," he said, "have you stolen something?"

"You are joking." Thankful to be released, she steadied herself on her feet and then looked up to see that he appeared to be completely serious.

"I assure you I am not. That was neither your father nor some fellow you have promised to marry."

"Oh?" Millie stammered as she smoothed her ruined dress as best she could.

"That was a police officer, sent up by hotel security to check the perimeter for a thief," he snapped. "Had I not given him proper identification, I might have been hauled off to jail. Explain."

"I might ask just what sort of identification you gave him, sir."

"Never mind that. I will have your answer."

"My answer is that I am not aware of any theft in this building." Ignoring for a moment the blustering man, Millie concentrated her thoughts on her current predicament. Father and Sir William still could make an unannounced visit. With her dress smudged and her hair in ruins, the situation would look worse than ever.

Plus, the hour had moved from very late to very, very early. At this rate, she would be seeing the sun rise soon unless she found a way home.

Home . . . yes, she could manage it. First she would need to slip down the back staircase. After that, she could make her way through the Peabody's kitchen, an easy prospect on a busy night. Then—

"And yet you are on the roof, hiding in a barrel?"

She forced her thoughts away from her plans to concentrate on the stranger's statement. "Any resemblance to the behavior of a thief is a coincidence."

Again he gave her a scathing look. "I am not given to believing in coincidences."

"Nor am I."

"No, I do not suppose you would steal jewelry," he said slowly. "You do not seem like the type. Not that I have found an algorithm yet that explains women and all of their possible reactions."

She smiled. A scientist, this one, and had she not agreed to give her life if not her heart to another, Millie might have found him quite interesting. Attractive, even.

"Point taken." She spied an ant crawling on her skirt and reached to swipe it away. "So what happened exactly?"

He frowned. "According to the police officer, someone broke into one of the larger suites and stole a piece of jewelry."

"Just one?" At his questioning look, she continued. "Wouldn't you think if a woman had checked into one of the larger suites, she might have brought multiple pieces of jewelry?"

"I suppose," he said as he gave her a sideways look. "One set of baubles would not serve multiple purposes."

"Of course not." She offered him a half grin as she assumed the thick Southern accent of her Cope cousins. "Perish the thought, sir. We women must be well dressed while in public. Surely your mama told you that."

"Repeatedly," he said dryly.

Her mind sorted through the possibilities. "What would make a thief steal only one piece of jewelry?"

"It was the most expensive? Or maybe he was interrupted before he could grab anything else."

"That is possible. What was it? Did the officer say?"

"A necklace. Sapphires, I believe. Do you recall anyone at your party wearing something of the sort? Perhaps her escort or someone else at the event was less than honorable. He could be the thief who took the . . ."

Necklace. Millie felt for the chain that never left her neck only to find it gone. "Oh, no!"

She looked into the barrel and at the bottom found the chain now broken and the two charms it held nowhere in sight. Millie tipped the barrel on its side and fell to her knees to retrieve the chain and search for missing pieces. She spotted the heart locket glittering in the moonlight. The cypher, however, could not be seen.

"What are you doing?" the aviator demanded.

"My necklace broke," she said as she inched toward the shadows. A moment later her fingers touched cold metal and she curled them around the familiar object. The cypher. Millie sagged against the wall, her heart racing.

"Here it is." Schooling her features, she returned her attention back to him. "What were you saying?"

● ● ●

What could he say when he could not get her to stand still long enough to listen? Kyle's gaze swept over her. She bore a smudge of something gritty on her nose and her dress was stained, and yet somehow she still managed to look absolutely breathtaking.

He had tried to be stern. Tried to act the part of an aggravated Pinkerton agent without actually admitting to his employment with the company. And still he could not manage the ruse for more than a few moments without succumbing to a grin.

"Why are you smiling?" she demanded as a glossy dark curl landed between her brows. She blew it up and away on a breath and then lifted her free hand to smooth it back into place behind her ear.

Again he had no answer. Instead, he sighed and said, "Let me see the cypher."

She placed it in his hand, brushing her fingers across his palm in the process. "So," he said as he turned the item over to erase the feel of her touch, "tell me about the piece."

She paused to fiddle with the locket and chain she still held. "It is of some value, according to my mother, and it is different than other wheel cyphers because there is something inside." She paused. "That much I have figured out on my own. What I cannot figure out is how to open it."

"What do you think is in there?" He gave the

123

piece a shake and felt the clank of metal against metal. "A smaller piece of jewelry?"

"Possibly." Her expression told him she knew more but was not offering it.

The light on the rooftop was insufficient for a good examination. "Hold this," he said as he gave it back to her so that he could retrieve his pocket lantern.

A moment later the device was lit and placed atop a nearby stack of crates. Now he could see quite well.

"Another of your inventions?" she asked as she returned the charm to his palm.

Kyle simply nodded as he turned his attention to the piece. This was no ordinary wheel cypher, and not only because the device was made of gold instead of the more customary wood. As with other coding devices of its kind, this wheel cypher was comprised of independently revolving rings. Normally, turning the rings and placing them into the correct order would break the code and reveal the message. With this device, however, there were no letters carved around the edge.

"It is different from anything I have read about in my research," she said.

"It is unique to me as well."

Under the light of the lantern, he could see that the rings appeared to be made of gold coins. The ends had long been worn down by age, a fact that added to the wheel cypher's uniqueness.

"The size and weight of the piece suggests these might be Spanish in origin," he said.

"Doubloons," his companion supplied. "Or at least that would be my guess based on the thickness and age."

"Possibly." Kyle moved the first of the seven cylinders to the right and felt a click. "And your grandmother left you no hints as to what the code is?"

She shook her head. "I have tried all sorts of things, and nothing has worked."

"Such as?"

"Normally, the first thing I would look for is any single-letter words, such as *A* or *I*. Because the edges have notches instead of letters, that principle is not valid. I did count the times each notch appears." She gestured to the cypher. "If you look closely, the notches are not all alike."

She was correct. Whoever created the cypher had gone to great detail to carve out a series of indentions that, when viewed as a whole, could be separated into patterns.

"Making sense of the patterns seems to be the key," Millie said as if she had read his thoughts. "However, I've yet to find any repeating patterns that can be sustained for the length of the device. I thought of the code telegraph technology uses because that seemed most logical, but I doubt that technology was available when the cypher was created." She met his gaze. "So therein lies the conundrum."

Kyle could not help but be impressed, and he told her so.

"Cryptology is a hobby of mine," she admitted. "So I find it ironic I cannot solve the one puzzle I most desire to solve."

He continued to spin the rings, both clockwise and counterclockwise, using several different variations on algorithms that had worked on previous cyphers. Each time he twisted the rings, the cypher failed to open.

"I have never seen a wheel cypher quite like this," he finally said. "It's an interesting piece of work. Who did you say made it?"

She lifted a dark brow. "I did not say, but I have no idea. Are you testing me?"

Kyle settled for a chuckle rather than an answer. Of course he was testing her, but everything about her expression when he asked told him she was telling the truth.

Still, there was something she was holding back. Something other than her name.

He thought briefly of inquiring. However, if she shared her name, he would have to do the same. And that was not something he was keen to do, considering the size of the city and the fact he had been given a lead that could mean any of the wealthier citizens were guilty of hiding Confederate gold.

From the looks of this one, she could well be related to his next arrest. So, though he would prefer to have a name to go along with the lovely lady, he would settle for anonymity rather than reveal himself as a Pinkerton agent.

"Well, Mr. Inventor, perhaps you should invent something to solve this puzzle."

Kyle grinned. "Actually, I have been playing around with a device that might just do the trick, but I don't happen to have it with me."

She reached to touch his sleeve again. Her fingers were small and unadorned by jewels. Kyle noticed the pearls at her wrist and thought of Lucas and the latest allegations made against Will Tucker.

"Stop teasing me," she said as she withdrew her hand.

"I'm serious. I have been toying with an idea that might work, but it's back in my workshop in . . ." Kyle bit back the remainder of his statement. "In another city."

"A workshop," she echoed. "I would so love to have such a thing."

Everything about her surprised him. This statement, however, topped the list. "Oh? You do not have one?"

He was teasing. However, he instantly saw from her thoughtful expression she had taken him seriously.

"It's more of a third-floor attic that I have

borrowed from the staff to make a room of my own."

Kyle gave her a sideways look. "And what sorts of inventions do you build in that room of yours?"

"Nothing yet, though I have done some drawings. Mostly I play with puzzles and numbers." She paused. "And read."

"Read?" He shook his head. "Are you not allowed to do that elsewhere?"

"No." Her answer came out softly, with more than a little wistfulness. He watched her carefully for some sign she was playacting and found none.

"So the reading of books is not encouraged in your home?" he asked instead.

"Not by a woman." Their gazes met. "Believe me. I am not such a shrinking violet that I have been cowed into hiding my pursuits out of fear." She paused and seemed to be considering her words. "Rather, I have learned it is much more convenient to allow my father to see only what he wishes to see."

Though her statement affected him deeply, Kyle chose not to let her know. Instead, he decided to change the topic slightly with a wink and a shrug.

"I do not suppose I could convince you to leave the item with me so that I can perform further studies." Her expression answered for her. "I didn't think so," he said as he returned the cypher to her.

She tucked the piece into the pocket of her coat and then surprised him by walking over to the edge of the roof. He followed and found her staring up at the sky.

"Beautiful, isn't it?" she whispered when he reached her side.

"Yes, lovely." Though he was not looking at the stars.

"We were up there tonight." Her voice was soft now, quiet enough to make Kyle wonder whether she realized he stood beside her at all. Then she nudged him. "Do you ever wonder if we will ever be able to fly as far as the stars?"

The thought was not a new one to him, though his calculations for such a feat were rife with unknown factors. Still, he hoped someday the answer would be yes.

"I think so," he said, though he had not realized he had spoken aloud until the lovely lady turned to look at him. He saw something in her eyes. Was it relief?

"You do?" she breathed.

When he told her why and gave her a brief description of the math involved in the project as well as some of the possible pitfalls using currently available methods, she seemed to hang on every word. Her questions were intelligent, and well thought out. His responses, he hoped, did her queries justice.

"So with the advancement of the science of

physics and the discovery of a fuel source light enough and yet burns with enough power to achieve the proper lift and thrust . . .”

"Space travel is possible," he supplied. "Science is an ever-expanding field. Eventually someone will find a material that will withstand the cold of that altitude and the heat generated by a swift fall to earth while keeping the vessel's contents safe. And when they do, yes, I'd say travel to anywhere would become very much a reality."

She looked up into his eyes, jolting his attention from the galaxies overhead to the woman at his side. "Then perhaps you should work on that project next."

He chuckled despite himself. "Perhaps I will."

There was no need to tell her that the principles behind the machine she had flown in with him tonight were, he hoped, building blocks upon which that very sort of invention might one day be created. That was a topic best kept to himself. Even Lucas hadn't quite decided whether the idea was brilliance or lunacy.

When they finally fell silent, a comfortable quiet settled between them. Kyle had no idea how long they stood shoulder-to-shoulder.

Finally, she turned to face him again. "Thank you."

He chuckled. "For what?"

"For taking me seriously and not thinking the

worst of me because I have an interest in the scientific arts."

"Thinking the worst?" He shook his head. "I have never met a more interesting woman than you."

The corners of her mouth lifted in the beginnings of a smile. "Interesting," she repeated. "I suppose that is a nice way of calling me odd."

"I meant nothing of the sort." He turned her to face him fully and then traced the length of her jaw with a knuckle. "Let me rephrase so you will understand."

She allowed the familiar gesture, her expression unchanged. "Please do."

"When I say you are the most interesting woman I have ever met, what I mean is . . ." Almost in spite of himself, he leaned in to the attraction. "Is that you are a woman of substance. A woman with a quick mind . . ." He paused only long enough to choose his words carefully. "A brilliant intellect . . ." He moved slightly closer. "And . . ."

Words failed him as his companion lifted up on tiptoe. "And?" she asked from just inches away.

"And . . ." He wrapped his arms around her and kissed her.

Softly. Gently. With a tenderness that belied the fact he knew nothing of her other than what he had discovered on two rooftops and the flight in between as well as on the Peabody's dance floor.

"Happy New Year," he whispered against her cheek.

"Happy . . ."

Apparently she could not manage more than that. Without warning, she slipped from his arms and turned away. "It has been quite the interesting night," she whispered.

An understatement. "It has."

"But it is time to say goodbye."

He should have let her go right then. Should have given her a swift nod or a word of agreement. Instead, Kyle opened his mouth and ruined everything by saying, "I will see you home."

"That's not necessary." She gathered up her skirts and swept past him toward the door and then paused to look back. "If my father or Sir . . ." She shook her head. "If anyone comes asking for me, will you please keep my secret?"

"How will I know they are asking for you?" he teased. "I don't even know your name."

As soon as the idiotic statement was out of his mouth, Kyle wished he could reel it back in. Instead, he stood firm and offered his most bland expression.

Or, rather, the blandest expression he could manage considering he had just kissed her. Thoroughly and completely kissed her.

In response, the lovely lady bested him with a broad smile. "No," she tossed over her shoulder, "you do not, do you?"

He easily caught up to her and turned her to face

him. "Lady, you need to understand that as long as I live, I will never forget you."

A smile began on the lips he had just kissed. "Nor will I."

"Stay here," he said before he could come to his senses. "I think you and I were meant to meet. I know it sounds crazy and yet I believe it."

"Not crazy," she said. "I think perhaps we are two kindred souls who chanced to meet."

"And now that we have, I cannot let you go. Not yet."

She shook her head. "We have no choice. Very soon I will be in England." A pause. "With my husband."

"Do not marry him. Stay."

The society scientist reached up to touch his cheek. "I can't," she whispered. With that she turned and was gone.

Going after her was the obvious choice. And yet what purpose would it serve? Waiting for the men in her life to make their way up to the roof so he could ruin her wedding plans was a tempting second option he quickly discarded.

He would allow her the wedding she wished, though Kyle knew he would long remember the flight over Memphis, their dance across the Peabody ballroom, and the conversation regarding science and the stars.

The kiss.

Oh, he would never forget that New Year's kiss.

As the song went, their acquaintance would not be long forgotten.

Nor would the place she had etched in his mind and, strangely, his heart. For something about the woman just seemed as if the Lord had made her for him. If that were true, then surely she was not meant to leave him. And yet she had.

Kyle sighed, and then an idea occurred. He had been raised a gentleman, and gentlemen did not allow a lady to leave alone at such an hour. So he followed as his flying companion slipped past the kitchen staff to leave the Peabody Hotel and make her way down the deserted city streets.

Keeping just far enough behind her to prevent detection, Kyle easily trailed her all the way to Adams Street. When she opened the gate of a redbrick mansion midway down the block, he waited a full minute before casually walking past and jotting down the address in his notebook.

As he had guessed, her home was expansive, though not more than the others on this block. Captains of industry, scions of wealth, and a few bankers and tradesmen thrown in were the residents of the homes on Adams Street.

Not for the first time, he wished for an end to his Pinkerton days. Were he simply an inventor, there would be nothing keeping him from paying a social call on the young lady of the house.

But he was a Pinkerton agent. A Pinkerton agent working a case that could easily involve any of the residents on this street. And whether or not he believed in the existence of Confederate gold, he still had a job to do.

Kyle ran his hand over the cornstalk fence that reminded him of his New Orleans neighborhood and then resolutely turned and walked away. He was tired, that was all. Tomorrow he would not give the woman he had spent this evening with another thought.

Nor would he consider the kiss.

He swiped at the lock of hair that had fallen into his eyes and picked up his pace. Indeed, he was tired. Exhausted.

Once back at the hotel, Kyle returned to the rooftop to gather up his flying device, and then he made his way back to his room. Dropping his things just inside the door, he loosened his collar, lay down on the bed, and fell asleep fully clothed.

He awoke to the sun's rude glare and a list longer than his arm of things to do. Then he recalled that it was New Year's Day. The banks would not be open until tomorrow. And while he could pull rank and gain access to the records he needed, he would not do that. Not on a case that still seemed like a waste of time.

Kyle rose and stretched the kinks out of his muscles. After bathing, changing into a fresh set of clothing, and then calling down to order something to eat, he snatched up the file folder Henry had given him and began to read.

As before, the beautiful dark-haired scientist tugged at his thoughts and caused him to read the same words over and over without comprehending any of them. This time, however, he pushed back against them, tucking all thoughts of a woman bound to marry another into the vault of his mind.

The key that sealed the lock on that vault of memories was comprised of the last words she had said to him. *Very soon I will be in England. With my husband.*

"And soon I will be hunting Will Tucker again." Kyle returned to the documents with renewed resolve.

Three days later he stepped out of the Union & Planters Bank, his last stop of the day. Bank president Napoleon Hill had left instructions to provide him with anything he needed.

The staff had been most accommodating, and so he had managed to rule out this bank as a possible depository of hidden gold. Should any new information be found, Kyle had the telephone number of Samuel Read, Union & Planters' second-in-command, written in his notebook. He had a similar experience at the other banks in the city.

Turning his back on the three-story brownstone building in the heart of the financial district, Kyle paused. All leads exhausted, he had no further reason to remain in Memphis.

Except one.

Eight

Three days.

Millie released her grip on the curtain and let it slide back into place. Sir William had kept her waiting three days . . . and then he had arrived unannounced on her doorstep an hour ago, saying he needed to meet with Mr. Cope in his study at once.

She had hurried into her best afternoon dress and called one of the maids to pin up her hair once again. And then she began to wait. And wait.

"What are they doing down there?" she muttered as she once again pulled back the lace window covering.

At any moment she fully expected her father to come storming up the stairs and announce that she had ruined her chances of marrying the Englishman and, in the process, brought embarrassment to the family. And so she steeled herself, leaning against the windowsill and making a feeble attempt to distract her scattered thoughts by watching the activity on the street below.

If Sir William were to leave without speaking to her, at least Millie would know before she heard it from her father, not that she was looking forward to talking with him. He had been exceptionally grouchy these past few days, and his lady friend had not appeared at any of the evening meals. Instead, Father sat silently brooding over his dinner plate and requiring more than the usual refilling of his wine glass.

Though the evenings generally found Silas Cope away, he had remained sequestered in his library until well into the night. Millie found the quiet almost as unnerving as when Father was shouting.

Millie owed this information to her inability to find a restful sleep apart from dreams of a handsome aviator with dark eyes and the loveliest way of kissing her goodbye. For it must be goodbye. She could not possibly entertain any idea of repeating the scandalous behavior of New Year's Eve.

Foot traffic on Adams Street was light this afternoon, likely owing to the chill that had overtaken Memphis. People hurried by in warm coats and winter hats under gray skies that threatened rain.

Too close indeed to her mood. She rang for her maid. "Is Sir William still here?" she asked when the girl arrived.

"He is, miss. Still in the library with your father."

Though she hated gossip in all its forms and generally avoided any pretense of it, Millie knew the walls in her home practically had ears. And the servants had eyes that rarely missed anything. Between Cook in the kitchen, the butler and the valet, and the maids—two pretty Irish sisters— little went unnoticed indoors.

Thus she knew with absolute certainty that her comings and goings on New Year's Eve were common knowledge among the help. Though Millie would never ask it of them, they would likely keep her secret against any inquisition on Father's part. They liked her. They merely tolerated her father.

"And is their conversation of a cordial nature?"

"It is, I do believe," the maid said. "There has been much laughter, and Cook is preparing a right delicious-smelling roast dinner just now. It is to be ready within the hour."

Millie glanced at the silver clock on the mantel. "Dinner? It's not even four o'clock."

"Yes'm. Cook did find it odd."

"As do I." Millie moved away from the window and squared her shoulders. "Please lay a fire in the fireplace of my private room and light the lamps. I will be having my dinner there this evening." She looked at the clock again. "But at a more reasonable hour."

A wisp of a smile softened the maid's stoic expression. "Yes'm."

"And should my father or his guest wish me to join them . . ." She gave the remainder of her statement some thought. "Please inform them I am indisposed."

"Yes'm."

Millie allowed time for her wishes to be carried out and then went to seek solace in her third-floor sanctuary. The attic room, while small in size, felt grander to her than any other room in the Cope home, especially when the lamps were lit and the fireplace shed a golden glow over the furnishings.

With three of the four walls filled with the books Father would never allow in her bed-chamber, the room might have held the scent and image of a tiny library save for the organized chaos on the table filling the center of the room.

It was there pieces of thoughts were made real, items she had crafted into partially working mechanisms and others still needing attention. Mixed in among the odd collection of metal, leather, and wooden objects were a stack of sketchpads that threatened to topple at any moment, one of Mama's discarded Spode gravy boats filled to the brim with fat charcoal pencils, and paint brushes in need of a good cleaning standing upright in an old jar.

The scent of the leather of the books mixed with the blended aroma of linseed oil and turpentine to offer a fragrance unique to Millie's private retreat. Thanks to a few spills, the priceless Aubusson rugs she had salvaged from Mama's bedchamber before Father sent all the furnishings away bore far too many paint splatters to be called decent for company to see. They would accompany her to England along with the books and her art supplies, for Father and her soon-to-be groom need not know the contents of her trunks. Surely somewhere in Trueck Abbey was a place like this one she could call her own, a room where Mama's Bible was the only item not likely to suffer some sort of minor damage due to her slight forgetfulness when returning the tops to jars of ink or keeping the metal shavings from her poor attempts at inventions from flying about.

Millie fitted the key in the lock and turned it, inhaling deeply of the intoxicating mixture as she opened the door. Repeating the process of securing the lock on the other side, she tucked the key back into her pocket.

She would have the maid check on the repair of her broken gold chain tomorrow. Or perhaps she would go herself. Yes, that would be the better option, as Mr. Parker, while a very discreet jeweler, had been abominably slow. His promise to return the piece intact today had apparently been forgotten.

Millie headed toward one of two wingback chairs, upholstered in tapestry with threads of deep burgundy and spun gold, that the maids had spirited away for her convenience. Likely Father would never miss them from the formal parlor, though his valet had let her know in no uncertain terms that he might be required to return them should his employer complain about their absence.

She had loved the oversized pair as a girl because they made the perfect place to hide in from her sisters. Never failing to win at their hide-and-seek games, Millie could easily disappear simply by sitting in one of the big chairs. It made her smile to know she still could, such was the height of the chairs' backs.

She went to the bookshelf to retrieve the novel she had begun yesterday and then turned with the intention of finding a warm place to read. Only then did she notice she was not alone.

She saw dark hair and a length of leg that began with a man's winter trousers and ended with a shoe that held not a single scuff. Millie froze. Who could have possibly found this room? Found her?

Inching forward, she held the book tight against her. Should her privacy have been breached by a stranger who meant her harm, the heavy leather volume was likely her best weapon.

A thought occurred. She could back slowly and softly out of the room and then report the breach of the premises to . . . whom?

Father would have the offending chamber torn apart and packed away. Still, she had to leave. To stay with a stranger about was lunacy.

Millie took one step backward and then another as she inched her way to the door. And then a traitorous board squealed beneath her foot.

At this, the intruder shifted positions to stand.

Recognition slammed into her, and she slumped against the door as if she had been shot. "You?" she breathed. "But how did you—"

"I was hoping I would find you here." The aviator's lifted brow belied his casual pose.

From head-to-toe he looked as if he had only just stepped out of the bank around the corner. And yet his rakish grin belonged more to a rogue than a captain of industry.

"What . . ." She gulped for air as she held the volume to her chest atop her galloping heart. "*What* are you doing here?"

"I came to see you. And the place where you hide away to read your books." He gave the room a sweeping glance, both hands in his pockets, and then returned his attention to Millie. "I like it. Very much."

"But how . . ." She shook her head, her pulse still pounding as her fingers tightened around the book. "How did you get in here?"

He stepped around the chair but moved no closer to her. He produced something that appeared to be metal spikes. "I am an inventor. Finding my way into a third-floor room is not a difficult proposition."

Curiosity almost had her walking over to examine the device he held. Prudence, however, caused her to remain in place. She thought of

Father and Sir William two floors below and drew in a deep breath. Finding her here with all her books and treasures would be bad enough. Adding a decidedly handsome stranger to the mix would be a complete disaster.

"You cannot stay."

"I have no intention of staying." He looked away from her to scan the room.

Golden firelight traced a path along the patterns of the rugs as he made his way toward the table in the center of the room. Bypassing the jumble of objects Millie had left there, he continued toward the bookshelves on the far wall.

"No, I mean you must go *now*." She nodded toward the window. "Now. Really."

"So you said." He ran his palm across the leather volumes, his gaze seemingly diverted to studying their titles. "You have an impressive library here." He lifted a book from its place and opened the cover. "This one in particular is one I have been keen to read." He set it back in place and reached for another. "Is this Goethe's *Faust* in the original German?"

She merely nodded. He asked in German if she had yet read the novel, and she responded in kind. And because she could not resist, she also told him how much she loved the story but disagreed with some of the character's choices.

In French.

With an admiring glance in her direction, the

aviator turned the pages until finally he apparently found the one he sought.

"In the end, you are exactly what you are," he read, translating to English. "Put on a wig with a million curls, put the highest heeled boots on your feet . . ."

"Yet you remain in the end just what you are," she supplied, this time in Italian.

He repeated the phrase. In Latin. "I can also offer Greek, Spanish, and a few other languages that might betray my penchant for traveling abroad."

Millie smiled in spite of herself. "Thank you, but no. I think I understand you just fine in English."

The stranger glanced toward her. So he was no stranger to the German language. Or any of several others, if what he claimed was true. She resisted the urge to test him.

"Yet you remain in the end just what you are," he again quoted.

Lovely words, though she would never again think of them in the same way. Not after today.

She watched in silence as he closed the book and returned it to the shelf. "And who are you?" he asked when he had once again found her gaze.

"I am sure you know by now," she said with more bravado than she felt. Inside, she quaked. Outside, she hoped she appeared at least somewhat collected.

"I do not, actually." He moved away from the

bookshelves, focusing his attention on her work-table.

"What do you mean?" She took a few tentative steps away from the door and then paused, her grip tight on the book. "You found me. How can you not know my name?"

"Because I choose not to."

Emboldened, she shook her head. "I do not believe you."

"Fine," he said. "But it is the truth. We agreed names were not necessary. You are to be married, and I am . . ." He paused. "You are going your way very soon, and tomorrow I will be going mine. What would be the point?"

She nodded, praying he told the truth. Her situation was already far too complicated without adding an inventor and his flying machine to it. Still, she glanced around the table, looking for anything that might bear her name.

"Of course. What would be the point? And I rather like it. It gives you an air of mystery I will not forget."

"An air of mystery," he echoed. "Yes, I like that. Nor will I forget you, my society scientist." The stranger reached for the topmost sketchpad in the stack. "May I?"

When she nodded, he began to flip through the sketches until he paused to study one intently. She came closer, curious as to what had caught his attention.

The Porter dirigible.

"You know about Rufus Porter and his plan to fly miners west to the gold mines in California with his dirigible?"

"Though he had some setbacks, the concept was a good one. It should have worked . . ." she said before falling silent again. There was no need to encourage the stranger to stay, so conversation on any topic was a poor idea.

"You understand then." He gave her an admiring look. "I see now why you were not afraid of flying with me. Well, not after I convinced you that the two of us together would not keep the device grounded."

Millie joined him at the table. "That is a copy of the sketch I found in Father's library. A pamphlet on aerial navigation he had kept from his youth."

" 'The Practicality of Traveling Pleasantly and Safely from New York to California in Three Days.' " He shrugged. "I own it. Brilliant work for forty years ago. As you said, his ideas were sound, but his dream was too big for the time." He paused as if to weigh the sketchbook in his hand. "This is a very good likeness."

"Thank you."

He turned to the next page and then the next, giving each drawing its due consideration before going on. The slow pace of his reading was maddening, as was her inability to capture his attention and channel it toward making an exit.

"Tell me something," she said and his head jerked up, his attention shifting again to her. Millie closed the distance between them to take the sketchbook from his hands and close it.

Their fingers brushed as he allowed her to set the book aside. Millie stood with her back to the table now, her hand gripping the edge. "Why did you go to the trouble of coming here?"

"This is going to sound foolish, but I had to see you one more time." He paused when a log cracked in the fireplace, sending a jolt of firelight up the chimney. "To see if you were real."

Millie let out a burst of laughter that died quickly when she realized he was serious. "I don't understand."

"No, I don't suppose you would." He allowed his gaze to travel around the room. "Do you have any idea how unique you are?"

"Oh, I am acutely aware of that. And lest I forget, my father takes particular care in reminding me."

"Forgive me for saying so, but your father is a fool." At her sharp intake of breath, he reached to follow the line of her jaw with his knuckles. "Let me rephrase," he said gently. "Your father apparently does not understand that a woman of your intelligence and beauty is a rare gem and should be treated as such."

"You are toying with me," she said, though her lip trembled. "And it is not appreciated."

"I am doing nothing of the sort."

She met his steady gaze, willing her heart to believe he spoke the truth. If she could believe that one man found her more than just an oddity, then perhaps the man she was to marry would too.

He bent his head, and then his lips followed the trail his knuckles had traced. Slowly the aviator leaned toward her. He would kiss her, this Millie knew. She should not allow it, should not want him to.

And yet she leaned into his embrace as he wrapped his arms around her and fitted his lips to hers. The kiss was one she would not forget. For when it ended and he pulled back, she felt his absence keenly.

"There," he said as he pressed his index finger to her lips. "I have done what I came to do." He shook his head. "No, that is not exactly right, is it?"

"No?" she somehow managed, though her knees threatened to betray her and send her tumbling to the carpet at any moment.

"No." He linked arms with her, led her to the chair by the fire, and then asked her to sit.

She obeyed, thankful for the excuse to give up the battle to remain upright. He knelt beside her, one hand resting on the arm of the chair, the other on his knee.

For a moment Millie was not sure he would

speak. Then he cleared his throat and let out a long sigh.

"This man you will wed, is he good to you?" He looked at her and then at their surroundings. "Will he allow you this?"

"He is not unkind. And, yes. It is our agreement that I shall have the freedom to establish my own household."

"Establish your own household? What does that mean?"

"It means I shall have the workshop I have wanted as well as the library I need. And I shall enjoy both without being made to feel that neither is suitable for a woman."

His smile was instant, dazzling. Dimples framed his grin and bid her to touch them. Were she made of lesser stock, Millie might have given in. But she had been raised a lady, and except for her unfortunate penchant for allowing this stranger to kiss her, she managed to keep within the strictures of those expectations.

"You have his assurance on this?"

She dipped her head in a nod that had the dual benefit of responding to him as well as removing his face from her line of vision. Without the aviator's countenance to cause her confusion, Millie found her thinking clearer and her resolve to avoid yet another kiss stronger.

"We have not discussed the specifics of the arrangement, but I intend to pack up all that you see here and send it ahead so that when I arrive at my husband's household, I will not be left without the things I love. This much I have already secured permission to do."

"Secured permission?" He rose abruptly and began to pace. "Were it not impossible, I would suggest you tell this man you have changed your mind. That you do not need his permission for such activities as reading books or—"

"Enough of that." She rose to follow him. "You are a stranger here, sir, and I will ask you to remember that. Unless you intend to exchange names and then perhaps go downstairs and meet my father and ask his permission to pay me visits, I will thank you to—"

A knock at the door interrupted her. Pure dread sent her stumbling forward. The stranger stretched out his arms to keep her from falling.

"Oh, no," tumbled from her lips. "They cannot find you. Find us. Or this room or anything such as . . ."

Another knock, this one more insistent. Millie fixed her companion with a do-not-move look and then tiptoed to the door to await another knock.

Nine

When the knock came, Millie edged the door open slightly. The maid. She let out the breath she had been holding.

"What is it?"

"Is there something wrong with you, miss? Are you ill?"

"No, I am fine," she snapped. She closed her eyes and took a breath. "Do not mind me, Bridget. I was involved with something that had me quite focused. Do you need something?"

"Yes, miss. Your father wants you down in his study. Something about an announcement that be long overdue."

"Oh, my," she said softly. "Were those his words?"

"They were, miss."

Millie collected herself and said calmly, "Please tell my father I shall be down directly."

She closed the door and then leaned back against it. The dark-haired stranger came to her, moving like a jungle cat across the room.

"Bad news?"

"Likely very good news." She put a smile in place and then offered it to him. "You must go now."

"I know," he said gently.

"And you cannot return."

Again he leaned in toward her, this time raining kisses on her temple. "For more reasons than you know, it would be impossible." His expression brightened. "Fly with me again before I go."

"Now?"

He laughed. "No, of course not. Later. Tonight. Or tomorrow. Or when I send for you."

"I cannot. Truly."

"And yet I think you just might."

"I will not." She pushed him back to hold him at arm's length. "I must marry this man. It is the only way. Promise you will not interfere."

"I promise, though I would extract a promise from you as well."

"And what is that?"

"That you will contact me should you ever have need of me."

Millie shook her head. "Impossible."

"I assure you it is quite possible." He reached into his pocket, drew out what appeared to be a small rectangle of paper, and handed it to her.

"A playing card?"

The aviator turned the card over and then ran his hand over the back to show her the almost imperceptible raised dots. She followed his example and smiled as she recognized what he had done.

"This is a code."

"It is, but I am sure it will be no problem for someone of your intellect to solve."

Millie smiled as she ran her hand over the familiar pattern. "It is a number. A telephone number," she said as she lifted her gaze up to meet his. "Yours?"

Dark eyes caught hers and then looked away. "Someone who can get a message to me."

She held the card in her palm. "I see."

"I will await your call to solve the wheel cypher or just generally save the day."

He paused, as if he longed to say more. And then he walked to the window and opened it. A moment later, he was gone.

"I will not call you, you know," she whispered as she tucked the card into her bodice and turned to open the door. "I cannot."

Millie hurried down the stairs to pause at the second floor landing and catch her breath. Kisses the stranger had pressed to her lips and dusted across her temple still fought for her attention, as did the playing card resting close to her heart.

Knowing she could reach the stranger again gave Millie only the briefest cause to second-guess her upcoming marriage. A world where a man understood, even praised, her intelligence was tempting to imagine.

But he was not offering her that world, only giving her a glimpse of what it might be like. Though temptation was sweet, reality was her true master. And the reality of her situation meant that Mildred Cope of the auspicious Memphis Copes would soon marry Sir William Trueck and flee to England. Perhaps it was not the best choice, but it was the choice most likely to happen. It did not take a genius to deduce this.

A door closed somewhere, hurrying Millie along. She found her father alone in his library. Millie wondered the reason for it. Had Sir William given the Cope family his last goodbye, or was he merely called away on other business?

Then there was the thought that news of her visitor had traveled down two floors to land squarely in Father's library and cause the Englishman to make his exit. That, too, could be possible.

He swiveled in his massive chair behind his massive desk and skewered her with a look that told her he was not pleased. But then when was Father pleased with anything she did?

Squaring her shoulders, Millie refused to cower as she made her way through his stare to settle onto the first chair she reached. When she was good and fortified against whatever charges she would be answering, she said calmly, "You wished to see me?"

"You took your sweet time," he grumbled. "But, nonetheless, your groom has not yet returned."

"Returned? Where did he go? I thought he was here with you."

"He was, and then he received an urgent message and had to step out to speak to his driver. Now I do not know where in the world he is . . ."

The sound of footsteps caused Father to cease his speech before he had gotten it sufficiently underway. The valet came in the room with a silver tray held before him. "A message, sir, from Sir William. He was called away and begs your forgiveness."

"Of all the confounded . . ." He shook his head. "Go on."

"Yes, sir. He would have Miss Cope read this. And he wishes you to know he shall see you tomorrow at the time and location previously agreed upon."

Millie met her father's inquiring glance before accepting the letter. Rather than the expected "Miss Cope," the name "Mildred" had been scrawled across the folded page.

She read through the contents and then said, "He wishes to make a formal request for my company tomorrow at a luncheon with several important persons celebrating our engagement." Millie paused. "And he thanks you for arranging the announcement to be printed in tomorrow's newspaper."

Father looked quite proud of himself. "Yes, well, it was no small feat, considering what passes for news nowadays. Quite nice of the lad to offer up a formal invite for you."

What she did not share was the last line:

Might I also have the pleasure of your company this evening? It is of the utmost importance, and I would beg your indulgence as well as your discretion in not making mention of it to your father. I will call for you at half past ten.

Half past ten? She read that again. Indeed, the Englishman kept odd hours.

"Anything else?" her father asked.

"No, no further message on that subject." The truth, and yet she hated the deception.

"You will attend, of course. And you will not embarrass the family with any of that nonsense you are given to chattering about. I want the story that runs in a week's time to be worthy of reading. 'Wealthy Memphis Heiress Weds English Lord,' or something of the sort. Ridiculous talk of inventions and books will muddy the waters, and I would rather not have it printed."

"But, Father, I—"

"None of that," he said. "Your marriage to Trueck is going to be good for business, and I will not let you ruin it. And while I am at it, I should remind you this goes for your conversations with Trueck too. What man wants his wife to talk of such things?"

An image rose unbidden of the handsome aviator, firelight slanting across his features as he leaned down to kiss her. She shooed it away.

"Exactly," he said to her silence.

On a less auspicious occasion, Millie might have attempted to argue his point. But with the goal of leaving Memphis behind so close in hand, she would do nothing to ruin things.

"Yes, Father," she said, giving the appearance of being the dutiful daughter.

He rang for the valet and then set down his pipe, ignoring the fact he had dusted Mama's lovely rosewood desk with ashes.

"Sir?" the valet asked from just outside the door.

"Have one of the girls see Miss Cope to her bedchamber. I will not have her leave the safety of her room until her appointment with Sir William tomorrow."

"But, Father, I—"

"I will hear none of it."

"As you wish." She rose and offered him a mild look. "I will not leave my bedchamber until my appointment with Sir William."

At half past ten.

Millie kept her word, slipping out under cover of darkness a few minutes before the appointed time. Consoling herself with the knowledge she was doing as she had said, she closed the kitchen door behind her and quietly made her way to the street.

Lamps were lit, but there was no sign of anyone about. What to do?

Just then a hansom cab turned the corner and

rolled slowly toward her. Millie pressed herself into the shadows until the vehicle stopped. Sir William opened the door and beckoned.

She went to him quickly, her attention focused on her surroundings as he helped her up and closed the door. Once she was settled, they were off.

Millie blinked as she waited for her eyes to adjust to the dim light from the lantern fixed to the roof outside. The hansom cab was quite roomy, and the evening's rain had tempered the windows with just enough moisture to offer some measure of privacy. With the driver riding outside in a seat suspended above the back of the vehicle, it almost seemed as though she and Sir William were alone as they traveled down the deserted streets.

"Are you chilled?" he asked.

"No," she said as her gloved hands clutched the lap robe her fiancé had kindly provided for the occasion. "I'm quite fine."

The hour was late for idle chitchat, but owing to her promise to Father she made no comment on the matter. Instead, she traced a raindrop down the glass with her finger, wondering when her companion would get to whatever point he intended to make by bringing her out on a damp and dreary night.

Sir William swiveled to face her, and pale lantern light slid over his handsome features. "Thank you for coming, Mildred." He voice faltered and he dipped his head. "I'm sure you had your reservations."

"I admit I was curious as to why you would arrange such a clandestine meeting when you could have either paid me a proper visit or merely remained for dinner this afternoon."

He glanced up at her, meeting her gaze. "Neither suited my purpose."

"Which is?"

"I wished to speak to you alone without fearing we might be overheard by your father or the servants. You see, I have come to care for you, and I wonder if you have developed any similar feelings for me."

His question took her by surprise, as did the way he seemed to study her with such open vulnerability. "Feelings are . . . complicated," she said gently. "Of course there are feelings . . ."

"But you do not love me."

"Well." Again she bunched the fabric in her hands. When she caught Sir William watching her, Millie rested her palms on her knees. "Not yet, no."

"An honest answer." He nodded. "Yes, I approve of your honesty." A pause. "And your use of the word 'yet' gives me hope you expect such feelings to evolve over time."

"I would say that is a fair assessment."

Millie suppressed a sigh. Talking about feelings was not her preference, nor was remaining in an enclosed hansom cab with a man who wished her to forecast her change of emotions into the future. For a moment the quiet lengthened between them, broken only by the clip-clop of the horse's hooves on the brick street.

He reached to adjust his tie, a gesture that appeared more nervous than due to any sort of need. "You have not asked of my feelings for you, Mildred."

"No, I have not." She slid him a sideways glance. "Should I?"

Sir William chuckled. "No, my dear, I don't suppose you should." He reached to place his hand atop hers. "I will admit that, though I cannot fathom why a woman of your beauty and intelligence would take me on as a husband, I think we shall make a good pair."

"Do you?" The question slid out before she could stop herself.

"Yes, I do." Sir William's fingers curled around hers. "We both have a purpose in marrying, and unlike other couples, we actually admit it. I say that alone should be the basis for what I expect will be a wonderful friendship."

"Friendship," she echoed. "Yes, I like the idea of that. We shall be friends first and then . . ." With the aviator's kiss still fresh in her memory, Millie could not continue.

"Then we shall see where that friendship goes."

"Yes, absolutely," she said. "We shall see where it goes."

Sir William reached up to knock on the ceiling, apparently a signal to the driver to turn them back toward Adams Street. They rode in silence. At the corner the vehicle stopped.

"Good night, Sir William," Millie said, assuming he was allowing her the privacy of walking up the block to the house alone. "I wager my father would not take it well if he caught us out here without a chaperone at this hour, so perhaps our next visit should take place in the parlor."

"I wager your father would be delighted. Is it not the point that I marry you, Mildred? Public indiscretion would only hurry that event."

"Public indiscretion?" She looked around at the deserted street, the darkened windows of her neighbors. "I see no one here but us."

"Ah, but your father might not see things the same." He shrugged. "No matter. We will make the announcement tomorrow and set the date for the ceremony. I thought perhaps three weeks hence. Or is that too soon?"

Three weeks. Was it possible to feel relief and fear all at once?

"Three weeks is fine," she said.

Sir William caught her wrist and brought her fingers to his lips. "The love you spoke of. I pray it for both of us someday."

As do I, she almost said. Instead, Millie settled for a silent nod.

The Englishman's attention went to her neck, as

did his hand. "Your chain," he said. "It is missing."

"It's being repaired."

"I see." His expression unreadable, his hand still lightly touched her neck. Then, slowly he moved to rest his fingers on her shoulder. "Where?"

"Parker's Jewelry. Now I really must go."

"Until tomorrow," he said as he released her to step out onto the sidewalk.

Millie set off walking toward home. Before she reached the gate, the driver had already turned the hansom cab around to leave by the opposite direction.

A precautionary measure, she told herself. And yet as Millie watched it disappear around the corner, she had to wonder just what sort of man would allow his fiancée to walk alone at this hour.

"The man I am to marry," she whispered as she let herself in and hurried upstairs to her room.

The next day he caught up to her as they left the newspaper office and wrapped a protective arm around her.

"I thought the luncheon and announcement went well," he said as he ushered her into her father's carriage.

"Yes," Millie said absently, looking out the window. The formal sharing of the news of their engagement left her feeling slightly depressed. Giving herself a mental shake, she looked over at Sir William in time to see him reach into his coat pocket and retrieve a small box covered in green velvet.

Smiling, he handed it to her. "Open it."

Inside was a breathtaking confection of diamonds radiating out from a sizeable emerald anchored in its center. Slowly she lifted the piece from its resting place.

"It's lovely," she said as she allowed him to take the piece from her and slip it on her finger. "Oh, but I fear it is too big for me." Millie illustrated her point by turning her finger downward and allowing the ring to fall into her other hand. "I fear I will lose it."

"No matter," he said. "You are obviously more delicate and finely made than my mother. I will simply have it refitted."

She smiled. It was a beautiful piece.

"I will have my man deliver it to the place where you are having your chain repaired. Then I can pick them up together. How would that be?"

"That would be very kind of you, though I had hoped to have my necklace sooner. I was thinking of sending one of the maids this afternoon to—"

"What is this?" Father called, his tone unusually cheerful. "Did I see my future son-in-law putting a ring on your finger?"

"Indeed you did," Sir William said as he tucked the box back into his pocket.

"Come over here, Mildred," Father said. "There is one last man you need to see."

Millie allowed Sir William to help her down from the carriage and then walked with him over to where her father stood talking to several of the newspapermen she had met at lunch.

They were ushered back inside to return to the expansive office belonging to Father's friend the editor. They had gone over the main points of the engagement article here in this room, and while Father and Sir William spoke, Millie had stood at the window and searched the roofs dotting the Memphis skyline.

"We are ready," one of the newspapermen called. "Just come this way."

Millie followed the two men in her life into an adjoining room, where a photographer stood waiting. "Ah, the happy couple. Let's show our readers how much in love you two are."

Father grinned, while Sir William looked none too pleased. For her part, Millie simply went through the motions, first posing with Father and then between the two of them. But the room was warm and the food she had eaten for lunch sat like a lump in her stomach.

Let's show our readers how much in love you two are.

Millie suppressed a sigh. Had she been required to give a response, which thankfully she had not, she would have declined. She would have admitted friendship but nothing more.

"Hold on there," Father said. "I am only just

noticing my daughter is not wearing the gift her fiancé has given her." He looked to Millie. "Put it on for the photographer, dear."

"It's a bit large for me. Sir William will be having it refitted."

"Put it on anyway. There is no danger of it falling off here. You will only just be standing still." He looked to the photographer. "Be sure you get that ring in the shot."

"Yes, sir," the photographer said as he began adjusting his camera.

"Is there a story behind the ring?" one of the reporters called out.

"There is, actually," Sir William said. "It belonged to my mother. She sends it along with her best wishes to my future bride."

Father frowned. "I thought you said your mother was dead."

Millie felt the man beside her tense. "She is, but before she succumbed, she asked that I would give her engagement ring to the woman I wed with her best wishes." He slanted a look down at Millie. "And with a prayer that my bride and I would be as happy as she and my father were."

"Isn't that nice?" Father said, and Millie almost believed him.

If she had not seen how he had looked at the ring, had not known what his feelings were about her marriage to Sir William, then she might have gone along with the others in the room and thought the father of the bride was quite proud of his position that day. But she knew. And the warning look he gave her told Millie that Father knew she knew.

"One minute more. Now, Miss Cope, will you stand there? And, Sir William, please would you just hold her hand like that? Be sure the ring is . . . yes, there, exactly like that." The photographer held up his hand. "On three, then."

As the flash went off, Millie looked up to see that Sir William was gazing into her eyes.

Millie could only stand very still and attempt a smile, though her stomach continued to churn. From the photograph that appeared on the front page the following day, the effort had been an abysmal failure. However, the ring did look lovely. For that, Father was happy.

And it quickly left her hand for a trip to Parker's Jewelry. For that, Millie was happy.

Two weeks later Millie had escaped endless talk of the wedding to find solace in her attic hideaway. Father had gone out for the evening, leaving her alone to amuse herself.

To her surprise, someone had left her copy of *Faust* on the chair nearest the fireplace. When Millie picked up the book, a playing card fell out. This time the code was no telephone number.

She smiled as she ran her fingers over the dots to be sure she had deciphered the letters correctly.

Fly with me again.

"Is that a yes?" the aviator asked from the now-open window. "Or have I risked my life and probably my career to come back here just one more time?"

Ten

January 16, 1889
Memphis

The telegram from Henry could not have come at a better time. Over the course of almost two weeks, Kyle had followed the trail of Confederate gold across three states and come up with nothing to show for his efforts other than more than enough proof that his metal detecting device worked even better than he had hoped.

He had stopped counting the number of cannonballs and other weaponry—as well as the iron skillets, nails, and cooking and farm utensils—he had unearthed since the beginning of the assignment, though he had kept copious records in his notebook. And other than an Alabama woman who promised her undying affection for returning her late husband's missing pocket watch, his time spent was not offering the results he had hoped.

With the new information from an anonymous

source in St. Louis, he would be following the trail of evidence up the Mississippi just as he had done in Georgia, South Carolina, and Alabama. And likely the investigation would come to the same conclusion. Confederate treasure had not been buried here.

But tonight he had managed a stop in Memphis for one purpose, and that was to fly. With her. Just one more time beneath a moon that would be putting on a special show for both of them.

She was never far from his thoughts. There was something to be said for a memory with no name. With a woman who could torment his dreams but with whom he could never really settle. For once he knew her name, he would then have to decide what to do about her. Whether to interrupt her obviously well-ordered life or whether to forget her.

Kyle had paced the length of his suite, staring out over the Mobile River like the fool he was becoming where this woman was concerned. With each step he tried to convince himself there were good reasons to forget about her.

Many good reasons, of course, though none had mattered enough to keep him from finding his way back to Memphis and into her third-floor library uninvited. Again.

"You have not answered," Kyle said as he became aware of the unsettling fact.

"I am trying to talk myself out of it," she said,

her lips turning up into the beginnings of a smile.

"And?" He leaned against the windowsill and tried to blame the chill air at his back for the weakness of his knees.

The real reason was her, of course, but a man bent on just one more evening with a woman—and nothing more—could never allow her to know just how much she affected him.

"And I am failing miserably."

"I see." He relaxed, though he was careful not to allow his companion to know. "Well then, why don't I relieve you of the responsibility of choosing and rephrase my question?"

She grinned. "How thoughtful of you."

"I am." He paused just long enough to make sure his casual demeanor had not slipped. "So, about flying with me one last time?"

"Yes?"

He lifted one brow and gave her a no-nonsense look. "Let's go."

"That is not a question."

"No, it's not." Kyle gestured to the window. "And thus I have relieved you from answering it. After you."

"Out the window?" She crossed the room to join him and then leaned past him to peer outside.

She smelled of something floral, feminine. Beautiful.

And then she turned those eyes on him. Her smile had broadened. It was all he could do not to trace the line of her jaw with his knuckle. To lean down for just one more kiss.

And yet there would be no more kisses. He had determined this when he bargained with himself to justify tonight's adventure. They were just two people watching an eclipse of the moon together. Nothing more.

And yet she seemed to be made for him. The why of it was still a matter to wrestle with God for an answer. And thus far, God was not offering any clear responses. At least He had allowed them one more evening together. For now, that was enough.

"Your flying machine is tethered to my roof." Her voice held a lilt of amusement.

"It is." Kyle reached past her to grasp the rope and pull the device down within reach. "Shall we?"

He assisted her out of the window and into place on the flying machine. Then he held up the spare coat he had brought for her and helped her slip it on.

"You have thought of everything," she said as she leaned back against him.

Everything except how to say goodbye. "I do my best," he said instead. "Now hold on, and we are off."

A few minutes later they were rising above the treetops on Adams Street. The night air was crisp, but there was no wind to impede them as Kyle set a course for the river.

The lack of wind was exactly what he needed to test the tweaks he had made to the steering system after recalculating for fuel use and wind speeds. If his theories were correct, he could vastly improve on his most recent test flight and, he hoped, provide the final numbers to the patent attorney next week.

Though the watch in his pocket read half past eight, it felt much later. Rooftops and buildings glittered beneath the half-moon, but those few persons still about kept to themselves and never noticed the flying machine above them.

"It's lovely," his companion said when they reached the river. "Look at how the moon shines so prettily on the water." She snuggled closer against him. "I have lived in Memphis all my life, and I must confess I have never thought of the Mississippi River as anything other than a muddy mess to be avoided at all costs. But it is just lovely."

"Lovely," Kyle echoed, but his attention was not on the river. Between the nearness of the woman and the importance of keeping track of the gauges and meters, the scenery below was not important.

"Look how many boats are down there," she said as he urged the device higher. "I never realized how busy the port was. It just seems so . . ." She let out a sigh. "I could do this all night."

He chuckled. "Hardly," he said, though he

allowed the thought for just a moment longer than he ought. "We have enough fuel to power the device an hour, maybe slightly more. Like it or not, I should have you back home well before your bedtime."

"And what if I don't wish to return quite so quickly," she said with a teasing tone. "Perhaps I would like to fly somewhere far away. Would you take me?"

"My schedule will not allow it. Not today."

"Why not?" she demanded as she attempted to swivel to look up at him. "Do you have other plans?"

"Be still," he demanded as he corrected the tilt she had caused and righted their course. "You cannot just move at will up here. And, as to your question, I actually do have other plans."

"Oh."

Did he actually hear disappointment in her voice, or was that a trick of the altitude and wishful thinking?

"As do you," he said as he glanced down to see her hand, so small and lovely, casually draped atop his arm.

"I do?"

"Your wedding," he forced himself to say.

"Yes," came out barely loud enough for him to hear. "It is to be next week," was a bit louder, though no less tentative.

"Next week?" Kyle felt the air go out of him.

He reached up to take a reading of the gauges, not because they needed it but because he did.

"I know. It's barely been time enough to announce the engagement. But I suppose that is for the best."

He removed his focus from the equipment. "Is it?"

"Yes, of course. Why wouldn't it be?"

"I could ask you the same question." He paused. "It seems pretty quick, considering you kissed me two weeks ago." Too late, Kyle realized he had said the words aloud. "So," he hurried to add, "I have to admit to an ulterior motive for flying tonight."

"That has nothing to do with my wedding?" He heard the teasing tone in her voice and grinned.

"Exactly. I wonder if you are aware that a lunar eclipse will occur."

"No. How wonderful." She lifted her head as if to study the sky. "What time?"

"According to my calculations, the moon has already entered the penumbra. See how it appears just a little darker than before?"

"I suppose," she said tentatively.

"The process takes hours, so it is not truly noticeable to the human eye until it is well under-way." He went on to tell her what the article in the *New York Times* had said on the topic and then paused. "What am I saying? You know all this."

"I know some of this," she corrected, "and I do

not mind hearing the other parts again." It was her turn to pause. "And I can assure you if the article appeared in the *New York Times*, I have not had the opportunity to read it. Papa would not hear of having a New York newspaper in the house. For him, the War of Northern Aggression did not happen so long ago. Do continue, sir, to enlighten me about the moonlight."

Light. Enlighten. Did she realize she was making a pun?

"Light? En*light*en?" His companion fell silent. "Hmm, I guess that was too silly for a man of your intelligence."

"Actually, I was going to say the same thing but figured you would think I was . . ." He shook his head. "Never mind."

"Of course you were."

"I was." Again they shared a chuckle. "So," Kyle continued. "We cannot possibly fly until it disappears and returns again. We will have a bird's eye view for part of it, though."

She tugged at his sleeve for a moment. "Did that article in the *New York Times* mention what time the eclipse might peak?"

He glanced up at the moon again. "Half past eleven. And it's only a partial eclipse."

"I would like to see it all the same."

"I told you, we do not have enough fuel to—"

"Just set this thing down somewhere and I will be content to watch from the ground. Or a rooftop. I do not care." She gasped. "Oh, look!"

He followed the direction where she pointed and saw that the edge of the moon was now obscured by a fingernail-sized shadow. As the partial eclipse proceeded, that shadow would grow larger and then eventually wane away to nothing again.

"It is brown. No purple. Or would you say it is mostly brown with a shading of purple at the edges?"

He agreed with her, not because he had any sort of opinion on the color of the shadow crossing the moon. Rather, he was considering where to land and how to explain to anyone who might come upon them exactly what they were doing sitting outside on a chilly January night with a partial lunar eclipse and a strange flying machine for company.

Going back to the Cotton Exchange was not an option. That area of the community was too densely populated, and the lights of downtown Memphis would likely obscure the view.

Taking her back home was an option, but he certainly could not remain there with her. Good sense told him that was the logical option.

"I must see this in its entirety. Or at least until the eclipse reaches its peak. I have never seen one, you know."

"Ever?"

She shrugged. "I've not had an opportunity until now."

"You will get a decent view from the city, but to really see it well, you will need to find a place where there are no city lights. Perhaps the next time one occurs you can arrange to be in the country."

Kyle stopped himself from asking where her fiancé's home might be. Better not to imagine her in city or countryside.

"Who knows when that will be? I want to see this one."

"Well, there it is." He nodded toward the sky above. "Look all you want. Until we run low on fuel, that is."

"I have a better idea. I know the perfect place. It's not far from here, and we can watch the whole thing from the upstairs porch. It has a lovely view of the sky, and the last time I visited, two porch rockers were still there, though the home has been empty for years."

"And what of your father? And your fiancé? Won't they miss you if I keep you away for hours?"

Her shoulders shrugged. "My fiancé has no way of knowing I might be absent from the house, and I am rarely missed by my father even when he is home, which tonight, once again, he is not."

And yet I will miss you terribly. "Tell me where this place is. And understand I make no promises."

She gave him directions.

"Near the Davies home, then?"

"Very near. Do you know the area?"

"I do," was his truthful response. A half-dozen pieces of property encircling the Davies home had been possible sites for hidden gold, though nothing had been found. He recalled this from the notes in the folder Henry had given him.

Kyle had followed up with several days of checking potential hiding places on the properties with his detecting device, confirming the previous agent's supposition that if any gold had been buried in that area, it had long ago been found and deposited elsewhere.

He turned east to follow a road cut through the trees and then veered to the south. Beyond a stand of pines was a clearing, and in the center of that clearing stood what appeared to be a dwelling.

In all, the trip had been brief. Less than ten minutes would be his guess.

"There." She pointed to the home. "That is the place."

Kyle guided them just close enough to see the house in question. Yes, he remembered this one.

The funds associated with the upkeep of the home and its surrounding lands had been deposited well before the Civil War began, thus eliminating them from the list.

"How do you know about this place?" he asked as he debated what to do next.

"It's mine, of course." She paused. "Technically, it belonged to my grandparents, though no one has lived here in ages."

"A pity. It seems like a nice enough place."

"I always liked it, as did my mother." She shrugged. "Because my father wants nothing to do with the country life, he rents out the pastures and pays to keep the home from falling down around itself. I think he does it all for Mama's memory."

After a trip around the perimeter, Kyle was satisfied the area could be considered safe enough for landing. "Hold on," he said as he adjusted the gauges and brought the machine down gently on the front lawn a few feet from the house.

He released the straps and then helped his companion to step carefully onto the grass. "Stand right there while I get this secured."

She did as he asked and then allowed him to lead her up to the front porch by the light of the personal lantern he always carried with him. Silence had fallen around them, punctuated only by the chorus of frogs and chirps of nighttime creatures off in the distance.

The wide porch boards appeared to wear a fresh coat of gray paint, while the home's log-and-chink exterior showed no need of repair. A smaller version of this porch ran half the length of the second floor and appeared to be in similar shape.

Kyle rested his palm against the worn wood and wondered how long a home of this type had stood in this peaceful place.

"Early eighteen hundreds," she said. "Maybe before that." At his astonished look, she continued.

"You were wondering how old the house was, were you not?"

Without waiting for his answer, she turned to walk the length of the porch. After shuffling around a bit, she returned to the door and produced a key that she used to let them both inside.

The front door swung open on hinges that could use a decent oiling. Following her, Kyle lifted the lantern to get a look at the interior.

A staircase of average size and design marched up the wall on the left side of the room and disappeared onto a second floor hallway. Doors on either side of the room were open, revealing two more empty rooms.

"Wait right here." Kyle pressed his palm to his revolver and did a quick check of the premises. When he was certain no one was about, he returned to his flying companion.

She moved toward the stairs, beckoning him to follow. "I thought we could watch the eclipse from the second-floor balcony."

He glanced at his watch. Almost ten. Ninety minutes of waiting time lay ahead, and that was only if they stayed until the midpoint of the eclipse.

It would be interesting to see if his companion could sit still that long. Kyle sprinted to the top of the stairs. By the light of the personal lantern, he made a thorough search of the two rooms on this level, all empty.

"Satisfied?" she asked and then nodded toward the balcony. "Follow me."

A moment later he extinguished the lantern and then stood still until his eyes adjusted to the lack of light. The moon was almost half covered in shadow now, the lawn shrouded in deepest black. Only the slight movement of the silk told Kyle his flying machine was still safely tethered below.

"Come and sit." She settled onto a cane-seat rocker painted brilliant white. He complied, resting his arms on the wide slats.

"We have a bit of a wait, do we not?"

"An hour and a half, or thereabouts." He slid her a sideways look. "Would you like me to take another look at that wheel cypher of yours?"

Her fingers went to her neck. "The chain is broken, and it seems to be taking an eternity for Mr. Parker to repair it."

"A pity." He paused to lift a brow in a teasing manner. "I don't suppose you have that Remington in your pocket? We could do a little target practice while we wait."

"Be serious," she said, though he could not help but notice she had not answered in the negative or the affirmative.

As their laughter died, silence covered them like a comfortable blanket. Kyle trained his gaze over the balcony and settled back with a contented sigh.

"Exactly," she said.

He rested his head against the wooden back of

the old rocker and tried to focus on the eclipse rather than the woman beside him. Unlike any prior experience with the fairer sex, Kyle found that he enjoyed sitting quietly with no expectation of conversation.

Apparently so did she, for a sideways glance in her direction found her watching the stars with what appeared to be a contented expression.

"You still do not know my name."

"I could find it if I wanted."

She continued her stargazing. "I know," came later, softer. Almost as if she had not said anything at all.

It was absurd, really, the way he felt in her presence. In her absence.

How long they sat side by side, faces turned to the sky, Kyle could not say. Though he was sorely tempted to check his watch, he resisted. The evening would end soon enough and then he would be wishing the time could be reclaimed. And though he was an inventor, the sort of mechanism that could remedy the limit of time and society was not in the realm of possibility. At least not yet.

His companion reached to close the gap between them by covering his hand with hers. "Do you ever think people are meant to find each other?" She glanced his way and then back at the moon. "That perhaps God has some special purpose in mind?"

"Yes," he said as he heard his own thoughts echoed in her statement. "Do you?"

"It seems reasonable."

"It does." Kyle waited in the hopes that she would turn this extremely theoretical discussion into a more personal one. That she might declare herself as the woman meant for him by the Lord Himself.

A melodramatic thought, and yet he prayed now that it might happen. Failing that, he prayed for the ability to say those words to her first and for her agreement to them.

But still there was silence. A long yawning quiet that no longer felt good or comfortable.

She sighed, though her attention remained on the lunar event unfolding in the heavens above. "You will not find me again."

A statement, not a question. An understanding upon which they had both silently agreed even as he had prayed against it. Kyle found no reason to respond.

He did, however, move his hand to place it atop hers. The better to show her that though he would honor her request not to be found as best he could, he would nonetheless keep her safe if the need arose.

The knowledge that he was acting like a lovesick fool hit him square between the eyes. Carefully, he removed his hand. If she noticed, she did not offer any indication. Instead, this woman with the affinity for foreign languages, for puzzles and astronomy and inventions, continued to stare up at the moon with something akin to a wistful expression on her beautiful face.

The idea that this society scientist could be the one for him just wouldn't let Kyle go. What the Lord meant him to do about it was another question entirely.

He did not even know her name, leaving him to believe that maybe God just wanted to show him there might be something other than work. That someday, somewhere, love could exist in his life. Love like Lucas had found with Flora.

He let out a long breath and trained his eyes upward into God's star-filled creation. *Lord, You know You made me hardheaded. If she is the one, I need a sign. And if I am to leave her be and not look back, I need to know that too.*

Then it came to him. *Give me her name from her own mouth or send her away.*

Slowly she turned to meet his gaze. "I need to tell you something." She closed her eyes briefly before looking at him again. "My name is Millie."

Eleven

Silence that was once comfortable now yawned painfully between them. Millie watched him rise to disappear inside, his boots echoing on the wooden floors. Then the footsteps stopped abruptly, or so it seemed.

Slowly, they returned.

"It's out now," she said. "I would rather be the one to tell you."

"Millie." He seemed to be weighing the word before nodding. "Yes, it suits you."

Her companion came and stood before her now, leaning against the porch post and blocking her view of the eclipse. "Kyle," he said simply.

Kyle. "I've never met a Kyle before."

"And now you have." He seemed to be sizing her up. Observing her, not as a man or even a scientist. Rather, as some other sort of puzzle-solver.

A thought occurred. "You are not just an inventor, are you, Kyle?"

Her companion was silent.

"No," she continued, "you are . . . what?" She thought a moment. "A detective of some sort? No, a policeman." Millie shook her head. "No, that cannot be right. You just do not seem like the sort."

"Really?"

Millie grinned. "I just cannot imagine it. You as a law enforcement officer?" Her grin became a giggle. "No. What about a Pinkerton man? Oh, that would be too much."

"Too much?" Kyle shook his head. "And why is that?"

"You just do not—"

"Seem like the sort. Yes, I suppose you are correct in that observation. I do not seem like the sort, do I?" Before she could respond, he continued. "And I am also not the sort to keep a lady out until well past her bedtime. So, with that in mind, I believe we have seen more than enough of the lunar eclipse. It is time for me to take you home."

"And if I do not wish to go?"

"I do not recall asking your opinion on the matter."

He reached for her, and she allowed him to pull her to her feet. With a nod toward the door, Kyle moved in that direction and she followed. Apparently their moon watching was finished for tonight, as was his willingness to answer her questions.

He lit the personal lantern he had stowed in his coat. "Walk carefully, keeping to the light."

Placing a hand on his shoulder, she moved at his pace until they reached the door and, a moment later, the front porch. While he went to the flying device, Millie returned the key to its hiding place.

She found him jotting notes in his book. As she neared him, he snapped the book closed and returned it and the pen to its place inside his coat.

"According to my calculations, we should have thirty-two minutes of flying time before the fuel reaches critical level."

"Should?" she could not resist asking.

He grinned. "It is far too late for you to pretend you are unsure of my abilities to captain this vessel."

Millie matched his smile. "And it is far too late for you to pretend surprise that I would make the attempt."

With a dip of his head he came up grinning. Oh, but that smile did things to her heart. Things a woman set to wed another should never allow.

"Fair enough." He slipped into place and then gestured for her to join him.

Instead of assuming the correct position, however, Millie moved forward to meet him eye to eye. Or, rather, owing to his superior height, eye to chest.

Her gaze met his as she kept a respectable distance between them. "I must marry him," she said plainly. "There is no other option. It's important to me that you understand this."

If her words stunned him, he didn't show it. "There is always another option."

"I will concede that point." She paused and

looked away, deciding what else could be said. "But never a choice so clear as the one I am making."

His finger lifted her chin as he once again captured her gaze. "And what choice are you making?"

When she did not respond, he filled the silence for her. "Do you love him?"

Millie said the truest thing she could manage. "Someday I will."

He let his hand fall away and she felt its absence acutely. "I suppose that is how you society girls have to look at things."

"I would not limit this sort of outlook to any social station," she countered, her feelings now feeling sorely trampled upon.

"Fair enough." Kyle paused. "I will admit I barely know you, Millie, but what I have seen does not tell me you are the type to barter yourself off for any cause." And then he shrugged. "I suppose I was wrong."

That did it. The comment was beyond the pale, even if it did have more truth in it than she wanted to admit.

She jabbed his chest with her finger. "You know nothing of this, so do not attempt to form a conclusion without all of the facts. There are always variables out of a person's control no matter the situation."

"And facts—or in this case, people—presenting

themselves at the most inopportune times?"

She could not argue, exactly. Irritation caused her to toss the question back at him. "If facts are missing, please enlighten me so that I can arrive at a better informed conclusion."

"You are not ready to be married." Kyle placed his hand atop hers and slanted her a look. "If you were, you would never have gone flying with me tonight. And you would certainly never have asked me to take you away on a flying trip of greater length."

"That is not true. I . . ." She took a step backward and let out a long breath. Slowly she looked up to meet his gaze. "All right, I am not marrying for love, but it is not at all what you are thinking. I have been praying for a way to leave Memphis, so when the opportunity to wed was presented . . ."

"You took it."

She nodded. "At the time it seemed like an answer to prayer."

"So you have said." Kyle tethered the balloon and stepped out of the restraints to envelope her in an embrace. "Millie," he said softly, "are you certain this is the only way? With your intelligence and creativity, would you not prefer to apply to colleges or perhaps accept a teaching assignment? There is no shame in hard work."

"You do not understand." She stepped out of his arms and moved toward a growing puddle of moonlight. Glancing up at the sky, she could see the lunar eclipse was on the decrease.

Kyle came to stand beside her, his face tilted toward the sky. "Explain it to me then."

"My father would not allow either of those things to happen. So I must—"

"Gain your independence?" When she nodded, he continued. "You are marrying this man so you can be free of your father?"

"There are worse reasons," she said as she shrugged deeper into the warm winter coat.

"Yes, that is true." He turned to face her. "Why did you bring me here?"

She gave him a confused look. "To watch the eclipse."

"No," he said as he shook his head. "What I mean is, if you were reluctant to share your name with me, why share the location of your family's farm?"

Why indeed? It was a stupid risk and yet she had taken it.

"Because I trust you. You seem very nice and . . ."

"And?"

"I don't know." She nodded to the flying device. "Can we leave now?"

"When is the wedding?"

"The twenty-fourth," she said slowly. A shadow crossed his face. "Please do not look at me like that, Kyle. Yes, I am getting married next Thursday. Now, can we please leave?"

He leaned in close, and she inched toward him. The chill of the night was what she wished to blame. Unfortunately, she could not.

"And yet you are here with me," he said gently as his hand went back to her jawline. "Alone."

Oh, but those dark eyes. That smile. Millie swallowed hard and forced her attention away from the pull of attraction.

"Yes, I am," she said with what she hoped was a steady tone. "I am here with you alone." She paused to regulate her heartbeat and voice. "Watching a lunar eclipse in the most reasonable place to see it without the lights of Memphis interfering. Two scientists observing a natural event, nothing more."

His gaze pulled her toward him. "All right, if you say so. But I have a question, Millie, before we go."

"What might that be?"

"Have you ever formed a hypothesis only to stumble onto evidence that refutes your theory?"

"Of course."

"What did you do?"

What an odd question. "I discarded the theory. Or rechecked the source of the evidence to be sure it was impeccable and irrefutable."

"No issue with the source," he said with what sounded like a touch of humor. "Though the source may have issues with me as I try and decipher what I'm to do next."

"You do realize you're making no sense."

"Neither is God right now." At her surprised look, he shrugged. "I assure you the issue does not lie with Him."

"We aren't talking about scientific theories anymore, are we?"

Kyle offered a wry smile. "You're quite the investigator. Are you sure you're not in law enforcement? A Pinkerton agent, perhaps? That would be too much."

Millie laughed even as she noticed that her companion had cleverly and smoothly changed the emphasis of the conversation. She decided to allow it.

He gestured toward the balloon. "After you," he said with an exaggerated bow. "But I still say no woman should marry for any reason except for love."

"Spoken like a man who was never told he was an embarrassment to his family," she tossed over her shoulder as she walked toward the craft.

"There is where you are wrong."

He caught up with her then, turning her to face him once more. His gaze swept her face as his knuckle traced her jawline.

The beginnings of a grin touched his lips. "Never apologize for who you are, Millie. You are a beautiful, intelligent woman. Be happy that is how God made you."

"Thank you," she said a moment later. "For making me laugh."

"What?" he said as he assisted her onto the flying device and then secured himself in place. "You didn't think I was serious?"

Millie shook her head as he buckled her in and then readied the balloon for flight. "I did not think to debate the point at all. There is no response for it."

Leaning back against his broad shoulder, she closed her eyes and inhaled the crisp night air. *Be happy that is how God made you.* If only she might.

When the device jolted upward, she opened her eyes. They ascended slowly and then turned away from the farm to retrace their path back to Memphis. By the time they arrived back on Adams Street, the brownish purple shadow that had covered most of the lunar surface was waning.

"Thank you for one last flight," she said when he had tethered the flying device and helped her to climb inside her sanctuary.

Now was the time to say goodbye and watch him leave. And yet she couldn't say the words. She didn't want him to go just yet.

"You know," she said as she shrugged out of the coat and handed it back to him. "It occurs to me that while my chain is still at the jewelers, the wheel cypher is not. I wonder . . ."

He made a great show of pulling out his watch

to check the time. "I suppose I have a few minutes to spare."

"Then make yourself comfortable and I will go get it." She paused. "I wonder if you would like some coffee. Or tea? Maybe cocoa?"

"Whatever you are having," he said as he closed the window and turned to face her.

"Coffee it is." Her gaze swept the room. Something seemed different, but she could not decide what it was. "It would be terrible if someone were to find you here, so would you mind staying very quiet while I am gone?"

"And hide should someone other than you come in? Maybe behind the drapes or out on the ledge?" He smiled as he dipped his head. "As you wish."

She looked him over carefully to see if he was teasing. As she left, she still was not certain.

Making her way downstairs, Millie slipped into her bedchamber and called for her maid. Her nightclothes had already been laid out, and the bed coverings were turned back.

"Do you need help, Miss Millie?" Bridget asked when she arrived.

"No, thank you. But a pot of coffee would be lovely." She paused. "With milk, sugar, and an extra cup."

If the maid thought the request odd, her expression gave no indication. "Yes, ma'am."

While she waited, Millie went to the place

where she had hidden the cypher and slipped it into her pocket. A glance in the mirror sent her scurrying for her comb and extra hairpins.

She had almost repaired the damage to her hairstyle when Bridget returned with the tray and placed it on the bedside table. "Anything else, ma'am?"

"No, that is all, Bridget. Thank you." Millie gathered up the tray. "Is my father home yet?"

"No, ma'am."

"Fine. Do not wait up for me. I can see myself to bed later."

"Yes, Miss Millie. Good night." She returned to the servants' quarters as Millie hurried down the hall and up the back stairs to her attic hideaway.

She found Kyle stoking the fire. When the door opened, he straightened, the poker in hand.

"It's just me. No need to hide behind the drapes." She shut the door and then moved to place the tray on the table by the fire.

A log cracked in the fireplace, sending a spray of sparks upward as she poured her guest his cup of coffee and then set the pot aside. Distracted, she watched the display a moment longer than she might have were she alone. Then she turned to catch him observing her.

"I take back my earlier statement," she said as she poured milk into his cup.

"Oh?"

"I think you just might be a Pinkerton agent. Or

a detective of some sort. The question is, what sort?" She gave him an appraising look. "Do you work for the railroads? Or perhaps you're a detective for hire. But that would bring us back to the Pinkertons, would it not?"

His smile was sweet and swift. "I would not be much of a detective if I admitted to it, would I?" He took a sip of his coffee and then said, "Did you bring the cypher? I've been thinking about this, and I may have a solution."

When Millie handed it to him, he set his cup on the tray. As he turned the wheels and contemplated the puzzle, she took the opportunity to study him.

Kyle was a handsome man, a man with that lovely combination of Gaelic features not altogether unpleasant and yet on him quite impressive. Hair of midnight black teased his collar and fell across his forehead as he busied himself turning the golden rings one by one.

Cheekbones dusted by thick dark lashes were turned golden in the fire's light, as was the cleft in his chin. His lips—lips she had kissed more than once—were soft, almost feminine in their fullness. Her gaze moved to his hands. They were strong and agile as he worked the concentric circles of gold into some sort of pattern he alone seemed to know.

When he paused to glance up at her, Millie felt no compunction to look away. "Having any luck with that?" she inquired innocently.

"I do not believe in luck," he said as he went back to his task.

And then there was a soft *clink* and the cypher fell apart in his hands. He chuckled as he opened his palm and produced the results.

"There you go," he said. "One opened wheel cypher, a very old scrap of paper, and a small key of some sort for the lady."

Millie reached over and allowed him to put the pieces into her hand. "How did you do that?"

He picked up his cup and leaned back against the chair cushions, his smile broad. "A guess."

She laughed. "No, truly."

"Truly," he echoed. "Because these are old gold coins, I thought maybe calling on the name of an old Barataria pirate might do the trick. I lined up the notches so that they spelled his name, and there you have it."

Her gaze met his. "Lafitte?"

"You've heard of him."

She laughed to cover the feelings bubbling up. "Oh, Kyle. Even in Memphis we know of Jean Lafitte. But I tried using his name and it didn't work."

"Perhaps our methods were not the same. At least the cypher has opened."

"Yes, it has." She reached for one of the coins. "They are small and hollowed out inside. Not at all what I thought a doubloon would look like."

"That's because this is not a typical doubloon."

Kyle held one of the coins up to the firelight. "These are gold escudos. Spanish in origin."

"Were they all so small? These are barely the size of a dime."

"The sizes varied, but yes, they were small." He flipped the coin over and held it where she could see it. "See that *S* there just barely visible beneath the place where the coin has been hollowed out?"

"Yes."

"That means this one was minted in Seville. And from what remains of the date, it appears this is a very early example. Likely prior to 1810."

Which would fit with the time when Jean Lafitte was prowling the waters and taking treasures for his own. Millie let out a long breath. Mama's tale was becoming all too real.

"What can you tell me about its contents?" Kyle asked. "Perhaps a connection from your family back to Jean Lafitte? That would certainly prove interesting."

"I know nothing of these things," she said carefully. "I'm seeing them now for the first time." As to his question about Lafitte, that would remain unanswered for as long as she could manage it.

Millie was almost painfully aware Kyle was now studying her. His had to be a fortunate guess, for how could he know? No one knew. Mama made sure to tell her that because of what the taint of scandal might bring, she was not to tell

198

anyone of the connection to the famous pirate. It was all conjecture, just theories of hers made with no substantiation from Mama or any other source.

And yet it all fit. Well, mostly.

The piece of paper, a scrap not much bigger than a folded calling card, fluttered to the floor. Kyle bent and retrieved it.

"This is old," he said as he carefully opened the creased page, "and there is nothing here, though we both know there are ways to hide writing that would stand the test of years." He held the page to the light. "Or it could have been folded around this tiny key to keep it from rattling inside and means nothing at all."

"Yes, I suppose that is possible."

"I have the capability to study the paper, though of course all of that is back home in my workshop." He looked up. "What were you expecting? Some kind of treasure map?"

His tone indicated jest, but something in his expression made her think he was serious. She smiled even as the teasing topic touched far too close to the truth.

The coins might bring a small sum, but nothing like what she anticipated as she listened to her mother's stories. And if there was a treasure map on the scrap of paper, it had been lost long ago . . . unless she could find a way to make whatever was missing from the page reappear, and then the real treasure would be found when the key met its lock.

Kyle took a sip of his coffee. "I find it ironic that a pirate's name opened the cypher. So, tell me, Millie. Is treasure associated with the contents of your charm?"

"That is a direct question," she said, smiling. "I will counter it with my own. Are you a railroad detective or perhaps one of those mysterious Pinkerton men?" She slid him a playful look. "Or are you merely a mad scientist who is clever enough to pose as one?" She shook her head. "No, I suppose you would be a detective posing as a scientist who . . ." She fell into laughter and he joined her. "Now I've confused myself. Who are you, Kyle?"

He dipped his head before meeting her gaze once again. "Persistence is a quality I admire, as is deflection when done well. And you have done both quite well. So I will answer one question, and then you must do the same for me, agreed?"

"Agreed."

"I am not a railroad detective." He paused. "So, the cypher. Tell me about the treasure. And yes, I am aware I have not phrased this as a question. Would you like me to?"

"Normally I would insist on following the rules, what with my background in the Descartes scientific method and all."

"Really? I am much more interested in his scientific treatise on *The Passions of the Soul*, but go on."

"I see," Millie said as she collected a breath.

Though she knew the treatise to which he referred was an analysis of emotions and their result in action, the very sound of the title in his unique mix of Southern drawl and something else set her pulse racing.

Her companion sat back, allowing the firelight to slant over his features, turning what God had rendered merely handsome into a man most breathtaking. That the inventor and aviator she knew only as "Kyle" was also brilliant . . .

"Millie," he said slowly, "You are stalling."

"I am."

She tucked the key, scrap of paper, and gold pieces into her pocket and picked up her cup. She thought a moment about the safety of confessing her secret and then decided to throw caution to the wind. If this man could fly across the Memphis sky and best the cypher that had eluded her for a decade, perhaps he could offer insight into other things of importance.

After a glance into his eyes, she took in a deep breath and let it out slowly. "I must depend on your word of honor to keep what I am about to tell you a secret." She shook her head. "What am I saying? I do not know you. I—"

"You have my word, Millie. However, I will release you from your part of the bargain if you do not feel you should answer."

Something in his eyes told her this was true. She

picked up the pieces of the cypher and its contents. She felt the chill of metal in her palm.

"The key," he said. "What do you suppose it opens?"

"A lock would be the obvious answer." She gave him a half smile and then shook her head. "Now to put the two together. That is where you could assist me."

Kyle set his cup aside and asked for a gold coin and the scrap of paper. She handed them to him and watched with interest as he studied first the coin, turning it all directions and looking through its hollowed-out center.

Then he turned his attention to the torn piece of paper and looked at both sides carefully. "If I could just get this back to—"

"Your workshop? Yes, well that is not possible at the moment. So, given what you see here, what are your thoughts?"

Kyle rose, set the paper and coin on the worktable, and began to scan the books. When he crouched down to inspect a selection of books she had thought were hidden well enough, she heard his chuckle.

"As I suspected." He bobbed up, a leather volume in hand. "You have an entire section of books on the pirate Lafitte."

"I also have a section of Jules Verne, Jane Austen, and William Shakespeare." She turned her practiced look of innocence on the man before her. "As well as many others. What sort of hypothesis are you attempting to prove?"

"A valid one. That we are, to some extent, what we read. Are the others as marked as this one is?"

Millie opened her mouth to protest but then thought better of it. Indeed, he was correct. None but the Lafitte books bore such marks. She must learn to be more careful in the future.

Kyle opened the book and turned to a page where Millie had placed a bookmark. "I believe you've noted the location of the Baratarians' suspected hideaway as well as . . ." He flipped to another page. "Oh, here. It appears you have taken an interest in the location of a home our pirate friend occupied in New Orleans." He looked over at Millie. "I know the place. I'm not sure I agree with the author's premise that Lafitte would hide his ill-gotten gains under his own roof. That would be poor judgment on the pirate's part, and nothing that fits with the legend of him burying his valuables in more obscure places."

Snapping the book closed, he pointed it at her. "Another question, and I will offer no bargain in the answering of it." He waited only a moment before continuing. "This treasure connected to your cypher. Did it once belong to Jean Lafitte or one of his men?"

Just then a series of loud bangs ended the con-versation. "Open this door, Mildred!" her father demanded. "Or I will have it torn off the hinges!"

Twelve

"My father!" Millie thrust the coin and foolscap into her pocket, darted a look at her companion, and then hurried to remove the book from his hand and return it to its hiding place. "You must go!"

Kyle grasped her arm, and she looked up to meet a determined expression. "I will not leave you in danger."

"It is your presence here that puts me in danger," she whispered. "He will not harm me. He wants my marriage too badly to ruin it."

The noise on the other side of the door increased. Her companion looked down at her and seemed ready to say something. Ready to go to battle for her.

"Daughter, you will open this door at once or I will ring for the police!" Father shouted.

"Now would be an excellent time to tell me you are a police officer. Then I could assure my father he has no need to make that telephone call." It was a poor attempt at humor, but fear kept her from moving or responding with any sort of intelligence.

"I am not," he said against her ear.

"Then please, Kyle, just go." Millie turned to

walk toward the door, praying he would heed her request.

Instead, he snagged her wrist and pulled her back. "I cannot leave you with that man in such a rage."

"He will get over it," she whispered. "He always does."

"What do you want?" Father said, apparently to someone else, and then another voice outside the door responded. The valet.

Oh, thank goodness. Millie pressed her finger to her lips and tiptoed to the door. Kyle followed, pressing his hat into her hand.

When she gave him a confused look, he turned the brim over to reveal some sort of gadgetry beneath. "The better to hear things with," he said softly.

With a wink he fitted the hat onto her head and then extended a small tube toward her ear. Instantly she could hear the conversation on the other side of the door quite clearly.

"No, sir, it is merely a place for storage," the valet was saying. "That door must be wedged shut again."

There was a pause as Father grumbled. "Yes, well it has always been locked when I have had reason to be in the attic."

The truth, Millie thought, *because the door is locked at all times.*

"I heard voices inside there," Father protested.

"A woman was speaking, and I know it had to be Mildred, for who else would be up here? Surely not one of the house servants. And I see firelight. Now, if you cannot open that door I will find someone who can."

"But, sir, if it is voices that has you thinking your daughter is in the storage room, I can easily clear that up for you."

"Go on," he said.

"Yes, um . . . you see, there is a chimney inside this particular portion of the attic. I believe the room was once used as a bedroom for the help many years ago."

"I fail to see what the history of my home has to do with my daughter once again defying my wishes and carrying on in an unseemly manner."

"Yes, well," the valet continued, "in any case, the same chimney flue travels between this room and the kitchen two floors below. And thus, if you did hear someone, it was just as likely the voices came from the kitchen."

Also the truth, for Millie had heard more than her share of conversations between Cook and the maids since finding this hideaway and making it her own.

"Likely?" her father demanded. "I did not become the wealthiest cotton trader in Memphis by using the word 'likely.' A thing either is or it is not."

Father punctuated his statement with a series of

sharp blows on the door. Millie jumped back, covering her mouth to keep from crying out in surprise.

"What I should have said, sir, was that it indeed is. The chimneys have ears. In fact, I wager the voices must have come from the chimney flue owing to the fact this is a storage space that has obviously been sealed shut for some time. And the light must be coming from the streetlight outside."

Father protested again, though this time with less enthusiasm.

"Indeed, I do understand, sir, but I did not see Miss Cope once she excused herself to retire for the night."

Unless Millie misunderstood, the valet was sending her a message to get out of the room and into bed somehow. But how?

She moved away from the door and handed the aviator his hat. He followed a step behind as she crossed the room and paused at the window.

Three floors up was a dizzying height to attempt creeping around the house on the outside, but she had to do something. There was a downspout just beyond the window that, if she stretched, she might be able to reach. From there it would be a matter of climbing to the floor below where . . .

She groaned. Her bedchamber was on the other end of the house. Though she might find a way to climb down one floor, there was no possibility she could somehow make her way to her bedchamber without being discovered, whether she made the attempt inside the house or outside.

After another look down, Millie completely ruled out anything to do with escaping around the exterior of the home.

"Do not even consider it," Kyle said softly against her ear as he returned his hat to his head.

"What?" she whispered.

"Nod if you are thinking of leaving this room without going through that door." When she did, he said, "Then we will do it my way. Follow me."

He stepped outside on the ledge and then helped her do the same. Just beyond her reach, the flying device bobbed in the light winter breeze.

"Where do you want to go?" he asked when he had closed the window behind her.

"I think the best plan is to somehow reach my bedchamber. If I can crawl into bed, perhaps Father will believe I have been there all evening."

"That is probably best. Which room is yours?"

"It's in the front. The eastern corner room with the balconies. The windows face the street, and that might be a problem."

His grin was immediate. "Not for us. Come on. Let's get you tucked in." At her sideways look, he amended, "I will get you to your window, and then you can take it from there. How is that?"

"We should hurry," she said as she allowed him to once again buckle her in to the device and set off into flight.

This time the ride was brief, just enough time to circle the back and go around the side of the Cope home. "I will anchor the craft just over there," Kyle said as he indicated the decorative rail on the balcony just beyond her windows. "Once I do that, you should have no trouble climbing out and getting inside."

"Thank you, Kyle."

Slowly the device descended until Millie felt the wooden bar beneath her feet scrape the iron rail. The sound of whistling drew her attention just as he was uncoiling the rope.

"It's the night patrol! We need to get out of here before he sees us."

"He?"

"The police officer who walks this beat at night. If he sees us here, we are doomed!" She glanced around and saw the man in question apparently occupied with something that had caught his attention several houses away.

"All right," Kyle said as he handed her the rope. "Hold this while I divert our landing for a while."

The device rose and moved back to the back of the house. And though Father was on the warpath inside, all looked quiet and well from Millie's vantage point. Perhaps the valet had convinced her father there was nothing to see behind the locked door. Or perhaps by now her sanctuary was in shambles.

Either option was possible, given the volatile nature of her father. However, Millie knew with absolute certainty if anything ever happened to the precious possessions inside that room, she would have no incentive to protect Father or to live any life other than one where she was free to sketch and invent and explore her scientific curiosities.

"I'm glad we didn't spend all the fuel in our travels tonight," Kyle said, interrupting her thoughts. "And I do have to praise my partner for thinking of using black silk. It makes the device hard to spot in the dark."

"You have not said much about your partner. What is he like?" She paused. "I assume you speak of a he. Am I correct?"

"You are correct in saying I have not yet said much about my partner. As to whether he is a he, well, his wife thinks so."

"I see."

"Now hush. If I have to leave this in your back garden for lack of fuel to take me back to the Peabody, both of us will have some explaining to do in the morning, and not just to your father."

Millie leaned against Kyle's shoulder, suddenly far too aware of the fact that she wanted to know more about him. And perhaps she wanted to tell him more about her. He already knew her name and address and that she had an extensive library and . . . enough. What harm could come from asking?

"So, you are an inventor who works with a partner who is male and married. Your workshop is not in Memphis, and you carry with you some sort of identification that, when offered to a policeman, convinced him you could not possibly have stolen anything from a hotel room. Who are you, Kyle?"

She felt the rumble in his chest before she heard his chuckle. "Quiet, Millie, or you will bring the policeman back here."

"Oh, my. Have I struck a nerve?"

"You have struck at the truth. And here is a little more truth for you. You have a fiancé and are to be married and shipped off along with all your worldly goods to England on Thursday. The last thing you need to know right now is more about me."

"Unless my hypothesis proves untrue due to new information."

When Kyle did not immediately respond, Millie reached to jab him with her elbow. "What? No witty comment on my little joke?"

"I have plenty to say on the matter, but in the interest of good sense, I am going to keep my mouth shut."

The whistling started up again, causing Millie

to fall silent. As the sound of the officer trailed off, so did her ability to keep from speaking.

"All right," she whispered. "What say you tell me something more about you? Anything. After all, you have bound us together several times, and my guess is I am the only girl you've taken to the moon and back."

Again he chuckled. "Millie, you are truly one of a kind. Now be still so I don't run this thing into the trees trying to land on the balcony."

"Are you saying you cannot manage this thing except under ideal conditions?" She shook her head as if she were attempting to absorb the information. "And I was under the assumption that a test flight was meant to test under multiple conditions." She lifted her free hand to cover his. "Here, let me console you. You poor, poor man. Your attention diverted by an ordinary female."

"Believe me," he said as he attempted not to laugh. "I am being tested right now."

"Well, excellent. Do not let me interrupt you."

"What is testing me is my inability to do justice to a response about your comment on being an ordinary female."

He paused to nimbly guide the flying machine around Mama's climbing roses and up to a gentle stop against the house. "Which, I will say, is absolutely untrue. There is nothing ordinary about you, Millie. I hope you understand that."

"Believe me," she said as she handed him the

rope, "I cannot recall a time when I did not feel out of the ordinary. But that's what having older sisters who are Father's idea of the perfect example of proper femininity will do to someone like me."

That was too close to the truth and an admission Millie instantly regretted. "Thank you very much for tonight's adventure," she said hurriedly as she tried to escape by releasing herself from the strap.

Unfortunately, instead of a graceful exit, she tumbled down from the flying machine to land in an awkward puddle of petticoats and dented pride. Before she could right herself, Kyle was at her side.

"What were you thinking?" he demanded as gentle hands helped her sit up. "Are you hurt? I did not realize you were about to step off the platform or I would never have allowed it until the device was securely tied up."

Parts of her smarted from the collision, but she would never tell him which ones.

"Millie, look at me. Are you all right? Did you hit your head?"

She looked up and met his gaze. And then she looked beyond him to something moving just beyond his left shoulder.

The rope that should have tethered the flying machine to the balcony floated past.

Had she been able to speak his name, she might have called it right then. Instead, Millie pointed as shock and surprise refused to allow the words to come forth. Finally she gasped, "There. Behind you. Flying away."

"Behind me?" Kyle turned and then tried to grab the cable, missing it by inches as it drifted out of reach. Muttering a few choice words that she was glad she couldn't quite make out, he let out a long breath.

And then he just stood there, watching the balloon as it made a slow arc upward.

"I have made you lose your flying machine," she said, ducking her head.

Her companion stood very quiet and still, not at all the reaction she expected from an inventor who was watching his prized gadget float away. When she looked up, she saw he had pulled some sort of metal half sphere from his pocket and was doing something with it.

"What is that?" she asked as she rose. "And why are you playing with one of your toys while the balloon is flying away?"

Kyle slanted her a quick glance. "It is not a balloon, and this is most decidedly not a toy. Now stand back."

The balcony was small, but not so small that she could not give him the space he requested. He moved slowly, deliberately. Meanwhile, the balloon was getting away.

Just before the black silk of the runaway machine disappeared beyond the trees, Millie decided if he would not take swift action, she must. Reaching into her pocket, she removed the Remington from her pocket and fired one shot.

It was a direct hit.

The balloon sagged and swayed, ceasing its upward motion in an instant. At the same time, Kyle threw the metal device toward the balloon. Because it was sinking fast, the metal object sailed past to lodge in the neighbor's rose arbor. A second later, the balloon snagged on the topmost branch of a poplar tree on the corner of the neighbor's property.

For a moment, it felt as if time stood still. And then he turned around to face her.

Unlike Father, whose face contorted in anger, this man merely wore his handsome features with only a bit less good humor. The real indication of his feelings, however, was his seeming inability to speak.

And then, "You. Shot. It."

Each word was spoken softly, his tone something between incredulous and deadly. And yet she felt no fear, only surprise.

"It was getting away," she said in her defense. "I knew the machine was important to you, and there it went flying over the trees. If I hadn't shot it, who knows where it would have gone before someone found it, and then what would you have?"

Millie ran out of breath and words at the same

time. Someone down the street called out, "Who is out there? Did someone shoot a gun?"

"Go inside," he said through his clenched jaw.

Her heart sank. How could he not see she was merely trying to help? "But I was only trying to . . . oh, I have really done it, have I not?"

"Did you hear it, Officer?" a neighbor called, presumably to the policeman who had only just disappeared down the street.

"Go," he said, this time in a slightly gentler manner. "You have enough trouble with your father, Millie. Best not add to it with this. At least there was no explosion."

"But I . . ." Tears threatened, and she blinked them back. "I am sorry, Kyle. Truly. I thought I was helping."

He let out a long breath and rested his palms on her shoulders, holding her at arm's length. "Thank you for helping. Now help me some more by going inside."

"I caused this problem, so I should help repair the damage—"

"Inside. Now."

She did as he asked and then watched as he put some sort of device on his shoes before disappearing over the rail of the balcony. By craning her neck, Millie could just barely make out what had to be his form crossing the lawn to disappear into the dark shadows of the shrubbery on the edge of the property just as the police officer appeared on the sidewalk.

Noticing her at the window, the man lifted his lantern in her direction and waved. Millie returned the wave in the hopes of giving Kyle more time to escape.

"Everything all right here, Miss Cope?" he called.

"Everything's fine. Thank you, Officer Wells."

"You didn't hear a gunshot, did you?"

"A gunshot?" she said in a bid to stall him. "On Adams Street? Oh, my."

"Now, don't get yourself all upset, ma'am. I'm sure it was nothing."

"Do you think so?" she said as she spied Kyle now halfway up the neighbor's tree. "I truly would not like to think that someone was causing a ruckus in our quiet little neighborhood. That is most distressing."

From behind her, she heard a knock on her bedroom door. "Mildred," Father said. "Is that you talking to someone in there?"

"Yes, Father," she called over her shoulder. "I was just speaking to the nice police officer down on the sidewalk. Apparently, someone has fired a gun and he was just asking me about it."

"A gun? Tell Wells to stay there. I will be right down."

Millie repeated the words to the officer, who nodded. And then Father knocked again.

"Before I go down there, I demand you open this door and show yourself."

She straightened the wrinkles the tumble onto the balcony had put in her dress and then smoothed her hair as she walked to the door. Breathing a prayer, Millie pasted on what she hoped would be an innocent look and then opened the door. "Yes, Father?"

"Step out here."

When she complied, he took two paces into her bedchamber and glanced around before returning his attention to her. His gaze swept the length of her and then stalled on her eyes.

"You have been in your room? What were you doing up here?"

She let out a nervous laugh, which she tried to cover by shaking her head. "What does a woman do in her bedchamber? Just now I was on the balcony speaking to the police officer about the shooting incident."

"You know I frown on your habit of climbing out the window to access that infernal balcony. I should never have allowed my mother to put those up. 'Looks like home,' she used to say. Well, I say it is not seemly to stand out in the open air when one has a perfectly good bedchamber in which to . . ."

He went on and on, but Millie's attention had already wandered. Somewhere outside her flying companion was attempting to retrieve the invention she had broken. What seemed like a grand idea to catch the flying device before it flew out of reach now made Millie feel awful. She should be helping him. Perhaps offer to replace the silk she had shot through. And there would likely be damages to the system he used to guide the machine.

At the words "attic room" her attention reverted back to her father. "What was that?"

"The room in the attic." He gestured toward the ceiling. "Third floor, Mildred. There is a room. Storage, the valet called it, but I must ask you what you know of this."

"What I know of this?" she echoed. What could she say? "Well, I do know of the attic. It is for storage, is it not?"

"Yes, yes. But the room behind the locked door—"

"Say, Miss Cope," Officer Wells called. "Is your father coming out or what? I cannot wait for him much longer."

Millie tried not to allow her expression to show her relief. "What should I tell him, Father?"

He gave her a long look. He sighed and shook his head. "I'm going down now, but should I get any idea that something funny is going on up on the third floor, I will not let you get by with it. Do you understand? If you and Sir William are meeting up in some sort of rendezvous, you will not be doing it under my roof."

Sir William? "Yes, Father."

"And here I thought Trueck was away securing some sort of business deal that was going to allow me to purchase a lovely piece of property next to your castle in Cornwall. If he is back here and sneaking up my stairs to play fast and loose with my daughter . . . well, he will not get another penny out of me until he marries you right and proper. I have certainly spent plenty on him."

Thankfully, Father did not wait around for any sort of response. Instead, he went down the hall toward the stairs and left her to walk back into her room.

"Miss Cope?" the officer called.

Millie made her way to the window. "He is on his way, sir," she called as she used the opportunity to see if Kyle had retrieved his craft yet.

Though the area where it had gone down was mostly hidden in shadow, Millie thought she saw movement near the tree's top branches. When her father emerged onto the front walk, she stepped back with the intention of going for help once the coast was clear.

In the meantime, she closed her curtains and sat down to wait. To busy herself, Millie took out paper and pencil and made a list of things she planned to do tomorrow. A new sketchbook was in order as the last one she purchased was almost full. And as long as she was purchasing a sketchbook, she would buy new pencils.

And, of course, she would check on the repairs to her necklace and engagement ring.

Shifting positions, she felt the cypher and heart locket clang against the metal of her pistol. Millie took out the small revolver, set it on the bedside table, and then returned to her list. At the top, she wrote *Parker's Jewelry*.

A peek out the window showed her that Father and Officer Wells were still engaged in conversation. Millie let the curtains fall back into place and set the paper and pencil aside.

Then a thought occurred. Sir William was away on business. Why had he not let her know? He also hadn't mentioned that Father would be their new neighbor in Cornwall. Although for the life of her, Millie could have sworn Sir William told her his ancestral home was in Somerset.

A trip to her desk and the collection of letters tied by a ribbon confirmed her thought. Trueck Abbey was in Somerset. And then she read a sentence that stopped her cold.

Mother will be most pleased to meet you and sends her regrets she cannot travel to attend our wedding.

So she had not imagined he had claimed his mother to be alive. Setting that letter aside, she thumbed through the remainder of the thick stack. Several months ago, he had written this:

I regret there will be no matronly figure to greet you when you come to live at Trueck Abbey, for my mother's passing in August has distressed us all and delayed my arrival in Memphis.

A check of the dates confirmed the mother who could not wait to meet her in December had apparently died in August. Interesting.

And then finally, on one of his earliest letters, this stood out:

Owing to my position as head of the family, I cannot abide in any way a weakness of character, though your father has assured me you are of the finest moral fiber. Untruths in any form would be considered a grievous trespass of our agreement to marry, so I rejoice that you are a woman of good Christian values.

She stacked the letters once more and retied the ribbon. If he was willing to lie, what else was he hiding?

"A grievous trespass indeed, Sir William."

And why had she been so blind that she could not see any of this? Of course, she knew the answer.

She had seen what she wanted to see. And what she wanted to see was a way out of Memphis and the stifling atmosphere of the house on Adams Street.

In that moment, her path became clear. Someday she would walk out the door and leave this place and its awful memories behind. But when she went, she would go with all the things she loved, and if that meant packing up the entire attic room and carrying it out under dead of night, then so be it.

All she needed to do was to figure out how. That puzzle could be left for another day, however, because right now she was more concerned about a certain dark-haired aviator and his ailing flying machine.

Surely the door would slam downstairs soon when Father came back inside. When it finally did, Millie opened the window and stepped out onto the balcony, but she couldn't see anything of Kyle or his balloon.

Going back inside, she shrugged into her coat, slipped down the stairs, and went out into the night determined to offer help or, failing that, at least a proper apology.

But there was no sign of the dark-haired aviator. Millie retraced her steps to look for clues as to something he might have left behind but found nothing. She knew he was likely still staying at the Peabody, but how could she find him if she did not know his last name?

Returning to her room, Millie spied the Remington sitting on the bedside table.

If she would shoot a flying machine for what

she thought in the moment was a good reason, what damage could she do to that lying, no-good Sir William Trueck the next time she saw him?

"You're nothing but trouble," she said as she picked up the gun and removed the remaining bullets before putting it away.

By the time she climbed beneath her blankets, the clock in the hall was chiming half past two. When it chimed three, she was lying on her side with her eyes focused on the roses climbing the wallpaper. At a quarter after three, she rose to move to the window.

If only she could reach Kyle and set things right.

Of course. Millie got out of bed, hurried to her handbag, and retrieved the playing card he had given her. Slipping into her dressing gown and slippers, she went downstairs to Father's library.

Even with the door closed, Millie worried the entire house would awaken at the sound of her talking to the operator, and yet they did not. When the call was finally put through, she relaxed, albeit only slightly.

"Yes?" was the simple answer when the ringing stopped. The voice was bland, neither deep nor high, and held no indication of any sort of accent. The only two things she could discern was that the person on the other end of the line was male and not Kyle.

"Hello?"

"Oh, yes! I . . . that is . . ." Millie paused to take

a deep breath. She had only used the telephone a few times and never had quite got used to the gadget. "I am terribly sorry to telephone at such an hour, but I was given this number and told I could reach a certain person should I have need to contact him. And I wish to let him know that . . ."

That what? That she was sorry she shot his balloon? That she wished she hadn't tried to help? That she wanted to make things right between them?

"That you have need to contact him?" the person supplied.

"Indeed," Millie said. "That is exactly it. To apologize. He will know how to contact me."

"And your name?"

"Millie." She debated whether to add her last name and then decided not to. Telling him that much did not appeal unless she could do so in person.

Silence fell between them, and she wondered if perhaps the contrary device had disconnected itself. "Are you there?" she finally asked.

"Yes, one moment."

Millie leaned against the wall and forced herself to breathe. If she got caught using Father's phone, he would absolutely—

"Your message has been delivered."

"It has?" Millie shook her head. "But you did not ask the name of the person I am trying to reach."

"There was no need, miss."

And then the line went dead.

Thirteen

January 17, 1889
Memphis

The call from Millie had come in after three a.m. Because the system of messages was arranged so that he had immediate information on any calls that came through, Kyle ended up spending the remainder of the wee hours of the morning trying to decide whether to respond or let the woman stew a while.

He was mad at her. Furious. Her reckless irresponsibility had nearly cost him an invaluable piece of scientific gadgetry, and along with that, the possibility of reaching the patent office before anyone else.

Almost, but not quite. For somehow the only damage was to the silk fabric. A lone bullet hole had downed the craft, and another strip of silk had been lost during the process of untangling it from the tree, but other than that, his invention was still in working order.

If he had any questions about whether God still performed miracles, they were answered when he returned to his room with the pieces of his machine and found them all still in working order.

Silk was easily replaceable. The gears and levers of his steering mechanism were not.

Leaning back in his chair, Kyle studied the note as he'd received it. Coded to carefully prevent detection, the message was brief.

Caller No. 7343. Female. Name given: Millie. Message: Has need to contact you to apologize.

He smiled at that last part. Likely those were the exact words Millie had told the call taker. "Nothing like a man who can follow instructions exactly and to the letter."

Unlike this woman he knew only as Millie. Discovering her last name would be tempting, and yet he would rather hear it from her if he saw her again. Which he knew he would.

He couldn't help but find her again. It was as if he had to. Which was ridiculous because she was an engaged woman with a wedding just days away.

"What is it about you, Millie?"

Even as he said the words, he already knew the answer. He'd even told her himself. Millie, his society scientist, was unlike any woman he had ever met. And the Lord had sealed any question with the admission from her about her name. But still the situation seemed impossible to resolve.

Sighing, Kyle picked up the letter from Henry following up on the telegram that brought him back to Memphis.

He decoded the message twice to be certain of its contents.

Confederate gold could be Lafitte treasure. Either way, we want it. Local involvement suspected. Await further instructions.

"It has been finished for quite some time, Miss Cope," the jeweler's assistant told her the next morning when she arrived at Parker's to inquire about her necklace and engagement ring. "We were beginning to wonder when someone was coming to fetch it."

"So my fiancé, Sir William Trueck, did not happen by? He mentioned he would be coming in."

The assistant shook his head. "I don't think so. If he had, then I would not still have the item."

"Well, that is true. But I actually have two items here: the gold chain and an emerald-and-diamond ring. Could you please check again?"

He returned with the news that there had been no such ring in their possession.

Of course not. That was just another lie told by the man she had very nearly married.

"How very odd," she said to cover her feelings as she pulled the reassembled cypher and the locket from her pocket. "Then might I trouble you to attach these?"

The assistant brought the pieces back to Mr. Parker, who came out with a smile. "Miss Cope, so good to see you," he said as he shook her hand with vigor. "You need these attached?"

"Yes, please. I will wait for them."

The old jeweler shook his head "I hate to keep you waiting. If you will allow me to deliver the necklace when I go home for lunch, I will give you my word I will not delay."

Her skepticism must have shown, for he grinned. "You young people. What if I have Hiram polish these before they are attached? You have not been diligent in keeping them up."

That was the truth, and she knew it. "All right, but I truly must have the necklace by this afternoon."

"I promise. And, child, I do not give my promise lightly."

"One more thing," she said, as she decided to make absolutely certain there was no misunderstanding regarding the claims Sir William had made. "Have you seen my fiancé here? Sir William mentioned he would be stopping by."

"A handsome couple you two are. I saw your picture in the paper. And that ring. Now, speaking professionally, that was certainly something of value. I do hope you will have it insured."

"As a matter of fact, it's supposed to be here getting sized, but your assistant says he hasn't seen it."

Mr. Parker frowned. "We definitely do not have that ring here for sizing, of that I am certain. Perhaps your fellow has forgotten. You might want to give his memory a little jab."

"More than just his memory that needs jabbing," she muttered as she left the necklace in Mr. Parker's capable hands and went on to complete her day's shopping.

Millie's next destination took her past the Peabody Hotel. Pausing across the street, she debated whether to go in and make an attempt to find the aviator. But what would she say? How would she, Silas Cope's daughter, explain that she was looking for a stranger named Kyle in one of the town's most prominent hotels?

Better to wait for him to respond to her telephone call than to take the risk. She walked on past the hotel to turn into her favorite bookstore. An hour later, she left with her purchases tucked in her handbag lest Father happen to see her on the street.

At the neighbor's tree, Millie paused. Looking closely, she spied a patch of black silk fabric dangling from a limb near the top of the stately poplar. Other than that small reminder of last night, it appeared Kyle had been able to retrieve his flying machine and, she hoped, could make the repairs it needed. If not, she would be responsible. Either way, she hoped he would contact her soon so she could make her apologies.

Oh, how she wished she could go back in time and redo the whole evening. But where would she start? Logic and prudence would say she should never have left to go moon watching. Her heart, however, told her she only wished she had allowed him to handle the problem of the fleeing balloon without her assistance.

"Hindsight," she muttered as she trudged home and headed upstairs to the safety of her bed-chamber, her brand-new copy of *The Black Arrow* by Robert Louis Stevenson securely hidden in her handbag along with several pencils and a lovely sketchbook.

To her surprise, the door to her room stood open and her bedcovers were a mess. The drapes had been drawn, and someone had moved her bedside table, knocking over a vase of fresh peonies from Father's greenhouse in the process.

Placing her handbag on the chair by the window, she threw open the drapes and then turned around. Brilliant rays of afternoon sunlight illuminated shards of what looked to be broken glass now glittering on the rug. A check of her hiding place told Millie the Remington was gone.

"She done it."

Her attention jerked to the doorway where Maeve, the younger of the Irish maids, stood with broom and dustpan in hand. Without invitation, the girl stepped inside and closed the door behind her.

"The new missus. She done all this."

Shaking her head, Millie asked, "Who?"

"That woman who is after your father. Mrs. Wilson or something."

"Mrs. Ward-Wiggins?" When Maeve nodded, Millie allowed her attention to sweep the room. "But why?"

"Cook says she was looking for something."

"My revolver?"

If the girl had any idea the gun was gone, she did not show it. "I don't think so."

Millie moved to the chair, picked up her hand-bag, and sat down. The weight of the novel and sketchbook shifted as she tucked the bag under her arm. "Then what does Cook think she was looking for?"

"She doesn't know, but she said the lady was as mad as a wet hen when she didn't find it." Maeve paused as she appeared to be studying the edge of the dustpan, and then she lifted her eyes. "Cook thinks maybe there was something she had took from her on New Year's Eve that she thinks you have. Me, I think she wanted that heart charm you used to wear before the necklace got broke."

"Oh, no!" Millie said. "The necklace. Mr. Parker was supposed to deliver it."

The maid reached into her pocket to pull out the item in question. True to his word, Mr. Parker had attached the charms and delivered the necklace during his lunch hour.

Millie accepted the chain and slipped it over her head. The cool metal chilled her skin, but she didn't care. "Thank you," she said as she met the girl's eyes.

"Cook instructed me to keep it safe until you came home because there was treasure inside it." She covered her hand with her mouth. "Oh, I was not supposed to tell that part."

Millie's handbag tumbled to the floor as she jumped to her feet. As the maid hurried to pick it up, Millie stopped her.

All her life she had heard Mama infer that treasure was to be had. Mama said Millie was the only one who could know. So how was it that there were others in the house who had also heard of it?

The chimneys have ears. Hadn't the valet said something of the sort? If the third-floor fireplace offered a listening post for the kitchen, why not other fireplaces in other locations in the house?

"Tell me what you know about the treasure," Millie demanded.

"Who, me?" Maeve shook her head. "I don't know anything, Miss Millie. Really, I don't. Cook, now she's the one who—"

"Tell me, please," Millie repeated.

The girl's shoulders sagged but she stubbornly kept her silence.

"All right, then. I will find that out for myself." Millie left the maid cleaning up the broken glass and headed downstairs.

The delicious smells of garlic and roasting meat swirled around Millie as she crossed the kitchen to the stool where Cook sat stirring a pot. As long as Millie could remember, Cook had been old, but only in the past year had she required a stool to complete her daily duties.

"I wondered when you would come see me. If you are curious as to how your bedchamber's got all which-way, you will have to look elsewhere for an answer. I will not be carrying tales."

"Not how," Millie corrected, "but why."

Cook swiveled to face her. "Well, that is a whole other question, is it not? And I believe you have an idea about that too."

"The necklace." Millie paused to pull it from her bodice. "Mama told me never to lose it. That might be what has Father's friend wanting it. Or was it something else?"

Cook went back to stirring the pot. Silence fell between them until Millie decided to press on. She touched the older woman's sleeve, causing her to look up from her work. "What did she tell you?"

Watery eyes the shade of a morning sky blinked twice as if calling Millie into focus. "By *she,* do you mean the missus your father took up with? Because *she* did not tell me nothing. Does not talk to the help, that one."

"I meant my mother," Millie said gently. "What did she tell you about my necklace?"

"What she told me is between me and her. She is gone, and I have said what I can. Looks like you have got all the answers you will get on the subject."

"The maids know."

"They know nothing but what they are told. They know they are to be careful that your father is not allowed near the charms your mama gave you. Even if that means they must be hidden from time to time when he is in one of those moods of his."

By moods, Cook meant those times when Father needed more funds than his business offered. Then he came raiding jewelry to pawn. That Cook knew this should not have surprised Millie.

Cook paused to reach for a tasting spoon. When she had seasoned the broth to her satisfaction, she set the spoon aside and returned her attention to Millie.

"Your mama made me promise I would train up anyone working in this house to keep your necklace with you." She shrugged. "I have kept that promise to her, and long as I can I will keep at it."

"Thank you, but I believe there is more to it than that. Tell me the rest. Please give me something of my mother back."

The elderly woman stepped away from the bubbling pot, her expression unreadable. "All right, child. Open that locket and show me what is inside."

Millie did as she asked and then offered it to the cook.

Wiping her hands on her apron, Cook cradled the open heart, gently touching the portrait it held.

"She did wear this proudly long as she could."

Memories of her young mother with the heart clasped around her neck on a dark velvet ribbon tumbled forth. Though as a child Millie never questioned why Mama stopped wearing the locket, as an adult she now understood why. What could not be found could not be lost. Or sold.

"When the cypher was opened, there was a key and a slip of paper inside."

Cook lifted one gray brow. "And what did that mean to you?"

She shook her head. "I don't know. It was just a torn scrap of paper, and if it had any writing on it, it was erased by time."

"That is too bad. I never heard anything about a key from your mama. That might not have anything to do with anything. The puzzle, it was a game to her. But the locket? That was special."

Fingers bent by age and yet still strong traced the miniature portrait. "Oh, yes. I remember you," Cook said to the dark-haired man in the portrait.

"Who is he?"

A wistful smile touched Cook's lips. She handed the locket back to Millie and resumed her stirring. "Maybe he was your grandmother's idea of treasure and that is how the stories were twisted up."

Millie snapped the locket shut and returned the chain to its place around her neck. "I don't understand."

Cook gave Millie a thoughtful look. "No, I do not suspect you would." She paused to swipe at her brow with the corner of her apron, and then her attention returned to the stove. Just when Millie thought the woman might be finished talking, she slid her a sideways glance. "A woman, if she lives right, has only two great loves in her life."

"Two?"

"Yes, indeed. Her first love, that will always be our Lord Jesus Christ. If He is not first, then a woman, she is sunk. You believe that, don't you, child?"

In theory, she did. In practice, she was still working on it.

"And then there is the other one. That one man the Lord made for her. Some say there is more than one, and I suppose there could be situations where that is the truth. Me? I do not know." She smiled. "But that one man, if we wait, he finds us."

"How do you know?"

Cook stood very still, her eyes looking past Millie. "Oh, sweet girl, if you have to ask, the fellow is not the one. Because when he comes along, you will know."

Millie smiled at the idea of the elderly woman as a girl young enough to have suitors. She watched as Cook stepped away from the stove to disappear into the larder. "Did you know?"

The old cook's giggle made her sound more like a young girl than a woman of many years. "Of course I did. Now get along with yourself."

Millie offered a quick embrace before hurrying away. Would she ever have faith like that? She couldn't imagine it. And yet, that sort of faith was what she wanted desperately. What she craved.

Back in the privacy of her bedchamber, she pulled the necklace from her bodice and held the charms up to the light from her bedside lamp. Again she opened the locket. "Who are you?" she asked the tiny painting of the handsome dark-haired man. "And what do you know about the treasure?"

For there *was* a treasure. Mama told her there was, Cook believed it, and Millie had staked her whole life's plans on seeking that treasure and finding her freedom. Until Kyle managed to open the cypher, she thought the solution to finding the treasure rested in whatever was inside that. To see it was a simple key and a torn and faded piece of blank foolscap had been a disappointment, but she had not discounted the fact the key might have some significance. What did a tiny key and a miniature oil painting of a stranger have to do with a treasure that Mama insisted would secure her future?

She sighed. For all that she did not know, there was one thing she did know for certain. Her future did not include Sir William Trueck.

Fourteen

While she decided the best way to end her ruse of an engagement, Millie slipped up the back stairs to the attic room to fetch the sharpener for her pencils. To her surprise, she found the door unlocked. A look around proved the room was unoccupied and presumably had been, leaving her to assume things had not been disturbed. She would have to remember to ask the maids to be more careful when they were in there.

Millie went directly to the worktable to find her sharpener. As she reached for it, her sleeve caught on a jar of linseed oil and sent it tumbling. With nothing within reach to stop the liquid as it poured across the table, Millie swept away the sketchbooks and Mama's Bible off of the table with her free hand just before the oil ruined them.

"Now I've made a mess," she said under her breath as she hurried to find the cheesecloth she kept for such instances. The spill was soon soaked up and the rags piled safely away from the books she now reached for.

The room was so cold she could see her breath, and her toes were beginning to feel numb, so returning the sketchbooks to their neat and orderly state would have to wait for another day. Millie retrieved the Bible, though, hoping she had done no permanent damage to the precious book by tossing it onto the floor.

The leather was old and cracked in some places, well worn in others. Millie lifted the cover and the book fell open to Mama's favorite verses in the second chapter of Proverbs.

My son, if though wilt receive my words, and hide my commandments with thee; so that thou incline thine ear unto wisdom and apply thine heart to understanding; yea, if thou criest after knowledge, and liftest up thy voice for understanding; if thou seekest her as silver, and searchest for her as hid treasures; then shalt thou understand the fear of the Lord, and find the knowledge of God.

"Searchest for her as hid treasures," Millie whispered.

Flipping back to the front of the book, she found the page where family history had been written in line after line of almost indecipherable script. There was Father's name and birthdate and then his marriage to Mama with the date, May 8, 1862. Below had been recorded the births of the Cope daughters along with the dates of their deaths—except for Millie's, of course.

Older entries had been faded by time, blurred to something akin to unreadable. Here and there she could make out a date—1837 for a marriage;

1812, 1815, and 1820 for births. Nothing that she could really read or understand, however, and nowhere did she find anything that might indicate the association to the pirate Lafitte.

She closed the Bible and returned it to the worktable, being careful to avoid the wood still glistening with the remains of the oil spill. Still, she could not yet let go of the one solid link that tied her to her mother.

Her eyes glistened with tears. *I need your wisdom, Mama. I miss you.*

"Miss Millie."

Millie nearly jumped out of her skin as once again the Bible tumbled. Lunging forward to try and catch the precious book before it landed on the floor, Millie's foot got caught in her petticoats and she fell.

The maid hurried to assist her and then snatched up the Bible. "I am fearful sorry, ma'am, but your father is home unexpected, and he is asking for your presence in the dining room. He wishes you to join him and Mrs. Ward-Wiggins for the evening meal." She paused. "Are you hurt?"

"No, I'm fine, Bridget." Her heart still racing, Millie leaned against the worktable to steady herself. "Please tell my father I will be down as soon as I have dressed properly."

"Yes'm." She held out the Bible toward Millie. "Here you are, Miss Millie. It's torn, though."

True enough, several pages were now sticking

out in a ragged manner where once the gold-tipped edges had all been orderly and straight. She accepted the Bible and then cradled it to her chest.

"Just go tell Father, please. We don't want him coming up here to see what the delay is."

"No, ma'am," the maid replied as she scurried off.

This time Millie carefully placed the Bible on the table and then opened it to repair the damage as best she could. When the pages were straight again, she closed the cover. The crack on the spine was larger now, revealing far too much of the book beneath. Millie sighed as she pressed ancient leather back into place.

And then she spied an odd sheet of paper wedged beneath the cracked spine. Pulling carefully, she saw that the page had something written on it, though the yellowing that came with extreme age had taken hold.

She pulled again, and this time the page gave way and tore, releasing all but a corner of the paper to fall into her hand. A quick glance revealed a letter written in French, apparently a missive from a father to a daughter named Sophie, lamenting their loss of relationship and requesting permission to visit.

The date was simply recorded as 1838. No other information was given, and the signature was smudged. An elaborate letter *J* and what might be the letter *L* or perhaps an *H* was followed by a name that only revealed three letters to be readable.

Arn.

Millie ran her fingers over the letter and found nothing untoward, nor did there appear to be any sort of tampering or coding in the text of the document. Instead, it appeared someone's father wished to have a reunion. Whether this Sophie agreed was a matter left to history, her answer lost.

"Where is my daughter?" came drifting up the stairs toward her.

Father. Millie hid the remains of the page back in the spine and then snatched up the pencil sharpener. She hurried to tuck the sharpener into her pocket and then set herself to rights. By the time she closed the door, she could hear his footsteps on the attic stairs.

Quickly she yanked at the first thing she found, a voluminous sack that covered her mother's wedding gown. Cradling the garment as if that was exactly what she had come to the attic to attend to, Millie walked briskly toward the staircase.

"There you are, girl." His grumbling sputtered to a halt when he saw the bundle she carried. "What's this? What have you got there?"

She pasted on a smile. "Father, I sent Bridget to tell you I was just putting away Mama's wedding gown and then I would be down to dress for dinner. Did she not tell you?"

"She mentioned something about a . . ." He paused. "No, no she did not tell me you were messing about with your mother's dress. Put that away this instant and come down to dinner." He glanced at her attire. "And what you are wearing will do. I would rather look at a spinster's clothing than have my meal delayed any further. Cook is already complaining that I have come home unannounced and too early. I wonder if she realizes just who works for whom around here."

"Yes, Father." Millie moved away from the stairs, resisting the urge to say anything further. As she returned Mama's dress to its resting spot, she smiled. Someday maybe she would wear this dress for her own wedding. And Kyle was right. No woman should marry for any reason other than love.

She arrived moments later at the dining room to find the seat beside her occupied by Sir William. "I had no idea you would be here," she said.

And then to Mrs. Ward-Wiggins, she said, "Did you find what you were looking for?"

If the direct question took the older woman by surprise, her expression did not show it. "Good evening, Mildred."

"What is she talking about?" Father asked her.

Mrs. Ward-Wiggins allowed her smile to slip only for a moment. "I am sure these gentlemen do not care to hear about such things."

"After our meal, then," Millie said firmly.

"While you are at it, might you give our Mildred some fashion advice? Apparently she is of a mind to wear her mother's dress for the wedding, and I do not think it appropriate in the least."

A covert glance at Sir William revealed he was much more interested in the food on his plate than the conversation taking place around him. At least until Father steered the talk in his direction with a brusque, "What say you, Trueck?"

"I beg your pardon?" he responded as he set aside his soupspoon. He looked to Millie for assistance.

"My father was asking your opinion on my wearing my mother's wedding dress when I am to be married."

"You are lovely no matter the garment you choose," he said as he reached to pat her hand.

She slid him a sideways smile and marveled that he did indeed appear to be genuine. Nothing about his expression, however, gave her reason to believe she had made the wrong decision regarding ending their engagement. Nor would she fool herself into believing anything he said, however sincere he might look.

"She is not paying the least bit of attention, Freda. You had best say it again."

Millie glanced across the table at the woman who had torn through her bedchamber while she was out. "I said that I would be happy to assist with your wedding plans, Mildred. You have only to ask."

"Thank you," Millie murmured as the servants came in to bring in the next course.

"Well, that has been decided." Father looked to Sir William. "Tell me, young man. When do you leave?"

"You're leaving?" Millie asked her soon-to-be former fiancé. "Again?"

He smiled in her direction. "Just a quick trip up to St. Louis. I expect to return on Monday."

"I see." Disappointment colored her tone, but she didn't care. The need to break off their engagement pressed her forward. "Is there perhaps some time you and I could have a private conversation before you leave?"

"Private conversation?" Father echoed. "Goodness, girl. Sir William and I have much to discuss this evening. Surely your frippery can wait."

"Yes, Father. I suppose it can."

"Until Monday, then," Sir William said as he reached beneath the table to squeeze her hand.

"Until Monday."

After an interminable period of business talk, the men finally rose to adjourn to Father's library, leaving Millie and Mrs. Ward-Wiggins alone in the dining room.

"I suppose you have questions," the widow said when the door closed behind Father. "And I do regret the broken vase. I will be happy to replace it."

Millie gave her a look that told her she would no longer suffer through friendly talk. "Thank you, but that will not be necessary. I would rather have an explanation instead."

"Yes, I am sure you would. However, the best I can offer is that there was something of mine purported to be in your possession. I merely went to find it."

"I see. And what was that?"

She looked away. "Silas will not be pleased that I have told you."

"Mrs. Ward-Wiggins," Millie said evenly, "I have long ago ceased succeeding in pleasing my father. I suggest if you wish to get along in this house, you will do the same."

"All right. A theft occurred in my hotel room on New Year's Eve. I suspected that your father took my gems and gifted them to you."

Millie erupted in laughter at the absurdity of the statement. Only when she took note of the woman's expression did she allow her laughter to fade to silence.

"You're serious," she finally said.

"I am." She paused. "I loaned him another piece with the understanding it was for you. Thus, when that one went missing and no one had been in my room except him, well, naturally I thought that perhaps . . ."

"Perhaps my father had stolen your jewelry and given it to me?" She shook her head. "If Father took them, you will find them at his favorite pawn shop. I can give you the address if you like."

Apparently the news that Silas Cope was capable of such behavior was not a complete surprise to Freda Ward-Wiggins. "And the emerald ring?"

"The one from Sir William? I have no idea where it is. He left with it after our photograph was taken for the newspaper, and I have not seen it since. Nor has the jeweler who was supposed to have it."

"I see."

Millie rose and pushed away from the table. "I'm sorry," she said, and she meant it. "I wish I could give you better advice on your missing jewelry. What I can tell you is if you wish to keep whatever else you might own, then do not spend any more time with my father. Things of value tend to go missing in his presence. Now if you will excuse me, it has been a long day."

Silence trailed Millie to the door and then the widow called her name. When she glanced back over her shoulder, she found Mrs. Ward-Wiggins sitting unmoved in her chair.

"Your father loves you, Mildred."

"I am sure he would like you to think so."

"No." Mrs. Ward-Wiggins rose to grip the back of the chair with bejeweled fingers. "He is hard on you, I know. And he uses your jewels for collateral when his business deals do not bring him the funds he needs. I know this too." She was silent for a moment. "He still holds himself responsible for losing your mother and sisters."

"That is because he *is* responsible." At her pained expression, Millie bit back on any further response.

"Don't you see?" she said softly. "You are a reminder of what he has lost. Of how he lost them. Looking at you?" She shook her head. "I have been told you are the very image of your mother. I cannot imagine what it must be like for him to see you and think of them every single day."

The words bore a hole into the hardened place in her heart. Still, Millie was not yet ready to let it crumble completely. "Then he shall be much relieved when I am married and away."

"Perhaps. However, if that were the case, then tell me why he is so keen on seeing that your fiancé provides him with a home adjacent to your own. Could it be that he does not yet want to release you completely?"

Millie had not thought of that. Still, any gesture of love or attention seemed impossible to explain. She waved away the question.

"I will bid you a good night. And in the future,

should you wish access to my bedchamber, I would request you ask me first."

She left quickly before any response could be given. Not that she needed one.

Bypassing the stairs, Millie's ire had her walking directly toward the library. Her father would be angry, of course, but at this moment she was willing to risk anything to keep from waiting until Monday to rid herself of an engagement that should never have happened. To rid herself of a man who had lied to her.

Hesitating only for a second, she lifted her hand to knock. Twice. Still the men continued to talk. She heard something about New Orleans and ships. Something else about promises. She caught only snatches, and yet they were spoken in a harsh tone that told Millie the men were no longer engaged in friendly conversation.

How much more would a disturbance irritate them? Probably not much.

"Please excuse the interruption," she said as she threw open the door, "but I need to speak to . . ."

Her voice fell silent as she caught a glimpse of the two men leaning over Father's desk with a set of blueprints laid out before them. Father quickly moved to block her view.

"You were not welcomed in here, Mildred. Leave at once."

As he spoke, Sir William cleared the desk of the suspicious paper.

"Again, I apologize for intruding, but I need to speak to you," she said to her fiancé. "Please."

The Englishman held back Father's bluster with a wave of his hand. "We will just be a minute," he said as he led Millie from the room.

They stopped in the foyer, and she shook her head. "In there." She nodded toward the parlor. "Where it is more private."

He smiled, moved into the room, and then waited until she closed the door behind her. "All right, Mildred. What is it?"

"I will come directly to the point." She drew in a deep breath and leveled at him a calm but determined look. "I wish to end things between us, Sir William."

"End? I'm afraid I do not follow."

"Our engagement. Had I a ring to remove and return to you, I would do that now. However, I shall settle for merely saying I no longer wish to marry you and leave it at that."

As her news sunk in, his expression changed. "But you cannot—"

"I am terribly sorry, but I already have." She turned and opened the door. As far as she was concerned, the conversation, as well as their relationship, was over.

"You will change your mind."

She turned back to see the Englishman looking less than confident in his statement. "I won't."

"And you will leave me without an explanation?"

"I simply cannot marry you." She paused to consider whether continuing the discussion was worth the effort and decided it was not. A liar rarely accepted being branded as such, so there was no need to press her case. "Please just accept that."

"Cannot or will not?" His question followed her as she walked through the door.

Millie paused, her courage bolstered by the fact that she had accomplished what she intended and had no further need of conversing with the man. Though she half expected her suitor to be at least a little disappointed, he did not appear so at all. Rather, he stood as a man scorned and appeared ready to remedy the situation.

"Will not." And then, before she could be made to change her mind, she left Sir William standing in Mama's parlor.

Whether he followed or went to Father to complain, she neither knew nor cared as she fled to her bedchamber, where moonlight filtered through her windows and teased silver stripes across the bedcoverings. Though she could not see the moon from where she stood, she smiled as she thought of the last time she had flown beneath it.

That memory would be a treasure to her. One that Father could not take away to pawn.

She traced the edges of the windowpane with her finger, recalling as much as she could of that night.

And though Father soon pounded at her door, she ignored him. Eventually he left her alone, though grumbles of threats he would never carry out trailed in his wake.

Then, finally, came relief. Relief that she had outlasted her father's bluster, and relief that the engagement that never should have happened was now at an end.

Millie let out a long breath and glanced around the room. *The Black Arrow* still lay hidden in her purse, and reading it tempted her. But what tempted her more was the new sketchbook and pencils. A glance around her room offered nothing of interest for her to draw. Then she thought of her necklace. She took the chain from around her neck and set it on the bed beside her.

Looking at the charms, she chose the cypher first, making sure each concentric circle captured the image of the Spanish coin it represented. She continued her work until the wheel cypher was completely depicted.

"Decently done," she said as she moved her attention to the locket.

But the simple heart shape offered no challenge to her artistic skills. She set it aside and closed her eyes to consider what she might capture next.

Kyle.

Yes, she should draw him before she forgot him. And so she did, pausing occasionally to close her eyes and recall a certain feature. The cleft in his chin. The thick sweep of lashes that outlined dark eyes. The way his lips turned up in the suggestion of a smile long before he actually allowed an expression of humor. The way those lips felt against hers as they celebrated the new year.

Drawing quickly now, she shaded in his hair, his dark brows, and the smile that touched not only his mouth but also his eyes when he offered it.

When she was finished, her fingers ached and her wrist felt almost numb from the constant motion of pencil against paper, but the likeness was unmistakable.

The aviator grinned back at her from the page. Memories threatened.

"Stop that," she said again as she took one more look and turned the page. "Draw something else."

Again she looked around. Again, she lifted the heart locket off the bedside table.

"I think I will draw you now," she said as she opened the locket to reveal the miniature portrait inside.

Only then did she see the resemblance. Were he twenty years younger, Father could have posed for this painting. They could have been brothers drawn at different ages and in different decades. The features that shaped them were similar and yet not exactly the same.

The locket tumbled from her fingers and landed

on the floor. Setting her drawing materials aside, Millie reached to pick it up and accidentally snagged an edge of the tiny portrait with her fingernail as she lifted it.

"Oh, no," she said as she attempted to press the portrait back into its frame. It would not stay in place, nor would the locket close with the frame now bent.

Finally giving up, she set the piece aside with the plan of returning it to Mr. Parker in the morning for a repair. "And this time I will wait while he works."

Fifteen

January 18, 1889
Memphis

The next morning Millie escaped down the back stairs to walk to Parker's Jewelry. Only when she turned the corner onto Second Street did she realize how early it was. Thankfully, Mr. Parker was unlocking his store when the building came into view.

"Has my repair not held?" the elderly jeweler said when she arrived at the door.

"Yes, it's fine, but I am afraid I have another repair for you."

Millie followed him inside and showed him the

locket. "Hmm, you do have a problem. Who is this lucky gentleman whose face you carry with you?" He gave the piece another look. "The portrait is old, is it not? So my guess is your grandfather? Perhaps great-grandfather?"

"I don't know. Mama said she was never told."

"I see." He shrugged. "May I?" he asked as he gestured to the back of the store.

"Yes, please."

"As my assistant is not yet here, I fear you will have to entertain yourself while I work." He paused. "Unless you would like me to deliver this later today?"

"No," she hurried to say. "I do not mind waiting at all."

Mr. Parker disappeared into the back room, leaving Millie to wander over to the window. Watching the traffic heading up and down the street amused her until the jeweler's assistant arrived.

"Did not Mr. Parker deliver your necklace, Miss Cope?"

"Yes, I did," the jeweler called from the back.

Millie smiled. "I received the necklace yesterday as promised. However, I have another problem that needed addressing. Mr. Parker is . . ." She noticed the elderly man coming toward her. "It appears he has already made the repair."

Holding the locket in his outstretched hand, Mr. Parker came around the counter to gesture toward the front window. "Come over here to where the light is best. I want you to see something."

She did as he asked and then accepted the locket when he offered it to her. The frame was no longer bent, and the portrait had been removed completely.

"This is what I wanted you to see." The jeweler retrieved the miniature from his pocket and placed it facedown in her palm. "You said you did not know who this man is? His name is Julian."

She looked down at the tiny scribble of words and marveled at the old man's ability to decipher them. As if he had guessed at her surprise, Mr. Parker reached into his pocket again and pulled out a magnifying device.

"Here. You will see it much clearer through this."

Millie lifted the glass to her eye and then edged closer to the sunlight now streaming through the front window. Indeed, there were several lines of miniscule letters, though the print was quite blurred.

"How did they make this so small?"

"The same way the portrait was painted. With a tiny brush and much patience." He gestured to the portrait. "Go on, read it. You may have to lift your head a bit or even move closer to get the words to focus."

"All right," she said as she brought the glass again to her eye. And then she saw them. Words that took her breath away.

Julian, the source of my treasure.

And beneath it a date that time and dampness had obscured. Then the last line.

"Oh, my. Does that say New Orleans? And then the date. It looks like 1837."

"That was my guess. Does any of that sound familiar?"

"Only the date," she said as she handed the looking glass back to Mr. Parker. "I seem to recall a marriage recorded in that year in my mother's . . ."

No good would come of mentioning the Bible, even though the likelihood Mr. Parker might somehow transfer that information to Father was extremely small.

"Miss Cope?"

She returned her attention to the jeweler. "Yes? I am sorry."

"Would you like me to put this back in the locket?" As if guessing her next question, he said, "And I will be sure to show you how to remove this portrait should you want to look at the message on the back again."

Though she watched what the jeweler did, it took several attempts to replicate his ability to slip the miniature out of its place and then return it again. That finally accomplished, she bid Mr.

Parker goodbye and hurried out of the store, the question of Sophie and the letter weighing heavily on her.

Such was her concentration that she might have missed Kyle had she not run directly into him going the opposite direction. Hanging on his arm was a lovely fair-haired woman who barely spared her a glance as she released her grip and kept walking.

"You're in a hurry," Kyle said as he steadied the pretty society scientist, decked out for the day in a gown of crimson that matched the color rising in her cheeks.

Millie gave a passing glance to Agent Sadie Callum of the Denver Pinkerton office before looking at him. He'd seen that look before. She was jealous.

How about that?

"Yes, well, I . . ." With another glance in Detective Callum's direction, she began to fiddle with the lace at her collar. "I was just going home. If you will excuse me . . ."

He gently captured her arm and held her still before she could flee. "I got your message," he said softly.

"Um . . . yes, about that . . ."

With another glance behind him where, Kyle assumed, his fellow Pinkerton agent was now waiting, Millie returned her attention to him. She seemed to have difficulty recalling her next thought.

"And . . . ?" he prompted, smiling in an attempt to help her feel a little more at ease.

"I just wanted to apologize for shooting your . . ." She shrugged. "Well, you know what I mean."

"Yes," he said as he moved out of the way to allow a trio of matrons to pass.

Out of the corner of his eye, Kyle could see that Agent Callum was watching closely, her cover as his ladylove in full effect.

"Am I interrupting something?" Millie nodded toward his companion, a vision in pink with a winter coat and hat to match.

What to say? "Actually . . ."

"Of course." Two words and yet they spoke volumes. "Then I will bid you goodbye."

With a nod she turned away. Long after Millie disappeared around the corner, he remained standing there, hoping like a fool she might return.

She would not, of course. Not since she surely figured he was sporting around town with Agent Callum. And that *had* been the plan. For who would expect that a stroll on a nice January after-noon would be, in actuality, a business meeting between two of the Pinkerton Agency's best agents?

She sidled up beside him and placed a gloved

hand on his sleeve. "I think I may have caused you some trouble with your friend."

"That one is trouble enough without your help." The detective would get no further response on the subject. He took her arm and walked in silence until Kyle felt it safe enough to stop. "Where were we?"

"I was about to give you your marching orders and remind you that, although your original assignment was to chase down rumors of Confederate gold, you are now following the trail of a different type of smuggler."

"Why not turn this one over to local law enforcement?" he wondered aloud. "If our suspect used stolen Confederate gold to fund his empire, then why not just go in and shut him down?"

"I asked Henry the same thing. Apparently he's hiding behind a dead mother." At Kyle's confused look, she continued. "There is a connection to Lafitte on his mother's side being claimed as the source of their income, or at least that is what Henry's informant is saying."

She paused to adjust her pale pink gloves and then turned her green eyes back in his direction. "Our informant says otherwise, and if he is right and our suspect built his empire with funds that came from stolen gold . . ."

"Then it all belongs to the government, which makes our mystery client very happy."

"Exactly." She reached into her handbag to

offer him an envelope. After a quick glance around to be certain they had not been followed, Kyle tucked it into his pocket.

"Field work suits you," he said when they resumed walking. "Or has your move to Denver meant you are no longer in the field?"

It was Agent Callum's turn to shrug. "Not as much as I would like, but that is the nature of our career, is it not? I mean, who among us isn't either planning our exit or still trying to justify why we joined up in the first place?"

"Agreed."

"We do what is asked of us so that someday we can do what we wish."

"Deep thoughts, Agent Callum," he said. *And far too close to true,* he did not say.

They were turning toward the dock now, and the wind blew raw and dirty off the Mississippi. To her credit, Sadie appeared not to notice.

She gave a passing nod to the ancient vegetable seller who plodded by atop an old gray mare and then continued. "In the meantime, it's not a bad way to get even with the bad guys."

The way she held his gaze told Kyle she was speaking from personal experience. Just what that experience might be was anyone's guess. And he certainly did not intend to ask.

"How long has it been since you went home to New Orleans?"

"Too long," she said. "You?"

A bell sounded at the harbor, announcing the departure of a steamboat. Kyle waited until the noise abated before responding. "I was supposed to be there for Christmas, but Pinkerton business diverted me."

"Then you will be happy to know it appears Pinkerton business will be sending you there after all." She glanced at the pocket where he had placed the envelope. "And for the record, it did not take any sort of fancy detective work on my part. Henry offered me the chance to go along."

"And you accepted?"

She shook her head and nodded toward the docks. "I declined. My business in New Orleans is not ready to be conducted just yet, and I'm needed back in Denver."

"I see."

"So that pretty brunette you nearly bowled over coming out of Parker's Jewelry?" she said as the beginnings of a grin touched her lips. "It does not take a Pinkerton agent to know she was not pleased to find you with me."

He thought of the hint of jealousy she had allowed and tried not to smile. "Why do you say that?"

"Just a hunch." Her grin broadened. "That, and the fact she is hiding behind those cotton bales next to the Cope Warehouse."

Kyle leaned just far enough in that direction to

allow his peripheral vision to catch a glimpse of crimson skirts shifting out of sight. "So she is."

"Far be it from me to give instructions to a fellow agent, but as a woman I believe I can safely say you will probably want to go and have a conversation with her." She shrugged. "You were heading that way anyway."

"I was?"

Sadie nodded again to the envelope now in his pocket. "Our suspect owns that warehouse and the other three beyond that one. He has a nice new office over in the Cotton Exchange."

The reminder of that building caused his attention to return to Millie, whose hat rode just high enough above the bales to look as if someone had left the latest fashion sitting atop the cotton.

"And, of course, he has the required address on Adams Street," she continued. When she rattled off the address, Kyle's attention jerked back in her direction.

"What? Does that address sound familiar?"

He nodded.

"Oh." She looked beyond him to where Millie was doing who knew what. "And your lady friend?"

"Lives at that address."

"Oh." She paused and her expression brightened. "Miss Cope?"

"Not sure but probably so."

"Well, I would say you are in an excellent position to prove or disprove the case. Any qualms about possibly ruining that girl's daddy if he's guilty, Agent Russell?"

She had every reason to ask, and yet her question stung. "None," was his brief response.

"Then I suggest you get to it." She reached to shake his hand, sliding kid gloves over his roughened palm as their eyes met. "I ought to offer some sort of sage advice regarding the duties of a Pinkerton agent, should I not?"

"Is that a rhetorical question?"

Sadie looked away. "It's one I hope someone would ask me should the situation ever require it."

Kyle was still thinking about that statement even after he bid her goodbye. After she disappeared onto a steamboat some distance away.

Turning his back to the river, Kyle allowed his gaze to lazily scan the docks. Or at least that was the appearance he hoped to offer. The feathered hat no longer danced atop the cotton bale, but by placing his long-distance spectacles on his nose, he did see a blur of crimson disappear behind a stack of boxes just beyond the cotton. Adjusting his bowler hat to be certain his listening device was in place, Kyle set off in that direction.

As he walked, he made a show of removing his spectacles and appearing to clean them with his handkerchief. All the while, he kept his attention focused on the spot he knew Millie would be hiding.

Millie Cope. Part of him hoped it was not true,

but there was no denying the facts that all lined up so neatly. He glanced at the Cope Enterprises sign over the door and then let out a long breath. *Lord, what are You up to with this?*

With no sign of Millie, he made an abrupt left turn and slipped inside to cross the warehouse and emerge on the street beyond. Though he would make it his business to see the society scientist very soon, this was not the time.

A little while later, Kyle opened the door to his room at the Peabody Hotel and went to his satchel, where his important papers were stored. Taking them out, he placed them on his desk and added the envelope Agent Callum had given him to the pile. It was then that he noticed an envelope from Henry he had apparently overlooked. He tore open the seal, tossed the envelope onto the desk, and unfolded the documents it contained.

Scanning the words his boss had written, his gaze stalled when he saw the name Mildred Cope.

Daughter of Silas Cope, owner of Cope Enterprises.

The letter went on to detail the business interests of the Cope family, the deaths of Mrs. Cope and two daughters, the possible connection to Confederate gold, and then finally the claim of a relation to the pirate Lafitte. All information he should have read and reported back to the Chicago office well before now.

Also included was a copy of an article that appeared in the local newspaper announcing Millie's engagement to a British nobleman, Sir William Trueck. Though the photograph was dark and poor in quality, there was no mistaking the society scientist's grim expression.

He tossed the letter and its accompanying newspaper clipping aside. Likely Henry had wondered why he had not received a response—and with good reason. Kyle should have opened the envelope the minute it arrived. How had he missed it? Undoubtedly by being absorbed in a distracting combination of beauty and science.

"That girl has been dangerous since the first day I met her," he muttered as he rose to walk to the window. He could not see the river from there, though the sound of the vessels and the smell of the docks were never far from this side of the city. Unlike Adams Street, where Mildred Cope lived.

Kyle let out a long breath and stepped away from the window. He owed Henry an explanation, and he would give him one. And then he would go and do the work he was being paid to do, even if that meant he had to steer clear of Millie Cope.

He wrote three versions of an apology letter and then settled on a fourth that he went down and mailed before he could change his mind. With a few hours of daylight still ahead of him, Kyle decided to go do some checking on the property he had visited with Millie. Finding the information he sought was a simple matter of showing his Pinkerton badge to the courthouse clerk.

Purchased fifty years ago by a J. L. Arnaque, the records had long ago been buried by time and inattention. What set this transaction apart was the manner in which the buyer had arrived in the county, made his purchase, and then disappeared.

The taxes were paid from an account set up for the purchase, the balance of which was substantial considering the humble purchase price. Had Kyle not come looking for anomalies such as this one, another fifty years might have passed without comment.

Or longer, given the amount of funds available for the property's tax burden. In his search for Confederate gold, Kyle had only given the information a cursory glance, but where money went out, there were records for how it came in.

The other curious fact was the issue of Arnaque himself. When the city of Memphis had its charter revoked by the state in 1879, changes were made to the taxing structure. Notifying landowners had proven difficult owing to the fact that many of those who had not lost their lives to yellow fever the year before had chosen to relocate their interests elsewhere until the epidemic had passed. Arnaque, however, was not reported dead, nor did he appear elsewhere. His lone contribution to public record seemed to be the purchase of that property.

Then there was his name. Perhaps it was his New Orleans background, but Kyle took notice immediately of the fact that the meaning of *Arnaque* in French was "swindle." Could "J. L." be an abbreviation for "Jean Lafitte," the pirate whose death had been claimed and retracted multiple times over the past sixty years? Perhaps the Baratarian had tired of the pirate's life and reinvented himself to spend the remainder of his days as an upright and law-abiding citizen.

The topic of Lafitte and his brother, Pierre, was a popular one in New Orleans. Experts and amateurs alike debated the truth of the reports that the pirate had been killed after taking aim at a pair of Spanish vessels in the Gulf of Honduras. But was he truly buried at sea on that foggy day in February 1823? Conveniently, no concrete proof existed on either side of the argument.

How it all connected back to Silas Cope and Cope Enterprises was still to be determined, as was any connection to Lafitte's treasure. Kyle thought for a moment about the Spanish escudo coins made into Millie's cypher. Coincidence? He tried not to hope but failed miserably. Again he wondered what the Lord was up to. On the one hand, the evidence of His approval of Millie Cope had been found in the confession of her name that she made at this very property he now researched. On the other hand, what if he had misunderstood?

Logic would settle on the second option,

although Kyle found himself hoping he was right about the first. In either case, he was a Pinkerton agent bound by duty to complete the requirements of his job, and right now that meant doing all he could to see just what kinds of secrets Silas Cope was hiding.

"Finding what you need?" the records clerk inquired.

"I believe so."

As soon as the clerk was once again out of sight, Kyle removed his newest gadget, a mechanized portable camera small enough to fit in his satchel, and quickly assembled the pieces. Then he spread the documents on the table and stepped back to look through the viewfinder. After an adjustment to the lens, he was ready to put in the glass plate.

That accomplished, Kyle pulled the lever and held the camera very still while the flash sparked and a photograph of the evidence was taken. As he waited for the requisite developing time, he heard the clerk come running.

"What in the world was that flash of light? Why, I could have sworn—"

"Nothing to see here," Kyle said as he continued to hold the camera still. "Pinkerton business."

A few minutes later, he braved a peek at the glass slide. "This will do just fine."

He summoned the clerk to retrieve the documents and then headed back to the Peabody Hotel.

As the building came into view, Kyle thought once again about Arnaque and the meaning of his name. Much as he hated to, he had to consider whether Millie might be part of a swindle involving a large sum of stolen money in a Memphis bank. Money that, should its provenance be determined as Confederate, he had been hired to find and return to the United States government.

He bypassed the hotel to retrace his steps to the wharf, where he found a beehive of activity but no one resembling Millie Cope. Turning away from the river, he walked toward Adams Street, unsure as to what he would do when he reached the Cope home. The photographic plate in his satchel would not wait much longer, nor could he spare a visit until he was fully prepared. He needed to search the Arnaque property thoroughly with the metal detecting machine to eliminate the obvious connection between buried treasure and the Copes.

Or to prove it.

And then Kyle spied Millie looking out the third-floor window, and he hoped she would be found innocent of any wrongdoing. He could not get her out of his mind. There was something special about her, a connection he had not yet managed to break.

And yet he couldn't possibly allow the possibility of feelings for a woman who was also a criminal. Surely God would not permit it, and neither would the Pinkerton Agency.

Millie let the curtain slide into place and turned her back on the man she had been foolish enough to kiss. Foolish enough to follow until better judgment took over. So Kyle had another woman. Of course. That would explain everything. The secrecy. The surprise arrivals in her attic hideaway under cover of darkness.

"And what sort of idiot dreams of a man whose name she does not fully know?" she muttered.

The question remained at the edge of her thoughts as Millie turned her attention to other issues. Foremost in her mind was the puzzle of just who Sophie and Julian might be.

Sixteen

January 21, 1889
Memphis

The question of Sophie's and Julian's identity was of sufficient importance to brave a trip to her father's library on Monday morning. Millie found him in the center of a cloud of pipe smoke, a copy of the day's newspaper spread before him.

"Father, may I have a moment of your time?"

"Unless you wish to discuss the ridiculous

conversation you had with Sir William last week, I have nothing to say to you," was the response he offered without sparing her a glance.

Indeed, Father had been absent all day Saturday, and on Sunday Millie had attended Sunday services alone. His absence had been welcome, but only he could answer her questions about the Cope family history. "It is of some importance." Millie inched inside. "And it does concern Sir William."

That got his attention. "Go on."

"Sir William once mentioned how very important family lineage is to the British." That was the truth, though certainly not in this context. "And I realized there are certain gaps in mine."

When Father said nothing, she tried again. "I wonder if the names Sophie or Julian mean anything to you."

He continued to puff on his pipe for a moment and then surprised her by sparing her a glance. "No. Now go away and leave me unless you wish to discuss how best to make your apology to Sir William." He returned his attention to the newspaper.

Millie sighed. Perhaps a small diversion was in order. "Do you suggest I write Sir William or would a meeting face-to-face be best?"

Once again, Millie caught his attention. "I think the latter, seeing that time is of the essence."

"Yes, right," she said, though she had no plans

to go forward with any such thing. "But first, could you tell me anything more about your family? Or perhaps about Mama?"

He paused to look at her over the page. "Very well, but only because I believe your husband would appreciate such family details. My father, Hugh Cope, came to Memphis from Virginia before the war. His people were planters, successful folk. Father took that success south to build up the family fortune with cotton and crops, but then you likely know all that."

"No, Father," she said gently. "I did not."

He looked surprised. "Yes, well, there were once cotton and indigo fields on that property outside of town. My mother, Genevieve Lacoste, preferred to live in the city. Your grandmother was gently bred and had no interest in country life. After all, she had come from New Orleans where her family maintained a lovely home on Royal Street. I visited it as a child, but the building has since passed to another owner."

The connection she sought. Millie's heart leapt. "New Orleans? I had no idea."

"Why do you think this house has those ridiculous balconies? It reminded your grandmother of her home."

"Would you happen to recall the name of Grandmother Genevieve's father?"

From his expression, Millie could tell she'd stumped her father. "I have no idea. I believe he died while she was still very young. Now, see that you make arrangements to mend your troubles with Trueck."

No answer was required, for he had already dismissed her, going back to his newspaper with the single-minded attention of a man who did not desire to be interrupted. So there were family connections to Louisiana that ran closer than even the fellow in the locket.

Interesting.

And a home owned by the family and yet long ago passed from her father's hands.

Even more interesting.

Could the key open that door? Or perhaps the door to a treasure? No it was too small to be a door key, but there must be some connection.

Millie reached for the chain around her neck and weighed the cypher and locket in her palm. A trip to New Orleans might offer the answers she sought.

And although Kyle might be spending time with another woman, there was no reason why two scientists might not meet to work out the puzzle that was her family's treasure hunt.

"Just one more thing," she asked, though Father likely had forgotten she still stood before him. "I wonder if you know of any stories about . . ."

"About?" he asked impatiently.

She drew in a deep breath, closed her eyes, and sent a quick prayer up to stop her should she not need to speak of such things to her father. When no such impediment came, Millie released her breath.

"Treasure," she said, her gaze locking with his.

His face went blank, and then slowly an expression of surprise formed. "Why do you ask?" He set the newspaper aside and gave her his full attention. "Has Sir William inquired of this?"

"No."

"Then what sort of foolishness has you bringing up such a topic, Mildred?"

Nervous laughter bubbled within her. Under her father's steady gaze, the years fell away and she was a chastened child again. "Well, I . . ."

"You what?" When she did not immediately respond, Father snatched up his newspaper once more. "Honestly, this is why I discourage reading for you. It gives you ideas."

"So there is no connection between a treasure and the Cope family?"

"None that need concern you."

The statement was made with the finality of a man well used to making them. Millie was still searching for a response when her father dropped the newspaper and rose.

"I believe we are done here, Mildred. And you will not ever speak of treasure or any such family nonsense outside of this room. Do you understand?"

Squaring her shoulders, Millie forced herself to

meet his gaze. "I have questions, Father. There is nothing wrong with asking them."

"Indeed you have asked. And you have had a response." He pressed past her to step out into the hall and then stopped to spear her with an irritated look. "And now you are to understand that any further discussion on this topic will be met with silence by me. Should your husband wish a conversation on this or any other matter, he may come and speak to me himself."

As she watched him walk away, Millie briefly entertained the idea of going to Sir William and asking him to speak to Father on the topic. Given their breakup, however, the idea was quickly tossed aside.

If Silas Cope knew anything about treasure, be it Lafitte's or anyone else's, he was keeping the information to himself. The conversation had not been a total loss, however, for she had learned there was a Cope home in New Orleans. Or, rather, a home owned by the family of Genevieve Lacoste Cope. Given that the books she read about Lafitte placed him in the city at approximately the same time her family was there, she had at least forged a tentative connection between the two.

A door closed at the far end of the house, adding to the finality of the situation. Or did it?

Millie looked around and found herself quite alone. Carefully she closed the door behind her.

Though her footsteps were muffled by the thick carpet beneath her feet, Millie tiptoed toward the telephone and slowly lifted the receiver. With no time to retrieve the card containing Kyle's information, she relied on her memory to give the correct number when the operator answered. As the call rang through, Millie held her breath. And then the same fellow answered with the same bland greeting, and her heart soared.

"I wish to make use of Kyle's workshop for scientific purposes as offered by him upon our previous meeting," she said with an assertiveness she did not feel.

Though there was static on the line, she could hear what sounded like the scratch of a pencil as he wrote down what she said.

"Is there anything else, miss?"

"Yes," she said as she gripped the phone and forced herself to sound as mundane as she could manage. "Please tell him I am willing to offer a negotiable portion of the proceeds for his services. He is to name his price and then—"

"What are you doing?"

Millie slammed down the receiver and pivoted to see her father standing in the open doorway. "Father, I thought—"

"Leave off telling me what you *thought* and enlighten me with what you were *doing*, Mildred."

"I was . . ." She glanced down at the telephone and then back at her father. "I was using the telephone." She eased into a reasonable explanation by starting with the truth. "How else will I learn if I do not practice?"

He crossed his arms over his chest as he regarded her. Then, by degrees, his expression softened. "With a husband in your near future and a houseful of servants to do things for you, you have no need of the telephone. Any attempt on your part to learn to use the machine is a waste of time."

Mildred bit back what she knew would be a useless protest. "I suppose you are right. I only thought that perhaps in case of emergency I might—"

"In case of emergency I would not rely on a woman, especially one of your age and abilities, and thus, I repeat, any attempt on your part to learn the use of the telephone is a waste of time. As is reading and all of that nonsense you do when you should be doing womanly work. Now leave me to privacy."

"Yes, Father." She scooted past him and hurried upstairs without so much as a backward glance.

A negotiable portion of the proceeds.

Kyle read that twice, and both times he grinned. So Millie Cope wanted to partner with him to solve the mystery of the Lafitte treasure. Life was indeed sweet.

The question was how to proceed. He had

spent the last four days going over the Arnaque property with his metal detecting device and found nothing beyond a growing stack of Civil War–era cannonballs, pots and pans, and quite a few tools and implements that must have been missing from the barn for at least twenty years, given their deteriorated condition.

If any Cope treasure existed, Confederate or otherwise, Kyle could say with absolute certainty it was not buried within the boundary markers of the Arnaque farm. And so he had been praying as to how to proceed when the message came in from Millie.

God's perfect timing again. Or at least Kyle hoped so.

That the call had been interrupted bothered him, as did the fact he had no idea how best to contact her. With Silas Cope as the prime suspect in what could become an investigation with far-reaching consequences, he couldn't exactly walk up to the front door of the house on Adams Street and knock.

And with the flying device temporarily grounded, he couldn't fly to her and carry her away for a private discussion, either. Notes might be inter-cepted, and she had no regular routine that might allow him to happen upon her.

He would just have to wait until the right moment to respond, but with the clock ticking on a March 4 deadline less than six weeks away, he couldn't afford to wait long.

There was also the problem of the steamboat ticket in his satchel. Though he was tempted to let Millie know he would soon be in New Orleans, instinct told Kyle it would be far more prudent to go and do the investigative work demanded of him first and then send for her.

He smiled as he rose to stretch out the kinks. Four days with the heavy metal detector had left him stiff and aching from the weight of the boxlike structure. He had already made notes on how to lighten the frame and would likely make that project his priority after the repair of the flying machine.

He spent the remainder of the afternoon securing the devices into trunks newly purchased for the purpose. Train travel generally allowed for gentler handling of baggage, but he would not complain about Henry's choice of transportation by water. Thus, by the time the sun had set, he had enough padding around his inventions to feel fairly secure they would survive the trip. Still, he supervised them closely as porters took the trunks from his hotel room to stow in the hotel luggage room in preparation for tomorrow afternoon's departure.

That task accomplished, Kyle picked up his copy of Robert Louis Stevenson's *The Black Arrow* with the intention of reading until sleep overtook him. What overtook him instead was an urgent need, despite his intentions to the contrary, to see Millie Cope one last time.

For the next time he saw her, he very well might be required to inform her of her status as a person of interest in a Pinkerton investigation. Tonight, however, she was merely a person holding his interest.

Grinning at the thought, Kyle tucked the items he needed into his satchel, slipped on his hat, and headed toward Adams Street with the intention of waiting for Millie to make an appearance in her third-floor hideaway.

Fortunately, he found the window unlocked, making his entrance into Millie's world an easy one. Lighting a lamp was out of the question, so he made do with his personal lantern adjusted to the lowest setting as he scanned the room for something to interest him while he waited.

The sound of muffled voices drew him to the fireplace, where he leaned against the chilled bricks to better hear the conversation taking place somewhere below.

"I don't trust that man," said a woman whose voice indicated advanced age. "There's just something about him that don't add up."

"Sir William seems nice enough," a younger girl said. "My guess is he and the mistress will patch things up and get married after all."

"Nice don't make no difference. Our Mr. Cope, he can be nice when he wants to."

Silence fell, though the clatter of what sounded like a pot lid on a tile floor rattled up. Kyle leaned his head inside to see if he could determine how the acoustics worked.

The women began chatting again, though their talk was of more mundane matters, such as seasoning for the soup and which of the neighbor's maids might be having a baby in the spring.

"Oh, and did I tell you I caught Mr. Cope snooping around Miss Millie's room again? Lord knows there is little left for him to take except what she wears around her neck." This from the younger woman.

"Oh, he could take a whole lot more, and I hear he has." The slam of what might have been an oven door drowned out the elder woman's words. Kyle reached for the hearing device in his hat and adjusted it until her voice returned to his ears.

"All I know is that if she gets caught, the mister is going to be terrible angry. He's been threatening to take anything like that away if he catches her."

Again the conversation went back to domestic issues, giving Kyle the opportunity to test his theory that the pipes sent the conversation up, and probably down as well. So it stood to reason that if he were to shut off the flue, the conversation would also be shut off.

With a tug on the proper lever, the two voices instantly fell silent. Pressing it the other way brought the conversation back. He made a final adjustment to close the flue and then swiped at the ashes on his hands.

On one of the chairs he found a copy of the same book he had left back at the Peabody. Opening *The Black Arrow* to the place where he left off, Kyle returned to the adventures of Dick Shelton and his quest to rescue the fair Joanna until he heard a key turn in the lock. Quickly extinguishing the lantern, he set the book aside and leaned back against the chair cushions to await Millie's arrival.

Millie knew the moment she stepped into the attic room that she was not alone. "You came," she said, sounding pleased.

A lantern flashed and there he was, sitting in one of the chairs before empty fireplace, though he stood politely as she came closer. "You called," was his simple response.

"I want to hire you." She gestured toward his chair, inviting him to sit again, and then took the seat opposite him.

If he had an opinion on the topic, his expression did not give it away. "Maybe we should talk about that."

She removed the chain from around her neck and held the charms in her palm. "You were able to solve the puzzle of the cypher. I want you to make use of your workshop and whatever gadgets and inventions you might have to solve another puzzle. As I said in my message, I can offer payment in the form of a percentage of the funds recovered."

He said nothing, so she continued. "You saw the blank paper for yourself when the cypher was opened. I need to know if there is something on that paper that will lead to . . ."

"The Lafitte treasure?"

"The Cope treasure. That is my name. Millie Cope."

"I know." He paused only a second. "Or Mildred Cope, according to the engagement article in the local newspaper."

"Yes, though the wedding has been canceled."

"Does your fiancé know?"

"He does, but those sorts of things never make the papers, do they?"

"I would beg to differ," he said. "Sometimes the story of the breakup makes a bettter headline."

"Well, it's possible my story may yet be told. But first I have to convince my father a nobleman will not be joining the family." She met Kyle's eyes. "He's having trouble accepting that fact."

He let the statement pass without comment. Instead, he reached for the necklace, and she allowed him to have it.

"What is it you think I can do to help you find the treasure?" he asked as he twirled the Spanish coins and once again easily opened the cypher. The key tumbled into his palm, followed by the torn piece of foolscap.

"You can determine if that is a clue to something or merely a blank piece of paper."

"Are you saying you would be willing to allow me to take this with me?"

"I would have to come along."

He shook his head. "Impossible."

"That point is nonnegotiable, Kyle. You cannot expect me to allow something so valuable out of my sight."

"My point is also nonnegotiable. You cannot follow me to . . . where I am going."

"I'm sure I could, though I am loathe to considering it *following*. More like traveling to the same destination for an agreed-upon purpose." She paused to consider her words. "I assure you our relationship would be business only."

Kyle looked as if he might laugh. "Well, that is slightly disappointing, but not the reason you cannot accompany me."

Slightly disappointing? She let the comment pass even as she tucked it neatly into her heart to be considered later. "You are leaving soon, are you not?"

He gave her a how-did-you-know look that told Millie she was on to something. "No comment."

"Oh, I see. It's to be like that."

They were both quiet for a moment, and in the stillness Millie grew aware of the cold seeping up through the floorboards. Though disappointed in his refusal, she didn't want to leave the dark, chilly room, didn't want to leave him. It was silly, really, this feeling she had whenever she was close to Kyle. No, silly was not the correct word at all, for the powerful mix of feelings he stirred in her was nothing less than intriguing and very close to dangerous.

"Tell me about the woman you were with." The words tumbled forth with such speed that she had no time to retrieve them.

Out of the corner of her eye, she saw him chuckle, though the sound was too soft to hear. "I wondered when we would get around to discussing her." He paused as if to study Millie. "She is a colleague, nothing more."

Millie did her own studying, and it only took a moment to decide he was telling the truth. Then came relief, crowding out the jealousy that had surprised her with its fierceness.

"You look relieved."

He was teasing her. His smile gave that much away. But behind the smile, somewhere between his words and his eyes, was that the tiniest bit of concern that she might not believe him?

Which would only mean . . .

"Millie?"

He was looking at her in a completely different way now. Indeed, he appeared to be amused again. "Are you woolgathering?"

"Perhaps. Now," she said as she turned the conversation toward a safer direction, "about the foolscap."

"I can make a copy, but that will not allow a proper testing of the paper."

"How can you copy a . . ." She shook her head. "Never mind. If you can fly, it should not surprise me that you could somehow copy pieces of paper."

Kyle shifted his attention to the locket and opened it. "What of this? Could there be a connection between this fellow and the treasure you're searching for?"

"I thought so, but I have come to a dead end in my search for who he might be. The jeweler found an inscription on the back of the miniature. Apparently he is Julian. The year is 1837."

"That is written on the back of the image?"

She nodded as she moved to kneel beside him. With care, Millie removed the miniature and turned it over. The tiny words could barely be seen.

"Look at that," Kyle said as he reached into his pocket to produce a pair of spectacles. "Let me see the locket."

She watched as he studied both sides of the piece. "If this side opens, what is on the other?"

Millie frowned. "I don't know. Let's see, shall we?"

He handed the piece back to her. After two attempts she gave up. "Apparently just the one opens," she said as she returned it to Kyle.

"Or it is jammed." He held the open locket up

and looked at it closely through the spectacles. "See here. It looks as if this side was meant to open like the other."

He offered her the spectacles. Millie fitted them in place and then blinked to focus on the locket. Indeed it did appear as though both sides were identical.

"Maybe what was once there is lost." She removed the spectacles, allowing her fingertips to brush his hand as she returned them to him. "What do you make of all this?"

Kyle's smile was brief. "All of what?"

"The clues . . . the puzzle pieces. A cypher made from Spanish coins that contains a key and a seemingly blank but very old piece of foolscap. Oh, and a letter I found in my mother's Bible."

She rose to retrieve the letter and then set it on the table between them. "See, it was hidden in the spine."

Kyle handled the torn page carefully as he read the words. "Arn," he said. "Interesting."

Seventeen

Kyle did not need the instruments back in his workshop to know what name those letters were part of. Arnaque.

J. L. Arnaque.

He sat back to make sense of the evidence.

Arnaque was the owner of record on the property Millie had claimed was hers. If Arnaque was Lafitte, then the connection between the society scientist and the Baratarian pirate was very close to being fact rather than supposition.

He gestured to the letter. "What relation are these people to you?"

Millie shook her head. "I don't know. My mother was a very private woman who was orphaned as an infant and knew nothing of her own parents. Do you suppose . . ."

"That your mother could have been an Arnaque?"

Or a Lafitte?

Kyle reached for the letter again and pretended to study it. Instead, he thought of the lovely woman beside him. How had he missed the delicate features of what must be a Creole heritage? The complexion that had to have been passed down from relatives of the French persuasion?

"My mother was far too young to have been the Sophie to whom Mr. Arnaque writes." She let out a long breath. "I wish my father would be more forthcoming. All he will tell me is that his father, Hugh Cope, came to Memphis before the war but somehow met and married Genevieve Lacoste in New Orleans and then brought her back here. There was a Lacoste home in New Orleans, but it has passed out of the family's hands. Beyond that, I know nothing else."

At this his brows rose. "So there is a Louisiana connection in your family. Interesting."

"Yes, but that does not answer the more immediate question of who J. L. Arnaque is."

One thing was certain. Arnaque translated to "swindler." But who was being swindled? If the answer was the federal government, then Kyle was obligated to act. Indeed, it was what he had been hired to do.

He would much prefer to sit here with Millie Cope and play the part of helpful assistant while she plied him with information and begged him to allow her to come along with him to New Orleans. Not that she realized he was going to the Crescent City. He hadn't admitted that much yet.

It was indeed a conundrum. And yet there was evidence spread on the table before him that must be catalogued.

Yes, of course. That was the answer. Photograph the evidence and then leave quickly before he could change his mind and allow her to inch her way any closer into his heart. For she had certainly already gained far too much real estate there. That much he had realized when she asked about Sadie Callum.

Given the right situation, he could see himself settling down with a woman like Millie. A woman whose wit matched her beauty and whose humor matched his. Could imagine working beside her. Waking up next to her.

The thought jolted him back to reality. This was not a woman he could consider making his wife. Not when her father could be at the center of the case he was currently working. He forced his mind back on the project at hand.

Kyle allowed only a moment's guilt at the possibility Millie might be incriminating herself by offering these items to him for photographing. He comforted himself with the thought that if anyone held guilt here, it was her father, not her.

He spread the letter open. "May I see the locket and cypher too?"

She handed them to him. "What are you doing?" she asked as she watched him arrange the items so they would all fit in the photograph. Deciding the engraving on the back was more important than the painting on the front, he turned the tiny piece of artwork over and placed it beside the locket.

The seemingly blank piece of foolscap presented a similar problem. He lifted the torn page to the lantern's best light to study both sides. Though they looked the same, he knew anything could be written there—or nothing.

"Millie, would you open the cypher? I think it might be best to show the Spanish coins."

She shook her head. "I cannot."

"Of course you can," he said as he played with the lantern light. "I told you the code is 'Lafitte.' "

"Yes, I know, but I have yet to manage it. Apparently you are the only one who can."

He watched her try and fail several times before taking the piece from her hand to align the gold coins into their proper places. "See how I have done this?"

"I do, and I'm spelling 'Lafitte,' but the cypher refuses to budge."

"Show me."

He pressed the cypher into her palm and then leaned close. The scent of her perfume, soft and floral, diverted his attention.

Her fingers moved. He saw that from his peripheral vision, for his attention was focused on the curve of her jawline, the dark lashes that swept her high porcelain cheekbones, and the way her pink lips turned up slightly as she concentrated.

"See, it's hopeless." She caught him looking. "What? Are you amused that I cannot open my own cypher?"

Had he been smiling? He hadn't noticed.

"Not at all." He reached to take the coins from her, and his fingers brushed her palm. "I should have been more specific in the method I used to spell 'Lafitte.' " She was close. Too close.

Kyle cleared his throat and continued. "See these notches here?" He indicated a set of deep indentions that, when aligned, traveled the length of the stacked coins.

"Yes, and I did notice those two were deeper than the others. I assumed that meant one was the starting point. The difficulty was in deciding which of the two was the correct one."

"Are you familiar with semaphore flags?"

Her brow wrinkled as she concentrated. "As in flag signals used by ships?"

"The very same." He aligned the seven coins so that each of them corresponded to a flag position of a letter. "See here, this is an *L*. And the next one is an *A*. Then an *F* . . ."

It was his turn to catch Millie watching him instead of the cypher. "What?"

"Nothing. I . . ." She tucked a strand of ebony hair behind her ear. "It's just that the code is so simple and obvious and yet so effective."

"Sometimes it's the simplest things that confound us, Millie," he said, no longer speaking of the cypher. He leaned closer. "And it's the obvious that we are apt to miss." Such as how the Lord had already answered his question about whether this woman was the one. And yet though the answer had come, the manner in which God would make such an impossibility actually happen eluded Kyle.

"Is there something wrong?"

"Wrong? No." He handed the cypher back to her. "Try it again. And should you find yourself unable to open it, there is a simple solution. Just break it. The gold is soft and can be managed without too much trouble."

"I hope it doesn't come to that."

Kyle finally had everything arranged as best he could manage. He lifted the camera and paused only a moment. "Once I take the photograph I have a limited amount of time to develop the plate."

"Wait then." She touched his sleeve. "Is there no way I can convince you to allow me to accompany you to your laboratory to do further research on these items?"

Oh, how he wanted to say yes. How he wanted to kiss her again and toss aside his Pinkerton assignment to see where the Lord was leading in a relationship with her. But responsibility and good sense must prevail.

"There is not," he said, though he had to look away from her to accomplish the steady tone he used.

"And what of my offer to help search for the treasure?"

"I'm taking that under advisement." This time he met her gaze. "That is the best I can do at the moment."

"I see." She laced her hands together in her lap and looked away in her turn. A moment later she returned her attention to him. "Then I shall require a gentleman's promise of confidentiality from you regarding the things I have shared."

"Including the kiss?" At her surprised look, he quickly amended, "Forgive me. I could not resist. And yes, you have my promise."

"Especially the kiss," she said as the beginnings of a smile showed on those lips that haunted his dreams. "Which was only a celebration of the New Year and nothing else."

"Of course." He lifted one brow. "And the other time?"

"What other time?" she asked as if daring him to argue.

A memory of kissing her lips and dusting soft kisses across her temple in this very room arose. Quickly he pressed it back into place in his mind. "Yes, of course. What other time?"

She nodded to the table and the items arranged there. "Go ahead, then."

He did as she suggested, making the adjustment to the level of brilliance the lantern produced until everything looked just right. And then Millie caught his eye, and he aimed the camera at her instead.

She laughed at just the right moment, or at least it appeared so through the viewing glass. "I have never seen a camera like that."

"No, you have not." He made quick work of exchanging the used plate for a fresh one. "Nor will you see it again."

"So this is another of your inventions? What is the principle behind it?" When he told her, she continued. "Well then, I just might see it again if I decide to travel on my own. When did you say you were going?"

"I did not say."

Those beautiful eyes held his gaze for a moment longer than was comfortable.

He cleared his throat. "Please lean away from the lantern. You're casting a shadow on the evidence."

"Evidence?" She did as he asked but her expression changed to one of suspicion. "You sound like a police officer."

Choosing not to respond to that, Kyle held the camera very still until he was certain the image would not blur. When he finished and looked up, her expression had changed again.

Millie reached to touch his sleeve. "I cannot believe I have forgotten to ask. Is your flying machine . . . that is, have I ruined it permanently?"

Kyle returned the used plate to his satchel and camera to his pocket before leaning back against the chair cushions. "No, it is not permanently ruined. Other than a bullet hole in the silk, it is remarkably free from damage."

"Oh, good." She released her grip on his sleeve, tears now glistening in the lamp's golden light. "I was terribly afraid I had cost you a patent. I'm so sorry. I—"

"Millie." Though he wanted to embrace her, Kyle set the satchel aside and regarded her from a safe distance. "I understand you were acting on instinct." He paused to offer her his handkerchief. "I'm just glad you were carrying a Remington and not a rifle."

Now she laughed, even as she dabbed at damp cheeks. "I no longer carry it."

He feigned horror. "Please do not tell me you have purchased a larger weapon."

"No, of course not. I cannot carry something I use inappropriately."

Kyle placed his hands on her shoulders and gently turned her to face him. "You were trying to help me. Other than the fact that you did a little bit of damage, you accomplished what you intended."

"I did?"

He nodded. "I did not lose the machine, did I?"

"That is true," she said softly.

"So you see, it all worked out." He released her and reached for the satchel. "Now, tell me goodbye, my society scientist. If I stay here much longer, I will have nothing left on these plates to develop."

He glanced past her to the fireplace. "Oh, before I go. Were you aware that the flue in this fireplace carries sound quite well? While I was waiting I could clearly hear two women working in the kitchen, which I assume is two floors beneath this one." Kyle shrugged. "I took the liberty of closing the flue. That should make this room soundproof."

"Yes, I was aware of that issue in this house, although I have never heard a conversation clearly. That may not be the same for those down in the kitchen."

Gesturing to his hat, Kyle grinned. "I did have the help of my hearing device."

She smiled back at him. "I shall have to be careful to instruct the maids to open the flue before laying a fire next time."

Small talk. He detested it. And yet he found himself wishing he could remain in this chilly attic room and talk about anything but what was really important. Instead, he moved toward the window and away from the woman who tempted him so.

"I shall continue to search for the treasure whether you accept my offer to help or not," she said when he met her gaze. "I have no choice."

"Nor do I," he admitted as he extinguished the lantern and plunged the room into silver shadows and puddles of moonlight. "Which is why I cannot accept." He reached for the curtains. "However, you have my word that what we have discussed here will go no further."

She was moving toward him now. "And the kisses?"

"I thought we have covered that point. Am I mistaken?"

"We covered the first two times we kissed." She stepped within his reach, her gaze holding his. "However, we have made no such arrangement with the third."

Only an idiot would have missed that hint. And he was a certified genius.

Gathering her in his arms, Kyle inhaled once more the floral scent that was all Millie. A scent he would commit to memory and recall often until the Lord showed him how the two of them might find their way back to each other. He bent his head toward her only to find her finger pressed against his lips.

"Do not think this is a goodbye kiss, Kyle," she whispered, "for I promise you I will see you again." She gave him a meaningful look and a wry smile. "And I always keep my promises."

"As do I," he said before he captured her lips with his.

She put her arms around his neck and kissed him back. Time stood still.

"I fear I have made a mistake," he finally managed with a whisper that sounded far too rough to his ears.

"Oh?" Her eyes widened even as he traced the line of her jaw with his knuckle.

"Yes, a terrible mistake." He smiled. "I should have waited to photograph you now. Like this." He reached to wrap a strand of dark hair around his finger and then met her gaze once more. "Freshly kissed."

"Yes, well," she said, her voice strained and soft, "as we have no agreement in place for any further kisses, I think we should probably say our goodbyes now. Unless you wish to change your mind about allowing me to go with you."

"Millie," he said gently as he released her curl, "I think under the circumstances traveling together might prove ill advised, don't you?"

She appeared to consider his question. Then slowly she nodded.

"Goodbye, Millie Cope. For now, at least."

A smile was her response. "One thing more," she added. "You should know that my interest in traveling to visit your workshop is motivated solely by professional curiosity and a need to find answers to a pressing question."

To her surprise, he bent to kiss her again. "As was that."

"Well . . ." she began, though she seemed unable to complete the thought.

"You have my promise of discretion, Millie. And who knows? Perhaps we will meet again soon."

It was only when Kyle had returned to the hotel and began to unload the camera and plates from his satchel did he realize he had not told her the truth about his ability to be discreet. For if the treasure was truly from the pirate Lafitte, or a more modern Civil War pirate, then he was obligated to alert the authorities.

Depending on the depth of knowledge and amount of complicity Millie exhibited, she might join her father behind bars. And he would be the man to turn the key and testify against them both.

• • •

Millie watched the aviator slip out the window and disappear into the darkness, knowing he had stolen her heart. She closed her eyes and allowed each nuance of their moments together to press in. The conversation, the embrace, the kisses. And then his promise . . .

A loud knock at the door made her jump.

"I know you are in there, Mildred Cope!" Her father paused as some sort of scraping sound began. "I've brought a workman, and he will be removing the door from its hinges. My suggestion, young lady, is that you save him the trouble."

She froze. This time there was no flying machine by which to escape. Nor could she wait out the man who was intent on coming inside by any means necessary.

Millie was finally well and truly caught.

"Coming, Father," she called. "I'm just looking for the key now."

She quickly slipped the chain back around her neck. Only then did she see the foolscap, now fluttering to the floor. She tucked it into her pocket.

How easy it would be to fly away. To escape the tightrope she walked between pleasing her father and buying time until she found the freedom she craved.

"I've located the key," she said as she tried jabbing it into the lock, only to have it fall to the floor.

"Mildred—"

"Just a minute!" Another try and again her shaking fingers failed her. She threw the key into the cold ashes of the fireplace.

"Daughter, I demand you cease your stalling and open the door this instant!"

"I'm afraid I'm locked in." She looking anxiously around the room and knew she had to move quickly.

Father swore a blistering oath, but by the time the workman had removed the door from its hinges, Millie had managed to fill some of the boxes that had been left in preparation for packing up her things.

Mama's Bible had already been safely tucked away, along with Millie's sketchbooks and some of her more precious possessions. In all, she was able to set aside three boxfuls of items she hoped she might save before Father pressed past the workman to barge inside. He found her placing *Faust* into a box as if were the most natural thing ever. Perhaps he would believe she had taken up with Sir William again and would be moving soon. Whatever it required to keep her things and placate Father, at least for now, she would gladly do it.

"What in the name of . . ." He stopped short, causing the valet who had been following him to nearly run him down. After a slow glance around the room, his attention finally landed on Millie.

"I'm terribly sorry," she said in her most innocent tone.

"What is all of this?" he demanded before turning to stare at his valet. "Did you know my daughter was hiding this place up here?"

"The responsibility is mine alone," she said, attempting to direct her father's anger back where it belonged.

"Mildred, you would have me believe you carried all of this up here without assistance?"

"Really, Father," she said as she closed the box and set it aside. "Does it matter? I've done as you asked and kept any hint of my tendency toward the pursuit of science and reading out of the sight of anyone who might be bothered by it."

Eyes the color of hers narrowed as her father rested both hands on his hips. "You know what I meant."

Straightening her spine, Millie pressed her palm to the table and refused to back down. "You asked that I not embarrass this family. Well, I have not. So if you take issue with anything, take issue with the fact that you did not specifically outlaw the practice of my hobbies under your roof."

He looked beyond her to the stack of boxes. "And what is all of that?"

Millie replied calmly, "That is a portion of the items I will be transporting with me when I travel."

"So you have mended your engagement with Sir William?"

She could have lied and soothed his temper, but no good would come of it. Instead, she remained silent a moment too long, leaving him the opportunity to continue.

"Indeed you have not. Or at least you had not as of this afternoon, when Sir William and I met."

His expression seemed to require her to respond. Still, she remained quiet.

"Well, no matter. I cannot allow such frivolity." He glanced over his shoulder at the valet. "Take these boxes out and burn them. Then come back and do the same with all the rest."

"No!" Millie exclaimed, stunned. "Please, Father, no. Mama's Bible is in there, and . . ."

Words failed her then, and she was left to fight tears. The valet offered a pitying look as he collected the boxes.

"I want this room stripped to the walls!" He shouted to the man's retreating back. "And because it is obvious my staff knew this den of iniquity was under my roof, you can gather every last one of them and send them up here to do the job."

"Yes, Mr. Cope," the valet said from the other side of the attic.

Millie was shaking now. Though her father was a strong man, Millie felt no fear as she stood before him. Just sorrow for the incredible loss she was facing. He had struck a blow to her heart for the last time.

His gaze swept her face, and a glimmer of some

unspoken emotion flickered in his eyes as his expression softened. "You look very much like her, you know."

"Father," she said carefully, "you've taken everything else. Please, do not take the rest. I am begging you."

But the words died away without so much as a reaction from him. And then, just when Millie thought he might speak, might relent, he grasped her necklace and pulled, the gold links tearing tender flesh as they broke and fell free. The locket landed in his palm, and the cypher went rolling away to lodge beneath the worktable.

"What are you doing?" she cried.

"Making good on a promise," he said as he regarded the locket for a moment and then slipped it into his vest pocket. "Sir William has assured me you may have your bauble back after the wedding. As he and I have formed a business relationship I am not keen to see end, I am in agreement with him on this. Now, compose yourself and find a way to remedy the trouble you have caused."

She could never wed Sir William. Not after the lies he had told, and especially not when thoughts of the handsome inventor had begun to steal her heart. Even to save Mama's locket, she could not do that.

"There must be another way," she blurted out.

"I assure you there is not." Father turned his

back to walk as far as the door before pausing. "I hope someday you will realize I am doing all of this for your own good, Mildred."

"My own good?" Her back stiffened and she clenched her fists. "It appears I am losing everything, while you and Sir William have gained it all. How can you possibly insinuate that I might—"

"You always were dramatic," he said, cutting her off. "You should find Sir William at my office tomorrow afternoon. Do not miss this opportunity."

"If I will speak to him, would you allow me to keep my things?"

"Don't be ridiculous. I doubt he wishes to be burdened with a wife whose mind is on something other than him." And then he was gone.

She fell to her knees on the stained rug and pressed her face into it. Out of the corner of her eye, she spied the cypher and hurriedly stuffed it into her pocket as tears joined the linseed and turpentine and the flecks of paint on the floor covering beneath her.

Vaguely she became aware of footsteps returning. The staff arrived, eyes downcast, and their attentions were focused anywhere but on Millie. Books and paintbrushes and all the other accouterments of her private sanctum went into boxes headed for the burn barrels, while she remained anchored to Mama's favorite rug, her heart too numb now to hurt.

Sometime later, she must have closed her swollen eyes and dreamt of flying machines and handsome aviators who thought her interesting and not an embarrassment, for at a tap on her shoulder she awakened with a start. Pale lamp-light illuminated the now nearly bare room.

Cook knelt before her. Without a word, she gathered Millie into her arms and held her while she cried.

Finally Cook held the younger woman at arm's length and offered her a handkerchief of fine linen embroidered with the stylized family crest.

"Land and sea," she said when she noticed Millie looking.

"The same as my pearls," Millie whispered as she looked up into the old woman's eyes.

"It was a gift, and now I'm giving it to you." She paused to take the square of cloth from Millie's hand. "Now, let's see what we can do to get you fixed up here," she said as she dabbed at Millie's face. "You're still just as pretty as your mama."

"Father said I look very much like her."

"You do," she said gently, "and that may be why he finds it so hard to see you when he just as well might be looking at her." She sighed. "Come on, child. Let's get out of this room. There's no reason to stay and watch it all go."

Millie allowed Cook to help her stand and then followed as far as the door. Pausing in the doorway, she turned back to see the effect of the dismantling of her sanctuary.

"Why did You allow this, God?" she whispered as her fingers curled around the edge of the door.

"Come on now," Cook urged. "You don't need to be asking things of the Lord Almighty unless you want to hear the answer. And I'm not sure you're ready for that."

Millie turned to face the woman who had known her mother since childhood. "I've lost everything—including the locket," she said as tears once again threatened. "I cannot imagine a better time to hear from Him."

An expression Millie could not quite define crossed Cook's face and then quickly disappeared. "He got the locket and the cypher too?"

"Just the locket," Millie said. "I have the cypher in my pocket."

"Then I guess maybe you're right, but you haven't lost everything." She touched her sleeve. "You got family it's about time you knew about, child."

"Family?" Millie's heart surged. "Really?"

"Come on down to the kitchen and lets you and me have a talk. See, a Mrs. Koch who is kin to your grandmama just might still be living on Royal Street down in New Orleans. I bet if I look for it I can find the paper where I wrote the house number down."

"A relative?"

"That's right. Now come on out of this room. You have not left anything you need. It is all right there in your heart."

Eighteen

Kyle circled around the Cope house to follow the plume of black smoke. There he found a raging bonfire in the alley with a half dozen servants milling about in the cold. Though he could not hear their grumbling, it was obvious their exercise in fire building was not one they were keen to complete.

He glanced up at the room where he had left Millie some time ago. Why he had come back was a mystery to him. He had developed the photographs and found all he needed within the pictures. The items he had lined up to document for evidence showed perfectly in the light, and even the writing on the back of the locket's miniature was visible if he used his spectacles.

Perhaps it was the photograph of her that had him loitering on Adams Street at this late hour. For what he had thought was lovely while looking through the viewfinder had been breathtaking once he developed the image.

And so he had taken a walk to remove himself from the picture that stole his attention from everything else. To set his mind back on the track where he needed it to be, where he could think objectively about the elements of the treasure case without trying to reason a way that Millie and her family were not guilty of wrongdoing.

He stuffed his fists into his pockets and shrank back into the shadows as a maid tossed what appeared to be an oversized sack through the window.

The bundle landed a few yards from Kyle's feet, and he craned his neck to see what was inside. A length of pale silk showed through the loosely tied opening. A gown of some kind, or perhaps a coverlet.

Shivering, he waited for one of the servants to retrieve the bag. Then he would make his exit. But no one came.

He glanced up and saw that the maid was gone, with the window shut tight and the curtains closed. Meanwhile, those at the burn pile now huddled close with hands extended, all the better to keep from freezing.

Kyle decided to retrieve the bundle. Should someone finally break away from the warmth of the bonfire to come looking for it, they wouldn't find anything to cause them to pause in his vicinity.

Carefully, he retrieved the bag and pulled it into the shadows to look inside. Fifteen minutes later, he was standing in his hotel room ready to examine it when a knock sounded.

Palming the revolver he kept at the ready, Kyle walked to the door and opened it just enough to see who had come to call ten minutes past midnight.

"Henry?" Kyle stepped back to allow the captain inside. On his heels was Lucas McMinn. "Luke?"

He closed the door behind them and then shook hands with both men. He then shifted the burlap bag aside and offered his guests a place to sit. Lucas made himself comfortable as he smiled at his friend.

Henry shook his head. "Long train ride down. I'll stand."

"All right." Kyle looked to Lucas. "Well?"

He shrugged. "I've been temporarily lured out of retirement."

"For what purpose?"

"We are going to catch Will Tucker," Henry said. He walked to the window and pulled back the curtain to peer out into the darkness. "I take it you are aware that Miss Mildred Cope's engagement to Will Tucker has recently been in the news?"

"Tucker?" Kyle could barely say the name. "She told me she was engaged to an Englishman."

"Trueck," Lucas supplied. "Sir William Trueck. But it's Tucker. The crook didn't even bother changing the letters of his name. He only rearranged them."

Tucker and Millie? The woman he had grown to care for had been engaged to the man he was determined to track down?

Kyle knew he had seen the engagement photograph. He struggled to recall the man standing next to Millie. Unfortunately, he had been so focused on the society scientist that her fiancé might not have been in the image at all.

"Will Tucker? Here in Memphis? And engaged to . . ." He scrubbed at his face with his palms before regarding Henry and then Lucas once more. "You're certain?"

"That is what Lucas is here to confirm," Henry said. "What I do know is that Silas Cope has joined up with this Trueck fellow on several high-dollar business deals in the last few months. From what we can tell, the money is coming from the Cope bank account, which is no surprise given the man we are dealing with."

Lucas met Kyle's gaze and nodded. "Looks like he's branched out from conning women to conning their fathers."

"It appears so. If Trueck is Tucker, then colluding with an escaped prisoner is reason enough to bring Cope in. It also gives us carte blanche to go over the company books in detail to look for irregularities." Henry paused. "And hidden treasure."

Kyle thought of the cypher. Of the locket and Millie's admission of links to the pirate Lafitte.

Of his duty to report all of this once he was certain there was a good reason. The enormity of the news, however, left him numb.

"So you want me to confirm it is him?" Kyle asked as he tried not to consider how close he had been to Tucker without realizing it.

"That will be Lucas's job. Of the two of you, he has spent the most time with the man." He turned around to face them both. "I am putting you in charge of keeping track of Miss Cope."

Keeping track of Millie would be a simple matter. All he had to do was allow her into his workshop. Which would inevitably mean allowing her into his life. And that, he knew with absolute certainty, would mean allowing her into his heart. No, that had already begun. For where it came to the society scientist, Kyle was pitifully unable to keep his feelings from straying into dangerous territory.

Lucas must have realized this, for Kyle caught him studying him.

"As to how you will keep Miss Cope busy and under surveillance, I will leave that to you," Henry continued, interrupting his thoughts. "But I figure between you and Lucas you are bound to find a plan that will work."

"And if I lose her?"

Henry crossed the room to close the distance between them. "You won't. You are our best agent. That is why you are on this case."

"Casualty of my retirement," Lucas said to lighten the mood.

Unfortunately, the attempt failed miserably. Instead, Kyle saw his career reduced to baby-sitting a woman who refused to listen to him and, worse, unwittingly enticed him to kiss her. Regularly.

"But I thought that was why you put me on the treasure case," he said, though he knew his protest was weak.

"They are one and the same now."

"Am I to trust her enough to take her into my confidence?" Kyle asked.

"I will leave that decision to you."

As Henry left the window and headed for his satchel, Kyle looked at Lucas. "Did you know about any of this?"

"If you mean the connection between your friend Millie and Tucker, then no. I had no idea." He paused to lower his voice. "Is she the one you took flying on New Year's Eve, or is there another young lady in Memphis who will be disappointed at your departure?"

"I am old but not deaf," Henry said as he took two folders from his satchel. "And I will register my disappointment right now that I have not been afforded the same opportunity to go flying in your machine as whichever young lady to whom you refer." He handed one of the folders to Kyle and then gave the other to Lucas.

Kyle set his on the table in front of him. "I would offer a flight tonight, sir, but the silk needs patching."

Lucas looked up from his reading. "Oh? Was the material defective?"

"Not exactly."

Kyle opened his folder to find a copy of the engagement photograph that had appeared in the local paper. Even now, knowing that the man was Will Tucker, Kyle had to look closely to recognize him.

"Not *exactly* defective? What does that mean."

"It means," Kyle said as he set the photograph aside, "that Millie Cope is an expert with a Remington pistol." He paused only a moment to wave away any further conversation with a sweep of his hand. "Don't ask."

"Had not planned to," Henry said. "But I will ask if you have any further questions before I bunk down for the night. I am used to sleeping in my own bed and definitely not comfortable in a sleeper car anymore."

"I think we can take it from here," Lucas said. "And I know I said this on the train, but I appreciate your including me on this. I don't miss Pinkerton work, but finishing unfinished business is something I have strong feelings about."

"And I appreciate your willingness to leave that beautiful wife of yours to offer us your expertise." He nodded toward the file in Kyle's hand. "The dossier on Silas Cope was enlightening, to say the least."

"I look forward to reading it," he said, though nothing could be further from the truth. "My only experience with the man was not a pleasant one."

"Oh?" Lucas asked.

"I heard him in action, and he does not afford his daughter the kindness a father owes to his child."

Lucas's brows gathered. "How a man treats his children is a measure of how he will treat anyone else."

"Agreed," Henry said. "Ideally, we can arrest Tucker here in Memphis and save us all some trouble. But if we cannot, then I expect a plan in place."

"Yes, sir," Kyle said as he rose to walk his boss to the door.

"And, son," Henry said, his hand on the doorknob, "I know she's a pretty girl, but I'm going to depend on you to keep your head on straight and your mind on the task at hand, at least until this case is concluded."

"Absolutely." Kyle shook hands with his boss and then plastered an I-do-not-care look on his face before returning to the sofa once more.

Of course Lucas did not believe him for a minute. "Tell me about Silas Cope's daughter," he said.

"There's nothing to tell. She is a fellow scientist."

Lucas held up the engagement photograph Kyle

had just cast aside. "A beautiful one." He turned the picture so he could see it. "I cannot blame you for not recognizing Tucker. Unless you were expecting it, who would think an Englishman with that facial hair was our clean-shaven scoundrel?"

"I suppose," Kyle said. "But I cannot help but think if I had been paying better attention . . ."

"Did you meet him or talk to him at all?"

"Not that I can recall." Kyle pressed his fists against his knees, frustration building. "I just cannot see it. Millie and Will Tucker?"

"I understand. Remember, I married a woman who was also engaged to him." He shrugged. "So, now that we have that out of the way, how are we going to manage this assignment?"

"If Tucker is in Memphis, we are going to find him," Kyle said with a certainty that grew the longer he thought of it.

"You mean *I* am going to find him. A steamboat is leaving for New Orleans in the morning, and I think it might be a good idea if you were on it."

"Me and Millie." He set the folder aside and scrubbed at his face. When he looked up, he found Lucas watching him.

"You have it bad for her, don't you?"

"It seems so. But for the life of me I cannot figure out how that happened. I was minding my own business and putting together the pieces of the flying device on New Year's Eve when there she was, the prettiest woman I've ever seen standing in front of me and quizzing me on my invention. Asking about drag and lift and talking about scientific theories and reading *Faust* in the original German."

"She was reading *Faust* on the roof of the Cotton Exchange? On New Year's Eve?"

"No, that came later. In the attic."

"I'm confused," Lucas said.

"So am I." Kyle rose to spend some of his restless energy on pacing.

"No, you are not confused," Lucas pronounced with the certain authority of a man who had known Kyle since both were children. "You are in love. And for that, you have both my congratulations and deepest sympathy. Now, let's see if we can come up with a plan."

"I have an idea," Kyle said slowly, "but it would involve purchasing a ticket to New Orleans for Millie."

"Go on."

"She's a scientist, and as such, she has been inordinately curious about my workshop." His best friend grinned, and it was all Kyle could do not to knock the smile off of his face. "A clue in the treasure hunt could be better analyzed if I had access to my laboratory. I could offer to allow her to accompany me on the condition that she bring a chaperone."

To his credit, Lucas did not scoff at the idea. "It

would certainly make the job of keeping track of her easier. And if she *is* in collusion with Tucker . . ." He paused to shake his head. "I'm sorry, buddy, but it's something we do have to consider, at least for now."

"She ended the engagement," Kyle offered. Then he sighed. "But yes, you're right. We need to leave that open as a possibility."

"Separating her from Tucker really isn't a bad idea," Lucas said. "Even if only to even the odds, as it were. So, how will we go about this?"

Kyle paused to think on the problem and then decided on the surest course of action. "I'll pay her a visit first thing in the morning and invite her."

The next morning Millie followed the scents of coffee, bacon, and biscuits down the stairs, her stomach revolting at aromas she might otherwise have called delicious. Sleep had eluded her last night, leaving her pacing the floor of the empty attic until dawn before giving up to change her dress and prepare for the day.

She reached into her pocket to feel the comforting shape of the cypher. The sound of a woman's voice stalled her on the stairs.

Suppressing a sigh, she gathered her handbag to her side and determined to hurry past the dining room in the hopes of not being seen.

Her gloved hand was already touching the doorknob when she heard her name being called.

Millie froze. Mrs. Ward-Wiggins? It could not be. And yet, unmistakably, it was.

Perhaps they would believe her already gone should she hurry and turn the knob. Unfortunately, Father's valet caught her attention before she could step outside.

"Your father wishes a word with you," he said, his expression unreadable.

"Thank you," she said now, though it was a response made by habit rather than with any meaning.

Her appearance in the dining room went unnoticed for a moment, such was the intensity of the conversation between Father and the heiress. The topic completely slipped past Millie, though that was intentional. She absolutely did not care what either had to say. She remained in place a moment longer, determining that should she continue to be ignored by the occupants of the dining room, she would count that as her permission to leave.

"Mildred, darling!" Mrs. Ward-Wiggins exclaimed just then. "Do join us."

Millie gathered her handbag closer and fixed her eyes on Mama's silver coffee server on the sideboard. "Thank you, but I cannot. I am on my way out."

"You look as if you haven't slept at all, my dear. Is she always in such a hurry, Silas?" When he ignored the question in favor of an overlarge bite of scrambled eggs, she returned her attention to Millie. "Well, then. I will just share our good news and let you go on with your day. Your father has saved your reputation, Mildred," she said with far too much enthusiasm for this early hour, "and you will want to thank him for it."

Father continued to salt his eggs as if neither of them were in the room. One of the maids stood just beyond the door, her eyes downcast, though Millie knew for certain she would not miss a word that was spoken. Nor would those in the kitchen, who likely knew Millie hadn't slept nor spent a moment longer in her room than it took her to exchange yesterday's dress for today's.

Millie returned her attention to Mrs. Ward-Wiggins. "Perhaps you can tell me all about it another time."

"I will tell you now." The ferocity of her statement must have surprised both of them, for it took a moment before she continued. "Had my darling Silas not handled the situation with the press, your disaster of a postponed wedding might have been . . . well, a disaster."

She smiled at what she must have thought her cleverness and then snickered. Apparently she was waiting for Millie to offer a comment.

Only in the interest of a quick escape did she oblige. "I see," was the best she could manage with Father now watching.

"So, it's really just the most brilliant thing. I am

in awe of the man, truly. Why, when he sets his mind to something, there is just no stopping him from—"

"Oh, for goodness' sake, Freda," Father interjected as his fork clattered to the table, leaving a yellow streak on Mama's best Battenberg lace tablecloth. "I called in a favor. This morning's paper will announce our wedding."

"Your *wedding?*" Millie's fingers clutched the strap of her handbag tighter. "Congratulations, but how does your marriage help my reputation?"

"Always the selfish one," Father said. "Never did know how to think of anyone but her own precious—"

"Now, Silas," the new Mrs. Cope said. "I think a bit more explanation is required."

When he did not move to make that explanation, she leaned forward and held out her hand toward Millie. A ring that looked suspiciously like Sir William's emerald engagement gift glittered under the electric lights.

"You and your Englishman provided just the diversion Silas and I needed to carry out our secret wedding without anyone noticing." She smiled widely. "That's what your father told the newspaperman. Is that not just the most clever thing?"

Millie shook her head and met her father's eyes. "Do you really think people will believe that my engagement was to draw attention away from your marriage?"

"It is an unfortunate truth that people will believe what the newspaper tells them to believe. And that is what today's edition will read. Freda and I wanted our privacy, and you and your young man were kind enough to provide it by pretending to plan a wedding. That, of course, would put off suspicion that Freda and I would marry. Your wedding to Sir William, however, will go on at a date to be named later. Or some such nonsense."

Resisting the urge to comment on the likelihood she would ever wed anyone, much less the liar Trueck, Millie elected to remain silent. With a glance at the door, she decided it was time to go.

Her new stepmother rested bejeweled fingers on her father's shoulder. "Oh, darling, do you think the newspaper has been delivered yet?" She turned her attention toward Millie. "Be a lamb and fetch it, would you?"

Any excuse to leave was a good one, Millie decided as she turned to hurry outside. Sure enough, the newspaper was waiting on the porch.

She stepped over it and kept walking.

Nineteen

January 22, 1889
Memphis

Kyle walked up to the front door of the Cope home and knocked as if he had not made his prior entrances by virtue of a third-floor window. When no one answered, he tried again.

Finally, an older fellow dressed in formal livery opened the door with an appraising glance and a bland greeting.

"Are you expected, sir?" he asked when Kyle had stated his business.

"No, but I'm certain Miss Cope will see me."

The longer she kept him waiting, however, the less Kyle believed his statement. When the door to the parlor finally opened, he rose expectantly.

A woman dressed in servant attire and well past middle age greeted him with a smile. "I expect you were hoping to see Miss Millie," she said as she closed the door behind her. "She isn't home at present, so I wonder if I might help you."

"You could tell me when she is expected." He softened his expression. "It is of some importance that I speak to her as soon as possible."

"I see. Shall I tell her that or is there another message you would like me to give her?" She paused a moment, and then asked, "Or are you leaving soon?"

"Actually, I am," he said with no small measure of surprise. "Very soon. And no, that message will suffice."

"And she doesn't know this? That you are leaving, I mean."

"Yes, she knows." He thought for a moment and then said, "I would appreciate it very much if you would tell her that Kyle has changed his mind. She knows how to reach me and will understand what that means."

"Changed your mind, have you? That might take Miss Millie by surprise, but it doesn't surprise me a bit. I knew that would happen."

He waited for her to elaborate and then decided she was just saying what she thought he wanted to hear. In his experience, servants had a penchant for that, especially ones who wanted to remain in the household and not cause any trouble. And from the looks of this one, she had been at the game for decades.

"You're not going to ask me how I know?" She smiled. "I will tell you anyway."

"All right," he said with a chuckle. "Go ahead."

"I knew you would be back here for Miss Millie just as soon as I saw you making off with that bundle little Bridget threw out the window last night."

"You saw me?"

"I knew it was bound to happen. If you want to catch Miss Millie, I suggest you head downtown for that. She stepped out of here about an hour ago and wasn't looking too happy, what with last night's bonfire and then learning she had a new stepmama and all. She may not come back, that one. You just never know."

So Silas Cope had married again. Lucas would need to add the new Mrs. Cope to his dossier.

"And whom did you say Mr. Cope married?"

"I didn't." She shook her head. "But she has already buried two other husbands. One a Ward and the other a Wiggins."

"Thank you for that. You said Miss Cope was headed downtown, then?" he asked as he pressed past her. "Could you be more specific?"

"I could, yes, but I believe the Lord will handle the details. You just go on with your plans, son, and wait and see. There she'll be."

"You will tell her, then?" he said as he moved toward the door. "Time is of the essence."

"You have my word, young man. And I wonder if there's a reason you haven't asked me about that Trueck fellow."

Kyle stopped and turned around to face her. "All right. I am asking now. What do you know about him?"

"Just that he is not who he claims to be. Miss Millie, she figured out enough of it to tell him just what he could do with that engagement ring he never bothered to get fixed to fit her. Sitting on Mr. Silas's new wife's finger now, that emerald is."

"And where is Sir William?"

"Don't know, except that he hasn't shown himself around here since Miss Millie broke off the engagement. Mr. Silas, he thinks that man hung the moon, so maybe you will find him up at the Cotton Exchange where Mr. Silas has his office, or he might be over to the warehouses since he and Mr. Silas have been doing business together." She shrugged. "Other than that, I couldn't say."

"Thank you again," he said as he turned back toward the door. "You have been a great help."

"Glad to do it."

After a search of downtown Memphis turned up no sign of Millie, Kyle returned to the Peabody to report in to Lucas.

But his friend was out, forcing Kyle to leave a detailed message with the information he had gleaned from the woman in Silas Cope's employ.

Back downstairs, he arranged to have his crates delivered to the steamboat *Virginia Anne*, and then he confirmed with the employee at the desk that no messages had been received. He was left to hope that the servant who assured him the Lord would handle the details knew what she was talking about. For right now the detail of getting Millie Cope onto the steamboat to New Orleans seemed impossible to resolve. But God had done the impossible more than once, and he was living proof of the fact.

"Just one more time, please," he whispered as he gathered up his satchel and bid Memphis and the Peabody Hotel goodbye.

Millie walked into the Peabody as if she owned the place. It was something she had learned from Mama and, until today, had never once attempted.

Though she left her home with only her handbag, Millie had placed quite a large order of clothing with a favored dressmaker, taking what fit and putting the balance of the substantial cost on her father's account. From there she went across Second Street to purchase two trunks to hold her clothing and then had them sent to the dressmaker to be packed and delivered to the Peabody.

Just to be sure, she took a sizeable draft from Father's personal account at the Union & Planters Bank with the explanation that she would be traveling and in need of funds for the duration of her stay. By the time the news got back to her father, she hoped to be well on her way to New Orleans.

What she would do once she arrived there was a matter yet to be decided, though her intention was to go straight to the relatives Cook had only just told her existed. The thought excited and terrified her in equal measure.

Whether the home still stood on Royal Street or Mrs. Koch, the woman who was her last living link to Grandmother Cope, still lived, Millie had complete faith that her steps were being ordered by the Lord. Why else would He allow her to lose absolutely everything of value to her only to have hope returned?

She smiled. Indeed God was ordering her steps. If only He would give her just a little hint of where she was actually going. In the meantime, she had one last errand to do. One last goodbye she hoped was only temporary.

"Morning, Miss Cope," the doorman said as he stepped back to welcome her with a tip of his hat. "Lovely day today, isn't it?"

"It is indeed," she said, smiling warmly. "I wonder if I might trouble you to be on the look-out for two trunks I will be having delivered here."

"Of course, ma'am."

She wandered past the front desk and surveyed the lobby with a casual glance. A fellow behind the desk caught her eye, and she sauntered over to smile in his direction. "Might I ask you a discreet question?"

"Yes, Miss Cope."

Millie suppressed a frown. Did everyone in town know her name? She recovered quickly to give the man her attention once more.

"A friend of mine is staying here. I wonder if you might tell me which room is his."

The question itself was scandalous. The act of brazenly marching upstairs and knocking on the door of an unmarried nonrelative of the male persuasion was even more so. But desperate situations called for desperate measures, and Silas Cope had given up any right to worry about bringing shame on the family when he set fire to her prized possessions in the alley last night.

"And this friend's name?" he said as he looked over his spectacles at her.

"Oh, yes. His name is Kyle." She gave him a bright smile, acting for all the world as if he should recognize his guest by the one name alone. "Surely you know to whom I am referring," she added with a bit of the confidence that was building inside her.

"Kyle," he echoed as he bent his head to once again consult the register. "Yes, well . . ." And then he nodded. "We do have a guest named Kyle."

"Oh, good." Millie leaned forward and tried to read the ledger upside down. She might have accomplished it had he not slammed the book shut so quickly.

"Well?" she said when he merely looked at her.

"It appears he has checked out, although he has not yet had his luggage delivered to the steamboat."

"Is that so?" She calculated the risk of asking for more information and decided to take it. "And which boat is he traveling on? Or perhaps he did not say?"

"I believe he did, in fact, though I would have to check with the doorman to get that information for you." He glanced past Millie and then met her gaze again. He leaned forward and said in a discreet voice, "And I apologize, but there are folks in line behind you."

Millie turned around to see there were indeed several prospective hotel guests waiting their turn. "Oh, I am terribly sorry. Why don't I just go and ask the doorman myself?"

"Kyle?" the doorman asked. "Yes, ma'am. Mr. Kyle Russell has already left to board the *Victoria Anne*, but right there's his things still waiting to be sent over."

"And where might that vessel be headed?" she asked as if the answer was of no consequence.

"New Orleans, ma'am."

New Orleans. Interesting. Had Kyle learned something about the Lafitte treasure that sent him heading downriver? If so, he'd be going with her.

Millie offered up her sweetest smile and a five-dollar bill. "Might I trouble you to have someone fetch my trunks from the dressmaker and have them loaded about the *Victoria Anne*?"

His brows gathered. "You'll be traveling with Mr. Russell?"

Millie slyly retrieved another five-dollar bill. "Not as far as anyone knows."

The doorman glanced around and then nodded before accepting the money. "I'll have those trunks fetched over right now, Miss Cope."

Now her lone impediment was a ticket, a matter quickly settled when the ticket agent recognized her as Silas Cope's daughter. As he was handing it to her, the wind gusted, whipping it from Millie's fingers. The agent scrambled to fetch it before it flew off into the Mississippi River.

"We're lucky we didn't lose that, Miss Cope. Please be careful with it."

"Very careful." Millie placed the ticket in her handbag and snapped it shut. Then she gave the ticket agent a sideways look. "And speaking of being careful, may I ask a favor of you?"

"Anything for Mr. Silas's daughter."

"Yes, well," she said as she made a show of looking around to be certain no one was near enough to listen in. "Please do not mention that you have seen me here," she said as she added a generous tip to the voucher she was signing. "I am hoping to surprise him, and, well, you can imagine it would be no surprise if he were to be told."

The statement made no sense, and yet Millie delivered it with enough charm that the ticket agent not only agreed but also wished her well and left his position to find a member of the crew to escort her to a nicely appointed first-class cabin.

By the time the bell rang and the *Virginia Anne* pulled away from the docks, the reality of her situation had begun to sink in. After a twirl around the room, she fell on the settee with a sense of relief. As much as she wished things had happened differently, Millie's only order of business for the remainder of the day was conspiring to be seated at the same table with her dear friend Mr. Kyle Russell. The friend who owed her an explanation as to why he was rushing away to New Orleans, of all places.

Then she would figure out just how to convince him to go along with her plan. Her plan and Cook's, for she would never have found the courage to walk out of that dreadful house on Adams Street had Cook not taken her into her confidence.

Now, instead of running away, she felt as if she were running toward something. Toward family. Toward the truth. And, she hoped, also toward the Copes' share of the Lafitte treasure.

Millie rose and walked to the window, watching through a fresh downpour of January rain as Memphis grew smaller.

Her fingers went to her neck, where the only reminder of Mama's necklace was the scratch the chain had made when it was torn away. Yet with every turn of the paddle wheel, her spirits lifted. Soon enough Father would discover she had escaped and taken a substantial amount of Cope funds with her. But he had Mrs. Ward-Wiggins now, or would that be Mrs. Ward-Wiggins-Cope?

In any case, perhaps the marriage had bought her enough time to become established in New Orleans, just as it had bought Father an addition to his bank account and social standing.

This thought carried her through the tedious process of dressing without a maid and pressed at her as she stepped into the vast dining room to await her assigned table. Traveling alone was not something she feared, and yet she had never experienced it.

The room was long and overly done with decorations a bit on the gaudy side and crystal chandeliers the size of wagon wheels that swayed with the rhythm of the paddle wheels. From the golden trim to the bandstand bedecked with every sort of flounce and trim imaginable, Millie could not quite decide where to focus.

Adding to all of that was the chaos of dozens of tables set for dinner with what appeared to be a king's ransom of gold and silver, while waiters in formal wear hurried about. The effect of it all was dizzying.

"Miss Cope," said the steward who came up beside her. "Welcome to the *Virginia Anne.*"

"Thank you," she said as the sparkling crystal lights above her head took a startling jolt to the right.

"Easy now," he said as he caught her elbow. "This weather has the river churning. What do you say to my getting you to your table before that captain of ours has you and all the other diners sprawled out on the floor?"

"Yes, of course." She leaned in slightly, nothing untoward but definitely in an effort not to be overhead. "Did you receive my request for dinner seating?"

"I did, ma'am." His sweeping glance told Millie that he was holding much more interest in her than was proper. "I must say that Mr. Russell is a lucky man."

"And I must say that your impertinence has me wondering how you managed to secure this position on the *Virginia Anne*." Her steely gaze punctuated her statement. "Perhaps I should take my concerns in this regard to the aforementioned captain for his opinion on the subject."

All color faded from the steward's face as he appeared to have a sudden difficulty with speech or movement.

"Shall we?" Millie said as she nodded toward the dining room with measured cheerfulness as the vessel once again shuddered beneath her feet. "I would prefer to be sitting rather than standing at this moment."

With a nod, he escorted her to her assigned seat. Two gentlemen rose at her arrival, but neither was the man she hoped to find there.

The younger of the pair, a fellow who looked to be about Millie's age, grinned beneath a moustache that had been trained to stand at attention on both ends of its drooping length. He put her in mind of a well-dressed walrus.

The other, likely a close relative, bore the look of a gentleman gambler or, perhaps, some sort of businessman. "Merle Milligan at your service, ma'am," he said as he hurried to pull out her chair.

"Thank you, sir," she replied politely as she settled into place.

"I'd be pleased if you called me Merle." A jab from beside him alerted the man to his companion's presence. He glanced to his side and exchanged an impatient look with the other fellow before returning his attention to Millie. "And this here's my brother Sawyer. Say hello to the lady, Saw."

He did as instructed and then both men sat back down. Merle continued with the conversation. "Saw and I are traveling all the way to New Orleans. Been seeing family upriver, but it's time to get home." He shook his head. "Where are my manners? Why, we haven't given you the chance to make your own introductions. What did you say your name was, pretty lady?"

Millie opened her mouth to respond, but a familiar and decidedly male voice answered for her. "Mildred Cope."

She was far too well bred to turn and see the source. Not that she needed to, for Kyle Russell pressed his hand to her shoulder and stepped into view.

"Will you excuse us, gentlemen?" He glanced at the two men and then back at her. "May I have a word in private, Miss Cope?"

"Certainly, Mr. Russell," she said.

He gave her a half smile. "So you know."

"A man who wishes to keep secrets should never put his name on his luggage."

"Fair enough. Now, shall we?"

She could not help but notice that Kyle did not appear to care whether their tablemates responded. Instead, he had her on her feet and out of the dining room practically before either could speak.

His palm against her back gently pressed her forward. When they paused in a quiet passageway off the dining room, Millie slid him a sideways look.

One dark brow rose. Oh, but he was handsome. And here in the lamplight, with his best formal attire, his hair freshly combed and the unmistakable scent of fresh soap lingering, with the sweet recollection of being kissed . . .

Millie leaned away abruptly. What was she thinking?

"So," she said to derail her errant thoughts. "Are you surprised to see me?"

From her demeanor, it was obvious that though the Lord had answered his prayers on the matter, Kyle's message had not reached Millie before the steamboat departed. She looked far too uncertain and more than a little nervous in his presence, behavior not in keeping with a woman who had been invited to accompany him.

He decided to play along and see just what she had intended when she boarded the vessel. "What are you doing here?" he demanded when they stopped in a quiet corner of the hall. Leaning against the rosewood panels that lined the walls and matched the stateroom doors, she worried the trim on her sleeve.

Pasting on her best smile, Millie looked up into his eyes. "I am traveling to New Orleans. Why are you here?"

"Business. And you?"

"To hire you."

"Really?" Kyle didn't allow his enormous feeling of relief that she was safe and sound in front of him to show. Or his gratitude that God had worked out everything so well after all. "In what capacity, Miss Cope? Perhaps a bodyguard or a fellow to carry your purchases?"

She couldn't help smiling. "While you are most welcome to fulfill both of those positions, Mr. Russell, my greater need is a fellow to solve a puzzle for me."

"And you have chosen me for that fellow."

"I chose you well before you decided to depart Memphis, and you turned me down flat." She gave him a dare-to-deny-it look. "However, the situation has changed, and I believe that under the circumstances I can now persuade you to—"

A door opened down the hall and a couple walked out, the woman's laughter echoing in the narrow space. Millie waited until the pair had passed before continuing.

"I will get right to it. I have new information," she said softly, apparently lest prying ears might be listening from behind any of the closed doors. "And I have recently acquired the funds with which to pay for a complete investigation into my aforementioned search."

"Paid research? That is a novel idea. I generally do not receive payment until after the patent goes through, and even then I must share a portion of that payment with Mr. Toulmin."

"Truly you are insufferable, Kyle. I know you are just as intrigued with the idea of treasure as I am." She waved away his response. "Do not try to deny it. You are not only working on a project, but you are also intrigued by the puzzles I have presented."

"Indeed, Millie, I cannot deny being intrigued by the puzzles you present," he said. The truth, and yet not meant in the same way as the words he echoed from her. This rare combination of beauty and brains, gumption and grace, had not ceased to intrigue him since the moment she buckled herself into his flying machine and made off with his heart.

"I'm only intrigued by the fact that you are hesitating to answer. In fact, while you have done some impressive stalling, I must point out that you have not yet responded to what I believe is an impossible-to-refuse offer."

Was that the beginnings of a smile? Before Kyle knew for certain, she mustered up her gumption and stuck out her hand as if to shake his.

"What do you say, Kyle Russell? Shall we strike up an agreement?"

He should not take advantage of the moment or of obvious lack of understanding on just how much he needed to be striking up an agreement with her. And yet he could only smile and play along.

"And the specific terms of this agreement?"

"They are negotiable. I can offer compensation, and you can offer expertise in solving a particular sort of situation."

"Go on."

Her gaze wandered past him and then returned to focus on his eyes. "I prefer to discuss this privately, which may prove difficult in the confines of this vessel."

"Tell me what has changed. You mentioned you are following me because the circumstances are not the same. What happened?"

Her expression told him she was sorting through answers and looking for the one she wished to speak aloud. "My father . . . has made some poor decisions, chief among them choosing to marry again and . . ." She looked away again. "Well, that would be the worst of it, I think."

"No, Millie." He reached to trace the line of her jaw as he had done several times before, the image of that bonfire, of the gown being tossed out the third floor window, in his thoughts. "I do not think that is the worst of it. What else has he done?"

"I suggest we keep to the discussion at hand," she said with only the slightest quiver to her lower lip. "What would it cost for me to hire you to help find my treasure?"

Kyle pretended to consider the question.

"You have the photographs," she said before he could form a response. "Which is more than I have."

His attention went to her neck, where her upswept hairstyle revealed a scratch, vivid red against pale skin. "What happened here?" His fingers traced the edge of the fabric of her emerald gown as he noticed for the first time that the chain she never removed was gone. "Did your father do this?"

Her lack of response told him all he needed to know. Kyle's blood boiled at the thought of Silas Cope drawing blood, even a small amount.

"He has taken your necklace, then?"

"The locket and chain, yes. I have the cypher." She closed her eyes as she considered what she might next say. When she opened them, he saw pain in their depths. "The worst of it is, he has given the locket to Sir William. I am to receive it back upon our marriage."

Kyle's fist curled at the news. Tucker would not have the locket long. Of that he was certain. And the next woman who received it as a gift would have no idea of its true value.

"I see," he managed through clenched jaw.

Millie's eyes were lit now with what could only be shared anger. "I will *never* marry that man, so if the locket held a clue, then I am left to find the treasure in another way." She forced back her emotions and almost managed a believable smile. "And we are back to our original topic. This is where—and why—I am seeking your assistance."

At that moment, Kyle knew he was capable of agreeing to do almost anything she asked. This knowledge, along with a growing need to protect her from all harm, terrified him.

"I'll do what I can," he said instead. "Within reason, of course."

"Of course."

"And you will not offer payment. I will not hear of it."

"But, Kyle, your time is valuable and—"

"As is yours." He shook his head at the determination in her voice, in her expression. "You are a stubborn woman, Millie Cope."

"I am persistent. I think stubborn is something left to debate."

His chuckle echoed in the narrow passageway. "You have just proved my point."

"Then you will allow me to compensate you for

your work. The Bible says a workman is worthy of his hire, so—"

"All right," he interjected. "I give up. But here is what you can do in exchange for my work on your puzzles." He reached to touch her forehead with his index finger. "Put your brilliant mind to work on a conundrum I've reached in my work on the flying machine."

Her eyes brightened at the challenge. "What conundrum?"

"I am not happy with the ratio of fuel used to distance traveled. Any assistance in that area would be greatly appreciated."

"Yes, of course. I can see how there would be an issue with adding the extra weight required for additional fuel, and yet without the added—"

"Why don't we table this discussion as well until we can find more privacy?" He nodded toward the end of the hall as a trio of women headed their way.

"Yes, it is a bit crowded aboard this vessel, is it not?"

"Indeed." The ladies pressed past, their chatter rendering them oblivious to all but their own company.

Complete lack of situational awareness. Kyle shook his head before returning his attention to Millie.

"So until then," he said when they were once

again alone, "perhaps you and I should concentrate on enjoying the trip, at least until I can orchestrate some manner in which to discuss things without being overheard. What do you say to that?"

She looked reluctant, almost as if she preferred the relative solitude of the passageway to the public dining room. And yet when he drew her arm through his and led her back in the direction they came from, she offered no protest. Instead, she fell into step beside him and then allowed him to escort her back to the table, where a pair of gawking males was waiting.

As soon as he had Millie seated, Kyle placed his hand protectively over hers. Neither appeared to notice, not that he blamed them.

"Welcome back, Millie," said one of them, who then quickly introduced himself to Kyle as Merle Milligan and his companion as his brother Sawyer.

"Kyle Russell," he said as he stuck his hand out to distract the elder of the two. His effort failed miserably, so Kyle reached over to place his arm around Millie.

That did the trick. Both brothers shifted their attention quickly to him. And then, for good measure, Kyle leaned close to Millie so that his lips could touch her ear.

"You can either play along and pretend you find me the most fascinating man in the room, or you can suffer the attention of these two fools for the remainder of the voyage while I take my meals alone in my cabin."

Millie's giggle was girlish, but the kiss she pressed against his cheek was all woman. "You are the most fascinating man, Kyle Russell," she said, looking deeply in his eyes.

And though her acting left a little to be desired, the kiss was satisfaction enough. The Milligan brothers regarded him with what could only be awe.

Awe served up with a generous side of jealousy.

Kyle could only beam while Millie picked up her spoon to turn it over and preen at her reflection in the polished silver. Thankfully the steward arrived with their meals before further conversation was required by any of them.

"That worked out rather nicely," Millie said when the Milligan brothers made short work of their meals and then begged off any further socializing to exit the dining hall.

"And all it cost was a kiss. I hope that wasn't too painful for you."

"Not at all, though I am not sure how much longer I can endure these swinging chandeliers. I confess they are making me a bit queasy."

Kyle glanced up to see the source of her troubles. "It's the weather. It should be fine by morning, but tonight the river will be rough."

"I am not looking forward to that, or trying to sleep alone with the weather so nasty."

"Then let's see if we can't remedy that, shall we?" When she gave him an inquiring look, Kyle nodded toward the passageway. "By leaving the dining room. What did you think I meant?"

"Yes, of course." She allowed him to escort her as far as the door to her first-class cabin. "It hasn't escaped my notice that you have put off answering my question regarding my offer of employment."

Millie's formal tone stood in direct contrast to her weary expression, giving her the look of a sleepy child. And yet he was careful to take her seriously. For the one thing he could not miss was her determination.

He pressed his palm against the wooden panel and chose his words carefully. "Before I left Memphis I sent a message to you. Apparently you did not receive it."

"I did not. If you told my father, you wasted your time."

"I asked for you, not your father, and was greeted by an older servant. She was a very nice woman."

"Cook."

"Perhaps. She was dressed in a way appropriate for kitchen staff, although I got the impression she was more than just a cook."

"She is, although I have only just become aware of it. So, what was the message?"

"That I had changed my mind."

A spark of interest flared in her eyes. "About?"

He grinned. "I did not say."

"Then prepare to say now, mister," she demanded as she folded her arms and fixed him with a stern look. "Or I will have a good reason why not."

Kyle traced the line of her jaw with his knuckle again and then stepped back to allow his hand to fall at his side. How easy it would be to kiss her now. To wish her good night with an embrace.

His chuckle escaped quickly. "To invite you to my workshop." A pause. "In New Orleans."

"You never told me your workshop was there. Why not?"

"Millie," he said softly, "I promise you and I will talk more about this tomorrow, but please get some rest tonight."

Exhaustion forced her to agree. "Until tomorrow, then." She slipped inside and closed the door behind her.

Kyle waited only a moment until he heard the lock turn in the door and then he walked away. "Until tomorrow, Millie Cope."

In his cabin, one substantially less grand than Millie's, he found a note that had been left for him. It was a telegram from Lucas. Written in code and apparently sent just before the vessel departed, his words were sparse, the message not what Kyle had hoped for.

Once again Will Tucker had eluded them.

Twenty

While Millie's stateroom was more than pleasant with its sapphire blue velvet bed hangings and matching slipper chairs, the silk-covered walls were threatening to close in by lunchtime. Even so, she was not quite ready to give up on the drawing she had been sketching for the last hour, an idea based on the principles that Rufus Porter had used to extend the distance his dirigible could travel without refueling.

Yet even though the concepts intrigued her, blue skies beckoned outside the window. Last night's storm had washed away the grit from the glass and brought sunshine streaming in. Someone knocked, and Millie set the sketchbook aside to rise and answer the door.

Kyle's grin was broad as he stepped inside. "I've come to escort you to lunch." He glanced around. "Very nice room, Millie. Does your father know he is funding such an elegant escape?"

The comment stopped her cold. "Why would you ask that?"

"It was a joke, and apparently a poor attempt at one. Please accept my apology."

"Only if you will accept mine. I am a horrible grump this morning."

He removed his pocket watch to consult the time. "Technically you are a horrible grump this *afternoon*. As of ten minutes ago, to be exact."

"Let's find some lunch. My stomach is rumbling."

"What is this?" He picked up the sketchbook and studied her drawing.

"It's nothing. Just an idea I had based on something I read in Rufus Porter's pamphlet on dirigibles. It might address your conundrum, though I am not yet ready to make that claim."

"Tell me what is going on here with this." He pointed to the edge of the diagram and a representation of a fuel system alteration that she thought might be more efficient.

"You rearranged the alignment of the valve system. This way the fuel is funneled down instead of up and is used more efficiently and thus . . ." Kyle looked up. "Millie, this is brilliant."

"I don't know about that. I just thought that because I nearly ruined your flying machine, the least I could do was to consider a way I might help with an operational issue. And when you mentioned your fuel troubles . . ." She paused and then looked him in the eye with a small smile. "Had I paid more attention to my tutors, I might have been able to sew a patch on the hole I put in the silk, but the womanly arts are not my forte."

"Anyone can sew a patch, Millie. But this—"

"Honestly, Kyle. I didn't mean for you to see this. It's not finished."

"Well, no, although I can see value here." He turned the sketchbook on its side and regarded the page intently. "And this will never work."

"What?" When he pointed out what he considered to be an error in her calculations, Millie defended the numbers vehemently.

"I suppose you could argue that point," he said. "But when you factor in the variation in wind speed, then what?"

Millie considered his question and offered an answer that had them debating design and theoretical physics.

And then her stomach rumbled. Embarrassed, she took the sketchbook and set it aside with the cover firmly closed. "It's all hypothetical. Right now I am hungry and our dining partners will be wondering where we are."

"Actually, we will not be dining with the Milligan brothers. I hope you do not mind."

"Not at all," she said as she allowed him to lead her into the passageway and then shut the door. "Though I wonder how you managed it."

As she turned toward the dining room, Kyle stepped in front of her to halt her progress. "We'll be going in the other direction. Thanks to our captain, we are dining on the hurricane deck."

"You mean the roof?"

"One and the same. With the passengers all down in the dining room, I thought it might be a good place to have a conversation without being overheard." He gestured toward the exit. "After you, Miss Cope."

A few minutes later, Millie stepped onto the topmost deck of the *Victoria Anne* to find a table set for two near the rail on the opposite side of the ship from the paddle wheel. The noise from it and the boilers was louder than down below but not so loud as to make conversation impossible. And true to Kyle's assertion, other than the captain and his crew, who were secured inside the wheelhouse, they were alone on the deck.

Millie allowed Kyle to help her to her chair and then busied herself adjusting her skirts and smoothing back her hair while her companion took his seat across from her. Other than a light breeze that blew from the south, the sunny deck was blessedly warm for late January.

The table had been set much in the same way as if they were dining downstairs. Formal china and silver and a tablecloth of white linen were a stark contrast to their rooftop location. Two silver-domed serving platters containing enough food for twice their number graced the center of the table.

"All right," Kyle said after he had filled both their plates. "About our discussion last night."

"I need you to help me find the Lafitte treasure, and in return I will assist as best I can with your fuel conundrum," she said as she leaned back to regard him.

"Agreed."

"Without your expertise and the photograph you took, I have nothing to go on."

"And you are certain your father has given the locket to the man you were to marry?"

She let out a long breath and reached for her water glass. "I am sure of nothing anymore. Not since Father burned everything of value."

"Burned? What did he burn?"

"My library. All the books and sketchbooks and . . ." She paused to gather her thoughts. "All of it."

"Including a dress?"

Her brows gathered. What an odd question. "I don't know. Why?"

"Just curious." He dug into his meal with gusto, sparing her a look only when he realized she was not sharing his enthusiasm. "I thought you were hungry."

"I am, but I'm also interested in what we were just discussing. Are you purposefully stalling sharing your thoughts on how we will proceed or is that accidental?"

Her direct question surprised him. Kyle set his knife and fork aside to give her his full attention. "Neither, actually. I just happen to enjoy a good

353

steak. But enough of that. You once told me you didn't know whether your fiancé knew anything about the treasure. Would you still say that is true?"

"No. I believe he knows something, though likely it is only whatever my father has told him. And according to Cook, my father does not know the whole story."

"Go on."

"Not until I have your assurance that any treasure we find will be a secret between us that you will neither acknowledge nor share with anyone else. If not, then I have nothing to gain by giving you any more information."

"I have agreed to help you, though in what capacity and at what level of secrecy is yet to be determined."

"I am not sure I follow."

He looked around and then back at her. "I am a Pinkerton agent, Millie. And right now I am working another case."

He could tell she had not expected that, but due to her earlier guesses, she likely was not altogether surprised. "I see." She paused as if to collect her thoughts and then continued. "I don't suppose I can ask what case you are working on."

He smiled. "You can certainly ask, but I cannot tell you."

"Does your current assignment conflict with my request for help?"

"It could." Once again he reached for his knife

and fork. "However, as long as what you are asking of me does not interfere with what the agency is asking of me or cause me to break any laws, then I see no problem with agreeing to help with your search."

"Thank you for your honesty."

"Honesty is important to me, as I am sure it is to you." While she considered this, he said, "What does Sir William know about the treasure?"

"He knows the locket is valuable. At least to me. If he did not know this, then he would not be in possession of it right now. Or perhaps Father still has it and is trying to solve the puzzle himself, if indeed the locket is hiding secrets that might lead to the treasure. It's impossible to know with any certainty at this point."

"Tell me what you know about this man to whom you were engaged."

"Apparently very little. I recently discovered how many lies he told."

"Such as?"

"About his background, his mother, the location of his home." She paused to sip her water. "It seems that none of what he told me was the truth. I would not be surprised to find out that even his name was false."

"Actually, Millie . . ."

"What?" She shook her head. "Of course he lied about that too. Just who is this man my father holds in such high regard?"

"We are fairly certain Sir William Trueck is one Will Tucker, a convict who escaped from Angola Prison and is wanted for a list of charges, including duping women into agreeing to marry him and then stealing an item of value from their jewelry boxes to pass on to the next young lady."

He watched as she absorbed the news. "But he did not give me any jewelry, Kyle. Even the engagement ring he offered me ended up on another woman's finger, so it was never really a gift to me at all. It was just something staged for a newspaper photograph."

If he needed any further proof that Will Tucker was a first-class fool, Kyle only had to look across the table at the woman who might have married him. To miss that opportunity took more than the average stupidity. "You are certain of this?"

Millie nodded. And then she thought of the conversation on the roof where she had been told that the fact she already owned a set of pearls had ruined his gift. "Wait. He brought jewelry up once when we were talking. He was disappointed I already had something similar to what he wanted to give me."

"How did the conversation end?"

"With him saying 'that would be different, would it not?' Those were his exact words. I remember thinking it was an odd thing to say, but I put it off to his English customs." She gave Kyle a pained look. "He's not English, is he?"

"Best we can tell, he comes from Texas."

"Texas. I would never have guessed." She swung her gaze to meet his. "He is good at what he does, Kyle. I am not a stupid woman, and he had me completely fooled. At least for a time."

"He *is* good at what he does," Kyle said gently. "Do not be hard on yourself."

"I suppose I was looking so intently for a solution that I cast aside the details that did not fit." She shook her head. "As a scientist, I know better than that."

"But as a woman . . ."

"As a woman I depended on my father's opinion of the man." She paused to gain control of her emotions. Now was not the time to show Kyle Russell that she, too, could feel humiliated even when she did not love the man. "He introduced us. Championed him, actually. Took him in as a partner in his business. I was just the glue that held it all together. Or maybe I was his reward," she said with a chuckle that held no humor.

"And he was the means of your escape."

To hear the words said aloud took the breath from her. "Yes," she said softly, her eyes on her clasped hands in her lap. "I was also using him, something I am not proud of."

"Millie."

She looked up at Kyle. The sun slanted across

the angles of his face while the breeze teased at his dark hair.

"Try not to focus on that. Your moment of recrimination can wait. Right now we need to concentrate on two things. Capturing Will Tucker and finding your treasure."

"Absolutely," she said, although she knew there would be a time of wrestling with her own responsibility in this situation.

"Let's discuss the first order of business," he said firmly. "In order to accomplish what I have in mind, I will need your full cooperation. And I will remind you that of the two of us, I am the professional here, so I will lead all aspects of this project and you will follow."

"Of course."

He lifted a dark brow. "Millie, our success and your safety will require an understanding of the meaning of the word 'follow.' Are you so informed?"

"I fail to grasp your meaning," she said calmly, trying not to laugh.

"I mean you must assure me you fully understand the concept of abstaining from making any decisions without first consulting me." He paused to rest his palms on the table. "I will have your full cooperation or we can dissolve this partnership effective immediately."

"Don't be ridiculous," she said as she tucked an errant curl behind her ear. "Why would you assume I would make some sort of decision without consulting you? I have just given you my assurance you will take on the lead role in this matter."

He sat back and regarded her with the beginnings of a smile. "I have a length of silk with a bullet hole in it down in the cargo hold that would argue the opposite point."

Would she never live that down? "Fair enough. From this moment forth, you are in the lead. The supreme commander. The decision maker and emperor of all you survey."

"That will do for a start, though it might help if you put it in writing. Just to give you something to consult should you suffer another regrettable memory lapse or happen to—"

"I understand. I agree. Now shall we get to the topic at hand? How shall we proceed from here?"

"You want your locket and I want Tucker. Your father said Tucker would return the locket once you married him."

"Yes, but I don't intend to marry him, and he knows that."

"Unless you can convince him you have changed your mind, and then—"

"You could catch him, and I could have my necklace back."

"To which I can do a test on the evidence to see if there are any leads we can follow to find this treasure you insist exists."

"Not just me, Kyle. Cook knows it exists too. As did my mother and grandmother." Millie paused to consider whether she should save the remainder of her information or tell him now. She decided to compromise and tell him part of what Cook had said. "There is more."

"Oh?"

"I told you I had new information. I didn't board this steamboat merely to follow you to New Orleans. There was another reason." She paused and then took the plunge. "I have family there. A relative who owns a home on Royal Street. Or did, anyway. Cook says she can tell me more about my mother and grandmother and, just maybe, about the treasure."

"But will she?"

"I can only ask. At least she may know who Sophie and Julian were, and whether there was ever anything on the paper in the cypher. And then there's the key . . ."

"Yes . . ." he said, and then he stopped as he noticed the captain coming toward them and waved.

"Afternoon, Mr. Russell," the captain said to Kyle. "Lovely day. I am very glad you and your lady friend accepted my invitation to dine privately here on the hurricane deck. Things are quiet up in the wheelhouse right now, so if you are still wanting me to answer those questions you mentioned yesterday, now would be a good time to do it."

"Excellent," Kyle said. "Would you care to join us here, sir?"

"Thank you, but I believe I will stand, the better to keep me from having to jump and run should my copilot need me."

"Fair enough."

As the men conversed, Millie made an attempt to sort out the facts as she now knew them. Unfortunately, she failed miserably, leaving her to wish for a notebook and pen like the one Kyle carried in his coat pocket.

Or her sketchbook. Though she generally drew likenesses of whatever machine or chemical process captured her imagination, today would have been an excellent day to draw the complicated graph of her family tree.

Just how this Julian fellow fit in was yet to be determined. However, she had a feeling that soon she would know the answer to that. And, she hoped, to the question of what happened to Sophie—

"Millie?"

She glanced up at Kyle and realized both men were looking at her with what appeared to be humorous expressions. "Yes?"

Kyle made the introductions and then added a comment about their shared interest in solving puzzles. "Here is the other reason I wanted us to dine up here today. While conversing with the captain yesterday, I noticed something. Captain, would you show Miss Cope your cypher, please?"

"I would be glad to."

When he produced a Jefferson wheel cypher from his pocket, Millie's eyes widened. It was of the same construction as hers, the only difference being the type of coins used. While her cypher had been made of gold coins, these appeared to be silver pieces of eight.

And while hers had been worn as a charm on a necklace, the captain's cypher was attached to a chain and used as a pocket watch fob.

"It's lovely," she said as she examined the piece carefully. "Where did you get it?"

"Been in the family for years," he replied as Millie handed the cypher back to him and he returned the piece to his vest pocket. "I understand these were a dime a dozen among a certain group." He nudged Kyle. "Guess I won't be arrested by the Pinks if I admit I have a few shady characters in my family tree."

"No," Kyle said as he met Millie's gaze. "That happens in the best of families."

"It does at that." The captain grinned. "I do love the story of how old Lafitte gave those out like party favors once one of his men learned to make them. Why, I have heard there are so many cyphers around that there is no good way to tell which ones are authentic and which ones are reproductions."

Millie's heart sank at the news. And yet her

cypher had a code directly linked to Jean Lafitte.

"I understand you can buy these in certain shops in the French Quarter," Kyle said. "People can then tell all sorts of tall tales about pirates in their families without any fear of actual pirates coming back to taint their social standing."

"Look here." The captain's face colored. "If I wanted to lie about my family, I would say they were decent and upstanding folk who were law-abiding citizens all their lives. That is something worth telling people."

"You have me there, Captain," Kyle said. "But that is not what you are claiming, is it?"

"It is not. What I know to be true and what I have heard has been tangled up in the time that has passed, but I do know there was a man who kept the Baratarians gainfully if not honestly employed. I take my riverboat skills from that man."

"Lafitte?" Millie asked.

"Not that I will admit, and likely not him at all but rather one of his lieutenants. Apparently, Lafitte fell off the face of the earth sometime in the mid–1820s. No one knows what happened to him, but the old people say the swindler lived a long life."

Millie noticed that Kyle's interest piqued at the captain's use of the term "swindler."

"Do you believe that?" he asked.

"Yes, I do," the captain said with a certainty that left no doubt.

"And what of the treasure he is purported to

have buried all over the coast? What have you to say on that topic?"

"I believe a man who lives that long has plenty of time to find all of the piles of treasure he has hidden, don't you think?"

"I suppose so."

And yet as Millie heard him say the words, she longed to disagree with him. If Lafitte had recovered all the treasure, that would mean there was nothing left for her. And that just could not be considered. Not until all the options were accounted for. Millie made up her mind he was wrong in his assessment. Jean Lafitte had left plenty enough treasure to go around. All she had to do was find it.

"So I am left to wonder how much is still out there," he continued. "Though I will say that my dear old grandpappy used to say that the owner of a cypher was given the right to whatever treasure went along with it. The keys to the kingdom, as it were."

Millie's ears perked up at that. "What do you mean?"

"Just that the real cyphers have a tiny key inside. They are linked to whatever lockbox is holding the treasure.

"Now me," he said with a laugh, "well, I have yet to figure out where my treasure is. But then I never did figure out how to open it to see if a key is inside."

"Are you familiar with how cyphers work?" Kyle asked.

"I've done a little research," the captain responded as he once again pulled the cypher from his pocket.

"As have I." Kyle nodded to the silver charm. "You might want to start trying familiar names to see if any will unlock the puzzle."

"Familiar names? I'm afraid I don't follow."

"It is just a guess, but what about trying the name of the man who built the puzzle? Don't bother with regular alphabet letters. Use semaphore flags."

"And if I do not know this man's name?"

"Then that is probably where your research should go next."

"That is a right good idea. Once we get to port I am going to have to pay my mama a visit. I bet she will know where to start."

"Mamas usually do," Kyle said as he rose to slap the captain on the back. "I know mine always has an answer for everything, even when no one has asked a question. Now, I do appreciate you allowing us the courtesy of a private meal here. We both are very appreciative."

The man grinned. "The least I could do to further the cause of young love. You two enjoy yourselves up here long as you want, but I have a steamboat to run and I cannot do it out here enjoying the sunshine."

"Young love?" Millie said when the captain was a few paces away. "Why do you think he assumed this?"

"Probably because he could see your admiration for me on your lovely face, Millie," Kyle said as he returned to his seat. "Or, it might be because I allowed him to think that during the course of a conversation requesting his permission for this private lunch."

She laughed. "I suppose I can go along with that for now."

And yet as she said the words, she knew that it was far too easy to go along with the ruse that she and Kyle were more than business partners in a treasure-hunting venture. More than two people seeking to solve the same puzzle. In that moment, the real puzzle was how she could continue to pretend to be his ladylove without allowing herself to believe that it might one day be true.

"You're smiling," he said. "A penny for your thoughts."

"That is an offer I must turn down."

"And I thought we had an agreement that you would follow where I led, playing empress to my emperor. Have you so soon forgotten this?"

"Empress to your emperor? I truly do not recall making such a promise." Oh, but the subject did need an immediate change. "How did you know the captain had that cypher?"

"Situational awareness," he said, as if that were the simplest answer in the world.

"I don't follow."

"It's part of my training. You would be surprised at the things a person can learn just by observing his or her surroundings and seeking out the person in charge."

"But how did you know he had a cypher?"

"I saw it on his watch fob and asked him about it. As you might have noticed, the man is not shy about the subject of Lafitte," Kyle said with a chuckle. "But then I grew up with the subject matter, so the old pirate is a familiar fellow to me. To most New Orleanians, actually. A select few take great pride in the connection. The rest accept it as just something interesting in the family tree."

"I see." She paused to consider this. "So there would not be such a taint on a lady's reputation if Lafitte is found hiding in her family tree?"

"Taint?" He chuckled. "Down in New Orleans, men have married for less."

"You are teasing me."

"A little, but to answer your questions, no, there is no shame in these modern times with a connection to Jean Lafitte. Maybe in Memphis, but certainly not down there. However, there is one thing I should mention about the treasure you seek."

"Yes?"

"If it can be proven it comes from ill-gotten

gains, the funds are subject to seizure by the authorities."

"And how can that be proven? Is it difficult to offer the correct provenance of the treasure? I mean, we could be talking about valuables that were purchased legally."

Even as she said the words, her heart sank. What were the odds that a pirate's treasure was obtained through honest means? For the first time since she began her quest, Millie wondered whether the search was an honorable one. Whether she was chasing after a fortune that did not belong to her.

"As to proving their case? It would not be any more difficult than it will be for the government to prove the case against you. Or anyone else," he hastened to add. "Theoretically the one with truth on his side wins."

"I like that theory."

"But enough of this topic," he said. "I want to know about those drawings you made. What else do you have in that sketchbook of yours?"

"Just that," she said. "I only bought it yesterday."

"I see." He regarded her with an unreadable look. "What would you think about seeing if your plans are workable? The ones you drew in the sketchbook, I mean."

"I don't know. It was just a doodling and not anything I can say for certain will pass muster."

Kyle shrugged. "Doesn't matter. We already know the flying machine works. What we don't know is whether your tweak of the fuel system will give us the abundance of lift we need to keep the fuel conservation at the level you say it can."

"That I *theorize* it can," she corrected.

"Fair enough, but theories can only be proven through testing. I would love to get those drawings into my workshop to see if we can prove the theory behind them." He smiled. "Of course, that will mean more test flights. Once the silk is mended, that is."

"A burden I am willing to bear," she said as she matched his grin.

"A willing and able assistant. I like that. Might you have any other ideas?"

"Other ideas?" She shook her head. "None at this time, although the day is still young."

Kyle rose and helped her to her feet. "I will not be responsible for causing you to freckle, Miss Cope, so downstairs with you." She followed the line of his sight over the hurricane deck at the passengers now milling about one level below. "Unless you would prefer to join the after-lunch crowd for a stroll."

"I would rather take up sewing," she said, for she had an afternoon filled with books and deep thoughts ahead. Or perhaps a nap to make up for her fitful sleep and dreams of a strange man who looked like a combination of her father and her former fiancé chasing her.

With a nod to go with his brilliant smile, Kyle ushered her to the stairs and then assisted her down to the level below. As they entered the passageway, the elder Milligan brother stepped into view.

"Good afternoon," was all he spared them before moving on.

"Oh, dear," she said when the door closed behind him without further comment. "It appears our little ruse is working. It almost makes kissing you worth it."

"Hey now." He stopped short and turned her to face him. "I need a clarification on that."

Her heart slammed against her chest. "And what sort of clarification do you need?" she managed. "I think opinion was clearly stated."

"I beg to differ."

Goodness, was he leaning close? It must be the noonday sun that had her face feeling flushed, for she had certainly seen Kyle Russell this close before.

"All right," she said as she swiped at a curl the wind had blown out of place. "Enlighten me on any corrections required to my statement."

"I will be glad to. You stated your opinion about our kiss," he said in a most scholarly manner, "and you connected that statement to an economic action, namely to the idea that the kiss's effect was worth the cost of giving it."

"Yes."

"There are two qualifications required: What cost and . . ." Now he was certainly leaning close, heedless to the traffic going up and down the hall.

So much for situational awareness. The only situation Kyle Russell seemed to be aware of was the one going on right in front of him.

"And?" she said in a voice that sounded very much like a squeak.

"And to which kiss do you refer?"

Wit bested wisdom, and there was nothing for it. Millie raised up on her tiptoes and repeated her stellar performance from last evening's meal.

"That one," she said as she turned on her heel and left the intrepid inventor apparently speechless. "See you at dinner, Emperor."

Twenty-one

Dinner did not disappoint, nor did the evening's entertainment of music and oratory readings afterward. As Kyle escorted Millie to her stateroom, he checked his pocket watch and was stunned at how quickly the time had passed.

"You turned me down for a walk this afternoon," he said when they had reached the now-familiar spot in the passageway.

Eyes the color of café au lait looked up into his. "Perhaps you should ask again."

So he did, and a few minutes later he was

escorting the prettiest lady on the *Virginia Anne* around the promenade with the other dandies. A nod here and there fulfilled their social obligations, for no one expected two people young and in love to actually engage anyone but themselves in conversation.

When Millie paused at the aft rail, Kyle moved to stand between her and the crowd. The protective gesture had been ingrained in him during his Pinkerton training, and yet that was not why he did it. Not this time. For Millie Cope was no client of his, even if she did insist on trying to pay him to help her solve the mystery of her family's lost treasure. As much as he didn't want to admit it, she had dug in deep and was holding on tight.

If only she knew.

He would not tell her. Could not. Because then the game they played that kept the predators away from the pretty girl would turn into something much more serious. And neither of them wanted that.

She was saying something, and he struggled to concentrate. Something about the alignment of the constellations tonight and . . .

It was no use. While his ears needed to listen, all his eyes saw were her lovely lips moving.

He was the worst kind of cad, thinking only of holding her. Of standing there with his arm around her and allowing every passenger aboard the *Virginia Anne* to believe he was the luckiest man aboard.

She had stopped speaking and was now looking up at him, turning those eyes in his direction as if waiting for him to respond.

"Orion," she prompted, and he looked up in the direction of that collection of stars.

"Yes, there it is." When he looked back at Millie, he knew instantly that was the wrong answer. "I'm sorry. What were you saying?"

"My science tutor."

"Ah."

Kyle prided himself on being able to fit in almost everywhere. To join in a conversation and appear as if he knew exactly what he was talking about. It was a skill that made him a top-notch Pinkerton agent. And yet at this moment, that skill was failing him badly.

"Mr. O'Ryan?" She shook her head. "You did not hear a word I said, did you?"

Just as he was about to open his mouth and give further credence to her statement, the *Virginia Anne*'s bell began to ring. *Thank You, Lord.* He shrugged as if helpless to compete with the noise.

"You know, Kyle," she said when the clanging ceased. "What with this steamboat stopping at every possible port and dock along the Mississippi, we still have a few more days of pretending ahead of us."

"We do."

Their progress downriver had seemed interminably slow. Not that he was complaining. Once they arrived in New Orleans, he would have a duty to be first and foremost a Pinkerton agent again. And Millie would go back to just being Millie.

She looked away. "I wonder if we should take our meals in our cabins. Separately, I mean."

"No," he said far too quickly.

Her gaze collided with his. "No?"

"No, I think that would be . . ."

"Inadvisable?"

"Yes, inadvisable." He reached out his hands to grip the rail beside hers.

Quietly, she moved to place her palm atop his. "All right." They stood side by side without speaking for what seemed like a very long time. "But no more kissing."

"No?" he asked as he looked down to see silvery moonlight washing across her features as she once again cast her gaze across the water.

"No. It would be . . ."

"Inadvisable," he supplied, curling his hand into hers to grasp her fingers.

"Yes," came out like a soft sigh, barely heard over the splash of the paddle wheel. "Inadvisable."

January 28, 1889
New Orleans

Stepping off the *Virginia Anne* felt like coming home. To be sure, Millie had not yet been to the city, at least not that she could recall. And yet everywhere she looked, she felt welcomed.

Not in actuality, of course, for the looks of the people were suspect, their language coarse. But they were citizens of a city she could now claim for her own.

To them it was an ordinary Monday in the dreary month of January. To her, it was her day to come home. And so she studied it all. The warehouses, the bundles of cotton piled high just as they were in Memphis, and the odd collections of vessels clogging what was indeed a wide and very brown river.

She looked to the south as thoughts of the pirate Lafitte came to mind. He had traveled this river, sailing down its depths to hide in bayous and plunder in the Gulf. And if she believed what she had been told, he had also sailed north. To Memphis.

"Move along," Kyle said firmly, his palm pressed against her back.

His tone held a note of humor his words did not convey. With a backward glance at the river, partially obscured by her companion's broad shoulder, she complied.

"Thank you. I had hoped to cross the distance between the vessel and our carriage in less than an hour," he said. He tugged on a curl and grinned.

"I believe the trouble here is that our agreement was that you would lead and I would follow. After you, Emperor."

His laughter filled the space between them as he reached to clasp her hand in his. For just a moment the world telescoped to a place where there was no dock, no ships, and no constant confusion from workmen and passengers. In that moment, it was just them. Kyle and Millie. Emperor and Empress.

And then, in an instant, it was gone and the world had returned. With it came the treacherous walk across muddy ground to the carriage awaiting them.

"I can carry you," he offered when he realized the difficulty with which she was treading across the wooden walkway.

"Don't be ridiculous. I can manage this."

And then she slid. Of course.

Had he not grasped her by the arm and kept her upright, Millie might have tumbled headlong into an amalgamation of mud, debris, and other things she preferred not to consider. She breathed slowly in and out and walked more carefully.

As she allowed Kyle to help her into a carriage, she realized the weight pressing on her heart was gone. In truth, with each mile the steamboat had rolled southward, the progression had begun. But here, in this messy, muddy, awful place, the process was complete. What had mattered in Memphis became memories to cherish or hurt to be slung off and thrown aside.

"What is wrong with you?" Kyle asked when he took his place beside her. "Or, should I say, what is right with you? Your entire countenance has changed."

"You will laugh." She struggled for a place to rest her attention and finally gave up and looked directly at him. But he was not laughing, nor did he seem amused in the least. To the contrary, his expression showed more than a little interest. Whether it was in her or the topic at hand, Millie could not say.

"Tell me anyway." His voice was low, husky almost, his eyes intent.

The carriage jerked into motion, and Millie grasped the edge of the seat with a gloved hand. "It's just that . . . well, I cannot exactly explain it, but I feel as if I am finally at home."

"Oh, that." He shrugged. "Well, as a son of this city, I suppose I should explain this is a natural phenomenon brought on by the high humidity and low elevation. Give it time and a generous dose of beignets and café au lait, and it will pass."

She reached to give his arm a playful swat. "See, I told you that you would laugh."

"I'm sorry," he said, and he truly appeared as if

he might be. "I hope you don't mind, but I have arranged for you to stay at my home. Scandalous, I know, but believe me, we will have plenty of supervision."

Millie gave him a sideways look.

"I command a staff of considerable size." He shifted toward her, warming to his topic. "And my parents are frequent visitors, even though they have a perfectly good place of their own not three blocks east. They will probably insist you stay with them."

"Would something be wrong with that?" she asked with a lift of her brow.

"Nothing except that in my mother's younger days she was quite the accomplished opera singer. Emphasis on *younger* days. Time has not been kind to Mother's vocal chords." When she giggled, he continued. "However, theirs is a marriage made in heaven, for time has also not been kind to my father's hearing. Or perhaps it has. In any event, he's practically deaf as a post, which means he cannot hear half of Mother's singing."

Now Millie was laughing out loud. "You're exaggerating."

"Am I?" He affected a wounded look. "Then you will be interested to know that in order to get in the requisite amount of practice that perfecting her craft requires, my mother has a penchant for singing everything rather than speaking it. At least behind closed doors. You should be fine in public with the two of them, but should you choose to stay in their home—"

"I think I will be fine with the original plan. It sounds as if you have quite an interesting family."

He shrugged. "I have quite an involved family. As much as I hate to admit it, I do love them, though. But then I'm rarely home."

"A pity," she said softly as the carriage turned off the wide avenue of Canal Street onto a leafy thoroughfare lined with lovely houses all fenced with variations of the same black iron.

As they rolled past wide lawns fronting mansions of red brick, white masonry, and lovely stone facades, Millie began to feel as if she were still on Adams Street. After another turn the street names switched to French, and the homes were more distinct and closer together.

"The Quarter is just up there," Kyle said with a nod. "That's where your relative lives. On Royal Street. And this is my street, the *Rue de Prytanée* or as the Americans call it, Prytania Street."

"Named for the hearth that each ancient Greek village dedicated to Hestia?"

A chuckle real and true this time. "Not that I put stock in these things, but yes, the ancients did honor Hestia, their goddess of the hearth in that way." He sobered. "Interesting in light of the fact you say you are feeling as if you are coming home."

"I am not of a mind to believe in coincidences," she said as the carriage slowed before a two-level home painted the color of buttercream and bordered with black iron railings on porches spanning both floors. Floor-to-ceiling windows spilled light out onto the manicured lawn and revealed lush drapes and what appeared to be chandeliers in every room.

Not at all what she expected of an aviator who flew about in a homemade contraption and quoted German and French.

"My humble abode," he said as the carriage rolled to a halt before a fountain of the same black iron. Splashing water vied for the sounds of someone singing off in the distance.

Kyle cringed. "Apparently we have visitors."

The front door burst open to reveal a liveried servant of extended years. On his heels was a lovely auburn-haired woman of middle age whose beautiful gown of vivid purple was accented with jewels to match.

Millie looked down at her serviceable traveling dress and sighed. Apparently she was about to meet . . .

"Mother." Kyle descended from the carriage and then reached to help Millie down. "Please won't you say hello to my friend Miss Cope? And without singing."

"Welcome, dear girl," Mrs. Russell said as she enveloped Millie in a perfumed hug. Abruptly she released her grip to point a finger at Kyle. "You did not tell me she was pretty. Why did you not think to mention it?"

"Inside, please," he said as he ushered his mother toward the door, leaving Millie to follow a step behind.

"But you are," Kyle's mother insisted as she glanced back at Millie. "You are absolutely lovely. When my son telephoned to tell me he was bringing home a colleague, I assumed you would be some stuffy college professor or something of the sort."

"Mother."

She patted her son's arm. "Kyle has an eclectic set of friends, you know. Other than dear Lucas. He is such a darling boy."

"You always did love Lucas McMinn more than me," he complained with a wink back at Millie. "And you use 'eclectic' to describe anyone who does not attend the opera on a regular basis. Now, please, let's go inside. I'm sure Miss Cope is exhausted after her trip. Might we spare her some of the family tales at least until she has had time to unpack?"

"Unpack?" His mother stalled at the door and cast a horrified look at Kyle. "You cannot have her here. I will not allow it."

He gave Millie an I-told-you-so look. "I appreciate the offer on her behalf, but Miss Cope and I will be working together on an assignment of great importance. She must have access to the workshop at all hours. Would you have her walking the streets at odd times of the night?"

"Oh." Mrs. Russell pursed beautifully painted lips. "And yet how can she possibly stay under this roof with you?"

"I have seven bedchambers, not counting the attic—an area of her Memphis home she was once quite fond of, I might add. I'm certain we can figure out something appropriate."

The reminder of her destroyed sanctuary prickled, but watching mother and son locked in battle provided entertainment enough to distract Millie.

"But the scandal, Kyle—"

"Mother, this is New Orleans. If one is not in the middle of a scandal, then that is a scandal itself."

The conundrum must have given her cause to stop and consider, for she quickly fell silent. "I do see your point," she said softly, "and yet we are good people, Kyle. Do take care to remember that, would you?"

He gave his mother a swift kiss on the cheek, an action that caused Millie to recall a similar kiss she had given him. A kiss they agreed would be most inadvisable to repeat.

"I was raised to be a good man, Mother, and I have you and Papa to thank for that. What if I were to give a dinner in honor of Millie and invite the pastor?"

"Really, that is not necessary," Millie attempted to interject.

"Would that be blessing enough for you to cease your worrying about my guest and leave us to our work?" Kyle asked, apparently oblivious to Millie's protest.

Mrs. Russell laughed then, and she gave his arm a playful pat. "You are incorrigible, but I adore you. And rest assured, dear. The pastor will be invited for dinner, and you shall regret teasing me."

"As today is Monday, I wish you luck in reaching him. You know he claims his day of rest for at least the first three days of the week."

She returned her attention back to Millie. "Impertinent, that one, but he gets it from his father. Shall we get you settled, my dear?"

"Yes, please."

"And you may stay downstairs, son," Mrs. Russell said firmly.

Kyle's amusement was hardly hidden as he offered a sarcastic, "Yes, ma'am. Though at some point I warn you I will very likely have need of my bed. Shall I just stretch out on the carpet here by the door? Or perhaps I should take my pillow and blanket and move out onto the porch. But then the neighbors might think I have passed out drunk. Where does that fall on the scandal scale?"

"This is why I like Lucas better," Mrs. Russell said with a twinkle in her eye. "He doesn't give me any sass."

"He is worse, and you know it," Kyle called as his mother led the way up the curved staircase.

After a mild debate between Mrs. Russell and the houseman on which room would be Millie's, she was ushered into a beautifully appointed suite hung with crimson curtains sprigged with gold and overlooking the lush back gardens.

It was, she noted, on the opposite side of the home from the rooms Kyle claimed for his own. This fact was made crystal clear when Mrs. Russell stated it three times between the lovely downstairs foyer and the far reaches of the second level.

"You seem quite nice," Mrs. Russell said after the houseman had left Millie's trunks and departed. "I believe we shall get along swimmingly."

"I hope so."

The older woman's eyes narrowed. "Unless you hurt my son. Then you will wish you had not darkened his doorstep. Do you understand, Miss Cope?"

Oh, my. "Yes, Mrs. Russell, I do," was the response she settled for. "And I thank you for loving your son enough to be protective of him. He is a good man and has been nothing but respectful to me."

Was that a smile? "Then you would not mind if I moved into the suite next to you for the duration of your stay?"

"Not at all," Millie said brightly. "In fact, I would welcome the female company. My mother passed away some years ago, and I miss conversations she and I had."

If Mrs. Russell was surprised at the statement, she did not show it. "I'll send a girl up to help you dress for dinner after you have had time to rest. She is not a lady's maid but she will do."

"I would be most grateful."

"You are telling me the truth, aren't you?" she said as she toyed with the bracelets on her wrist.

"That is how my mother raised me, Mrs. Russell, and so yes, I am." Millie knew a test when she heard one. If only she knew whether she was anywhere close to passing it.

"You and I shall get along just fine."

Millie finally exhaled when the door shut with Mrs. Russell on the other side of it. She exchanged her traveling clothes for a more appropriate dress of sprigged navy with linen pocket bows, this time with the help of a sweet young maid named Eliza who also dressed her hair.

"It's lovely. Thank you," Millie said when the maid had finished. She set aside the silver mirror and found Eliza watching her intently. "Is there something else?"

"Actually, there is. We were all wondering what you said to the missus."

"I don't understand. Is she upset with me?"

"Oh, no, ma'am." The maid reached to adjust a curl that had gone awry and then stood back to nod before returning her attention to Millie. "It is just that none of us have ever seen the mister's mama be so . . ." She looked away as if searching for the word. "Well, so nice. There it is. She just is not very nice when it comes to the ladies. We all know she's protecting Mr. Kyle, but goodness, the man is grown and well and able to—"

A knock was heard at the door and she went to open it. When she returned she had lost none of her exuberance.

"The mister apologizes for the earliness of the hour but wonders if you might join him downstairs for a tour of his workshop."

"I would be delighted." Millie rose and gave the mirror one last look before moving past the maid toward the door. A footman met her in the hall and led her downstairs.

She found Kyle waiting for her in an elegant circular library paneled in rosewood with bookshelves spanning the space from floor to ceiling. Overhead, a leaded glass panel with electric light illumination behind it glowed in rich colors of purple, gold, and emerald green. Here and there small baubles of gold or silver were tucked into the shelves. As she neared she noticed they were miniatures.

"A hobby of my grandfather's. When he was not making money hand over fist selling land to the Americans, he fancied himself a silversmith of some talent."

Millie turned at the sound and smiled. Kyle rose from behind an ornate but masculine desk, its top neatly set with stacks of papers and file folders. "Hello again."

"Oh, Kyle," she said on an exhale of breath. "This room, these books, and . . . oh, look at the paintings." She turned to find him watching her. "It's breathtaking."

"Much the way I felt when I saw your attic room. There is something about books one has not read that raises the curiosity level, don't you think?"

"Oh, yes. I do."

Moving toward the nearest bookshelf, she traced the title of an oversized leather volume with her index finger. By degrees, Millie became aware of her host standing behind her.

He leaned in, his arm brushing hers as he reached over her head to retrieve a slender volume. "Here," he said as he placed it in her hands. "A welcome gift from me to you."

"*Faust*," she said gently.

"In the original German."

She opened the flyleaf and then turned to the first page. The familiar words served to remind her of the book that she had lost to the flames.

Her fingers followed the words across the page as her vision swam with tears.

"Look here," Kyle said as he removed the book from her hands to set it aside. "I didn't mean to make you cry."

"No, it's just that . . ." She blinked back her tears and then mustered a smile. "I will enjoy reading it while I am here, but I cannot possibly claim it for my own."

"We shall see about that." He nudged her toward the door. "Now will you indulge me? While I like this library very much, there is another room I am even more proud of."

"Your workshop?"

Rather than take the stairs, he pressed his palm against a carved wooden panel and then stepped back as if to wait. To Millie's astonishment, the panel slipped away to reveal an opening he walked right into.

When she did not immediately follow, he stuck his head out. "Are you coming?"

"Yes, of course." She walked forward and then found herself in a metal elevator alongside her host. As the doors closed, she began to wonder what she had gotten into.

"Worried?" he asked when the lights dimmed.

"A little."

He reached into his coat and lit the pocket lantern. "I am used to the low light in this area, but it has been so long since anyone accompanied me to my workshop that I confess I did not consider that the darkness might be disconcerting to you the first time."

"Thank you."

And then the floor began to move under her feet.

Twenty-two

The sensation was somewhat like an elevator and yet the feeling was as if they were moving much slower. Very much like climbing stairs without moving her feet.

Kyle reached to grasp Millie's hand. "You are awfully quiet," he said. "We're almost there."

She looked up at him and mustered a smile. Though she was disconcerted, Millie was also fascinated. What an interesting way to access a workshop. And then the feeling of movement ceased.

"Just a moment and the door will open." He released her hand. "But first I must enter the code."

He lifted the lid on a small box to reveal a brass wheel the size of a dessert plate. Turning it right and left and then right again, Kyle convinced the door to open. Extinguishing the lantern, he stepped out into the darkness and then reached over to once again hold her hand. "Follow the sound of my voice and trust me."

"Wouldn't it be better if you just turned on the lights?" she asked as she inched forward, the platform beneath her feet moving slightly as well.

"I suppose so, but then you would not get the full effect of . . . well, you'll see." He pulled her close and then put his arm around her. "Ready?" he said.

She nodded and then realized the gesture was futile. For as much as the light in the elevator was dim, it was dark as pitch here.

"Yes, absolutely."

Millie felt him stretch off to the side, and then a blast of light blinded her. Blinking to adjust her vision to the brilliance of the electric lights over-head, she gradually began to see what appeared to be a most magical place.

Chalkboards covered with scribbling of all sorts lined one wall that seemed to go the full length of the house. Here and there they were covered with lengths of paper pasted into place or, as she observed when Kyle released her and she drifted in that direction, of a map of the world that could have covered the broad side of a barn.

She went to it and began to read. Between travelogue and scientific notes were notations about weather and barometric pressure, names of hotels alongside the Latin names for flora and fauna, and even a restaurant menu beside a chain of chemical formulas.

"Interesting," she said as she turned to face the center of the room.

Unlike her small sanctuary, this workshop could easily accommodate a dozen worktables and still have room to drive a wagon through it. Not that she would put the feat out of the realm of possibility, for it was likely he had another elevator hidden somewhere that could suit the purpose.

Looking up, she noted lamps hanging at regular intervals from beams spanning the width of the room. Each set of lamps was situated exactly to produce the best light on the table below. "Oh, Kyle. This is . . ."

He came to stand beside her. "Yes, it is." A nudge and he had her attention. "Come and experience the grand tour."

And grand it was. From one end of the room to the other, he amazed her with the contents of the vast space. Finally they came to the end, and Millie was speechless, her head swimming with ideas.

"How do you decide what you will work on first?" she asked as she settled onto a settee in a seating area built into the half-circle of windows at the far end of the workroom.

Kyle sprawled on the chair opposite her, a grin touching his lips. "It is a nice problem to have. Now, about your locket and the foolscap. I have the photograph, and I want to try something." He nodded toward the center of the room. "Come see my cryptography machine."

"Oh?" She rose and followed him, weaving around tables and all sorts of equipment, some of which she could identify and some she could not.

He stopped in front of a device that looked like an oversized box with brass plates inside and some sort of mechanism attaching one to the other. "It is only a prototype," he hedged, "but I want to see if we can get some sort of code off of the message written on the back of the miniature."

He retrieved the photograph and held it up to show her. "If you will read the inscription exactly as it is written, I will see if there is any possibility of a code there."

She did and then watched in awe as he manipulated the letters and then cranked the dials to cause the machine to begin making a low humming noise. Carefully covering the box with another piece of wood, Kyle stepped back, presumably to wait for some sort of result. After a few minutes, the noise stopped and he opened the box.

His expression of disappointment showed quickly. "Nothing."

"Oh, well." Millie set the photograph aside. "I suppose that would have been too easy."

"I suppose," he said as he stepped away from the worktable. "Now that you have seen my workshop, may I interest you in some dinner?"

She paused to choose her words carefully. "While dinner does sound lovely, the thought of spending just a little more time in here . . ." She looked up to meet his amused expression. "I have to admit I am fascinated with all of this."

"So you would like to stay here a little longer?"

Millie laughed. "I could stay here all night."

"I do not think my mother would approve." He gave her a sideways look. "And speaking of my mother, what did you say to her? She came downstairs smiling, and though I cannot recall the last time I had a woman who was not a relative staying under my roof, I can recall in excruciating detail the times my mother has sent someone away crying."

"Honestly, I do not know." She leaned against the worktable. "Maybe she just likes me."

"No, that cannot be it. My mother does not like any woman she thinks may have designs on me."

Her smile gave her away.

"Oh, so that's it. You convinced her you had no designs on me. Very clever."

"But I do not." Millie wanted the statement to be true. And yet, if pressed, she might have to admit she did indeed have something that might be the beginning of designs. Not that she would act on them. But it was definitely time to change the subject.

"I wonder if tomorrow I could arrange a visit with my newly discovered relative." She glanced his way. "That is, if you would not mind giving me assistance in finding the address."

"You will not go alone," he said, and from the look of it, his final word on the subject.

"Thank you. I have no assurance she is still there or that she will agree to see me. But if she does, and she actually knows something of my grandmother and the treasure, then we may have a solution very soon."

Kyle reached to pat the top of her hand with his palm, and the warmth instantly calmed her. When he removed his hand, she felt its absence keenly.

"So, of all these projects," she said with a sweep of her hand, "which is the one you are most keen to work on next?"

"Clever. And yet I am going to allow you to get away with that diversion because I do have something over here I think you will find fascinating. Come this way, Empress."

Her laughter echoed in the vast cavern of a room. "Now see here. Do not get carried away with this emperor and empress designation. I never officially accepted the title."

"Shall we have a swearing-in ceremony then?" He reached behind him and retrieved a length of copper piping that had been capped with some sort of red wax. Emerging from the wax were electrical wires in a rainbow of colors.

"Your scepter, m'lady," he said in an exaggerated accent.

Millie looked askance at the makeshift scepter. "And if I do not accept?"

Kyle affected what she assumed was supposed to be an angry expression. "Then you shall risk invoking the wrath of the emperor."

Again, she could only laugh. "Well, I believe I have already done that by shooting his balloon, so I am not sure what I should be concerned with."

"That's true," he said as he cast the pipe aside. "I suppose I shall have to continue on as emperor without an empress. It is a sad day."

"Oh, come on," she said as she nudged him with her shoulder. "What do you say I accept the position on an honorary and temporary basis? Then will you forgive me?"

"Consider yourself forgiven. Come and see this."

Hours went by as Kyle answered Millie's questions about the projects and drawings he showed her. She gave surprisingly good advice and even repaired an issue with the ladies' automatic umbrella he had been struggling with.

Finally he stepped back and removed his pocket watch to check the time. "Millie, we have officially missed dinner."

Hunched over a page of calculations, she didn't even spare him a look. "Oh?" was all she said when he repeated his statement.

He came to stand beside her. When she continued to work on her mathematic calculations, he sighed. And then the page slid away from beneath her pencil.

"Come back with that," she said as she

watched Kyle walk away, the paper dangling from his hand.

"Tomorrow, Millie," he said as he turned to face her. "All of this will still be here tomorrow, but tonight we must eat."

Her stomach had rumbled a few times, a situation easily ignored. However, Kyle Russell was not easily ignored, and that trumped her lack of concern for dining. So she returned the pencil to its place and walked toward her fellow scientist.

He set the paper aside with a smile and offered her his arm. Together they walked to the elevator. While he twirled the dial to open the door, Millie turned back to look at the workshop one last time.

Indeed, the room would still be here tomorrow. However, she wouldn't take anything for granted since her father burned her dreams. Thus, if tomorrow all of this vanished . . .

"Millie?"

He pulled her into the elevator and drew her close as the doors closed. This time he didn't bother with the personal lantern. Instead, he just held her hand as the lift descended.

"Thank you," she whispered into the dark.

"For what?" was his soft reply.

"For sharing."

His chuckle warmed her heart. "You're welcome. But, Millie . . ."

"Yes?" she said as she felt the lift slow to a stop.

"I am the one who should be thanking you."

"For what?"

The doors opened but he remained in place. "For . . ."

"Kyle?" She squeezed his hand. "Are you all right?"

He was not, but he could not possibly tell her that. He had already come close enough to telling her far too much anyway. But standing side by side in the elevator, her hand feeling so small and warm in his, he had almost blurted out things he had no business speaking aloud. Such as the reason he ought to be thanking her.

Going through the motions of releasing the lock on the door and escorting Millie out consumed precious little of his time. Too soon he found her looking at him, waiting.

And he still had plenty to say. But now was neither the time nor the place to tell her that on that elevator ride down from the workshop, he had felt like a king holding her hand.

Like emperor to her empress.

Husband to her wife.

And that thought terrified him, especially with the specter of Silas Cope's potential legal entanglements looming large.

"Kyle?"

"Oh, yes. Sorry." He reset the lock and then stepped away to allow the panel to close over the door. "What say you to a midnight supper, Millie? Just the two of us."

She grinned. "Lead on."

And so he did, escorting her toward the kitchen he had built onto the back of the home just last summer. It was a spacious and modern room with the latest in gadgets, few of which his staff were willing to use.

"Is this a machine that makes coffee?" Millie asked as she wandered toward the far side of the room.

"It is. That was Lucas's idea. He swears the day will come when a man will not want to wait for a cup to brew the old-fashioned way." Kyle shrugged. "I'm not much for it, but my father claims it makes the best coffee he's ever tasted."

Millie met his gaze. "I am not much of a coffee drinker either, so I will have to take your father's word for it." She moved on, tracing the pattern on the carved marble backsplash and then toying with the hot and cold nozzles on the sink.

Meanwhile, Kyle put together a decent meal from the remains of what might have been the evening's formal dinner. Then he motioned to the stool he had pulled up to the slablike marble counter in the center of the room. "I have shrimp gumbo over rice, fried soft-shell crabs, and what is this?" He lifted the lid on a Wedgewood serving bowl and grinned. "Bread pudding for dessert."

At her blank stare, he said, "You have never had any of this, have you?"

Millie shook her head, but her smile told him she was willing to give these strange foods a try. When she had settled onto the stool, he placed the feast in front of her.

"Where do I start?" she asked with a laugh. "With the soup, I suppose."

"That is not soup. That is gumbo, and yes, there is a difference."

"All right. Please educate me."

"Watch and learn," he said as he retrieved a bowl and placed a generous portion of rice in the bottom. Then came the gumbo, and after that he topped the mound with an unusual-looking garnish.

She took the container from his hand and wrinkled her nose. "What is that?"

"Ground sassafras root. Best thing in the world on shrimp gumbo. Go ahead. Try it."

"Oh," she said when she had tasted her first bite of gumbo. "This is good."

Kyle could only nod because his mouth was full of the best thing he had eaten all day. When he heard Millie's spoon clatter, he looked over to see she had emptied her bowl.

"Looks like you were hungry after all."

"I was curious," she corrected. "And that led to hungry."

"Fair enough. Now for the soft-shell crabs." He collected two plates and set them out, filling each with cold fried crabs.

Millie studied the plate before her and then looked at him. "I give up. How do I eat these?"

"With your hands. Like this." And then he demonstrated, making short work of eating the crab.

"You ate the whole thing!"

He nodded. "The shell is soft and edible." He paused. "Hence the name."

This time when she sampled the dish, Millie did not dig in with the same enthusiasm. Instead, she nibbled daintily.

"Not your favorite?"

She shrugged. "I generally make it a rule not to eat anything that is looking at me."

Kyle grinned. "I can fix that," he said as he came around to her side and took the crab from her hand. A moment later, he handed it back to her facing the other way. "There. Now it is not looking at you."

"You are such a help."

The clock over the fireplace mantel began to chime, rendering any response impossible. Millie swiveled to follow the direction of the sound. When she turned back around, she wore a stunned expression.

"It's midnight."

He took another bite of crab and nodded. "I told

you we were having a midnight supper," he said when he had swallowed.

"I know, but I thought you were teasing." She paused to push her plate aside. "If it is midnight, then we must have been up in your workshop for hours." A calculation was happening somewhere in her amazing brain. He could see it on her face.

"You sent for me well before dark. What was that, five? Certainly no later than six? And now it is midnight?"

He shrugged as he pulled another crab off the platter. "I find it easy to lose track of time when I am doing what I love."

And there it was. Love.

Not spoken in conjunction with the feelings churning in his heart, and yet he had certainly contemplated that term as he lay on his bunk in the dead of night aboard the *Victoria Anne.* Unable to rid himself of the idea, he had instead allowed it, made every attempt to argue against it, and failed.

The object of his thoughts smiled back at him. "As do I."

He let out a long breath and reached for the bread pudding. "Now for the only thing in the room sweeter than you, Millie Cope." A wink accompanied the statement just to keep the mood light.

She tasted the concoction and then nodded. "Oh, this is . . ." Another taste. "Amazing. And it is made from bread? I can hardly believe it."

"Day-old loaves from the French Market."

"Tell me what is in this," she said as she savored yet another bite.

And with that request, the conversation had veered back into safer territory. By the time Millie had scraped her bowl clean, he had done the same.

All thoughts of discussing how they would catch Will Tucker or find the Lafitte treasure were banished. Tomorrow would be a new day, but tonight there was nothing but a workshop, a kitchen, and a very happy Millie Cope.

Especially when he served up another helping of bread pudding.

Twenty-three

January 30, 1889
New Orleans

A winter gully-washer, as the maid termed yesterday's rainstorm, kept Millie indoors and away from making contact with her newfound relative. Instead, she had made good use of Kyle's library, zipping through the copy of *Faust* she still insisted was merely a loan and then moving on to a volume of critical essays on Shakespeare's sonnets.

With Kyle otherwise occupied with business

matters that had piled up in his absence from home, she found the hours passing at a leisurely pace. Even as she tried to lose herself in a book, Millie was aware that very soon all of this would end, and she would be forced to decide what to do next.

With Kyle occupied in his workshop, she found the hours passing at a leisurely pace. She could have joined him. He certainly had made the offer. But after the day before when they lost track of time and ended up dining at midnight, Millie determined she would be more careful. Very soon all of this would end, and she would be forced to decide what to do next.

If the treasure were found, the choices were much simpler. The only complications came in the warning Kyle had given her that the government might become involved and declare the treasure to be ill-gotten gains.

But if there was no treasure, if Sir William or Will Tucker or whatever his name was could not be found, then she would have to make other arrangements. For she could not go home to Memphis again. Not after all that had happened. Not after what her father had done.

Father.

Millie smiled as a plan emerged. Donning her wrap, she adjusted her new hat and set out down the stairs and into the brilliant late-January sunshine. Though she had not taken much notice of her surroundings, she felt sure she could find a telegraph office if she just set off walking.

And so she did, past wide lawns and narrow alleys. Picking her way over muddy patches that rivaled the ground she had traversed at the port, Millie kept walking. Now the homes were smaller, closer together, and some looked to be in need of repair.

A woman sweeping a sidewalk looked up as she passed. "*Bonjour*," she called.

Millie returned the greeting, and then asked in French where the nearest telegraph office might be. Ten minutes later, she walked out of the office, her mission accomplished.

If Father did not pass on the message of her wish to reunite with her former fiancé, then she would figure out something else to attract the man to New Orleans. And if he did, she hoped to have a response very soon.

Now to decide how to tell her host that she had given an escaped criminal his telephone number. She thought he would be proud.

Her next errand was not so easily accomplished. Finding a way to Royal Street seemed an impossible task. Writing a note and having a footman deliver it, however, was certainly something she could manage.

Millie stepped into a tiny stationer's store tucked into what almost appeared to be an alley and purchased a lovely set of writing papers and a pen. Sealing wax and a seal with a lovely floral design completed her purchase. Tucking the wrapped parcel under her arm, Millie retraced her steps toward Kyle's home.

When she returned to the house on Prytania Street, however, he was furious. She was just climbing the stairs when he came out of the library, his expression as thunderous as yesterday's weather.

"What do you mean you just walked out of here and found a telegraph office? And a stationers? Are you serious? This is New Orleans, and you have no idea of the city or what could happen to you here! And for goodness' sake, we have more paper in this house than we will ever use."

"But there was a lovely shade of crimson sealing wax that I—"

"Millie, please listen to me. No lovely crimson sealing wax is worth the risk you take when you just go walking around without an escort."

He paused, and she made an attempt to interject, her fingers gripping the curved bannister as she looked down at him from the odd vantage point of superior height. Perhaps if she could manage to tell him about the steps she had taken to contact Sir William, then he would cease scolding her.

She smiled. "Kyle, I did something you will—"

"Millie, you did something that could have put you in danger." His expression softened as he leaned against the newel post. "Has it occurred to you that people know who I am in this city? That a number of them know I work for the Pinkerton Agency?" He nodded to the secret door behind him in the foyer. "Have you not considered why I go to such extremes to keep certain things away from prying eyes? I assure you it is not my mother's penchant for nosiness that gives me concern."

"That is a relief," Mrs. Russell said as she made a grand entrance through the front doors. Resplendent in yellow silk with matching hat and trim, the older woman handed off her fur to the footman.

"Mother," Kyle said, his voice even and his expression anything but.

"Good morning, Kyle dear. While you are lecturing your lovely houseguest on safety, you might want to give consideration to the fact you left your doors unlocked."

She moved across the marble floor to give her son a kiss on the cheek before turning her attention to Millie. "Good morning, my dear," she said. "I have come to take you away from all of this for the day." And then as if she only just thought of it, Mrs. Russell glanced over at Kyle. "That is, if you can spare her."

"As a matter of fact, Mother, we do have plans—"

"Change them, unless it is something that absolutely cannot wait." Again she turned to

Millie. "Are you expected at an appointment of some sort?"

Kyle met her gaze over his mother's head and appeared to be trying to send a message that he wished her to turn down his mother's offer. At least, that is what she assumed the shaking of his head and narrowing of his eyes meant.

"There is no actual appointment, ma'am. I only thought to pay a visit to a relative."

"And this relative will still be at the same address tomorrow?" When Millie nodded, Mrs. Russell turned to Kyle. "You see, darling? Problem solved. Now do be a dear and finish your rant so that Millie and I can get on with our day." She reached to give Kyle another kiss on the cheek. "I will be waiting in the carriage, so get to the point quickly."

Millie covered her smile with her hand until the door closed behind Mrs. Russell. And then she began to giggle.

"I fail to see what is so funny," he said through clenched jaw. "Can a man not make a valid point in his own home without someone interfering?"

"Is that a rhetorical question," she managed when her giggles ceased, "or are you speaking of something specific, Emperor?"

His glare quickly softened. "Your ability to tame my mother is beyond my understanding. Therefore, I am giving you the day off to do whatever it is women do when they are allowed to roam free."

"Roam free? You do realize you sound as if you are allowing the horses out of the barn."

Ignoring her comment, Kyle pointed a finger at her. "But I warn you. My mother is relentless in her search for information, especially where it concerns me and my life. She refuses to make peace with the fact that although she manages to control my father most of the time, she cannot seem to get a handle on how to do the same thing with me. I insist you not say anything about me, my workshop, or any of the things you and I have said or done since our first meeting. I will have a promise from you on that."

Though Kyle Russell was nothing like Silas Cope, at this moment the conversation was taking a dangerous turn in that direction. Her amusement vanished. Millie crossed her arms as her temper flared.

"Well, now," she said as she carefully measured her tone. "Just look at who is trying to control whom."

If he caught any veiled reference to her father, he did not allow that to show in his expression. Instead, he turned his back on her to walk toward the door. Millie followed, in part because she wished to be gone from the conversation and from his presence, and also because she refused to allow him to so easily dismiss her.

When he turned abruptly, she nearly smacked

into him. Kyle caught her by the shoulders and held her upright.

"How can I keep you safe if you do not cooperate, Millie?" he demanded, his tone still edged with the steel of his irritation.

The door opened, and a footman cleared his throat. "Excuse me, sir, but your mother has expressed an interest in collecting Miss Cope before she ages another year."

His penitent expression almost gave Millie another round of giggles in spite of her anger with Kyle.

"Her words, sir. Not my own."

"We will continue this conversation when you return," he said to her firmly as the footman slipped outside and closed the door behind him. "And I will assume you understand the reason behind the request I have made of you."

"So it is a request now?" she asked as she slid from his grasp.

"No. Yes." His frustration showed in his tone and in the way he scrubbed at his face with his palms, leaving a lock of dark hair to fall across his forehead. "Millie, stop twisting my words. It always was a request, for I cannot possibly make demands on you, now can I?"

"Well, that is somewhat better."

"Though a woman of your intelligence should have understood I was merely stating the obvious," he continued, plunging himself right back into the inky depths of a poorly constructed argument. "A woman like my mother cannot be trusted. She is devious."

"Yes, I am." Mrs. Russell now stood at the door, a smile touching her perfectly painted lips. "And you should remember that, Miss Cope. I will stop at nothing to learn all of my son's secrets." She fixed Kyle with an amused look. "Really, son. You are a grown man. Why would I possibly wish to meddle?"

"Because it is your strong suit, and the skill you have honed best above almost all others."

"Except loving my husband and child," she said before turning her attention to Millie once more. "I believe Miss Cope can handle her own with me."

"And you claim I am one to control?" he said to Millie. "I dare you to think otherwise after you have spent a day in my dear mother's presence."

"I adore you, Kyle," Mrs. Russell said. "And, Millie, he is completely correct. I plan to try in every way I can to extract all sorts of personal information from you." She smiled warmly. "I am very good at it, so I find it only fair that you be warned."

Kyle gave Millie an I-told-you-so look before he left them. "Enjoy your day, ladies." He stalked off in the direction of the hidden panel, likely to spend another day in his workshop.

Kyle need not have worried, for from the moment

Millie entered the Russell carriage, his mother did all the talking. And singing.

For all she knew of the world of opera, Millie had never been fond of the musical genre. Perhaps it was Father's penchant for it that had turned her against it. But here in the confines of the carriage, it was Josephine Russell's vocal stylings that were completely responsible.

"Are we here already?" Mrs. Russell sang as the carriage stopped. "My, that was fast." She allowed the footman to help her out and then waited for Millie to join her. Linking arms, she marched her charge into the nearest dressmaker's shop and demanded a new wardrobe forthwith.

"But this one is fine," Millie protested. "It is not what I was used to back in Memphis, but I left rather quickly and had to settle for what I could find."

"And it shows." Mrs. Russell spoke in rapid French to the trio of merchants. Two hours later, Millie had been primped and prodded and poked with pins, but she also had the beginnings of a lovely spring wardrobe.

"Remember, I want that emerald ball gown ready for a final fitting on Friday," Mrs. Russell told the staff as Millie watched.

"Friday? But that is only two days away, madame. One and a half, if you consider it is already past lunchtime today."

The elderly man with the pincushion affixed to

his wrist began arguing in rapid French. However, Mrs. Russell seemed completely oblivious to his concerns.

"Thank you for that reminder, Jacques," she said as she moved in to give him a kiss on both cheeks that did not quite touch lips to skin. "Millie and I are famished. These fittings are absolutely exhausting. I do not know how I endure them."

When the dressmaker continued to argue the impossibility of the timetable she demanded, this time in a combination of French and English, Mrs. Russell reached out to touch his sleeve. "You are such a dear. This is why all the ladies love your work. Mr. Worth has nothing on you and your brilliance. He could learn from you, and that is the truth."

"Yes, well, Worth, he is good, but I am . . . well, I am modest. But Madame Russell, I must protest the request you are making of me."

"Oh, dear." In an instant, she affected a pout Millie could only marvel at. "And I had so hoped our dear friend would be introduced to the best of the best New Orleans society at a ball I am giving. But if the dress is not ready, then I suppose I could find one of Mr. Worth's garments for her to wear. A pity, I know, and yet . . ."

With that, Josephine Russell had calmed the dressmaker and secured an appointment for an interim fitting on Thursday at three o'clock sharp.

"I will not be available to come with you to the

fitting tomorrow, but I am sure Kyle will accompany you," she said as she settled into the carriage. "I am absolutely certain he would do anything you ask." Millie's laughter was met with an astonished look. "Do you doubt me?"

"I am afraid I do."

"Well, then." Mrs. Russell gave instructions to the driver. Turning back to her guest, she said, "You are simply not asking him correctly."

"A ball in your honor?" Kyle thundered over the sound of the carriage wheels as they rolled out of the courtyard. "Absolutely not!"

"Apparently I have not asked you correctly," Millie said softly as she shrugged deeper into her winter wrap.

He gave her a sideways look. "What was that?"

"Nothing," she said with what she hoped would be an innocent look.

"It is bad enough that my mother assumed I would have nothing better to do this afternoon than accompany you to a dressmaker's fitting."

"To be fair, you did throw quite a tantrum when I left the house unescorted. It was over sealing wax, as I recall."

"I do not throw tantrums," he stated firmly. "And if I had spoken in a forceful manner, it would have been because of the danger you put yourself into. This, however, is a dress fitting. What could possibly happen?"

"Spoken like a man who has never been poked with a pin or required to stand still practically without breathing for what feels like hours."

After a look at the expression on Kyle's face, Millie decided a change of topic was in order. "Enough of that. I wonder why there has been no response from my letter."

"You must be patient. It is possible the woman is away or . . ."

"No longer alive," she supplied. "I have thought of that. I wonder if we could check on that. Perhaps find the house after the dressmaker's fitting. Maybe just knock on the door to see if Mrs. Koch is at home."

"Unannounced? And without invitation? I don't know if that is advisable."

"Perhaps, but it is something to consider. I know you think I am impatient, but I have lived for years with the belief I had no relatives left other than my father. Though Cook has been more like family than anyone else, she is not a blood relative." She swiveled to face him. "But to find another person who shares my lineage? It is such a nice surprise."

"Agreed, but I wonder why your servant took so long to mention it. Have you considered the possibility that she has made this woman up and that there is no Mrs. Koch? Or that there is no relative of your grandmother living on Royal Street at all?"

She had, but hearing Kyle say the words aloud still stung. The carriage clattered on while Millie mulled over a response.

"There is something else, Millie. I know you feel your cook is as close to you as family." He paused as if considering his words. "Would she have any reason to want you out of your home in Memphis?"

"I am sure she has plenty of reasons for wanting me out of that home, most of them with my father as their source. She has always been quite sympathetic to my cause, as have all the other servants. Cook has been there the longest and is the most willing to speak up."

"And she knew about the treasure?"

"She did." Millie frowned. "Do you really believe she concocted a reason for me to come to New Orleans? If that is true, then—"

He reached across to grasp her hand. "Do not get ahead of yourself, Millie," Kyle said gently. "These are all suppositions."

Ahead she spied the dressmaker's shop, a welcome sight that served to distract her for the better part of an hour until finally Kyle finally declared the fitting over.

"But *monsieur*, you cannot simply take the *mademoiselle* away. These garments are works of art, and as such, the greatest care must be taken in seeing that they are executed with precision."

"Sir, these are dresses. Simply dresses."

When the dressmaker began protesting in French, Kyle matched him with an equally compelling argument.

Millie listened to the discussion from behind the curtains as the dressmaker's assistant pinned up the gown that Kyle's mother had insisted would be for the upcoming ball.

The event Kyle had decided would not take place.

"It's lovely," the girl said when she had placed the last pin into its spot.

The gown was beautiful, an elegant confection of embroidered velvet and satin that fit in all the right places and set off her figure like no other she had ever worn. Indeed, the creator of this garment was quite skilled.

He was, perhaps, every bit as good as Mr. Worth, whose garments filled her closet back in Memphis.

Or had before she left without so much as a goodbye. Who knew what Father might have done with her things as soon as he discovered she had made good on her escape.

"Perhaps you would like to show the gentleman."

She glanced up, her sad thoughts scattering. "Yes, perhaps that's a good idea," she said as the argument outside continued to escalate.

Taking one last look in the mirror, Millie walked to the curtains and slowly parted them. Instantly the room fell silent.

Kyle moved toward her and then stopped short. His admiring glance slid across her before returning to her eyes. And then he let out a long, low whistle.

Millie felt her cheeks flush as she basked in his approval. She wanted to look away but couldn't as the dressmaker began fussing with the garment, tugging on the bodice and kneeling to work pins into the hem. All the while, Kyle remained silent.

Speechless.

"Wherever you were planning to wear that dress," he finally said, "you will not be going without me. Understand?"

She grinned. "Absolutely. Though I wonder if you are insistent on that. Should I promise?"

Her teasing tone made him grin. "Yes, you should definitely promise."

"All right, then. I promise I will not go without you to the ball being held in my honor on Saturday."

Before he could respond, Millie scurried behind the curtain and remained there as long as she could manage it. Finally, she emerged to find that Kyle was no longer waiting. A glance out the window revealed him pacing back and forth.

Bracing herself with a smile, Millie stepped outside. "All done," she said cheerily.

"You tricked me."

"I did nothing of the sort." She allowed him to help her into the carriage. "And if you will recall, the conversation began with you, not me. You issued an edict, asked for a promise, and I merely agreed."

She had him there, and he knew it.

"Where to, Mr. Russell?" the driver asked.

Kyle glanced over at Millie and then gave the driver Mrs. Koch's address on Royal Street. They set off, and after offering her companion a brilliant smile of thanks, Millie concentrated her attention on the scenery, on the streets where Lafitte and his men once walked.

"Driver," Kyle called, "would you pull over up ahead at the corner of Bourbon and St. Philip Streets, please? I would like to show Miss Cope the Lafitte place."

"Very good, sir."

The carriage veered to the curb and slowed to a halt. Before the driver could open the door, Kyle was out and reaching back to assist Millie. "There it is," he said as he gestured toward a rather shabby building constructed of stucco over red bricks that showed in spots. Two windows on the second level looked out over Bourbon Street, while three doors and a smaller window were open below.

"The Lafitte brothers operated a blacksmith shop from this location," he said as he reached for her elbow and guided her around the treacherous spots in the sidewalk, or as the locals termed it, the *banquette*. "Of course, there are rumors that the brothers used the property for purposes other than the shoeing of horses."

"Yes, I know of this place from my books, but it looks very different in person."

They stopped at the door, and Millie peered inside. The space was dimly lit, a fireplace rising up through the wooden beams to fill the center of the room.

"Some say that fireplace was Lafitte's favorite place to hide his gold."

Millie smiled. "I suppose that would keep things close at hand, at least while he was in port."

"Maybe," Kyle urged her back from the door just as a pair of rough-looking fellows barged past. "But who knows? I think it is most likely just another of those Lafitte rumors."

"Surely some of the rumors have to be true," she said as she allowed Kyle to lead her to the carriage and help her inside. "I mean, he did exist, and there is no dispute that he was a pirate."

"None at all." Kyle called for the driver to continue on. "What is in dispute is what he did with all of his gains, of course, and what became of him."

"According to the books I read on the subject, there are varying theories about his exploits in his later years." She sighed. "All conjecture, I am afraid. And we know what the captain of the *Victoria Anne* believes."

Kyle settled back and made himself comfortable. "Something I have learned in my time as a Pinkerton agent is that behind most rumors and conjecture is a germ of truth. I would assume the same could be said for the Lafittes. Both Jean and his brother, Pierre, were instrumental in keeping the city safe from the invading British during the War of 1812."

"So a little good and a little bad? That describes us all at one time or another, I suppose."

The carriage turned the corner and Millie spied the sign for *Rue Royale*. "Royal Street."

"Are you ready to find your answer?"

"Yes, I think I am."

He helped her out of the carriage in front of a tidy two-story home with galleries above and dark shutters on the windows.

Millie went first, walking straight to the door to grasp the ornate brass door knocker in her hand. Kyle moved into place beside her and then nodded.

Millie rapped twice and then stood back to wait for someone to answer the door. She had almost given up when the massive iron knob turned and the door opened to reveal an elderly woman dressed in a maid's black dress with starched white cap, cuffs, and apron.

"May I help you?" she asked.

"We've come to see Mrs. Koch," Millie said with a confidence she did not feel.

"Is that so?" The woman gave them her full attention but otherwise made no move.

"Might she be at home?" Kyle finally asked.

Ignoring Kyle, she focused on Millie. "Who are you?"

"Mildred Cope. I am Genevieve Cope's grand-daughter."

"I'm sorry, Miss Cope, but I cannot help you."

And then she closed the door.

Twenty-four

February 1, 1889
New Orleans

If yesterday's visit to the house on Royal Street had upset Millie, she did not let on. At least not in front of Kyle.

Instead, she rode quietly back to Prytania Street and then went to her bedchamber, where she remained until this morning. And now she sat across the table from her host, sipping café au lait and dusting herself with sugar while attempting to enjoy a breakfast of beignets.

"Did you rest well?" he asked for lack of anything better to say.

"Very," was her sparse answer. And then, "What do you suppose she meant when she said she could not help me?"

Kyle sighed as he thought of how he had wrestled with this question in her absence.

421

"Honestly, Millie, that answer could hold a number of meanings."

"That is what I thought."

"How do you wish to proceed?" he asked as he stabbed at his eggs with a fork.

"I think the only thing to do is wait. She did not deny Mrs. Koch lived there, nor did she confirm it."

"True."

Silence fell between them. When the footman brought in a folded note written on the paper only used for telephone messages, Kyle set his fork aside.

He glanced at it and then nearly dropped it. "Millie," he said slowly, "did you give anyone my telephone number?"

"Oh," she said as she returned the sugary fried donut to her plate. "Yes, I did. I tried to tell you but you were not amenable to listening. You were having a tantrum."

"I do not have tantrums." He waved the paper at her. "However, I would very much appreciate it if you would not tell anyone else how to reach me without my permission."

Completely ignoring his stern tone, Millie's expression brightened. She leaned forward in a futile attempt to read the note he held. "Is it him?"

He placed the paper on the table and then folded it over. "To whom did you give this number?"

"Technically, my father." Before he could

comment, she held up her palm to silence him. "Hear me out, Kyle. I sent a telegram to my father asking him to contact my former fiancé. I may or may not have phrased my telegram in such a way that my father may or may not believe I wish to speak to the crook regarding how I might retrieve my locket."

"You told your father you wish to reunite with Tucker?"

"Not exactly, although if he were to surmise that from my very carefully worded telegram, then that would be his choice, not mine."

Kyle shook his head. What was it about amateurs that made them believe they could play at investigation and law enforcement?

However, much as he hated to admit it, this time Millie just might have scored quite the coup. "Apparently your Englishman has been unable to forget you and wishes you would return with him to Memphis to wed." He thumped the page. "His words exactly."

"I see."

"Do you?" Kyle let out a long breath. "You have made contact with an escaped convict, Millie."

She tilted her head toward him. "And for that you are most welcome."

He lifted a brow, unable to believe the audacity of her tone. "What do you mean?"

"*I* contacted him and now *you* can catch him."

"It's not that simple," he said as he read the

message again. "Tucker wishes to meet with you here in New Orleans. How do you propose we manage that and still keep you safe?"

"First of all, I am in no danger from that man. He has never once threatened harm. My belief is he wants my father's money and is willing to accept the role of trying to convince me to change my mind about marrying him."

He thought a moment. "Possibly. Or he has figured out that the locket he holds has a connection to a treasure he believes you can help him find."

"I suppose that could be an option, but does it matter? The goal is to send him back to prison and return my locket to me."

"Agreed. And I know how I am going to do that."

"I or we?" she asked.

"I am in charge of this matter, but I will concede I need you to play a part. If you are willing, that is."

She gave him a look that told him no answer was necessary.

"Yes," he said, smiling. "How would you like to go to a ball, Millie?"

"With you?" she asked as a grin formed.

"Technically, although Sir William Trueck will believe you are attending with him."

"If you're referring to the ball your mother is giving in my honor, that is tomorrow night. There is no way to get Sir William . . ." She shook her head. "To get Mr. Tucker to New Orleans in time."

"He's already here, Millie. The telephone number he gives here is a French Quarter exchange."

"Oh." She worried the edge of her napkin. "So . . . he is very close by."

"Apparently."

Millie pushed away from the table, her breakfast obviously forgotten. "We may have driven right by him in the carriage yesterday and not even known about it."

"Possibly." Kyle steepled his fingers and studied the now not-so-brave crime fighter. "I will not allow him to hurt you, but I need to be sure you feel up to helping catch him. I know you have agreed, but you should be aware of what you are agreeing to."

She thought only a moment. "You say he has done this to other women?" At his nod she continued. "How many?"

"I have definitive proof of four others."

"I want to help you catch this man. What would you have me do?"

"You would return his telephone call and then invite him to the ball. Be specific that you want him to bring the locket. Tell him it will be his token of good faith, and without that, you will not know whether to trust him." He watched her intently. "Can you do that?"

At her nod, Kyle tossed his napkin aside and pushed back from the table. "Then shall we get this over with? If you are ready, that is. If not, we can wait until later."

"No. Now is better."

They went to the library, where Kyle placed the call and then handed the telephone to Millie. When a male voice answered, she let out a long breath and then said, "Sir William? This is Mildred. I have received your message and wish to meet."

The remainder of the conversation was brief and to the point, at least on Millie's end. She listened intently as he said something Kyle could not quite hear.

"No, not this afternoon," Millie said, her frightened eyes meeting his gaze. "Of course I trust you. There is a ball being given in my honor tomorrow at the French Opera House, and I would very much like you to be in attendance."

Kyle gave her a nod of encouragement and she continued. "Will you do just one thing for me, please?" There was a pause and then Millie met Kyle's gaze again as she said, "Yes. How did you know?"

Tucker said something, and Millie responded with, "Then we are at an impasse. Do not think for a moment I will accept your apology without a peace offering."

She was angry now, impressively so. "Yes, a

peace offering. Returning my mother's necklace would be considered an act of good faith on your part, and that is nonnegotiable. If you do not bring it, I will consider our association permanently at an end."

When she hung up the telephone, Kyle waited for her to inform him of the results.

"He knew I wanted the locket before I asked for it." She shook her head. "He said it was worthless and he had a better gift for me."

"Probably something he has stolen from his next victim. Or a previous one." He studied her. "Do you think he will show?"

"I cannot claim to know him at all, Kyle. However, he sounded angry."

Not what he wanted to hear. An easy arrest in a public place such as the French Opera House was the way to go. Finding the locket if Tucker did not bring it along might prove impossible.

But who was he kidding? Even if the locket were returned, the possibility that it continued some link to the Lafitte treasure was far fetched at best.

He would not tell Millie that, of course, for she had set her mind on the fact that the missing information was somehow contained in that locket. Not until it was absolutely necessary.

"We can still find this treasure without the locket." She looked to him for verification.

"Eventually," was his best answer.

"And the foolscap that was folded around the key? Are you certain there are no traces of a map or some kind of clue?"

"Not completely. When not squiring you about to dressmakers, I have been spending considerable time working on it."

"I see." Her smile was immediate and exquisite. "And what are your plans for the remainder of today? I would like very much to see your work and assist you with anything further."

The idea sounded promising, but there were other items that must be handled before they could retire to the workshop. "First you and I have an errand to run."

"Oh?"

"I recall that when I first met you, your gown had a peculiar feature sewn into it. It almost got me shot."

"The pocket for my Remington," she said with a wistful look. "But I have no need for such a thing anymore. After the damage I caused with that weapon, I set the gun aside."

"Well, Miss Cope, you are about to pick it up once again because I am having the dressmaker add a pocket into tomorrow night's ball gown."

"I doubt he will be pleased at the late addition."

"I am willing to pay any extra fees he might require, and that will soothe his complaints."

As Millie fixed him with a skeptical look, he paused to think of the odious Frenchman with the

428

temper that matched his attitude. And yet, if Kyle had to spend his life appeasing women who complained about the cut of a skirt or the lace on a sleeve, he would very likely have a nasty temper as well.

"I do not want another gun, Kyle."

He sighed. "All right. You made one other threat on the roof of the Cotton Exchange that night. Do you own a knife, or was that just an empty warning?"

Her laughter answered for her.

"Are you at all acquainted with using a knife for protection?" When a shake of her head indicated she was not, he continued. "Then we will scrub our visit to the gun seller and spend some time practicing that art." When she appeared about to argue, Kyle held up his hand to stave off her protests. "Either you go into this endeavor able to defend yourself if need be, or I will summon Agent Callum to come and assist."

That did it. The change in her demeanor was subtle, and yet Kyle did not miss the narrowing of her eyes and the straightening of her spine.

"I look forward to our lessons, Kyle. I do not think any assistance will be necessary."

As it turned out, the only occasion where assistance was necessary was when he explained to his mother that the belle of the ball would be attending with an escort who was not her son.

"I just cannot have it," she sang, her operatic

response grating on nerves already rubbed raw from dealing with the purveyor of fine silks and, as of today, secret pockets.

"It was not a question, Mother, nor do I come here as your son. This is Pinkerton business," he said as he spied his father walking into the parlor. "Papa, tell her I am trying to save a woman and her stubbornness could cause her harm."

"I will not allow you to harm your mother, son," his hard-of-hearing father said. "Indeed she is stubborn, but that is no cause for—"

"That is not what he means, my dear." She reached to touch Kyle's sleeve. "You are serious. There could be danger to our Millie."

"There is some measure of risk. More than she knows, which is why I elected to come here alone."

His mother smiled. "I wondered if perhaps you were here to seek our approval of your young lady. A ball is a lovely place to propose, and you do have that exquisite ring that belonged to Grandmother Russell. What was that, darling, a Burmese ruby?"

"No, sweetheart," Papa said as he moved to give Mother a peck on the cheek. "Grandmother Russell was named Rosalind. Ruby was her sister."

Mother rolled her eyes and then returned her attention to Kyle. "So is there to be an announcement? Perhaps a declaration of some sort?"

"Let the boy be, Josephine," Papa said. "He will announce when he sees fit. Now allow him some privacy and, for goodness' sake, give him some cooperation."

His mother's astonished look was priceless. So all this time his father had only been pretending to be hard of hearing? Kyle stifled a laugh.

"Yes, all right then." Mother reached for her fan and began fluttering it beneath her nose. "If you both will excuse me, I believe I am feeling a bit faint."

Once she had scurried from the room, Papa began to chuckle. Kyle soon joined him.

"That Lucas McMinn is a good man," Mr. Russell eventually said. "The last time he came to visit, he convinced me I ought to be wearing that hearing device you made for me. He said it was better to be informed, even if I kept that detail to myself. And I must say he was right."

A close look at his father's ear revealed that the tiny receiving device was almost hidden and yet obviously fully operational. "Well, how about that?"

"I still turn it off when she sings. I guess now I will have to explain how I managed to perform the miracle of hearing her. Or maybe I will just turn the thing off so I will not hear the question. Yes, perhaps that is the way to go. The gal I married does not care whether my ears work. She loves me in spite of all that."

Kyle clapped a hand on his father's shoulder and grinned. "I hope I find something lasting like you and Mother have."

"What about this young lady your mother is all atwitter about?"

Kyle scrubbed at his face with his palms. "I do not know. She is infuriation and fascination in equal measure. When I am not with her, I wonder what she is doing, and sometimes when I am with her, I wonder what I have done for the Lord to allow me to know her." He sighed. "That sounds ridiculous."

"That sounds like love, son." He placed his hand atop Kyle's. "My advice is to marry her. You'll never find another who gets under your skin like that. The Lord only makes one per fellow, and I think you have found yours."

Ah. "Like Mother?" he managed by way of diversion.

"Oh, I hope so." Papa grinned. "No man should be without a woman who thinks she can tell him what to do. Just never let on that you are the one in charge. Once you try and convince her of that, you are sunk."

Kyle thought of his conversations on that topic. "So having her call me emperor is a bad idea?"

Laughing, Papa glanced up in the direction Mother had gone. "She can call you whatever she wants and it will not matter. What matters is whether she comes when you call her."

"Millie is not a pet spaniel, Papa. And I can assure you she will never come when I call."

"Not on an everyday basis, but when it really matters. That is when you will know." He paused. "But I think you know already, do you not?"

"Based on your criteria, yes, I think I do. Except for the spaniel part. Millie is definitely not one to answer my whistles."

Papa laughed. "Why would a man want a lapdog when he might have a feisty companion? Personally, I like a little spunk."

"So do I. Now, sir, if you will excuse me, I have some work to do."

His father fell in step beside him as he headed toward the door. "This woman is not Angelique."

That stopped Kyle cold. "No, she is not."

"Then do not find her guilty of sins she did not commit."

Kyle gave Papa a sideways look. "What are you talking about?"

"If you had no reluctance to see the end of your relationship played out again in great detail on the society page of the *Picayune*, would you be so uncertain that Millie Cope is the one the Lord has provided for your wife?"

His engagement, a society coup between two well-placed New Orleans families, had been the talk of the best circles. The upcoming wedding was an eagerly anticipated event that took over nearly every conversation for months. Had Kyle been more focused on his bride and less focused on doing well at his new position as a Pinkerton agent, he might have noticed the way Angelique spoke less and less to him about anything.

About how long conversations about wedding details and honeymoon travel gradually faded to brief discussions and then eventually to snippets of talk between two people who found little else to say to each other.

And then Angelique's grandfather let slip during Christmas dinner that he'd been instrumental in facilitating a crooked business deal between a city politician and a wealthy planter the Pinkertons were investigating. It wasn't a case Kyle was working on, but he knew of the matter through Lucas. To remain silent went against everything he knew to be right, so he told his best friend.

Angelique was furious when the scandal broke, and yet she seemed determined to go through with the wedding. Only when Kyle stood at the altar with a cathedral filled with the city's elite did he see the results of his bride-to-be's wrath. The speech on family loyalty she made at the altar, the highlights of which were transcribed in a front-page article in the *Picayune* the next morning, left no question as to whether the wedding would occur.

And the slap she landed on his cheek sealed the deal and made the headline: *THE CASE OF THE BELLIGERENT BRIDE.*

Kyle shrugged off the reminder. All of that had happened more than five years ago.

And yet had he ignored clear signs that Millie Cope was the one for him because of this? For a moment he was simply stunned at the thought.

"You cannot answer because you do not know. Figure that one out, and you will figure out the other puzzle. And I do not mean one of those cyphers you toy with."

Kyle returned home as confused as ever about his feelings for Millie. A check of his messages revealed nothing pressing beyond a request from Henry on any updates he might have.

He jotted off a note in return saying he had nothing further to report regarding the treasure hunt but did have a good lead on Tucker. He included a coded line about his plan to capture the convict tomorrow evening, and then he sent the footman off to the telegraph office.

Kyle would likely have a call from either Henry or Lucas by tomorrow. In the meantime, he turned his boots toward the workshop where Millie had been toiling alone since he left her to visit his parents.

The lift door opened to reveal her beaming face. "Come quickly, Kyle!"

Banishing the image of a spaniel hurrying to his mistress's call, he made his way toward her.

"Look at this." She gestured to the torn piece of foolscap now securely held between two pieces of glass. Where there had been nothing but aged blank paper before, a map could now be distinctly seen.

He picked up the slide and held it to the light. "Millie, how did you do this? I tried everything."

"It was an accidental discovery. I was examining the paper under the microscope to see if there was any uniform pattern to the uneven edges, thinking perhaps of a code. And then I reached for my coffee cup." She nodded to a splash of coffee on the worktable. "My clumsiness caused the liquid to spill across the microscope, an issue I was able to repair quickly. And I might have cleaned up the table had I not been distracted by the map that appeared as I dabbed off the coffee. I suspected the map was somehow hidden in the locket, but here it was all the time."

"And it only took a strong cup of chicory coffee to bring it out." He chuckled. "Apparently, Monsieur Lafitte was a coffee drinker. It is a very good thing you pursued the investigation of the foolscap." Evidence he had already discarded as irrelevant.

Decision before all options are explored is a novice's mistake. His science instructor had required this quote be memorized well before Kyle was tall enough to reach the worktable without a stool.

The map indicated a decent depiction of the Mississippi River with small tributaries marked

436

on either side. The letters *BI* were clearly drawn on the lower right quadrant of the map beside a tiny cross mark and a violin.

A note scrawled in French said four words: box inside cypress knee. Something else had once been written beneath the words, as evidenced by tiny marks that might have been letters or numbers. Unfortunately, that part of the page had been long ago torn off, the piece lost.

"After looking over the book of maps on your shelf down in the library, I believe that *BI* refers to Bell Island." She gave him a triumphant look. "If I am correct, then the treasure will be found there."

She reached to press her index finger atop the *X*, her shoulder brushing his. Millie looked up into his eyes, and her smile broadened. "We have found the treasure."

"*You* have found the treasure," Kyle corrected as he set the glass panels aside and turned his full attention on her. "You have found the treasure," he repeated. "You, Millie Cope, have achieved what no one else could."

Her giggle began softly and then bubbled up into a full chuckle. Enchanted, Kyle could only sweep her into an embrace and join her in gales of laughter.

And then he knew for sure that she had achieved what no one else could. For somehow she had caused him to not only fall crazy deep in love with her, but she had also managed to make him not care one whit what might appear in the social pages of the *Picayune*.

He would court her. Properly, as befitting a woman worthy of great love. But first Tucker had to be caught. And then there was the issue of the treasure. And her father's business dealings.

Abruptly she backed out of his embrace, her smile still in place. "Oh, Kyle," she said in a husky whisper that derailed all his thoughts. "Do you know what else this means?"

With an admission of love still on the tip of his tongue, he could only shake his head.

"It means that the locket is not needed to find the treasure." She grasped his wrists. "What Will Tucker has might have great personal value to me, but it has absolutely no value in gaining him Lafitte's treasure. I could absolutely dance with happiness."

"Dance? No. Save it for when you need it."

"What are you talking about?"

"Dancing when you are happy is easy," he said with a grin. "Too easy for someone of your brilliance. Save your dancing for when things are hard."

"That is the silliest thing I have ever heard." She gave him a playful swat and then pressed past him to gather up the slide. "We have to find this. Should we hire a boat?" She didn't wait for him to respond. "Yes, of course we should.

Making our own way there is best. Now, what do you think—"

"Millie." Kyle reached down to press his index finger against her lips. "Stop talking now."

Giggling, she did as he said.

"I am beyond proud of you, but we cannot go anywhere until the question of Will Tucker has been settled. Nod if you understand."

She nodded.

"All right. Where is your knife?"

She gestured to the adjacent worktable.

"Go get it," he said as he removed his finger from her lips. "You still have practicing to do. And then I want to show you this paging system I've been playing with. I think it will be just what we need to keep each other in sight."

"Kyle?"

He looked down at her, and it was all he could do not to kiss her right then and there. "What?"

"Thank you."

"For what?"

She shrugged. "Just . . . well, for everything."

As he watched her move off to fetch the knife that would fit beneath her pearl bracelet tomorrow night, Kyle felt his heart swell to near bursting. She was perfect, and he loved her.

Thank You, Lord. For everything.

Twenty-five

February 2, 1889
New Orleans

"At no time will you be left alone." Kyle's hand clasped Millie's, his eyes sweeping the horizon in both directions as they drove around the side of the French Opera House.

Rather than exiting the carriage up front with everyone else, Kyle had secured permission to drive around to a back entrance where their arrival would not be witnessed by Tucker or anyone else.

"Even if you do not see me, I will be there. You have my word," he said as he assisted her from the carriage and into the building.

She looked up trustingly into his eyes, and at that moment Kyle felt as though he could conquer the world.

"I believe you," she said simply.

"I'm glad." He gestured to her skirt. "Do you remember the signal?" At her nod, he said, "Test it now."

Millie reached into the nearly invisible pocket that had cost Kyle more than the price of the entire gown. At her touch, the paging button sounded a series of clicks that were audible only through the device hidden behind his ear.

"Perfect. Now the self-protection device."

"Kyle, truly it is . . ." At his look she ceased her complaint and nodded. "All right."

Stretching out her right arm, Millie slid aside the pearl bracelet to reveal a leather band hidden beneath it. With a flick of her wrist, a small knife slid into place just as they had practiced.

"Remember," he said as she returned the blade to its hiding place, "once the knife is exposed, you will have just a couple of seconds to remove the protective sheath or the blade will retract and return to its hiding place again."

"Darling, I thought my son would never part with you," Mother called as she hurried toward them.

Kyle allowed his mother to fawn over Millie for a moment and then he nudged them both inside. "I know it is fashionable to arrive late, but I think it is time you ladies made your grand entrance. What do you say, Mother?" He looked around. "And where's Papa?"

"Goodness, I have no idea where that man has got off to. He said something about having a surprise for me and then away he went." She nudged Millie. "That is what a man will do, darling. They will run if you give them a chance, and don't you forget it."

"You are being dramatic again," Kyle told her, and then he took Millie aside. "Do not let her distract you. Keep in mind situational awareness."

Millie waved his comment away and then followed his mother inside. Kyle gave the ladies a couple of steps lead time before falling in behind them.

Never had he wished for Pinkerton backup so much as when the doors opened to reveal the entire ground floor of the French Opera House filled with party guests enjoying a brisk waltz. Somewhere among them Will Tucker was lurking. Or he could have figured out that this ball was given by the mother of a Pinkerton agent bound and determined to see him tossed back in Angola and avoided the event.

Either was possible.

Rows of empty theater seats cascaded up into the rafters like layers on a cake. Behind any chair a convict with a weapon could be hiding.

Kyle looked around to find each of the fourteen policemen he had met with this morning. All appeared comfortably dressed as guests. As he buzzed each one with his contacting device, they took turns nodding almost imperceptibly.

Finally Kyle drew a relaxed breath. Until something happened, now all he could do was watch.

He faded into the shadows and leaned against the wall as the orchestra ceased their playing and his mother took the stage. Kyle had his weapon at the ready, his gaze roaming the crowd.

"Dear friends," Mother said when the applause

died away. "I have made such a wonderful discovery recently, and I had to share her with all of you."

He prayed the unpredictable woman would keep to the script upon which they both agreed. To say the wrong thing in Tucker's presence could ruin everything.

"I wish to present to you a young lady new to this city but very dear to me and my family."

Kyle frowned. She was not supposed to refer to him even in such general terms. He moved closer, with a clear view of the stage and yet out of sight of anyone who might look in his direction.

With three steps he could reach the risers. Three more and he would be center stage protecting the women who stood there. And still he felt impossibly far away.

"Mildred Cope, I would like you to meet four hundred of my nearest and dearest friends."

He rolled his eyes and then, as Millie stood beside his mother, found he could not move. He could not take his attention off of the woman who had stolen his heart.

This time the applause lasted much longer, or perhaps it just seemed that way. When she finally stepped forward to offer a smile, he held his breath.

"Thank you so much for such a wonderfully warm welcome. I may have been born in Memphis, but tonight I feel as though I am a

New Orleans native being welcomed home to family."

Again the cheers arose. Again Kyle waited them out, his nerves taut.

"So, because we are all family here, I would like to make a special introduction."

Kyle froze. What was she doing?

"Sir William Trueck, have you arrived yet?" She shaded her eyes as she looked out into the crowd. "Sir William?" she repeated.

Just as Kyle was ready to pounce and remove the crazed woman from the stage, the crowd parted. And there he was. Will Tucker in all his glory.

"Dear friends," Millie said with a smile, "please give my English friend a warm New Orleans welcome."

Tucker apparently relished the spotlight more than he allowed for caution. A moment later he had pressed past Kyle just quickly enough to prevent being collared. With three steps up the risers and three steps across the stage, he reached Millie.

What they said, Kyle could only guess at, for her smile never left her. Tucker shook hands with Mother and then waved to the crowd.

"Thank you all," Mother hurried to say. "Now shall we dance?"

As the music began again, Kyle punched the button to alert the deputies that plans had changed. Once the men had made their way up to the second level, he pressed a second code to warn them to have weapons at the ready.

He then stepped out of the shadows and traced Tucker's steps up to center stage, keeping just far enough out of the crook's peripheral vision to keep himself from being spotted.

By the time he reached up to move Millie into a place of safety, he had a tight grip on Tucker's arm. "I have fourteen deputies stationed around the perimeter of this room. One false move and you're a dead man, Will Tucker."

Tucker looked past him to Millie, who was watching them closely. "So this was all a setup."

Kyle didn't bother to respond.

"Well, good luck finding that locket, Pinkerton, because I'm not going to tell you where I hid it."

"I don't need it," Kyle said as he discreetly moved the criminal toward the risers and then down the steps. From there two of the New Orleans Police Department's finest accepted custody of him.

"Nice job, sir," one of them said as he placed handcuffs on Tucker.

Millie came up to stand beside Kyle, watching quietly as the officers hauled the defiant man away. She gently took his hand in hers. Much less gently, he freed his hand to pull her into a close embrace.

"I made a dangerous decision," she said, her face pressed against his chest.

"Yes, and just as soon as I can manage it, I am going to have a tantrum. Understand?"

"Completely," Millie replied as she attempted to smile through her tears.

"Ladies and gentlemen."

"What in the world? Papa?" Kyle shook his head as he held his companion at arm's length. "Millie, are you ready to return to the party? Because my father is on stage, and I have no idea what he is about to do."

"I am sure you all thought this little party was for our dear Millie," Papa was saying. "But those of you who have known me for any length of time will recall that I had the good fortune to marry a woman of certain vocal talents."

A smatter of applause, politely given but not sincere.

"Josey, come here," he called to Mother. "You have gifted me with your lovely voice for almost thirty years. Tonight in front of all our friends, I would like to return the favor."

Mother was beet red, her expression somewhere between shock and apoplexy. For once, she appeared to be speechless.

But when someone brought out a chair and set it on the stage, Mother settled there comfortably. A queen on her throne might have been an apt description.

Kyle placed a protective arm around Millie and led her to a spot near the stage where he could have a better view of both his parents. If a man's family was acting the fool, it was best to get a good look at them.

The orchestra leader raised his baton and nodded to Papa. Then the music began. And Papa began to sing.

The room fell silent.

Stunned silent as Papa sang to Mother from the fourth act of the *Barber of Seville*. His notes were perfect, his phrasing brilliant, his stage presence mesmerizing. Kyle could only watch in awe as the man they had all underestimated brought the crowd to tears as he sang of his love and devotion.

To Mother. In public.

"Oh, Kyle." When the song was over, Millie reached up on her toes to whisper in his ear. "Your parents are so romantic."

He groaned. "I think I need to have that tantrum now."

She shook her head. "I think you need to have that dance now."

And then the woman he loved took him by the hand and led him to the dance floor. After ten seconds in her arms, he forgot all about the fact his parents had just made fools of themselves with all of New Orleans watching.

February 7, 1889
New Orleans

The meeting between the four Pinkertons took place the following Thursday in the downtown office Kyle used when he needed complete privacy. Formerly Papa's suite of law offices, the space was rarely used unless his father decided to take on a case or needed some time out of the house.

Allowing Henry Smith the place of honor behind Papa's oversized desk, Kyle situated himself in one of the wingback chairs flanking the desk with Lucas McMinn claiming the other. Sadie Callum found a spot on the settee under the painting of Grandfather Harry Kyle, the original lawyer in the family and Mother's father.

His stern Scottish demeanor and the rimmed spectacles behind which his eyes followed all who walked past gave him the nickname Scary Harry. That Harry Kyle had a namesake in Kyle was but a small testament to the sway the old man held over Papa and Mother.

And though he had been dead almost twenty years, Kyle still looked at the painting and recalled crossing to the other side of the room rather than coming too close to Scary Harry and invoking his wrath.

"It looks like we are all here," Henry said as he

slid a file from his satchel and opened it. "So let's get this meeting underway, shall we?"

Two items were on the agenda that day: Will Tucker's arrest and the pending conclusion of the government-requested treasure hunt. While Kyle was anxious to discuss the first, he was reluctant to report on the second.

"First of all," Henry said, "I want to congratulate all of you for a job well done. And an extra thanks to you, McMinn, for agreeing to this brief return to the agency to help us with the case."

"Glad to do it, sir," Lucas said. "It has always been a source of vexation that he slipped away on my watch and I couldn't go after him."

It happened on Kyle's watch too, but unlike Lucas, he hadn't taken any bullets in the process. That the Tucker case had caused Lucas to leave the Pinkertons due to injury was what kept Kyle on the job.

"I received word this morning that Tucker is officially back in his cell and will not see the light of day for many years, thanks to that escape. The boys up at Angola send their regards, and I plan to take the whole lot of you out to Antoine's for a nice thick steak and some *Pompano en Papillote* just as soon as we finish here."

Indeed the *Pompano en Papillote* was a favorite of his, but Kyle's stomach was tied up in too many knots to be concerning himself with the thought of the fish the Alciatore family somehow cooked to perfection inside a paper pouch. Instead, all he could think of was the grilling he was about to receive.

Lucas reached over to clasp his hand on Kyle's shoulder, drawing him back from his thoughts. "We have Agent Russell here to thank for that."

"Actually," Sadie Callum said, "the way I heard the story, we have Agent Russell's lady friend, Miss Cope, to thank. And his mother gave the party that drew Tucker there in the first place."

Heat rose on Kyle's face. It figured Agent Callum would point out the accomplishments of the females.

"Well, nonetheless," Henry said, "Tucker has been captured. And much as that makes me happy, it also makes me wonder how much longer you will be with us, Agent Russell."

Kyle shifted positions, grateful that his boss had so smoothly changed the subject. "As I understand it, sir, I am still working a case, so that question would not yet be appropriate to ask until after its conclusion."

"Through March four," he said, "and duly noted, Agent Russell. Which brings us to our next order of business. Where do we stand on the Confederate gold investigation?"

Finally a question simple to answer. "From what I have been able to determine, any gold that fell off a wagon or generally went missing is long gone. Not a single contact in any of the Southern states could find any trace of it."

"Could it be that people are covering for each other?"

"Possibly, but without digging up every cow pasture and backyard south of the Mason–Dixon line, I don't see how we are going to find any of it."

Henry seemed to think on that a minute. Finally he nodded. "Then that is what I will tell our client. I'll wait until the deadline just in case one of your informants comes up with something, but am I correct in understanding you do not hold any hope in pleasant surprises?"

"You would be correct," Kyle said. "However, I will follow up with telegrams and let you know."

"Thank you." Henry consulted the document in front of him and then sat back and steepled his hands. "McMinn, would you and Agent Callum kindly give Agent Russell and me a minute alone?" He went over to open the door and then closed it when the pair had made their exit.

Kyle released long breath and waited for Henry to return to his seat. A moment passed before the chair squeaked and he leaned forward to rest his elbows on the desk.

"All joking aside, I can see you are in this up to your eyeballs with Silas Cope's daughter." He paused. "What I cannot see is where your loyalty lies. That I need to hear directly from you."

Kyle opened his mouth to respond, but his boss waved him off.

"Understand I am questioning neither your dedication to your duties nor your loyalty to the Pinkertons. But, son, you need to let me know if you are having any doubts about your ability to bring this matter to a conclusion."

Kyle gave the request the thought it deserved and then shook his head. "No, sir, I am not."

"And if Silas Cope is tangled up in the case you are working? What are you going to tell that pretty little lady?"

"That pretty lady and her father are not exactly on speaking terms. And after what he has done to her, I welcome the chance to prove he deserves jail time." He paused to let out a long breath. "However, as I sit here right now, I can look you in the eye and promise I will not allow any of this to affect the job I have been paid to do."

Henry took it all in and then nodded. "And this link to Lafitte?"

"Miss Cope has found a map." When Henry's brows rose, Kyle continued. "Which I will turn over to you if you believe that is the right thing to do."

"And where did she find this map?"

"In a charm her grandmother gave her, a piece of paper was folded around a key. Until a few days ago, that paper appeared to be blank. In fact, we thought any clues to the treasure might have been lost with the locket Silas Cope gave to Tucker."

"And how did you discover that was not the case?"

"I allowed Miss Cope the use of my workshop while I was occupied elsewhere, and during the course of her experiments on the paper she uncovered the hidden image."

"What, if anything, do you or Miss Cope plan to do about this treasure map?"

"We plan to follow it to see what is there." He shrugged. "And yes, I will keep the agency informed of anything we find."

"Admirable," Henry said. "However, I am less concerned with what you find than I am with how it got there."

"Well, sir, I am not sure how any of that could be determined."

"I see your point." He leaned back and appeared to be concentrating. Then he met Kyle's gaze. "I think I can help you with that."

"Oh?"

"We are in a gray area here, son, so here are the rules. I don't need to know about anything found with a date before 1812. If Louisiana was not a state, then there is no basis for claiming a tax, understand?"

"I do, sir."

"And if Miss Cope owns the map by virtue of the fact her granny passed it down to her, then whatever she finds using that map belongs to her unless someone can prove otherwise."

Kyle nodded. "A clarification, then. Theoretically, if we find coins or some such treasure, how would we prove someone else owns them?"

Henry's expression remained neutral, but Kyle couldn't help noticing what appeared to be a gleam in his eye. "Unless there is a receipt, I do not suppose you could."

He held Kyle's gaze a moment longer. "I wish you well in your retirement, son, whenever that might be. Unless there is something I can do to change your mind."

"No, sir. There is not."

"Fair enough." He nodded toward the door. "Go get your fellow agents."

When McMinn and Callum returned, Kyle settled back into his chair. Henry stuffed all but one of his file folders back into his satchel and then stood.

"Just have a few things before we adjourn to Antoine's for that fish. Callum, first thing tomorrow morning I will be putting in for a transfer for you from the Denver division to the one in Chicago so that you will be under my direct supervision." He held up his hands to still any protest. "It's temporary, mind you, but with McMinn already out the door and Russell heading that way soon, I need my best man . . . er, woman . . . on the Tucker case until the judge makes a final ruling."

"With all due respect, sir, Will Tucker is back in jail. All's well that ends well."

"I'll agree with that statement as soon as the judge rules on the extension to Tucker's sentence. I need a Pinkerton representative present at those proceedings, and you are the only one of the three agents who have worked the case that I can guarantee will still be in my employ a few months from now."

"So I'm not required to stay here in New Orleans until trial?"

"Not at all. The agency will inform you when you are needed here. Until then, you will continue to work the other cases you have been assigned."

"Yes, sir," she said, relief evident in her voice.

"One more thing. As of this moment I am officially removing Russell from the Silas Cope investigation due to a conflict of interest. He will transfer all his files on the matter to you by the end of the business day tomorrow."

Relief flooded Kyle as he managed a nod. "Yes, sir," came a moment later.

Henry retrieved the last remaining file from the desktop. "Callum, you are now the lead agent on the case. If you're lucky, you may get Agent McMinn to stick around long enough to give you some assistance. Otherwise, it's all yours."

Kyle looked at his friend just in time to see

Lucas shake his head. "Not unless you can convince my wife. And good luck trying to talk sense to a woman who is in the family way."

"It seems as though the investigation is all mine," she said as she took the folder from Henry's hand.

"Any more questions?" Henry asked. "Then I move we adjourn this meeting and reassemble over at Antoine's."

Kyle grinned as he offered to pick up the tab. Deep inside, he was thanking the Lord for the blessings that had been bestowed and the grace that had been given.

But most of all he was praying that if Jean Lafitte left Millie any gold or jewels, the pirate at least had the good sense not to leave a receipt.

Twenty-six

February 13, 1889
New Orleans

The treasure hunters left for Bell Island one week later. When Millie was not fending off Mrs. Russell's attempts at taking her out for teas and other social events, she had been spending her time in one of two places: the library or the workshop.

Twice she had convinced Kyle to drive past

Mrs. Koch's home on Royal Street, but both times the windows were dark and no sign of life could be seen.

Today began well before dawn with a trek through the dark to the vessel Kyle had hired for their trip down to Bell Island. Heedless to the wind chilling her face, Millie stood on the deck of the little vessel and watched as the sun rose on the horizon.

With each mile that passed, she was that much closer to whatever lay beneath the cross on the map. Kyle came to stand beside her, and for what seemed like a very long time, they remained silent.

Finally he turned to face her. "Are you sure you are ready for whatever we find?"

She looked up into eyes that were kind and concerned. "No," she said honestly, "but I cannot imagine anyone I would rather have with me right now."

They stood quietly for a moment, and then Kyle glanced her way. "The agency took me off your father's case."

Millie could only nod. She had given very little thought to Silas Cope since escaping his home, and the reminder of him prodded what was a nearly healed wound.

"Sadie Callum is taking it over."

She smiled then, no longer concerned that the pretty Pinkerton agent might have designs on Kyle.

"Mr. Russell," the vessel's pilot called. "A word, please."

Before he turned to go, he traced her jaw with his knuckle and offered her a look that promised more. She watched him walk away and knew that no matter what was at the end of this treasure hunt, she would be much richer for the experience of having known Kyle Russell.

By the time the sun was above the trees, the little fishing village of Santee came into view. Kyle ushered Millie onto land that was mostly marsh but just dry enough to walk on.

All around her the greenish brown waters of the bayou flowed lazily into the distance. Cypress trees pointed skyward, their bald knees jutting up here and there while gnarled fingers of Spanish moss teased the water's edge. A cabin not much bigger than the carriage she had ridden to the docks in was nearly hidden under a stand of pines. Kyle asked her to wait a moment as he moved to the door. When he approached it, a light flickered in the lone window.

It wasn't long before he was coming back to her with a gray-haired man at his side. The pair walked toward a stack of pirogues, those flat Cajun boats that allowed passengers to glide easily across shallow muddy water.

When Kyle beckoned, she hurried to his side. "We can take it from here," Kyle told the older gentleman.

But he appeared not to have heard. Instead, he was staring intently at Millie. "You have returned," he said softly as if awe was modulating his voice. "I told you that you would be back, but you did not believe me."

Millie inched closer to Kyle and grasped his hand. "I am sorry, sir," she told him, "but I have never been here before."

"Yes, you have," he protested. "I was just a boy, but I remember you." His gaze narrowed as if the vision were escaping. "Like sunshine on the brown bayou, your eyes." And then he shook his head. "No," he said softly. "That was so long ago. And yet, those are her eyes."

"Her?"

The man nodded. "Sophie's."

Millie's grip tightened. "Sophie? Did you know Sophie?"

"Oh, no, of course not. I only saw her the once, but I never forgot her. My granddaddy, though, he knew her. Always had a kind word for us, she did. Last I heard, she went up north and married up with some rich man. I always wondered if Julian knew."

"Julian?" Millie asked carefully. "Can you tell me about him?"

"He was something, that Julian Girod. Could catch fish like nobody's business, and when he put his mind to it, he could trap a month's worth of pelts in a weekend. He taught me how to fish and hunt on account of my granddaddy liking the bottle too much and me having to fend for myself."

"Sounds like quite a man," Kyle said. "Whatever happened to him?"

The old man shrugged. "Guess he's still living. Don't travel into New Orleans much."

"But the last time you heard from him, where was he?" Millie asked.

"That I do remember. Had him a nice house on Royal Street." He repeated the address, and Millie nearly fainted. Mrs. Koch's house.

When further questions of Julian Girod were met with no answers, Kyle supported Millie with an arm around her and then nudged her toward the pirogue, making his goodbyes as they walked.

"Just get the boat back before dark," the old man called. "Else the gators might make a snack out of you."

"No danger in that," Kyle said as he rowed toward the gathering shadows.

"Sophie and Julian were from Bell Island?" Millie asked when they were far enough from the cabin not to be overheard.

"And there appears to be a connection with the house on Royal Street." Kyle shook his head. "But one puzzle at a time, all right?"

"Right."

With each stroke the pirogue jolted forward, cutting through the coffee-brown water and leaving a rooster's tail of ripples in its wake. Here and there patches of sunlight told Millie that somewhere outside the bayou it was still midday. But in here it might have been late afternoon or, perhaps, gathering dusk. Long shadows danced across the water and teased the sides of the ancient wooden boat.

Kyle abruptly pulled back on the oars, halting their progress. "Where now?" he asked as he gestured ahead. Two paths beckoned, but only one could be correct.

Millie retrieved the map. "Left."

He steered in that direction until he found another crook in the bayou. This time he knew the direction was to the right. A few minutes later, Kyle gestured to the cypress stump shaped like a violin.

Had there been an *X*, it would have marked that exact spot. The pirogue came to a stop as Kyle reached to grab the ancient wood.

"What now?" Millie asked.

"I am going to see what is inside that stump." He reached down into the water while she prayed nothing would snap up his fingers before he could find the treasure.

"I have something." He began to pull up what appeared to be some sort of chain. At the end of the chain was a loop attached to a metal box. A small padlock secured it.

"Oh, Kyle!" Millie exclaimed. "The treasure!"

"Not so fast," he said, smiling at her enthusiasm. "Let's see if we can get this thing to open."

He held out his hand, and Millie placed the tiny key from the cypher into his palm.

"I always wondered what kind of lock such a small key would fit." She paused to watch Kyle insert the key into the lock. "Now I know."

"It fits," he said, "but rust is keeping the lock from opening." He sat back and seemed to be studying the lockbox, oblivious to rivulets of dark bayou water staining his trousers. When he looked up, Millie expected to find discouragement. Instead, his expression brightened.

"What are you going to do?" she asked as she watched him reach into a carpetbag that looked very much like the one he'd brought up onto the roof of the Cotton Exchange weeks ago.

"I'm going to open this box, Millie. That's what we came to do, isn't it?"

It took some work, but he managed to pry open the rusted top only to find the box empty. Millie's heart sank.

"I'm so sorry," he said gently. "I know you were hoping for something more."

The trip back to New Orleans passed in a blur of sights and sounds, most of which Millie ignored. Returning to Kyle's lovely home on Prytania Street was bittersweet.

It was the end of one journey and the beginning of another.

February 14, 1889
New Orleans

The next morning Millie dressed early and then waited until the hour was late enough for visiting. Slipping out without attracting Kyle's attention, she made her way to Royal Street and the house now familiar to her.

Knocking, she held no hope of an answer. And yet the door opened, and the same tired-looking servant woman sighed.

"I figured you would be back," she said, and this time she stepped aside to silently invite Millie to enter.

The home was narrow and long, a gently shabby building of elegant proportions and fading grandeur. "Come on back here. They're outside enjoying the sun. Don't always happen like that this early into February."

Millie followed, barely noticing anything but the sliver of sunshine that rippled through a pair of French doors and spilled across faded carpet at the end of the long hall. The servant paused at the doors and sighed again.

Peering around the woman, she could just see the edge of a small New Orleans courtyard, its splashing fountain dominating a lush green landscape only just returning to its spring colors. Two chairs had been set up in the sun, their backs too tall and wide to reveal the persons sitting in them.

The only evidence of anyone inhabiting the space was the pair of hands stretching between the chairs to clasp in the middle. One was small and feminine. The other larger and definitely masculine.

Millie looked over at the servant. "I don't understand."

"Don't you?" she asked, one brow lifted.

"Is that Mrs. Koch?"

"No, that's Miss Hebert. Now go on. I told her I would let you in the next time you came. The Lord Almighty must have led you here just on the day when she is visiting." At Millie's confused look, she continued. "They only get today, you know. After that, she leaves and doesn't come back until next year."

"Miss Hebert?" Millie stepped through the open door, her heart pounding. Family. At last.

The hands remained clasped, fingers entwined. Still Millie moved toward them.

Great arching ferns shaded her as she circled around the couple. A few more steps and their faces would come into view. Millie sucked in a deep breath and let it out slowly.

And then she closed her eyes and propelled herself forward. When she opened her eyes again, the first face she saw was Cook.

"Child, it took you long enough to find us," she said. "Now come here and meet my Julian."

Julian.

He was wrapped in a quilt of brilliant red and yellow hues, a patchwork of stitches covering a man whose health had long ago left him. And yet his eyes followed her. Searched her face. And she searched his, looking for the man in the locket.

He was there. In those eyes.

"Hello," Millie said. Just then she realized he was unable to respond, and she looked back to Cook. "Are you Sophie?"

"No, honey," she said with a gentle laugh. "Not hardly. I'm just plain old Cook."

"But this is Julian. *The* Julian from the locket. Am I wrong?"

Cook patted her companion's hand. "No, child. You are not wrong."

She shook her head. "I don't understand. And how are you a relative of mine? There is no Mrs. Koch, is there."

"No, just me, Miss Cook, or you could call me Miss Hebert, but I had to come up with something on short notice to get you to New Orleans, and I am terrible sorry about that. Now come sit by me." Cook released her grip as she leaned to place Julian's hand back beneath his quilt. "Bring that stool over here."

When Millie had done as she asked, the old woman sighed. "Oh, honey, where to begin?"

"At the beginning."

"The beginning, it is. Your grandmama, she was

Sophie," Cook said gently. "And Julian was hers, but not before he was mine."

"But—"

Cook held up her hand. "Let me tell this straight through, child. It's the only way I can." When Millie nodded, she continued. "I loved that man, I did. But I was only the daughter of a cook in a servant's house. What did I know about anything but hard work? But Sophie, oh, now Sophie, she got what she wanted, and what she wanted was my Julian."

She paused now, looking off past the fountain and the ferns as if recalling things just as they were happening. Millie waited, wishing she could hurry the process but knowing she could not.

"Julian's people, they were poor. Fishermen from out on Bell Island, they were. When the hurricane hit, the waters got churned up and the fish, they all died. They had nothing. Couldn't eat, couldn't fix the roof, nothing. The little ones they were sickly, about to die. So Julian, he tells me we have to do something. I said I would get me a job and would send money, but he was a proud man. He told me that wasn't what a man did, taking money from a woman like that." She fell silent for a moment. "So Julian, he goes into New Orleans to get him a job. And Sophie, she hears of it and follows him."

When Cook once again fell silent, Millie

reached to touch her hand. "My grandmother, Sophie . . . she was from Bell Island too?"

"She was Baratarian, honey. Lafitte's baby girl. But nobody knew that except me and Julian. She took my Julian, but when he wouldn't marry her she got him drunk and had her way. I know that's shocking to you, but I believe it happened just like that." She reached to pat the old man's leg. "He wouldn't tell me something that wasn't true."

"Of course," she said for lack of a better response.

"When Julian came back to me, Sophie was furious. She hunted up her daddy's treasure box out in the bayou, got that key, and went down to the bank to get herself enough money to forget all about where she came from. It worked too. And just in case, she buried Sophie. Put her dead in the ground and held a funeral and then told everyone she was Sophie's grieving cousin, Genevieve. All the menfolk was falling over themselves to console her. And while they were drying her tears, she was picking herself out a husband."

"Grandfather Hugh?"

"The very one. He was older than the rest and had himself some money from the cotton business and a big house up there in Memphis. And Sophie, she couldn't afford to be too choosy, what with Julian's baby in her belly."

Millie gasped. "Father?"

Cook nodded. "That's right, sweet girl. Why do you think your grandmama never trusted your daddy with nothing? Because he wasn't Hugh's. Every time she looked at Silas, she saw the only man who didn't want her. And Hugh? That old man, try as he could, never did put a baby in Sophie. Your daddy was the only one she had." Cook paused. "And that ought to tell you why I put up with the man, insufferable as he is."

"Because he is Julian's son."

Twenty-seven

Millie searched the face of the woman who had offered wise council in the past, still unable to believe her connection to the Copes ran deeper than expected. "Does Father know?"

"He figured it out, I think. Probably got told by Sophie a time or two. Just don't know that he believed it." Cook shrugged. "Me, I leave that part of it be. It's enough to spend my days close to the child of the man I love. That he is Sophie's too? Well, that explains the part of him I don't much like."

"Staying at that house and being a mean and spiteful man's cook is what you want?"

"Millie, if I didn't want that, I could have moved out to the house he gave me years ago."

"Father gave you a house?"

"That's the story I was told. It's a pretty place just far enough outside Memphis to make a body feel like the city's far away."

Millie's brow furrowed. "The farmhouse that remains empty?"

"That's the one. I'll admit I was curious, so after Sophie—or, rather, Genevieve as she wanted us all to call her—well, after she died I went downtown to check the records and see just who did own that place. The clerk at the city office, he said that a man named Arnaque had set up a fund to keep that house paid up on taxes and taken care of real nice. Me being from the bayou, I knew who Arnaque was, but I didn't say anything about it."

"Lafitte. Sophie's father," Millie said. Cook nodded. "Arnaque wrote a letter to her. I found it in Mama's Bible."

"That don't surprise me. The old man, he had plenty to apologize for. But then so did Sophie. Whether it was him who arranged it or Sophie who did it and then just tried to pass it off as Silas's idea, I don't guess I'll ever know. But it was a nice gesture, wasn't it?"

"It was." Millie was quiet for a moment. "I always thought I would inherit that place, but I'm very glad it's yours."

"Oh, child, you can have it. I'll stay in the house on Adams Street until the Lord Almighty takes me home. Or takes Silas. Like I said, everything is paid for and taken care of in perpetuity.

That's banker's terms, but the Union & Planters men, they have been good to me." She smiled. "You know, it's a myth that old Lafitte didn't like banks. He did. At least, once he found bankers who were sympathetic to him. Why, in New Orleans he was considered a hero."

Millie was lost in thought about all of that for a moment, but then by degrees she became aware of the man watching her again.

"He hears you," Cook said, "but he can't respond."

"How long has he been like this?"

"It's been a long time now. He come home to Bell Island looking for me. Told me what he'd done wrong and how sorry he was he let Sophie turn his head like that. Said he wanted me for his wife. Even told me he made an appointment with the preacher for Valentine's Day."

"Today," Millie whispered.

"That's right, only it didn't happen, this marriage of ours. The yellow fever he brought back from New Orleans almost took him, but he didn't die. And neither did I, though there was times I wished I had."

"I'm so sorry," Millie said, and then she shook her head. "I don't want to call you Cook anymore. That is just not . . ." Again she shook her head. "What can I call you?"

"Mildred." This from the man in the blanket, a soft word that came from lips pitifully unused to speaking. "Mildred Hebert," he said with a bit more strength.

Tears shimmered in the old woman's eyes as she reached to clasp Julian's hand again. And then she nodded.

"That's right, child. My given name is Mildred. The one good thing Sophie did was to see that you was named after me. Your mama, she always did what Sophie, I mean Genevieve, said."

Millie rose to leave some time later, her heart full. The woman she now knew as Mildred walked her to the door and kissed her on the cheek. "Will you write to me?"

"Yes. As soon as I am settled."

"And Julian, he's your blood granddaddy. You don't be a stranger here, understand?"

"Yes, ma'am. I promise." Millie paused to look around. "But if you don't mind my asking, how did a poor fisherman from Bell Island—"

"Come to live here? That came from Sophie, though she didn't know it. More than that is for you to find out, child, all in good time."

That seemed a little cryptic, but Millie was willing to let it go for now, trusting that Cook would share more with her when she was ready.

They parted at the door, and Millie carried the story all the way back to Prytania Street.

As Millie approached the house, the front door opened and Kyle met her halfway down the carriageway. "Where have you been? I thought you were gone for good."

"Why would you think that?" She clasped his hand. "I took a walk. To Royal Street."

"But that is too far for you to walk. What were you thinking?"

Millie smiled. "I will tell you all about it. But first, do you think there might be some bread pudding in the kitchen?"

"We can do better than that. It's Valentine's Day, and we will not be spending it eating cold leftovers. Now upstairs with you. I think the dressmaker has delivered that haul of garments you and my mother purchased. Maybe you can find something suitable for dinner."

She grinned. "I don't know. Where are you taking me?"

"Antoine's. I think it is time to introduce you to my favorite places in this city. And I mean other than my workshop."

Millie chose a gown of deep crimson silk with a velvet trim. A little while later she found herself across the table from Kyle in the most elegant restaurant in New Orleans dining on scrumptious food and telling him the story of Sophie and Julian.

He listened patiently to every detail, and when she finished his smiled broadened. "What you have just shared makes what I have for you even more special, Millie." He reached into his pocket,

472

pulled out a small wrapped package, and handed it to her.

Beneath the wrapping paper, she found a lovely black velvet jeweler's box. She hesitated a moment, looking up at him with luminous eyes.

"Open it," he said softly, smiling.

Millie gasped when she looked inside to find her locket and cypher, this time secured to a breathtaking necklace of diamonds and rubies. "But how . . . where?"

"Your father," he said. "I had chance to speak with him. This morning, actually. He returned the locket and I handled the rest."

She shook her head. "What? Father is in New Orleans?"

Kyle rose and came around the table to stand beside her. "He is here, Millie. In Antoine's."

Her companion gestured, and then she saw her father come out of the shadows and walk toward her, stopping just out of her reach. Kyle stepped back as if to observe, or perhaps protect.

"Millie." Father's voice was hoarse, his use of her shortened name surprising. "Oh, Millie, I have been such a fool."

He moved closer. She could only watch as words failed her.

And then closer still. "I . . ."

"You what?" tumbled from her lips with acid she instantly regretted. "What is it you're asking of me, Father? To forget the treatment I've received from you all these years? Is that what you want?"

"I deserve your anger—"

"And I did *not* deserve yours." She gripped the edge of the table. "You were all I had after they died, and you . . ."

"I'm asking you to look at the face of an old fool and try to find your father there." His lips trembled. "And yet as I ask, I am painfully aware I deserve nothing but your scorn."

She thought of the years of scorn she had received at this man's hands. And yet her heart softened in spite of it all.

"You're a brilliant girl, Millie," he continued. "So very smart. Enough to make a father very proud . . . and fearful."

"Fearful?" She shook her head. "How so?"

"I feared you would find no man to be your equal. When Trueck, or Tucker as I've been told, came to me and offered for you, I jumped at the chance to secure your future." He let out a long breath. "Apparently, my haste was my downfall, for a wiser man might have asked for more than assurances of an impressive bank account and that my daughter would be cared for."

"You asked Trueck to care for me?" she asked as she released her grip on the table.

He looked up sharply. "I required it."

The man who appeared to care nothing for her had somehow become the father who had looked to secure her future. "But the books. The disdain for my love of learning . . ."

"Equal parts my fear and my complete understanding of your superior intellect. In short, Millie, you were gifted with so much more than me. I . . . I am not proud to say this, but I was jealous. Of you."

Father ducked his head, his shoulders shaking slightly. He dropped to his knees beside her, his eyes now filled with tears. "Millie, will you forgive me? I never knew what I risked losing until you walked out," he sobbed as he wrapped his arms around her waist and rested his head in her lap. "Please say you will forgive me."

She looked past him to Kyle, who nodded almost imperceptibly. "Yes," came out as a mumbled mess. "Yes," was a bit stronger. And then she wrapped her arms around her father and rested her head atop his. And cried. And told him she forgave him.

How long they remained there, she could not say. Then Father lifted his head and stood, bringing Millie to her feet. "No matter what happens to me, just know that I love you, daughter."

"I love you too, Father," she said and found that though there was still much to work through in her feelings toward him, she meant it. "Thank you for returning the locket."

"I should never have taken it."

He looked past her to where Kyle still stood guard. "Thank you for allowing this."

The younger man nodded, and then an awkward moment of silence fell, ending when Father cleared his throat. "I met my father today. Cook was still with him, so while he was not able to speak clearly, we did have a successful first visit."

"Oh," she said softly.

A lone tear slid from his eye. "My mother claimed it, but . . . well, I never believed that my father was anyone other than . . ."

He reached to swipe at the tear with the back of his hand. "I understand from Cook that you did not find the treasure, and I'm very sorry. I hope you know you will always have a home with Freda and me, though I realize that living with Jean Lafitte's illegitimate grandson is poor consolation when compared to finding Lafitte's treasure."

"A father is a father no matter the provenance," Kyle said. "And I'm sure that once Millie has had time to consider that, she will understand that fathers sometimes make mistakes out of love."

"Yes, but sometimes those mistakes are made out of selfishness. I claim both." He turned his attention back to Millie. "Will you come back to Memphis with me? I don't know what will happen when the Pinkerton agents are finished with their investigation . . . if I will remain a free man or . . . but I wonder if . . ."

She let out a long breath. Too much pain was still there. "No, Father," she said gently.

"Yes, of course." He offered a curt nod. "I understand. Please write. To Mildred too."

"I promise." She touched the necklace now circling her neck. "And thank you." She looked to Kyle. "Both of you. I thought Will Tucker would see that it was gone forever."

Her father shook his head. "I meant to give it to him but I just couldn't." He embraced her again and then offered a handkerchief to dry her tears. She looked down at the embroidery and spied the familiar logo.

"Land and sea."

And then he was gone, a proud man walking straight and tall through the front doors of Antoine's and out into the New Orleans night.

"Will he go to jail?" Millie asked as Kyle returned to sit across from her.

"He might. Everything depends on what the facts are."

"I see." She reached for the necklace and secured it around her neck. "It's lovely."

"You're lovely." He smiled at her with pride and something warmer shining in his eyes. Then he reached out to cover her hand on the table with one of his own. "I know we had dessert planned, but what would you say if I offered you bread pudding in a certain kitchen on Prytania Street?"

"I would say yes!"

"Then follow me."

She did, and when they were settled in the carriage he turned to fix his attention on her. "Millie, I have a question for you."

"All right," she said as she arranged her skirts.

"If it was important, would you come if I called you?"

"What? I have no idea what you're talking about." She smiled, though. "But of course I would."

"You're sure?"

"Yes, Kyle, I would. If it was important."

He grinned. "That's all I need to know."

Kyle's kitchen staff had two bowls of bread pudding ready before Millie could get situated on a stool. "It's almost as if you had this planned," she said as she touched the necklace she still could not believe she was wearing.

"Well, perhaps I did. Are you pleased?"

"More than pleased. Thank you." She paused. "But I wonder if I shouldn't give the locket to Mildred. After all, the miniature inside is of Julian."

"I think that is a grand idea. Tomorrow I will have the piece sent back to the jewelers to be separated. You'll keep the cypher in place, won't you?"

"Oh, yes, definitely."

He nudged her with his shoulder. "Why don't you try opening it?"

She grinned at him as she opened the clasp

and set the necklace down in front of them. "I was given an excellent lesson in semaphore flags not long ago, sir. I know just how to do it. Watch."

She turned the coins as he had showed her and nothing happened. After another attempt, she gave up. "Something seems to be wrong. You try it."

"Actually, I modified the code." He gave the cypher a few turns and then it opened.

"Ah. What's the new code?"

"I'll tell you later. Right now I would like you to hold out your hand and close your eyes."

Smiling, she did so, and then she felt something fall into her palm. "What is this?"

"Open your eyes, Millie."

She found him kneeling before her. In her palm was a breathtaking ruby-and-diamond ring.

"It was my grandmother's," he said softly, his eyes locked on hers. "She told me not to put it on a woman's finger until I was certain I couldn't live without her. Well, I'm certain."

"Oh, Kyle—"

"Hush now. I have rehearsed this, and if you insist on talking you will get me off track. Just listen. Millie Cope, I love you. I have for longer than I wanted to admit, and I want you for my wife. Will you marry me?"

"Is it time for me to speak?" When he nodded, she said, "I love you too, and yes, I will be your wife."

He placed the ring on her finger and then stood

to pull her into his arms. "There is just one more thing," he said. "A wedding gift."

With the ring sparkling on her hand and love filling her heart, Millie could not imagine anything that could best that gift. He led her out of the kitchen and toward the entrance to the workshop's secret elevator.

Once inside, Mille skipped the hand-holding to fall into his embrace and offer Kyle the best kiss she could manage while crying.

"You're going to have to stop this before we get to the workshop," he said.

"Why is that?"

The doors opened just as he said, "Because tears stain silk, and I don't want your wedding dress ruined before the big day."

"My . . ." She gasped when she saw it hanging a few feet in front of her. "My mother's wedding dress. And it's beautiful. Just like I imagined it would look. But I thought . . ."

"It was burned?" He shook his head. "No, and neither was this." He gestured toward a box on the worktable beside her.

"What is it?"

"Open it."

"My mother's Bible! My sketchbooks . . ." She looked through the box quickly before turning to once again fall into his embrace. "But how?"

"Your father brought it when he returned the locket. Apparently, he had second thoughts about destroying your things. Two more boxes filled with books are downstairs in the library, but I understand these things are your favorites."

"Yes, they are." She folded back the Bible's spine to see the old letter still tucked inside. A letter from father to daughter.

"Oh, it's all too much. I just can't take it all in. The dress . . ."

"Fitted to your size by my mother's dressmaker. And without tantrums," Kyle added. "From either of us."

She smiled then, and she sniffed. When she pulled out her father's handkerchief and saw the distinctive embroidery, she started crying all over again.

"All right. Enough of that." He marched her across the workshop to the far window where a pair of winter coats were draped over the chairs. "Put that on," he instructed as he donned the other coat. "And then come with me."

She shrugged into her coat, still sniffling, and then dried her eyes and tucked the handkerchief into the coat pocket. When Kyle disappeared through the window, she peered out to see where he had gone.

And then she saw it. The flying machine, newly inflated and tethered to the rail awaiting its next voyage. Kyle stepped in and she followed, allowing him to buckle her in place just as he had done several times before.

"So," he said as he reached up to adjust the valves. "Where would you like to go?"

"Surprise me."

"All right," was her fiancé's cheerful response. "But I should probably warn you that I have implemented the fuel adjustments you suggested. By my calculations, we are in for a long night."

Millie's laughter echoed in the starry sky. "Fly me to the moon, then. Or maybe just around the Gulf of Mexico and back."

Mildred Hebert sat in the courtyard of the home on Royal Street long after Silas left to find Millie and make amends. Julian had long since been put to bed, leaving her alone with her thoughts. She could only marvel at the events of the day.

Though she ought to be halfway back to Memphis by now, as she had been every other year, the choice to stay for a while set well with her.

"What a Valentine's Day we had, didn't we, Lord?" she whispered. "Thank You for the miracles and the grace, and for the words my Julian—"

Laughter from overhead stopped her in mid-sentence. Looking up, Mildred saw what appeared to be an exact copy of that infernal flying machine Kyle Russell insisted on parking on the roof of the house on Adams Street.

It flew on past, taking the giggles and sweet snatches of conversation along with it but leaving thoughts of the inventor and Mildred's namesake. Silas had told her of the engagement, of how Mr. Russell's grandmama's ring likely sat on Millie's finger by now. And of the dress that man had fixed up just to fit Millie for their wedding.

"Oh, yes indeed, Lord, You are good. So very, very good."

She leaned back against the chair cushions, this time in the spot where Julian normally sat, "I wonder what that girl will do when I tell her where to find the treasure."

Mildred chuckled. "Even Sophie didn't know what happened to the rest of it. Old Lafitte accused her of taking it, and she turned right back around and claimed he's the one who took it." She got the giggles then, laughing until she started coughing.

When Mildred caught her breath again, she said to herself, "I'd like to see it found in my lifetime." Again she closed her eyes. "It's just a pity none of that treasure's been seen in more than fifty years. Not since Sophie took it all down to the Bank of Louisiana back in 1837."

She paused only long enough to look up toward the heavens, toward the moon that was just one day shy of being full, and winked. "And I took it all out the next day and put it where neither of them could find it. You know I intended to make sure it would go to Julian's baby, Lord, but he didn't turn out all that nice. I'm so glad instead it will go to his sweet granddaughter."

Closing her eyes, she let the tired sink into her bones. Still she made no move to go inside. "Indeed, those Union and Planters bankers have been good to me. And when the time is right, I will help Millie Cope figure out that what she's looking for isn't in that old lockbox anymore."

Mildred laughed softly. "But then, treasures are not that hard to find, are they, Lord? Not with Your help."

New Orleans Picayune
May 10, 1889

RUSSELL-COPE WEDDING CAPTIVATES CITY'S ELITE

Mildred Genevieve Cope of Memphis, Tennessee, was united in marriage to Kyle Russell, son and grandson of prominent members of our fair city's legal community, on Thursday last at nine o'clock in the morning. A wedding breakfast was held at Antoine's with the couple departing soon after for a honeymoon trip to an undisclosed location. Husband and wife will make New Orleans their home.

The couple returned from their honeymoon to find the formal parlor of their home on Prytania Street filled with wedding gifts and letters from friends and family wishing them well. One of those letters was from Mildred Hebert. Amid warm wishes for a wonderful life together, she suggested they use the key from Millie's cypher to open a particular lockbox at the Union & Planters Bank in Memphis, Tennessee. They would find her wedding gift there.

New Orleans Picayune
June 1, 1889

NEWLYWEDS ESTABLISH MILLIE'S TREASURE FOUNDATION

Mr. and Mrs. Kyle Russell are proud to announce the establishment of a multimillion dollar charitable foundation they have called Millie's Treasure. According to Mrs. Russell, the former Mildred Cope of Memphis, the foundation's sole purpose is to make good use of a recent inheritance from her great-grandfather.

Though Mrs. Russell declined to discuss the windfall, she did indicate that some of the funds will go to support the building of libraries and the encouragement of young-sters, both male and female, to study the scientific arts. The first of these will be the Julian Girod Library, set to break ground on Bell Island, Louisiana in the fall of this year. A school and medical clinic are to be included in the plans.

Author's Note

Thank you for joining me on a whirlwind trip through the South with Kyle and Millie! I hope you enjoyed reading this book at least as much as I enjoyed writing it.

Treasure hunting lore abounds, and Jean Lafitte is at the center of many of the tales. A legendary pirate (or privateer, as the case may be), a patriot during the battle of New Orleans, and an enigma long after he sailed out of exile at *Maison Rouge* in Galveston and disappeared into history in the mid–1820s. There were sightings in Cuba and around the Caribbean, but some believe he lived many years—decades perhaps—under assumed names and in multiple far-flung locales.

Growing up on the Texas coast just a stone's throw from Louisiana, tales of Lafitte and his men abound. Many of those tales center around lost treasure. Time, tide, and hurricanes have churned up much of the landscape, leaving some to believe pirate treasure is all along the coast. Some even believe Lafitte came inland to hide his loot. One story even has the pirate aiding conspirators bent on stealing Confederate gold. That is the tale I've borrowed in part for this book.

In addition to researching people, I also learned so much about the locations in this story.

Memphis is such a wonderful city, although when Millie lived on Adams Street, the town was still struggling to come back from a terrible epidemic of yellow fever that left Memphis without a city charter for more than a decade.

I had a great time researching the city, and I was surprised at how much Memphis had changed since the turn of the last century. While both the Peabody Hotel and the Cotton Exchange still exist, neither are in the same building they were in 1889, nor were their addresses the same. In a few instances, I have added places to the story that are fictional, such as Parker's Jewelry and the Arnaque home. Others, such as the Davies Mansion, are real and still standing today and open to visitors.

Further south in New Orleans, the homes in the Garden District and French Quarter still look as if nineteenth-century men and women might live inside. Stately, lovely, and well-preserved mansions are the highlight of the city tour and one I highly recommend taking. And while I enjoyed visiting the sites in New Orleans, I also loved seeing the Louisiana bayou up close. From New Iberia down to Barataria, the cypress trees, Spanish moss, and murky water give way to some of the loveliest spots in the state. Even today it is easy to see how Lafitte and his band of pirates slipped into the dark bayou and remained concealed; easier still to imagine there are untold riches in the form of treasure hidden in the coves and inside cypress knees.

As with all my novels, whether historical or contemporary, I endeavor to be as correct and accurate in the research and writing as possible. To that end, any mistakes made are mine alone. However, this is a work of fiction and much license was taken to create characters and a story that departs from known fact.

But no story is written alone, and I am grateful to the many people who assisted in seeing this book to publication. Many thanks to the amazing Wendy Lawton, Janice Thompson, Cara Putman, Betty Woods, and Kathleen Fuller for reading this manuscript and offering encouragement and advice while it was a work-in-progress. You all are such a blessing to me. In addition, I also owe a debt of thanks to Jeane Wynn of WynnWynn Media for her tireless work spreading the word about my novels.

I also wish to thank the fabulous team at Harvest House Publishers for making the experience of turning my idea of a science-loving Pinkerton agent who meets his match into reality. I am blessed to be considered a member of such a wonderful and supportive family.

Speaking of family, I cannot forget my husband Robert Turner, who played chauffeur, tour guide, caterer, and roadie as we traveled across six states in search of material for the Secret Lives of

Will Tucker series. Later, he added line editor and brainstorm expert to his list of skills as he read through the manuscript and helped me get unstuck when a scene or character refused to cooperate.

And, finally, to my readers. Without you there would be no Millie or Kyle or even Will Tucker. If you would like to find out more about me or connect with me on social media, please visit my website at www.kathleenybarbo.com.

Thank you, thank you, and thank you!

Discussion Questions

1. The story opens with Millie's curiosity sending her to investigate a crate full of curious objects that eventually lead her to Kyle and love. Because she was looking in out-of-the-ordinary places, she found something that changed her life. Has this ever happened to you? Looking back, did you almost miss something—or someone—that ended up being important? How would your life be different if you had missed this?

2. Millie's father does not appear to be a good role model. In fact, he does things that are hurtful to her. Even so, she does not use her earthly father as an example for what her expectations of a heavenly Father should be. Are you lacking that example of a good earthly father? If so, how have you been able to get past that to allow a clearer picture of the kind of loving Father our God is?

3. Millie thinks she wants to fly around Memphis on the aviator's invention—until she gets the chance. Then she hesitates and might not have gone had she been able to find any other way down to the ground. Have

you ever been right on the edge of a big idea only to allow fear or something else to cause you to doubt whether you should do it? Is there something in your life right now you've longed to do but are afraid to try?

4. Millie and Kyle do not learn each other's names until several chapters into the book because both prefer anonymity. Later, this becomes a barrier to their relationship and they choose to reveal who they truly are. Have you experienced this reluctance to show someone—perhaps God—who you really are at first? Why? What did you do about it?

5. Kyle wears dual hats as a Pinkerton agent and an inventor. While he loves using his knowledge of science to create new things and solve problems with gadgets he has invented, he also uses his creative mind to solve Pinkerton cases. This is one example of how God gives us all gifts that can be used in more than one area of our lives. What are some of your gifts and how are you using them? Is there another area of your life you can use these strengths to bless others?

6. Millie disobeys her father's wishes and creates her own hidden space—a kingdom-of-her-own in the attic. Her father is furious

when he finds the room, and eventually the things she lied about owning are taken from her. While her father was not a good man, he did hold Millie to a standard of honesty, and when that standard was not upheld, he took action. Have you ever been disappointed to find out someone has lied to you? What did you do as a result of learning this?

7. Millie's grandmother was so desperate to protect the secret of her identity and that of her son, Millie's father, that she pretended to be someone else. That action changed the course of many lives, including her children and grandchildren. Though you have most likely not gone to the extent she did, have you gone to great lengths to keep a secret? Did it come out anyway? What were the repercussions of this? What do you wish you had done differently?

8. Millie is the recipient of a locket passed down from her grandmother to her mother and then to her. It is a reminder of her family history and a precious possession she guards carefully. Is there something special you now own that once belonged to a family member or beloved friend? If so, what is it and what memories does it hold for you?

9. Kyle has promised his best friend, Lucas McMinn, that he will see justice done and Will Tucker returned to his rightful place behind bars. It is a promise he has made, and one that keeps him working for the Pinkerton Agency until the promise has been fulfilled. Have you ever been called upon to make a sacrifice for a friend or family member? What did you do? Do you regret it?

10. Millie and Kyle share a love of science and learning. For Kyle, having a woman who is unique in this aspect is something he likes very much. Millie, however, is reluctant to believe that what most in her generation find odd in a woman is something that Kyle actually likes about her. What is most unique about you? If you cannot answer this question, ask someone who can.

11. Will Tucker is on the run, and he must never stay in one place too long or he will be caught. Was there ever a time when you felt as though you were on the run—from a memory, a responsibility, or even from God? What did you do about it? Or is it still something you're dealing with?

12. In Millie's private sanctuary, she surrounded herself with some of her favorite things. Many

of those things reminded her of her mother and sisters, while others were in the room because she enjoyed them. From the books on the shelves to the sketchbooks and pencils on the table, everything in her room was there because it was special to her. Close your eyes and imagine your dream room. What does it look like? What is in it? Why would you choose those specific things?

13. In addition to the wheel cypher made of gold doubloons, Millie wears a heart-shaped locket on her necklace. Inside is a painting and a message that causes her to believe a clue to treasure is hidden there. When the locket is taken away, Millie fears she has lost any chance of finding the treasure. Ultimately, however, this proves not to be the case. Have you ever had the feeling that all is lost only to find out later you were wrong? Why did you feel that way, and what changed to make you realize you were wrong? Could this apply to something in your life right now?

14. Millie Cope is the last woman Kyle needs to be thinking of as he tries to fulfill his duties as a Pinkerton agent on an important case. Not only does love take his mind off the mission, but Millie was once engaged to the man he is hunting. To fall in love with her meant taking

a huge risk, but he knew in his heart she was the woman he was meant to spend his life with. Have you ever taken a risk because you knew in your heart it was what you were supposed to do? What did you do? What was the result? What, if anything, do you wish you had done differently?

15. The Louisiana bayou is a dark and interesting place full of hidden coves and abounding in rumors of buried treasure and pirate gold. Some doubt these rumors, but many believe that time and the abundance of hurricanes that batter the southern coast of Louisiana have forever obscured markers that hide treasure beneath them. What do you think? Are you the type who might go on a treasure hunt if you had a map and a means for doing so? What would you hope to find? What would be inside your ideal treasure chest?

About the Author

Kathleen Y'Barbo is a bestselling author of 45 novels with almost two million copies of her books in print in the US and abroad. *A Romantic Times* Top Pick recipient, she is a proud military wife and an expatriate Texan cheering on her beloved Texas Aggies from north of the Red River.

Find out more about Kathleen at www.kathleenybarbo.com.

Center Point Large Print
600 Brooks Road / PO Box 1
Thorndike, ME 04986-0001 USA

(207) 568-3717

US & Canada:
1 800 929-9108
www.centerpointlargeprint.com